The Sparrows Who Dream

JR Szpila

Beluga Point Press

Copyright © 2023 by JR Szpila

All rights reserved.

www.jrszpila.com

No part of this publication may be reproduced, distributed, or transmitted in any form or by any means, including photocopying, recording, or other electronic or mechanical methods, without the prior written permission of the publisher, except as permitted by U.S. copyright law. For permission requests, contact Beluga Point Press LLC.

The story, all names, characters, and incidents portrayed in this production are fictitious. No identification with actual persons (living or deceased), places, buildings, and products is intended or should be inferred. This is a work of fiction.

Library of Congress Control Number: 2023900088

ISBN: 979-8-9872020-0-5

Book Cover by Maria Spada

Editing by Kate Angelella, Enchanted Ink Publishing, and Chandra Fisher

First edition: 2023

To my dear readers who were forced to be less than you were made to be, to those who felt like not enough or just too much, and to my mother who taught me that all boxes were meant to be broken and that all finish lines are crossable if you put your mind to it.

Love you more than the moon and the stars <3

Sky Islands

Agolya Mountains

Morsaw

Neven

Hickman

Casto[n]

Eastern Sea

a Sea Star Island Kuclan Warriors' Island

PARA

Frengress Mountains

Sparrow Castle

Boltos Mountains

Blaque Forest

Barlow

Finn

Dear Reader,

This book deals with some topics that might be triggering to some people. There are characters with mental health and eating disorders. There are also toxic and abusive relationships. If you are easily triggered please read with care. As much as I would love for you to read my book, your mental health is more important. So please take care of yourself first. This book was healing for me but it might not be for you.
I am hugging you tight!
<3 JR

Prologue

Twenty-One Years Ago

Every day for the past few moons Rhella checked the vibrant glen where the young woman was supposed to appear. She sat cross-legged, her fingers buried in the dirt, feeling the silky worms as they slithered over her pointed nails. The blue-stemmed grass was taller than her, hiding her perfectly between the wispy stalks.

She always thought this side of the world was beautiful, so unlike her home. There was no snow here, no mountains; just flatlands of grass. The valleys eventually gave way to rolling green hills to the west and beyond that, sands, but never the mountains. She would have to cross the Blaque Forest in the north to see them. At times, it felt like they were trapping her in.

She was unaccustomed to the heat. Sweat dripped down her spine, but that didn't stop her from arching her chest toward the sun, soaking up every last ray. It was liberating. It was freedom. Time always seemed to move intoxicatingly slower when she lived among the humans. She wished above all else that she could feel what they felt, knowing tomorrow could be their last day, but her immortal soul could do nothing more than imagine it.

It wasn't like her to be gone from her family for so long. Every time she left, she missed home, her children, and her *kupal*. He had begged her not to leave this time and told her that the children needed her more than the humans did. That he needed her. Her fear for her children, especially the twins, almost stopped her from leaving. Their destiny and powers were all a part of this unknown future. She had kept that secret even from her *kupal*. It ate at her every day. Rhella hated lying to him, but this was far more important than the bond that tied them for eternity. More important than even their immortal lives.

It was her youngest child, second born of the twins, who had given her pause before she left. He was so introverted, so gentle. She only saw parts of his future, and she was afraid for him, for all of the choices he would have to make alone. He was on a journey few would take. Even if she were there, she couldn't help him.

Rhella had kissed them all goodbye, her heart breaking as it did every time she left. But the moment she cleared the mountains, something lifted. A pressure released off her shoulders even though she knew it would be years before she could return.

Today was going to be the day. Something tickled the back of her mind, telling her not to move from her spot, to stay silent and observe. So she did, sitting patiently for hours in the warm morning light. She knew the girl would appear; deep down, her bones screamed it.

In the late afternoon, at the edge of the glen, the river that normally flowed black shone yellow. A small fishing boat with chipped teal paint carried two passengers through the water. The boat had no flag, no kingdom's colors. It pushed up into the grass, docking with a jerk. Rhella could barely see the pale-haired young woman tucked under the man's arms that circled sweetly around her shoulders. Gently, he helped her out of the boat. They wrapped themselves in each other, kissing and tumbling into the grass.

Everything about the scene made Rhella's hair stand on end.

Her amber eyes saw far more than they should. She didn't just see two lovers in the wild tangles of grass, the green wrapping around their almost naked bodies like sheets. No. She saw the two long, winding paths these lovers could take. Both were dark and crooked, overflowing with blood. But while one had no end in sight, the other carried a minuscule fleck of light within its cobalt and wine pools. She focused on the light; it was the only option.

The war between humans and Spitarians must come to an end.

Rhella stretched her long chestnut fingers in front of her. A warm buzz ran through her veins as her skin turned from taut to wrinkled and pale, her veins protruding. Her other features responded as well, transforming her into an average human female's height and build, her hair from black to silver and her eyes sky blue. Her back hunched, changing her perfect posture into something less threatening.

Would her words make the blond girl choose the right path? She never knew what choices a person would make until after she spoke her premonitions. She couldn't see whether her words helped or hurt in the end.

Ignoring these glimpses of the future brought on pain that wracked her whole body. It shot through her like a raging fire, then shattered her with shards of ice. It seemed to turn her blood to solid metal, freezing her in place for hours. The pain was more than one could bear. The words needed to be spoken to end it, and that was what she did. She spun her dreams, her visions, into a story that would make them want to listen.

The words Rhella had to speak had haunted her for far too long. She knew the pain they would bring this couple. She had prolonged this moment long enough for the girl to reach eighteen, to know right from wrong. But she couldn't wait any longer, for the girl was already headed down the dark path. The words spoken today would tear the poor dear's heart in two.

Tear but not break. Never would it be broken.

Rhella sucked in a breath and hobbled toward them, cursing her gift. Some called her a witch; others called her a demon. Most heeded her words, knowing who she really was: a Spitarian with the cruel gift of sight.

Chapter One

River

A flame in the mist
When death shall come
Only she will stand the fight
Only she can end it all
One war
One right

The third and final bell trilled, bouncing off the stone walls as River tore through the castle. She flicked her gaze away from the gold-painted script on the walls. The prophecy had become a prayer for most humans, a promise that one day the bloodshed would end, but for River, it was no more than a curse, a burden she could never live up to, and yet was hers alone to carry.

Her feet slapped against the marble floor. She barely avoided a collision with the guard as she turned the corner.

"Aren't you supposed to be inside?" he said with a sly look, pointing at the door.

River didn't have enough time to flash him a smile before she threw open the wooden door to her chambers.

Her handmaiden rose to her feet. "Did you find him?" Laya's voice raised an octave the way it always did when she expressed any sort of emotion.

River's eyes trailed to the portrait that hung above her four-poster bed. In it, her brown curls bounced as she straddled her horse and looked down on a blond boy several years older, his face caught mid-laugh.

"No." River controlled the tremble in her voice.

Laya moved to the window, pushing aside the large emerald curtains. "They're still unloading his carriage. He must be here somewhere."

River peered over her shoulder. "I don't remember him leaving with so many trunks."

"Do you think he spoke with your mother yet?" Laya's unlined face scrunched.

"Please stop making that face. I swear, it's like every time you speak of him, you could—"

"Strangle him?" Laya finished.

"Don't, please. Not today."

Laya *tsk*ed and twirled her finger. "I expect better from him, yet I am never surprised."

River spun, allowing Laya to undo the buttons of her brown day dress. "He's different with me."

"I'm sure they all say that."

River rolled her eyes. Laya couldn't understand how she felt about Bass, the way he made her feel like she was the only person he ever needed by his side. She pressed her thumb into the circular silver scar on her palm, the first one her mother had given her. River had only been four, and it was Bass who had stepped in to take the remainder of the punishment. Her stomach seized at the thought of the twin scar on his palm. How many times had he done that for her? More than she could count on her fingers and toes.

"I think this dress will work." Laya held up a stiff, velvet emerald dress and helped her inside it.

"A little formal for—"

A loud thud sounded as her door slammed against her wall.

"You're late," a gravelly male voice slurred.

Of course, Bass was right. By the third bell, she should have already been at her place beneath her mother's throne to await the council members' arrival.

River spun on him, clutching her dress to her chest. "Sebastian Michael, I have been searching this castle for you since before lunch! Where in the Heldours have you been?"

She couldn't help but rake her eyes over his body hungrily. It had been three moons since he had left to go to his father's sickbed, and every day her heart had ached to be near him, hear his voice, or feel his lips against her skin. His honey-colored hair was cropped short, dark circles fanned out under his aqua eyes, and his uniform was unbuttoned at his neck, showing the top of his muscled chest.

She put her hands on her hips, the dress collapsing in on itself.

Bass's eyes flickered to her chest and then to the wall next to him. "I've been busy." But the *s* was too elongated, and he stumbled over his words.

River gestured to Laya to finish buttoning her up. "You're drunk."

"So what if I am?" His jaw clenched.

"Suck in," Laya stated as she drew the laces back.

River tried not to watch in the mirror as the layers fell just right to hide her curves. She was thicker than most women in the court, bottom-heavy for her short stature. The emerald dress had capped sleeves and was cut low on her chest, where a jewel was strategically placed to ensure it as the focal point. Laya handed her a pair of fingerless gloves that matched the dress to hide her arms.

"I'm sorry about your father. He was a great king. We'll celebrate him."

Bass shook his head vigorously. "The monsters, they did it. Those evil demons from the north—"

River let out a breath, tired of this argument. "Sebastian, they didn't kill your father."

"That magic of theirs did. It ruined our world. It does something to our people . . ."

His ramble went in one ear and out the other. She had never been beyond the castle grounds to know whether what he spoke of was the truth. River only knew stories of the Spitarians—the bloodthirsty, winged monsters that lived to the north and haunted children's nightmares. They were the enemy of the whole human race. But River had never understood the irrational fear of the unknown.

"Do you really believe that?" she asked.

Bass ignored her as he strolled to her dressing table, grabbed a small circular bottle, and handed it to Laya. She didn't comment as her pale, thin fingers worked the cream over River's skin, covering the imperfections and scars that marked her. Unlike men, princesses were not meant to have scars from swords and daggers. Laya made sure to pay special attention to the two jagged scars that peeked out of the back of the dress and ran down her spine, an accident by the healer at birth. Finally, Laya braided River's unruly dark brown curls into a low bun covering the birthmark that rested below her hairline.

River caught Bass's arm as he tried to pass and spun him back toward her. "What's going on?"

He looked at the floor.

Look at me. Please. She had never seen him this way—without that ever-present infectious smile—and it pained her.

"Tell me," she whispered as she wrapped her hand under his stubbled chin and yanked his bloodshot gaze to hers.

He blinked his blue-green eyes slowly. "The stupid prophecy always gets in the way."

"What way?"

"This. I—"

Laya cleared her throat. "I think there's another time to discuss this, no?"

Bass pulled back but not before planting a kiss on her forehead. "I'll meet you outside." He was out the door before she could respond, leaving a wet mark atop her head.

"Why wouldn't he look at me?" River breathed, brushing her hand over her stomach, her callouses catching on the way down.

"His father did just die," Laya said, pulling out her skirts. "Give him some space."

But River didn't want to give him space. His father's death only made the discussion they'd had before he left that much more important.

Bass had promised that he would make a request to the queen for River's hand in marriage on his return from attending his father. They had planned for any argument her mother would make against it—the Finn and Castor thrones would be stronger if the kingdoms were united as one. As their domains bordered each other, it would only help strengthen their armies in the newest series of attacks from the Spitarians. River's hand began to shake.

Laya snatched at it. "Did you eat today?"

River let out a huff. "Must you always ask?"

"My concern is that if you continue bottling these emotions, you are likely to explode. And frankly, I don't want to be around when you do."

"I have more control than that."

Laya squeezed her hand gently before she opened the door. "You must go."

River pushed her shoulders back, taking the strength in Laya's squeeze with her as she exited her chambers. Humans didn't show affection other than to their lovers. Had it been anyone else, she would have shied from the touch, but River trusted Laya.

The corridor was empty, other than the guard stationed to her left and Bass on her right. The silence cut through her façade, and her shoulders slumped. She was late, which would undoubtedly mean consequences.

River sucked her lip in, trying to find a loose piece of skin with her teeth. She put one foot in front of the other, forcing herself forward. The candelabras flickered against the wall, shining light onto the tiled floor.

"Has something else happened?" River said, trying to slide her hand onto Bass's arm, but he pulled away.

Before he had time to answer, the oak door groaned, opening into a well-lit portion of the throne room. Crystal chandeliers lined the ceiling, their candles glimmering softly. The white marble walls were inlaid with gold swirled in patterns and shapes, all leading to a center spot on the ceiling: the Heldours's crest. A sword, featuring jewels of the five royal families lining its hilt, pierced through a crescent moon.

"Her Royal Highness, Princess Castor," the guard boomed, "and His Royal Highness, Prince Finn."

River kept her head high as she strode into the room, her shoulders braced in perfect posture. Before her sat two massive gold thrones, one with emerald stones for the Castors and one with red rubies for the Devlyns, her mother's family name. The gold shimmered stark against the crisp, clean walls; the high-backed thrones were the centerpiece for the whole room.

The king's throne sat empty except for his emerald-and-gold crown. She tried to remember what her dead father looked like, but she couldn't conjure more than the images painted around the palace.

The council stood at an angle below the thrones, all twelve men's gazes fixed on River and Bass. Their faces were a mix of pity, eagerness, and disappointment.

Queen Castor's long hair cascaded down onto her soft rose dress. A small gold crown lay atop her head. No one could deny how devastatingly breathtaking she was; they said she was the most beautiful queen ever to live. River's features were structured the same way with high cheekbones and large red-wine lips. The significant difference was the paleness of the queen's skin, a flawless complexion with piercing green eyes. River's hazel eyes blended into her tan skin.

The queen's smile was calculated. "It seems as though you two have finally decided to grace us with your presence."

The council laughed at her joke.

River tried to control the twinge as it seethed through her stomach. She dipped her head in the requisite apology before continuing toward her customary place.

"Don't bother as you were late. You both can stand." Her mother didn't meet River's eyes but instead stared intensely at Bass.

"Yes, my queen," River and Bass repeated in unison.

River blinked rapidly, trying to clear the tunnel vision as panic raced through her body.

"As I was saying, upon his return, Prince Finn informed us that Queen Finn has concluded she is no longer physically able to rule. Which, of course, changes our timeline a little. River's first assignment was to be on her eighteenth birthday, but that is still five moons away, and Sebastian will be crowned by then." The queen drummed her long fingers on her throne.

River tried to process all her mother was saying. Bass being crowned was no surprise, but him leaving so soon was. He had been living in her kingdom since he was seven, fourteen years ago. The Finn kingdom was too small to provide the training he needed, and River's parents had felt giving her a male competitor would make her stronger. They were to learn from each other the customs of the other kingdoms and become a seamless part of their traditions; they were to become better rulers for it.

"Council, you each trained River in different areas to prepare her for the prophecy and throne. Do you feel she is ready for her assignment? Is she ready to begin taking on the prophecy?" The queen's gaze fell on each of her advisors.

The men of the council whispered among themselves.

"Yes, we feel she is," one said.

A smile lifted the corners of River's mouth. She had gone through rigorous training her whole life to prove she was worthy of not only the crown but could live up to be the savior the humans needed and the prophecy promised.

"Proficient in all, master of none. Isn't that what they say?" another whispered.

Her smile fell. They were correct, of course. She could hold her own, but would it be enough? It had to be. The prophecy had chosen her to save them all.

The queen's nostrils flared. "Well, is she ready or not?"

"As long as she follows orders. In her fragile state, we worry that if she isn't under someone's thumb, she will flounder," the oldest one's voice croaked.

Under someone's thumb?

The queen turned her eyes back to Bass. "And you have trained River to look out for herself. Do you feel she is ready to be on her own?"

River turned to him, watching the blond stubble of his clenched jaw. He lifted his chin to the queen, his piercing blue-green eyes boring into her. "No readier than she would be in six moons." The slur was still present in his voice.

How could he say that?

You will be the greatest queen ever to live. You will save the world from the beasts and live a long life. Your people will worship you. He had said those words before he had left three moons ago.

River stiffened. "I am ready!"

"No one asked you to speak," her mother chastised.

Something coiled in River's stomach as her hand began to shake. Bass's eyes fell on her hand, then he looked away, rubbing his palms over his eyes.

The queen sighed. "Sebastian, dear, I know you have been through a lot these past few days, but would you rather someone else take over for you? I am certain your new wife would miss you if you were gone so long."

"What?" River choked.

She felt it as if it were a physical blow. She closed her eyes as the dizziness overtook her. She couldn't breathe. It was as if someone very heavy were sitting on her chest.

"Riv, I—"

The queen chuckled. "Oh, I am sorry. I thought since the two of you were arriving together, he would have told you he would soon be marrying your cousin. Did you think you would have that honor?"

Everything began to collapse as if the whole castle were falling on her. She felt his strong hands clasp at her elbow, but she shook free of him. River couldn't breathe. This was all too much. The weight of the future she had dreamed of was crashing down on her.

"Sebastian, I ask you again. Is she ready?"

"Yes," he breathed.

Chapter Two

Ky

At the edge of the human territory, Ky felt like his father's son, and he hated himself for it.

He shook his bloody knuckles out as he balled his fist and prepared for the next blow. A fist flew toward him, and he ducked his head. It whooshed through the air above him. Ky brought his leg up, slamming his knee into Kisling's side. Kisling, his rightwing; why did it have to be him?

Kisling clutched his side and spat cobalt blue blood into the muddy earth.

"Finish him!" someone shouted from the circle of warriors around him.

Ky looked into Kisling's face. His dark skin showed signs of fading, and wrinkles formed in the corners of his eyes, which were turning from brown to milky white. His large burgundy wings had begun to lose their feathers. By the looks of it, Kisling had maybe another hundred years. Would his daughter return home to him before it was too late to say goodbye?

"Finish this, *Heiralomun*," Belladonna's sadistic voice growled.

He wanted to turn around and fight her instead. Not Kisling. Not his mother's faithful comrade.

The northern winds blew, shifting his midnight hair off his shoulders. The wind smelled of snow, cold and bitter, like home. That was where he wanted to be, not here hiding northeast of the Castor's last rolling green hill, stuck between the sawgrass and the edge of the decaying Blaque Forest.

Kisling stood, beckoning Ky forward. He had been holding back, making sure his blows were half speed as if his mobility reflected his age. Ky knew the truth, though. Kisling might look every bit his age, but he was still a fearsome fighter—far better than Ky.

The male flipped forward into Ky's path and struck out with a quick combination of punches. Left. Right. Under. Upper. Right. Ky blocked everyone with a short shake of his head. Kisling was allowing Ky to assert his dominance in this fight because of the disobedience he had shown to Ky when he'd spoken out against the orders given.

But when Ky looked into his rightwing's face, all he saw was the one who had stood by his mother's side throughout their lives. A male who was loyal to a fault and who had fathered someone precious to Ky, who they'd both lost nearly a century ago.

Their gazes locked, and as if in understanding, burgundy cords of magical energy began to pulse out from Kisling's hand to create a magical barrier around them. Ky felt and heard an audible pop in his ears as Kisling's magical sound barrier protected their words from outside ears. It was one of the reasons Ky had appointed him his rightwing. Kisling was a magical shadow. He could come and go unseen and unheard. For terse bursts of time, he could do the same for those around him.

"It's okay, Kylane," Kisling whispered. "I will kneel to you."

"This is wrong," Ky said through gritted teeth. "I don't want to do this."

"I know."

They had to make this conversation quick. The crowd would see their lips moving and know Kisling was using his magic.

"Then why did you make your opinions known? Why did you openly defy my father's orders? You could have kept quiet or told me alone. This would have gone easier." Ky ducked the next blow and kicked Kisling in the stomach upon coming to a standing position. His feet sank into the muck beneath him.

Muffled cheers went up around them as his rightwing doubled over, coughing.

"How will we ever learn and change if we are too scared to tell the truth?" Kisling said.

He was right, of course. He almost always was. But because Kisling had spoken out against someone in higher authority in public view, they needed to duel it out until a neck snapped to prove who was the stronger male. If Kisling won, it would challenge Ky's position, and that was trouble he didn't need. Other than Kisling, this group was full of Spitarians who didn't like or even respect him for his forward-thinking. Elsewhere in the land, his views would get approval or at least acknowledgement but not with the hunting party.

A pop exploded in his ears again, and Ky shook his head.

Kisling bent his face toward the ground, extended his neck, and tucked his wings.

This male has more honor than the rest of these dragon-damned bastards.

Ky placed his hands on either side of Kisling's head and twisted. The crack of the bone snapping sent a shiver down Ky's spine. He flinched, hoping no one had seen.

He turned in the circle around him as fists pounded in unison against their chests.

Ky repeated the sign as he stepped out of the circle and began barking orders. "Now that's over with, we shall feast and further discuss the plan." Ky pointed back. "Make sure he has food upon waking."

Ky silently thanked Kisling, not only for being an honorable male, but for helping him stall. He looked over his shoulder, hoping to see the male move. But he knew it would be hours before Kisling woke. He was old, and the magic would take much longer to refill in his body than someone who wasn't as close to fading.

Snippets of the Spitarians' conversations wafted toward his ears as he moved farther away. They believed Ky had gone too easy. Some even wanted Kisling's wings cut off, something they only did to traitors. If any part of the body was struck by a unicorn blade, it wouldn't regrow.

Ky didn't hate his own kind; quite the opposite. He thought they were magnificent and evolved, which was why he wanted nothing more than this war with the humans to be over and peace to cover the land the way it once had. He schooled his features, making sure his face was still cold and distant.

Something wet hit Ky's cheek as he walked. He didn't reach up to wipe it away.

"Did you hear me?" Hunter Victumis, the hunt's pack leader, asked. His down-turned eyes pinned Ky with a glare.

Ky cocked his head. "Mm-hmm?"

Light green lines of magic spun in lazy circles around the hunter's body. He spit out another piece of bone. This time it landed by Ky's feet.

Ky continued across the sunken ground but lifted his eyes to the hunter with disdain. "Hunter, I would've thought you had better aim."

"You haven't told me why you're here."

Ky stopped and looked at him. "I thought I made it pretty clear when I landed. Head Axel had new orders to leave the border and head into the closest human town in the Kingdom of Barlow to destroy it. He wants to make a point that he can get to anyone at any time."

"Again, I ask you, why are *you* here? He could've sent word another way. I don't need you interfering with how I conduct this party," Hunter Victumis growled.

"Maybe the Head no longer trusts you."

Ky sensed the shift in the magic. The magical cords around the hunter began to thicken into a sturdy emerald rope. It wanted to be let loose.

"So, you're an errand messenger now?"

Ky ignored him. The hunting party only respected the Head, the ruler of all the clans, despite Ky's high rank.

"Then I'll take the party, and we'll go tonight."

"We'll go in the morning," Ky said. "I'm hungry. Plus, the humans aren't going anywhere."

He needed to stall the Spitarians as long as possible. After hearing Head Axel's plans this morning, Ky had sent word to his contact in the human land to let them know they needed to evacuate the humans as quickly as possible. If they knew about his secret work for the humans cause for peace, his wings would be the next to go.

Hunter Victumis's face twitched, and his jaw clenched for the briefest of moments before his attention returned to Ky. "That land is ours. It belongs to our people."

The land had initially been the Spitarians', founded by their ancestors after they had escaped human captivity, and yet, humans had still been brought here by the Spitarians. In Ky's mind, it was as much their land as his.

He moved to walk away from Hunter Victumis, but the magic shifted again. The green cords formed into a hand of sorts as if to wrap itself around Ky. He sent his own crystalline threads toward the green hand, striking like a serpent.

"I would tread carefully if I were you, Hunter." Ky's tangible sense of magic was his greatest weapon. He saw the magical abilities and strengths of those around him in vibrant colors in a way others could not.

Hunter Victumis ignored the threat and used the toe of his boot to dig a stone from the earth. He pressed the stone between his black teeth, pushing at strands of meat to loosen them. "Heel, youngling."

There was something in the way the hunter looked at him. Ky was glad Hunter Victumis couldn't read his thoughts like the hunter's son Wrynn could or, worse, control minds like his eldest son. Hunter Victumis could simply tell the truth from a lie.

Can he tell the fine line I walk?

Ky placed his hand slowly on the hunter's shoulder and squeezed, his magical crystalline hand inches away from the hunter's energy. With one thought, Ky could use his power to rip the magic from him, absorbing it with just one touch of his bare skin.

Hunter Victumis flinched, shrugging off Ky's touch. "Well, I'm sick of waiting. It disinterests me." He spread his emerald wings behind him, then placed his black leather helmet with its spiral horns over his head, transforming himself into the beast the humans thought they were.

"Noted." Ky moved away from him toward a divot in the earth created by the ever-changing river. He tucked back the wings that protruded from his shoulder blades. They were large, nearly double his arm span, but nowhere near the largest of the Sparrows. His wings were adequate enough for him as he tended to stick close to home. Ky removed his armor, untying the leather straps that held the animal bones to his body one by one.

"Would you like help with that?" a female voice whispered in his ear.

He shook her off, lifting his head to glare at Belladonna, who stood far too close for his comfort. His eyes ran up her long legs, covered in coral pict-paint, a solid yet breathable substance they used to cover their bodies for rituals. But underneath the hard layer of paint, Ky knew her skin was nearly transparent. Her light hair was swept up into a braided crown. Her dark eyes and eyelashes contrasted with the rest of her.

Ky shook his head. "I'm good." He couldn't allow himself to be distracted by her attractiveness; it was far more important to stay away from her. She was deadly.

Belladonna was the only female in the hunting party. It wasn't because Spitarians believed females weren't capable of fighting—they did their fair share. But the hunting party was different from any of the others. They were the ones who killed the humans, guarded their borders, and followed out any of the Head's more twisted orders. She had been the only female up for the challenge, and not just out of duty. She relished in it. Belladonna had killed more humans than all of these males put together. Spitarians like her were one of the reasons the humans called them monsters.

The few pieces of armor that remained on her body were grayer than his. He had taken care to treat his animal bones before turning them into armor, while her human bones had never been adequately treated. His nose flared at the child-size bone that interlocked with others along her outer thigh. A few gaps remained in her armor, and he didn't want to be around when she found what she needed to fill them.

"Pity. I hear you're lonely these days." Her voice was like a dragon sharpening its claws on rocks, and it set his nerves on edge.

"Find someone else to play with tonight. I'm not in the mood."

She let out a huff but didn't withdraw the long nail she trailed up his bicep.

Ky raised his lips until his teeth showed and growled at her.

She didn't flinch. "Your father thinks we would be a good match."

Ky took a step back and removed his chest plate, leaving his bare chest open to the light breeze. The feathers of his wings ruffled behind him.

"You've been making your way through the females. None have complained, even though the *kupaling* bond hasn't formed with any of them. Should I be offended that you haven't tried with me?"

She didn't speak lies. Ky had spent the last few years trying to find his *kupal,* pretending to sleep his way through the mountainside. It was something that needed to be done before his father passed on with the other fadelings.

"It's not going to happen."

Coral lines swirled slowly around her body as if they were dancing. Soon the lines danced faster, and her head snapped to the right. Her brown eyes flashed coral. She blinked, then nodded. The magic that swirled around her grew stronger.

"Mm-hmm. I understand."

"Learn anything?"

"They always tell me the most interesting things." Belladonna nodded again as she listened to the fadelings around her. Her magic allowed her to speak to them after they had passed.

Ky let his shoulders sink a little. "And?"

"And why should I tell you?"

"I'm not in the mood for games." Ky could feel the rest of the hunting party's eyes on them now. The twelve males probably wondered if she would tumble him right here.

She rolled her eyes. "You're no fun."

"Bella," he growled. She was his father's favorite, and that bothered him.

Belladonna grabbed the human skull helmet—multiple skulls hammered together, intertwined with metal—and placed it on her head. There was a row of mismatched teeth across her brow, and an eye socket had been smashed and flattened for her ears.

"Human riders approach from the southwest."

Ky snapped his head in that direction. "From the Castor's land?"

She ignored him, instead turning to the others and shouting, "We've got company!"

All around them, the males put their armor back on. Ky barely had time to retrieve his chest plate before he heard the riders cresting the distant hill.

Ky didn't want to keep sticking his wings out to save the humans. He felt like he was stabbing his own people in the back. On the other hand, he felt obligated to his murdered mother. She had been so determined to find a way for peace. Did he disrespect her by continuing an ancient war or follow in her footsteps by limiting or even ceasing bloodshed on both sides?

He looked back to Kisling's unconscious body and swore. If he were awake, he could have helped keep the bloodlust to a minimum.

It would take mere minutes for his Spitarian brethren to devour their ranks. It was a waste—of energy, of life, of so much. He couldn't fathom it.

"This is not what we're here for!" Ky shouted, but no one turned around. The standing orders from Head Axel about killing humans on sight would always trump his. "I've been going all day long. I want to rest. In the morning, you can slaughter the town."

"Well, then, you relax. We'll take care of it," Belladonna said over her shoulder as she adjusted her armor, her bare feet slushing in the mud.

The Spitarians around him started to shift. Some readjusted the bones that covered their bodies, while others simply dusted off the scales of leathery skin that covered their vulnerable chests. The Spitarians had the advantage of speed and enhanced senses, but they also only had one true weakness—a weakness the humans had yet to discover.

A Spitarian could only die one way—a unicorn horn straight through the heart. It was a secret the Spitarians held close to the chest so this world didn't become like the one they'd escaped almost three millennia ago. A world in which humans and their technology enslaved every magical creature.

"Dragon-damn," Ky grumbled. Nothing was going to slow them. They were bloodthirsty, just like his father. While the Spitarian people were all trained warriors, most were home living in peace, as it should be. These thirteen, though, seemed to want to make Ky's role as hard as possible.

Someone whooped and ran forward as fifteen soldiers all clad in the Castor's emerald green crested the hill. Brown wings spread wide to blow a fierce wind at the human soldiers whose horses stumbled back.

Ky watched in horror as one of the human soldiers advanced. His spear flew through the air and plunged into a male's outstretched wing. The screech of pain rang in Ky's ears as the Spitarian tumbled to the ground, clutching his wing. It would heal quickly, though not fast enough for him to fly tonight.

Hunter Victumis stomped his foot, mud splashing as they spread in a wide circle around the humans. One human had been smart enough to retreat over the hill from whence they'd come.

"Let him go and tell this tale," Hunter Victumis shouted as they enclosed the remaining soldiers into the circle.

Ky released a string of curses as he ran toward the impending slaughter. Within a blink of an eye, the circle closed in, and the shrieks of pain began.

The Spitarians used teeth, claws, daggers, wings, and whatever else they had to pulverize the humans. Human body parts flew in every direction. Blood splattered as easily as the mud at their feet. Ky could have sworn at one point he saw a spine already stripped of skin. He reached out and caught a small object that flew toward him—a toe.

The screams of terror and pain quickly died off. By the time Ky reached the soldiers, it was too late. He knelt by a human whose chest had been ripped open; his intestines spilled over his emerald uniform. He gasped for breath as blood bubbled up from his lips.

Fadelings, forgive me, Ky prayed to his ancestors' spirits. *Guide me.*

He gripped the human around the chin and twisted, snapping his neck.

"I will celebrate your life," Ky whispered. The human words he had learned were meant to help them pass on to the afterlife.

He gritted his teeth, loathing his own race in that moment for making him do this. He moved to the next human and the next until the dirty business was done.

Belladonna's gravelly laughter brought his attention to one of the remaining soldiers.

Two Spitarians hunters tossed a human back and forth in the air like some sort of toy. Belladonna was a few feet in front of him, slowly plucking the eyeballs from a man who pleaded for his life to end.

"You're all acting as if you're no better than the human animals who tortured our ancestors. The fadelings would be ashamed. End the games. Finish them off, then rest." Ky pointed to the injured Spitarian. "Zuo, you were reckless, and now with that wing, you're of no use until morning. We'll move out when that wing is fully healed."

"Can I at least have a femur to brace the hole in my wing so it doesn't tear more while I wait for it to regrow?" Zuo almost whined as he pointed at the nearest human body.

"Of course," Belladonna said, licking the blood from her sharper-than-knifepoint claws. She walked past him and began to rip flesh from bones. "I need a few femurs as well." She shouted to the other males, who were also picking apart the corpses to mend their armor.

Ky's jaw clamped down.

"Found a letter," someone shouted.

Of course. He'd wondered what was so important that the Kingdom of Castor would risk crossing their border.

"Give it," Hunter Victumis said, advancing farther into the mess.

Ky intersected him and grabbed the outstretched envelope sealed with the Castor crest. "You can't even read the human tongue, so don't be stupid." He slipped the letter into his helmet.

The males' eyes flicked back and forth between him and Hunter Victumis.

"You should leave, then, and take that directly to the Head. It clearly was important," Victumis growled.

Ky ignored him and turned to everyone else. "Per Head Axel's orders, at dawn you'll fly out and destroy that town. If dawn arrives and Kisling hasn't awoken, you'll wait as long as it takes." *Hopefully, another day.*

He turned, not waiting to see if his order was obeyed. He knew it would be.

He was their future Head, after all.

Chapter Three

River

The smell of sweat and cleaning supplies assaulted River's nose the moment she burst into the training room. The stone slab walls were the oldest part of the castle, once the grand ballroom of the High King Heldours's summer home. The first human king before his sons had broken off into five smaller kingdoms, ruling separately. On the ceiling, River could still see the vestiges of what had been a beautiful painting centuries ago. The only remnants from a simpler time, a time before the war. The colors were now dim, muted ghosts of the fields of wildflowers on the rolling green hills.

The image calmed her, though not enough. She stripped off her gloves and began yanking at the buttons on the back of her gown, tearing at it until all that was left was her undergarments. Yet even those covered her skin too much.

Someone had propped open the window, and a sticky breeze flowed in. She stuck her head out, trying to gulp down the air. Through it, she could see those same rolling hills from the painting with a variety of wildflowers, every color of the rainbow spread out onto the lawn. It was one of the only spots left with wildflowers. The rest had been trampled and never returned. Each year the castle got bigger and bigger, expanding and destroying the natural landscape.

River stretched out her muscles, trying not to think about all that had just gone wrong or the feeling as if she was drowning. Yet the thoughts kept coming. Bass was marrying her cousin Lilith. He hadn't even bothered to ask her mother for River's hand, and to make matters worse, he didn't believe she was ready for her assignment, despite the fact he'd been telling her for almost a year that she was.

A ripple of anger washed through her and tears pricked her vision. She set off into a brisk jog, every slap of her feet against the floor vibrating up her legs, causing her muscles to contract. Physical exertion was, at times, the only thing that kept her mind sharp and the hysteria away. She ran as fast as she could around the perimeter of the room before she came to a stop and doubled over. Her breaths became ragged rasps as her vision went dark. She took a few steadying gulps of air. Yet again, she had gone a whole day without eating. If she continued down this path, she was going to land herself another visit from a healer.

River collapsed onto the large mat, letting her body sink into the material. She was ready for this assignment. She had to be. It wasn't just herself or her mother she would let down if she couldn't fulfill the prophecy. It was the whole human race.

She buried her face into the crook of her elbow and sighed. River would do this to get it over with, get out of the castle, and maybe after it was all done, she would be able to breathe for the first time in her life.

Her body shifted as another weight lay on the mat. The lemon smell was a dead giveaway.

"You didn't even stay long enough to hear the assignment." Bass's breath was warm against her cheek.

"And I'm sure you're here to tell me what that is."

"No, River, I'm here to tell you the queen didn't dismiss you."

She scoffed. "Is that all?"

"Riv," he whispered, his lips grazing her ear.

She clamped her jaw shut as her body betrayed her. She didn't want him this way. Not if she couldn't have all of him. She reluctantly pulled away and rolled off the mat.

"I did what I was instructed."

River threw up her hands. "Did you even speak to my mother?"

"Riv," he said again, grabbing her arm to pull her back toward him. He placed his lips on her knuckles and spoke against them. "You have to understand my place—"

"Your place!" she croaked. "You are a prince about to be king, not some random soldier under my mother's command."

A guard cleared his throat from the doorway.

"We should get to it then," River said, pulling her arm from Bass's grasp. She strolled from the room, leaving her dress in her wake.

River's hand shook on the brass doorknob as she opened it and stepped into the hall. The guard to her left didn't catch her eye as she walked, running her hand on the painted chair rail, steadying herself. The gold-framed paintings hung above it, and she resisted the urge to smash them all down. The gold-inlaid stairs lay ahead of her, each step designed to honor her family. She ascended them slowly, pressing her shoulders back and repeating the words etched below her bare feet.

Honor. Glory. Loyalty. Love. Ferocity. Courage. Duty.

She entered the throne room from the back this time, slipping through the emerald curtain. River could hear Bass's heavy footsteps falling behind her as he called her name.

She halted in her tracks at a new figure seated on her dead father's throne. Her blond hair was swooped into an elegant, ruby-lined bun as she leaned, whispering to the queen. The fact that Lilith dared to sit in a space that River had never been allowed sent her further over the edge.

"Cousin," Lilith said, arching one perfect peach eyebrow. "Would you like us to get you something to wear?"

River pursed her lips and ignored her. She walked past them and bent into a curtsy in front of her mother. "Forgive my abrupt departure earlier. I am ready for the assignment."

"Thank you for getting her, Sebastian," the queen said over her shoulder as he entered the room, his face flushed.

River gritted her teeth as Bass bent down and planted a kiss on Lilith's delicate pink cheek. River looked away quickly as he stepped back from the thrones.

"River, your cousin has so graciously said that she doesn't mind if Sebastian accompanies you on the way to your assignment." The queen squeezed her niece's hand. "Isn't that wonderful?"

"Of course," River agreed through the twist in her gut.

"Well, thank your cousin," the queen prodded.

River looked at Lilith's petite frame in the gold throne. Her head barely reached the emerald crest behind her. She looked childlike, just as River had when she'd snuck in as a small girl pretending she was queen.

That is not your throne. It is mine, and I will rip you from it if I have to.

"Thank you, Lilith, for that kind gesture. I am sure Sebastian is just as thrilled with my company as I am with his."

One perfectly shaped pale eyebrow rose on Lilith's face, the corner of her pink-lined mouth sliding up. "You're right. I'm sure he is quite sick of me. After all, we have spent the last three moons together, haven't we, my sweet?" Her eyes flicked to Bass, and River's stomach hit the marble floor.

River's eyes bore into Lilith's as she imagined throwing a small blade into her symmetrical face. She pressed her hand to her thigh, wishing she had strapped a blade to it earlier. She could almost feel the bulk below her palm.

Her vision wavered as little prickles of goose flesh spread from her heart outward. She felt afraid, and she wasn't sure why. It was a sensation she got every now and then when her emotions ran too high, one that generally resulted in a bad headache that left her in bed for days.

She pinched the back of her neck to steady herself.

"River. Dear cousin, you don't look so well. Are you having one of your hysterical fits?"

She ignored Lilith and squeezed harder until the fear ebbed.

"She's fine," Bass said, stepping closer.

"My queen, may we discuss the assignment?" River nearly pleaded. "I'm anxious to get started. Also, I don't feel Prince Finn's presence on the journey is necessary. I'm sure any old guard will suit his place just fine."

"Riv!" Bass whispered next to her. "You don't understand what you're saying." He grabbed for her elbow, but she shook him free.

"While you might not feel he should be there, I do insist. This assignment is of the utmost importance. King Morsaw has written us a letter requesting our aid in dealing with a delicate matter. His estranged son Barthomule—I am sure you remember the story of the prince who killed his mother." She waved her hand theatrically. "We celebrate her life."

"We celebrate her," the room echoed in remembrance.

Of course, River knew the story. Who hadn't heard the bloody tale of King Morsaw's first wife, though it had happened nearly ten years before her time? She remembered how Laya had always told the tale slightly differently than the rest of the castle.

The queen continued, "King Morsaw has learned Barthomule has been passing Morsaw military secrets to the Spitarians."

If Barthomule had been passing secrets to the Spitarians, it could, of course, account for the number of increased soldier deaths the five kingdoms of Heldours had seen in the past few years. It would certainly account for the recent invasions on the towns bordering the north, which had increased so much that the towns had been abandoned altogether.

"With that, River, the council and I feel your first assignment toward fulfilling the prophecy should be the elimination of this threat."

River lifted her eyes to her mother. "Elimination of . . ."

"You are to kill Barthomule." She paused and then declared, "*Only she will stand the fight. Only she can end it all.*"

The room exploded as the words repeated all around her.

River had heard the line so many times. Whispered as a prayer every time someone walked past her, written on the wall or in the gifts she received from the townsfolk. She had known that killing would be involved in bringing peace, leading a battle of some sort, but somehow, she hadn't expected the assassination of one man to be the start of it all. It had been naive of her, she realized now.

The five kingdoms were supposed to be united, though they weren't fighting as one. Instead, they all stood alone against the same enemy passing similar messages back and forth about the need for strength, yet never rallying together. Each kingdom was too proud to choose a leader among one of the rulers, each feeling they alone were the best suited for the job. How would she amass a great army and bring peace when the humans could barely stand one another?

Eliminate. Assassinate. Murder.

The words rattled in her brain. She clamped down the gnawing feeling in her intestines, pushing away the fear that began to spread.

She cleared her throat. "When would I leave?"

"You both will ride out tonight—if that is agreeable to you, Sebastian. I'm sure you are ready to return home to your throne."

"I think at first light would be better . . . for us to be well rested."

Because he's still drunk.

"Of course. Whatever you think is best. I have sent Leftenant Leon ahead, and he will meet you outside of Neven with all the information you will need."

"Thank you, my queen."

"Chosen!" the queen shouted, rallying the room.

The room erupted, echoing her, "Chosen!"

Only River didn't repeat them. All she wanted was to hold the words—and the bloody prophecy—at bay.

Laya's thin fingers worked the bar of soap through River's thick clumps of hair, combing through the knots. Laya gently massaged her scalp to ease some of her tension. The lavender smell wafted up from the warm water and into the air.

River flicked one of the wildflower petals across the water.

"I presumed Barthomule was dead," Laya said. "No one saw him since the day he left the castle."

"Evidently not," River said, dipping her head under the water. She wished she could stay under the water forever, where she could block out all the noise and where no one could hear her screams.

Tiny yet strong fingers raised her back up. "And they think it's the Prince of Morsaw selling secrets?"

River plucked at the shedding strands of hair clinging to her legs. "Well, he's not a prince anymore. Though how would he get this information? Someone on the inside must be telling him."

"Did they at least say where you were to go?" Laya braided the thick curls into a crown atop her head.

"A town called Neven to meet Leftenant Leon. I think he's one of my mother's personal guards."

"Leon?" Laya's finger stilled.

River looked over her shoulder at her friend's pale face. "Do you know him? I don't believe I've met him. Has he been stationed here before?"

Laya pursed her lips.

"What?"

"It's nothing," Laya said, her voice squeaking. She turned her away toward the window, where she raised another bucket of hot water.

River stood and crossed her arms. "It's not nothing. I can tell by your voice. Have you heard something? Is he not trustworthy?"

"No, it's not that." Laya turned. A pink streak of blush ran from her neck to her cheeks. "Sit down. You'll catch a chill."

"So I will," River said, remaining standing.

"Oh, fine!" She gestured for River to sit, and she obliged. "Do you remember the boy from my childhood? The one from my stories?"

"The gray-eyed fisherman's son?" River said, smiling. Laya's childhood had been her favorite stories growing up. Though Laya was less than five years her senior, her stories always made River feel as though she'd grown up in Hickman, the small seaport kingdom that smelled of salty air and fresh fish, alongside Laya.

"Yes, that one."

"Is Leon . . . your Leon?"

"He was never my anything," Laya said, dumping the bucket onto River's upturned face.

River sputtered, wiping her face. "Just as Bass was clearly never mine."

"River Rowan, I warned you about him over and over. You refused to listen. It was that smile."

River rolled her eyes and stepped out of the tub. She wrapped herself in the warmed blanket Laya handed her. "Unlike Leon's smile, then?"

"Enough talk. I'm sure when you come home from seeing him, you can tell me all about it." Laya ushered her to her bed and tucked her in.

"Goodnight, Riv." Laya bent and pecked her on the cheek. "I'll see you before the sun breaks to ready you. Sleep well."

Her touch and voice had always been such a comfort to River when no one else had ever shown her any kind of familiar love. The closest she'd ever had were the stolen moments with Bass.

River hesitated only for a moment before she grabbed Laya's hand. "Will you stay and tell me a story of your home? I'm afraid I won't sleep if you don't."

Laya smiled, and her lyrical voice wove a tale of two sisters swimming in the largest body of water River could ever imagine, of stringing shell necklaces, and of a boy whose eyes looked like the sky after a perfect night storm.

Chapter Four

Ky

Wrynn's fist flew toward Ky's face with just enough time for him to duck away from it. But Wrynn's foot was too fast, swiping behind his ankles. Ky landed on his back in a heap, his breath coming out in a whoosh.

"Brother," Wrynn said, reaching down a taupe-colored hand, "you're distracted." His eyes locked on Ky's.

"It's nothing." Ky grasped at the hand that pulled him to his feet.

"Really? Is that why you came here rather than taking the letter I know you carry to your father first?"

Ky felt Wrynn's magic as it swirled around his head. "Knock it off."

"What?" his leftwing said, feigning innocence.

Ky frowned, stepping back. He couldn't let Wrynn's magic anywhere near his mind. Despite their love for each other, Wrynn wouldn't understand.

"Just testing the boundaries," Wrynn joked, but when Ky's expression didn't change, he held his hands up. "Sorry, brother. You know, sometimes thoughts just float toward me. I can't help but snatch them up. It's instinct. You know I'd never enter your mind without permission."

"I know," Ky said with a crooked grin, trying to release some of his own tension. He needed Wrynn not to pry. "Because if you tried, I would beat the dragon-damned bones out of you." He leaned down, ducking his head, and stomped his feet like a dragon as if to charge.

"I seem to remember you being better at that," Wrynn said.

They both laughed, remembering their childhood games.

Wrynn turned his back and headed toward the nearest water basin, his blond-and-green hair braided down his back. Ky squeezed his eyes shut, trying to hide the truth written in them. Wrynn knew nothing of Ky's secret life. Even if he did, his leftwing would stay by his side no matter the cost, as was his duty: to fly into battle on Ky's left, second in command.

For Ky, the cost of losing his best friend, his sister's *kupal*, wasn't worth the risk. He could put his own life in danger, but he would do anything to keep the people he loved from harm. So Ky lied to Wrynn about his business nearly every time they spoke. Wrynn's face needed to be shocked when the Head's rule crumbled beneath his feet.

"Azalea sends her love," Ky said, changing the subject.

Wrynn turned, his hands cupped with water. "Does she fare well?"

"As well as can be expected." Ky didn't mention her fainting spells or the odd bruises. Azalea's relationship with the Head always went unspoken between them. Despite Wrynn's loyalty to the crown, his *kupaling* bond would force him to kill the Head if he knew of her health.

Wrynn's slate-gray eyes narrowed as he closed the distance. The rare times he was allowed to see Azalea, they had made a pact not to talk about their problems. Wrynn's father was Head Hunter Victumis; his and Azalea's lives were constantly endangered, so they spoke nothing of it. Ky honored them both by keeping each of their secrets.

Wrynn simply nodded, picked up his staff, and clicked it against Ky's, the wood vibrating in their hands, initiating round two.

Hit after hit, Wrynn came out on top. He was the superior fighter, and typically Ky could almost match him blow for blow. Recently, though, as Ky's promise to his mother to help the humans became harder to hold true to, and his father's cruelty was destroying so many lives, he couldn't see the point in training.

Another blow from the wooden staff smashed against Ky's face.

"Nice hit." He spat deep navy blood onto the ground.

"You're an easy target just standing there. I think we should call it quits for today, brother." Wrynn took the staff from Ky's hands.

Ky nodded. "I need to check on the girls, anyway."

"You check on them every day. Do they change that much?" Wrynn smiled over his shoulder as he walked off the dirt training field.

"We all have our vices."

"Yes, yours comes in the form of massive beasts that don't like the word no," Wrynn said, reminding him of the time one of Ky's dragons had stolen the lamb leg Wrynn had been roasting over a fire.

"You're still so bitter. That was years ago," Ky retorted.

"You could've stopped her."

"What fun would that have been?" Ky said, still rubbing his jaw. "Plus, the look on your face is one we'll remember for centuries."

Wrynn laughed. "I'll leave you to it then, but maybe deliver the letter to Head Axel first?" He gave Ky a pointed look. "I'll see you at the festival in a few moons?"

"Az and I will both be there," Ky said, answering the question Wrynn was really asking. He turned his back on his friend, walking toward the shelves that held the weapons.

"Brother?" Wrynn said hesitantly

"Yes." Ky did not turn as he placed their staffs back in their proper places, then sheathed his dagger.

"Can I ask you a question?"

Ky turned at the hesitation in Wrynn's voice. The look of pain that was so evident on his normally happy face made Ky's heart sink.

"Do you think it's possible for . . ."

Ky crossed the distance until he was nearly face-to-face with Wrynn.

"I'm not even sure you'll know the answer. I just thought because you read so many of the written records of our ancestors, you might know something about it. I just . . . Has Az ever mentioned offspring to you?"

"Offspring?" Ky said, taken aback. It usually wasn't the kind of thing he and Wrynn talked about. Nor was it something his sister had ever brought up to him.

"Well, a normal *kupal* is pregnant quite quickly after their *kupaling*—"

"Just because I'm not a *kupal* doesn't mean I'm not aware of what happens. You tumble like damned dragons for the next few months and some romantic dragon shit about your magic intertwining to create life."

Wrynn laughed. "Right, but your sister and I barely see each other, and when we do, trust me, we 'tumble like damned dragons,' as you put it. But, well, nothing. I've never met a *kupal* that hasn't created an offspring within the first year of *kupaling,* and it's going on ten years now." He sighed, looking Ky square in the eyes. "I was just wondering if you've read anything about that from the old world. I mean, I know we're *kupaled.* I can sense her even now in ways I couldn't with . . ." He didn't need to mention the females he had been with prior to Ky's sister.

Ky's stomach sank. "I haven't, but I'll look into it," he said, grasping Wrynn's shoulder.

Wrynn nodded, bringing his hand to his chest before unfurling his massive green wings. The interlapping emerald scales shone in the sunlight. He pushed off the ground, and in two beats, the dirt swirled all around Ky. Wrynn was in the air and out of sight.

Ky let out the breath he had been holding the whole time Wrynn was speaking. He had never felt the *kupaling* magic, but he had read plenty about it. It was one of the most powerful forms of magic. He didn't know for sure, but he guessed the issue was that it took so much magic to create life; in all of those times Wrynn and Azalea were together, he'd bet her magic level wasn't even halfway full.

How could he tell his best mate that not only was Head Axel taking Wrynn's *kupal* away from him, but also robbing him of his chance of an offspring?

Head Axel Sparrow stood hunched over his desk. The shiny, unnatural white of the bones stood out against the darkness that was his office. The bones of unicorn horns intertwined to create an extensive desk that took up nearly half the room with a slate glass plate laid on top.

"Kylane, welcome home." Head Axel beamed up at him, pounding his fist to his chest.

Azalea didn't flinch as she sat cross-legged in the middle of the floor. Small *Crystolas* stones formed a circle around her. The *Crystolas* were the ultimate source of all of their magic: raw energy. A larger one sat in her lap, clutched between both still hands. The milky white stone's magic created a flowing barrier that encircled her as smaller lines of energy shot off the circle and directed toward the center.

Ky clenched his jaw tight as the power was slowly drained from the smaller ones into the large one in Azalea's lap. She was creating a supercharged *Crystolas*, allowing her to use her powers longer. "She looks exhausted. How long has she been at it?"

Transferring magical energy was a tricky pursuit. His sister, unlike the rest of the Spitarians, had to physically touch the *Crystolas* to steal and use their power. Though they were a naturally occurring mineral that grew deep down in the rock bed beneath the soil, they didn't regrow like trees. Once the energy was used, the *Crystolas* disintegrated.

Head Axel walked around the front of his desk and placed his hand on Ky's shoulder. "She insists she is fine. And you, son?"

Ky's gaze flicked back to his sister's long gown, the rust-colored fabric too thick for her body temperature. Her blue-black hair was untamed, and beads of sweat slowly trickled down the point of her nose. He wanted to reach in and pull her from the trance.

"Fine, my Head."

"Hunter Victumis sent me a report."

Ky balled his hands into fists as he crossed his arms. "I was coming here to do that myself. He didn't need to."

Head Axel withdrew his hand and rubbed his temple. "Why is it you didn't try to *kupal* with Belladonna? She would make a great match for you. You don't have that much time, and if you can't produce *heiralomun* before I *fade,* civil war will break out. Is that what you want?"

"I know my duties." Ky's voice sounded so eerily similar to Head Axel's. He shifted his helmet behind his back, shoving the letter in, hoping his father hadn't been told about it by the hunters.

"Maybe if you spent less time worrying about your sister and her duties, you would have enough time to make a match with a female." The Head picked up a knife from his desk, flipped it in his hands, blade side coming down, and sliced open his palm. A few drops of blue blood welled before the wound knitted itself back together. Ky could sense the amount of magic in those few drops of blood, almost like a taste on his tongue.

He wouldn't find a *kupal*. Belladonna had accused him of sleeping his way through the mountainside. The rumors placated his father. It proved that Ky was trying to find himself the Heart that would guide him once he was the Head. Though if Belladonna had asked the females more questions, they would have informed her there was nothing magical about the experience; no exchanges of energy were made. He didn't want a *kupal*. All that had ever brought his father and sister was pain.

Ky could feel the levels of magic rise, sense the threads as they pushed against the Head's.

"Leave her out of this. It isn't something you can force, like some fickle human marriage. You have no power over the *kupal* bond," he said, flexing his twitching hand at his side. He couldn't be crowned Head without a *kupal*—proof he could produce an heir. "I'm trying." He fought the urge to turn toward the window. He wanted to look anywhere but at the Head.

"Your sister managed to find her *kupal* decades ago. Though I would've chosen differently for her—"

"You would've been pleased if she wasn't *kupaled* so she didn't feel the pull to leave you."

Head Axel slammed his fists down on the table. The slate glass vibrated under the pressure of his meaty fists. "Kylane! I want what's best for both of you. Why do you fight your duty?"

Ky had gotten his build from his father, the height and the thick expanse of his shoulders, the muscles that ran down each of their bodies. Their faces looked almost identical as well, except for the age that appeared on the Head's, with their prominent jaws with broad cheekbones. The Head's long midnight hair was tied back where Ky let his hang about his shoulders. Ky had grown to hate everything about this man, hated staring at him as much as he hated looking at himself in the mirror.

His father stepped toward him and tapped his fist against Ky's heart lovingly. The Head's large onyx membrane wings trembled behind him. His dark brown eyes watered a little. "I just want to protect you."

"I know, Father," Ky said quietly. He hadn't always hated his father. While Head Axel loved his children fiercely, it was a twisted love, the kind grown from unimaginable loss.

Head Axel walked to the balcony and stared out. "I don't want to fight with you. Your mother would have hated how much we're at each other's throats all the time. Just promise me you'll try?"

"We have another option."

Head Axel ignored him. "The Hunter said you had a letter. Read it, please."

Ky stiffened. *Damn the Hunter.*

He pulled it from his helmet, sliding his finger under the seal, breaking it. He hoped he wouldn't have to lie to his father about the contents of this letter. He had done it before, several times, altering words here or there. He was the only one who'd bothered to learn to read the human tongue. No one else could tell the truth from a lie.

"Report, Kylane." Head Axel's voice came out strained. He still hadn't turned to face Ky.

The rough paper trembled in his hands. He scanned over it quickly, his brows wrinkling. "It's an invitation."

"Well?"

Ky cleared his throat. "The first paper reads: 'The honorable and beautiful Queen Castor of the Castor Kingdom requisitions the honor of the magnificent and duly honorable King Morsaw of the Morsaw Kingdom to join in celebration. Prince Finn will be wed to Lady Lilith Devlyn on the full moon of the first day of the winter moon.'"

"Anything else?"

Ky flipped the paper over seeing a handwritten note. Printed in small lettering. "'Princess Castor has left the castle.'"

The Head turned slowly, his face a broad, demonic smile. "Well, isn't that perfect."

"What?" Ky asked, confused.

"We will need your sister for this."

"For what?"

"Azalea." Head Axel's voice boomed toward his sister's form.

The magic flickered all around her, and then the line of energy disappeared, returning to its original form.

Azalea tilted her head up. "Ky! Welcome home."

She got to her feet and wobbled a little before he caught her. She pressed a kiss to his cheek. Ky noticed right away the dark circles that ran under her brown skin, the blue almost as blue as her cobalt eyes.

"There is no color in your cheeks. You're exhausted," Ky chided.

She ignored him, turning to her father. "Most of the magic is transferred, Father." She placed the large *Crystolas* on his desk. "What's this?" She grabbed at the paper in Ky's hand.

"A wedding invitation for one of the human princes," Head Axel said. "What a perfect opportunity for us."

Her face broke into a smile to match his. "Are you thinking like the Stars?"

Ky's head began to fill with so many questions. What did the other Spitarian royal family that had been killed have to do with the humans?

Head Axel stroked his daughter's cheek with his long white claws. "You are just like me. Can you handle it?"

Azalea's head tilted to the side, her lips moving back and forth as she thought. "We would have to find a poison that affects them all, but yes, it could be done."

"Poison? Can I be included in this conversation?" Ky said.

Azalea rolled her eyes. "Father wants to poison the whole wedding. If we're lucky, the kings or the heirs will be in attendance."

Ky's stomach turned. It was precisely how she had killed off the whole island on which the Stars had lived because they'd refused to help in Head Axel's war on humans. Az had blown unicorn dust through every inch of the island. It was a slow and painful way for a Spitarian to die. A body was utterly immobile while the blood pushed all the dust into its heart until it exploded.

"And we would do that why?"

"It would leave the humans in a frenzy and allow us to invade with little effort and wipe them out for good. They will be too busy trying to recoup. It gives us the perfect opportunity." Head Axel turned back to Azalea. "I'll reach out and see if anyone knows of such a product."

Azalea nodded.

"And there was another note about the so-called chosen princess finally leaving her keep."

Ky wished he had never read that part. When his mother disappeared, it had been just after she had spoken a prophecy over Queen Castor's daughter about bringing peace. His father had been waiting over twenty-one years to punish the human who had taken his *kupal* from him. Elora Castor.

"Where is she headed?" Azalea directed the question at her brother.

Ky could almost see the bloodlust in her eyes. "It doesn't say."

"Ky should go after her, Father. Poison would be too easy for her. It should be one of us that watches the light leave her eyes. I would do it myself, but I am too busy with the *Crystolas* forging." Azalea had been working for almost five years now to recreate a new source of magical energy; the *Crystolas* weren't going to last forever.

"I am not going to go out and kill the princess. This plan—no, *both* plans are asinine."

Head Axel began to pace, his hands covering his face. "You're just like your mother, believing the humans can be trusted. That got her killed. If I had known you were going to cause this much trouble, I would have never appointed you to be *Heiralomun*."

"As if you had any other option. Which one of your other sons is still standing?" It was an argument they'd had many times before. When Ky's brothers had reached maturity, their magic at full strength, each had to fight to the death with the Head for the right to become *Heiralomun*. With Axel's *kupal* dead, he had no way of creating more heirs. Conception was only possible with a *kupal*, leaving Ky the only option for the throne.

"Azalea, it seems your brother isn't up for the task. Maybe you can do it?"

The thought of his sister viciously ripping apart the princess like Belladonna had done with the humans earlier flashed in his mind.

Ky stared at his father. "I will take care of it."

Head Axel nodded knowingly. "I thought you would see reason."

"Of course, Father." Ky needed to get word to his human contacts right away. This was going to be a disaster.

"Take Belladonna with you. It will give you a chance to see how well your magic plays together, maybe even *kupal*."

"Belladonna isn't someone I want as my Heart. Not to rule alongside me."

"I think she's perfect," Azalea chimed in before she began scribbling a note on a piece of paper. "I will reach out and let her know to meet you here promptly."

She clutched at her *Crystolas* with one hand and the letter in another. Closing her eyes, the note began to flutter from her hand. She opened her palm as a silent breeze picked it up. Ky still marveled at her magic. She was a siphoner and could do anything she wanted with her power except for that small catch. The paper floated toward the closed balcony. The doors banged open as the paper flew out. Ky wanted to fly after it to make sure it never reached its destination.

"Oh," she whispered just as the *Crystolas* at her neck dissolved and turned to ash. His sister's body crumpled to the ground, and the letter plummeted to the earth below.

Chapter Five

River

A gentle hand stroked River's cheek, easing her awake. No sun streamed through her large windows, but Laya had opened the curtains anyway. River stretched, feeling the instant discomfort in her belly and the unease of all she had to do.

Laya held out a piece of fresh-baked cinnamnut bread, and the spicy-sweet smell made River's mouth water. She sat up and snatched the piece of bread eagerly. "Oh, save me. It's even warm."

Laya beamed. "It's like I know you."

River pushed up, kissing Laya on the cheek before she took a small bite, letting it melt on her tongue.

"Eat it all," Laya said sternly.

River's aversion to food had never seemed to be in her control. Sometimes she was ravenous and ate everything in sight. Other times even the thought of food sent bile up her throat.

"I am." River sighed, slowly enjoying the warm bread as it slid down her throat. "Can't you come?"

"No, dear, but I would if I could." She reached out and pulled River to her feet.

"I am to spend all that time with Bass. What am I even supposed to say to him?"

Laya's face pinched, and then she turned to the bundle on the velvet chair by the bed. "Try the truth, and maybe you will feel a little relief after."

"Mm-hmm."

"Here," Laya said, helping her into a scratchy men's trouser and white tunic.

River tucked in the shirt the way she had seen it worn by the villagers who sold their wares by the front gate. "So I am to be a man?"

"I think you are to be hidden."

"Well, then we might need to do something about this." She pointed to her crown braid. Large chunks of brown curls had come undone in her fitful sleep.

Laya's nimble fingers worked quickly to undo River's braid and redo a stronger one that ran down River's back. She tugged on it gently before spinning River back to face her.

"Listen to me. No matter what happens out there"— she pointed to River's heart—"don't let anyone tell you to do something you're not comfortable with. Think before you act. And don't let your emotions get the better of you." She placed her hands on either side of River's face. "You are stronger than you know." She kissed River's forehead.

River's own mother had never pressed her lips to River's skin. Laya's sisterly affection warmed River's heart, keeping her raging feelings at bay.

She threw her arms around Laya and wrapped her in a fierce hug. "I love you."

Laya held her tightly for a moment and then pulled back. "It's time."

Hand in hand, they walked from the room, ignoring the eyes that followed them through the castle.

River tried not to panic as she walked toward the front gates. They loomed in front of her, the Castor family crest in twisted ornate metal—the doors to her cage. Her back was to the castle, and her gaze focused ahead on an unknown future. She didn't scuff her feet as she walked, but she still felt the gravel as it caught in the cracks of the worn boots.

If Laya's hand hadn't been in hers, she wasn't sure the palace staff would have recognized her on her way out. Bass sat, shoulders high, on his beautiful palomino, facing away from them as he waited. Another horse stood beside his, but it wasn't River's chestnut stallion; it was a dappled gray mare.

"You're late. Mount, and let's go." There was no friendliness in his voice.

River scowled at him. He wore almost the same outfit she had on, except for one minor difference: slung around his hip was his sword, the snake's head staring at her.

"Well, hello to you too," River bit out.

Bass didn't turn his head. He simply kicked his stallion into a canter.

River mounted the mare, studying her coloring.

She looked down as Laya patted the mare's rear. Their eyes locked, and Laya bowed her head, something she hadn't done unless required in years. River inhaled, the sign of respect sticking in her throat. She grasped Laya's hand, squeezing tightly.

"Remember my words."

River nodded, but she stared straight ahead, kicking her heels into the horse's sides.

She didn't turn to look at the castle as they rode down the path leading them away. She had only seen her mother venture out under her personal guard. She wasn't under heavy guard now and knew it was because she was within the human kingdoms. In disguise, they were relatively safe. As safe as a kingdom at war could be, at least.

War was what they called it, though there had never been an actual battle between the humans and the Spitarians. The five human kingdoms of Heldours had never gotten along with the ancient race to the north. The human borders had always been heavily guarded in fear of magic crossing over and the stories passed down of what the creatures could do. They were monsters only out for blood. In the years since River had been born, they had proven just that. All of the towns on the border had been invaded, and the human villagers slaughtered. The humans couldn't rally the soldiers fast enough to protect the border towns. Pulling back to regroup, over and over again. Eventually, anyone old enough to hold a weapon was forced to defend their home; farmers became soldiers and boys became men.

Any village close to the borders was abandoned, and the inner towns overcrowded.

"Keep your eyes alert," Bass yelled, pushing his horse faster over the rolling green hills.

River looked up to the blue sky. She had never seen a Spitarian, so she really wasn't sure what she was even looking for. She knew only the drawings from her studies about their grotesquely misshapen forms. The pictures depicted large, mangled wings sprouting from bone backs that doubled their arm span.

Bass once described them as sadistic, feral animals. He told the same battle story any time she questioned their humanity—he'd once seen a Spitarian soldier kill a human. With one bite, its massive teeth punctured gaping holes in the man. Instead of dropping the corpse, it continued to rip the flesh from his bones until the man was no longer recognizable. The first time Bass told her that story, he had given her a bloodied black feather that had fallen off a Spitarian's wing. The feather was long, the length of her forearm, black as night, and speckled with human blood. It was the first and only gift Bass had ever given her.

"And what am I supposed to do if I see one?" River shouted back. "You gave me no weapons." She patted the saddlebags looking for a quiver or a dagger.

"Ride faster then." He chuckled. "Ride like Euphrine River."

She knew that playful tone. His words brought her back to her childhood when they had raced around the castle's lake until her legs were numb. They would throw themselves into the lake and float until the sky turned dark and the stars shone down. She didn't bite the bait, though she did speed up until she was next to him.

"So, you plan to leave me defenseless?" she shouted into the wind.

Bass's smile faded. "You know as well as I that our weapons are no good against them." He pulled his horse ahead again, and she followed.

He was right. They had learned it over and over again in their studies. No weapon, sword, arrow, or fire seemed to kill them. They did bleed and could be wounded, but nothing could kill them. Small children who were unable to hold a weapon were taught to run and hide rather than try to fight. She didn't see how a race could be unbeatable, and if that was the case, how was she expected to bring peace if they were indestructible?

"And how am I to kill Barthomule with no weapons?"

"You will know when you need to know."

River dug her heels in, speeding past him, and shouted over her shoulder, "That seems to be the way these days. You seem to be keeping a lot of things to yourself!"

She bit her tongue as she pushed the horse, riding far ahead.

Chapter Six

Ky

Azalea's body fell almost in slow motion into a large heap. Her midnight hair with shades of blue fanned out around her.

"Azalea!" Ky screamed as his hand trembled at his side.

Her eyes didn't flutter as Ky whispered her name, cursing himself for not stopping her, knowing how drained she already was. He bent and gently scooped her body up into his arms. Although they were nearly the same size, he didn't struggle. She still looked beautiful even though her normally brown skin was so pale.

"Is she breathing?" his father asked, frozen in shock.

"Maybe if you would stop using your daughter as a magical weapon, this would stop happening to her!" Ky shouted.

He cradled her body to his. She was still cold; only in death would she be warm. Their thick skin kept them impervious to all climates. Fury burned inside him as he felt for the power that generally emanated off her body. Ky sent his power in waves, searching for hers, but as it curled around her, it snapped back with what he always feared. Her magic was dangerously low.

"Kylane," his father whined.

Ky ignored him. He couldn't stay here. He tore from the office with his twin in his arms and ran down the hallway until he reached what had once been a grand marble staircase. The stairs were cracked and eroded. Slick moss grew on every surface. He descended, the tips of his wings pulsing with anger as he leaped over the holes. He knew where each crack was without having to look. Years of practice made this path easy. It wasn't the first time he had found her like this and, what was worse, he knew it wouldn't be the last.

Ky pressed her body close to his, ducking into the hallway. He didn't bother taking the stairs one at a time. He simply shot up through the center of the staircase, his wings maneuvering the turns effortlessly. He reached the bird tapestry, trying not to jostle Az's body as he flew them up to the second floor. He passed several doors before he reached the door painted blue and kicked it open with his foot.

Her four-poster bed stood prominent in the center of the room. Her royal blue blankets were straight and neat, as if she never slept in them. Her room was the opposite of his. That was the pattern of their lives. She had been born moments before Ky, and, as she liked to constantly remind him, she was the superior twin.

Ky placed her body gently on the bed, smoothing the hair back from her sweaty face and tracing his fingers first over the dark circles under her eyes and then down the bruises on her neck. His magic flickered with anger, and Ky pushed it down as he reached over to the end table, picking up a small white *Crystolas* no bigger than a human pinky finger. He placed it in the center of her chest. Then he grabbed a yoligs leaves candy out of the bowl and placed the small amber shard on her tongue. Ky took a few steps back, not wanting his magic to interfere with hers.

The *Crystolas* began to glow, its magical light bouncing off the walls of the room. Azalea's fingers twitched, her chest rising and falling steadily, and the coloring of her skin returned to normal. As the magic flowed from the gem into his sister, Ky sensed her magic refilling. The *Crystolas* turned to dust on her chest, all of its magic gone.

"I think you rather enjoy playing the hero, Ky." Azalea's voice came out in a croak.

"Don't joke, Az. I don't have the patience today."

She turned her head to meet Ky's gaze. Her cobalt eyes bore into him.

"Don't think you're getting away with not explaining to me what happened this time. I saw you merging the energy from the smaller *Crystolas* into a larger, more powerful one. What else did he have you doing?" Ky's question came out louder than he'd intended, though it wasn't her he was mad at.

She blinked lazily at him before looking away. She wouldn't tell Ky; she never did. What Azalea did with the Head, the missions he put her on, she kept secret. He would use her and her power until she blacked out, until he used every last drop he could without killing her.

"Az," Ky almost whined. "Why didn't you refill your necklace? You had all the power in your fingers, and you only used it for him?"

"Don't start." She patted the bed next to her.

He obeyed, not wanting to fight with her. He would get her out of here one day. Let her be free so she could be more than a weapon. She was one of the only things he had left in this world, and there wasn't anything he wouldn't do to please her.

She propped her feet in his lap playfully. "So, tell me, what else happened at the border? Was it as bad as your face is making it out to seem?"

"Why don't you ask what you really want to know?" Ky teased her. "'Did you see Wrynn? Did he look well? Was he with any females?'" he mimicked in a high-pitched voice.

"He wouldn't dare be with any females. If he was, he wouldn't walk for another century," she commented. "But, yes. How is he?"

"He wasn't with the hunting party. Hunter Victumis had sent him on some family errand, but I saw him later at the training pit, and he . . ." Ky wasn't about to tell her that Wrynn was concerned about offspring. "He was excited for the next festival and seeing you."

She nodded, but a slight frown appeared on her face. She was one of the lucky ones, having found a *kupal* so easily. He pitied her, though—despite their bond, Head Axel still refused to let them be together. His reason was purely selfish. If she were off in a household of her own, like other females, he wouldn't be able to use her powers at his will.

I will never kupal and allow that to become me.

Despite that, Azalea wouldn't leave him, believing deep down her father, the man who used to sing her to sleep, was still in there somewhere. Ky didn't believe their father still existed. He was only the cold-hearted Head, but Ky wouldn't leave her, not here and not with him. So, he stayed.

"But Belladonna was there? Father seems very taken with her."

"He can have her," Ky grumbled.

"I should send that letter."

Ky shook his head in disbelief. "Rest. A few more hours won't make a difference. The human princess is traveling slowly, probably by horse. I can catch it easily."

"Mm-hmm. So tell me, did you finish off the last of the human towns? Any injuries on our part?"

"Why do you say that with such joy? Loss of life isn't something we should be happy about."

Az scoffed. "Why do you care? They took our mother from us. I wish you would care for ours the way you care for the memory of something she wrongfully believed in."

Ky swallowed the hurt he felt. Azalea was right. His mother had died believing the humans could be reasonable and peaceful. After her passing, he had sought the humans for whom his mother had such fondness, finding them to be just as good as she had described. This was why he still held a torch for peace.

With hesitation, he told Azalea about the most recent attacks on the humans and how they had conquered the two towns before he had arrived. Hundreds of humans had been slaughtered for no purpose. Ky's stomach turned with every gory detail. And though he was sure his sister pitied the humans, she believed what most did, that humans were lesser beings. Yet she—also like the rest—feared the day when the humans' technology caught up with magic and plunged the Spitarians back to the enslavement of the old world.

No, Az wouldn't risk her own life to save theirs. But Ky was going to do everything in his power to stop the Head's reign of terror.

Ky removed his hand from his sister's sleeping body, opened the door quietly, and crossed the hallway. He looked over the balcony to the room below at the long wooden table that had once been lined with his brothers' smiling faces. Ky studied the names they had each carved on the table before their rightful place. Some places had multiple names because each seat had seen different brothers over the years. Ky lingered on the names of the siblings he remembered. His siblings' faces popped into his mind the way they'd looked frozen in death before they faded. All the names of males who had died at his father's hand, except one. He blinked away Fiskane's face.

How was he going to protect Azalea, the humans, and the chosen princess all at the same time? He slowly banged his head on the railing, trying to come up with a solution. He didn't trust anyone but himself with this.

The last time he had trusted someone with his loved one, Kisling had come back with that gaunt face and the story of his mother's death. Elora and her husband had slaughtered her once she had finished speaking the prophecy of peace over their future daughter. Kisling had been waiting in the distance like his mother always requested. They'd never been able to recover her body, and it was the inability to help her fade that ate at Ky the most. She'd been so concerned about everyone else's peace. Who was concerned for her eternal peace?

He let out a sigh. *I need a plan.*

But first, he needed a little sleep and a clear mind. The balcony wrapped around to his bedroom, and he pushed open his door, the cracked wood rough under his fingertips.

"Dragon-damn!" he cursed as he stepped over clothes and piles of books he had been using for research, making his way to the bed. He had forgotten to do his laundry before he left. Despite only ever wearing pants and his body armor, it still seemed to pile up. Selfishly, he missed the times when they were younger and the castle had been bustling with people who took care of these things for him. His father had forbidden anyone to be in the castle, his way of protecting them from unforeseen threats. With all Ky's duties, sometimes it was easier to buy a new pair of thin, lightweight pants than to come home and hand-launder these. At least his armor only ever needed to be wiped down.

Ky removed his pants and flopped onto his large bed, face down. He spread his wings out behind him, stretching them until they were at their full length, and let them be. They twitched slightly; his body was exhausted. The pillows and blanket felt like silk underneath him. He didn't understand how other Spitarians slept without these luxuries. His mother had introduced them after one of her trips to the human world, and he knew he could never live without them.

He relaxed and drifted off into a fitful sleep.

"I wish every day could be like this."

Her voice was like a song. It wrapped around him, giving him warmth. Her brown curls blew in the wind as she laughed; it lit up the flecks of green in her hazel eyes. They were on the edge of a field playing in the tall grass that threaded between their toes. She reached for his hand . . .

Ky went to grab for her, but when their skin touched, their surroundings shifted to a battle. Mangled bodies lay all around them. His insides squirmed as if he already knew something terrible was going to happen. The smile on her face was gone. Instead, her mouth was open in a scream as she flung herself in front of the blade coming right at him.

All he could do was watch and scream.

Ky's palms were sweating and his body shook uncontrollably. He pushed himself up, leaning his bare back against the wooden bedframe. He threw the covers off, the beads of sweat rolling down his naked form. Everything inside him screamed, his magic reaching out in every direction, trying to grasp onto something, trying to kill. It needed a release.

Every night, when Ky closed his eyes, he saw it.

They were the same dreams he'd been having for months. He couldn't stop himself from meeting her, loving her, and watching her die. No matter how his mind warred with the dream world, he couldn't change a dragon-damned thing about it. He still held her small, frail body in his arms with the blond brute's sword, its snake handle protruding from her gut. Her blood spilled out over Ky's fingers, the wound so small compared to his large hands. No matter how hard he pressed down, the blood wouldn't stop, and he could only watch as her hazel eyes fluttered to a close. His heart broke, and everything inside exploded.

Was that how his father had felt when his mother died? Like his world had ended? Like there was nothing left to live for? Because that was how Ky felt every time the dream ended. He watched her die, and the power exploded from his body. As though he'd lost everything.

Ky wanted his mom. It sounded childish, but if his dream was a premonition like he thought, she would have been the only one who might be able to help interpret it. Ky's mother was known for having powerful premonitions. Each time she left to seek out the source of her latest premonition, she would leave with no real explanation. Her power had been far more potent than his. It caused her physical pain until she found the source and could tell them what they needed to know. Twenty-one years ago, when she left, she'd known she wouldn't return. It was in the way she had said goodbye to Ky, the extra-long embrace. She made him vow to do anything in his power to help bring peace with the humans.

But now, after having his first premonitions, he didn't simply want to help the humans from his mother's premonitions. He also wanted—no, he *needed*—to help the hazel-eyed girl from his dreams, to stop her from dying. He had no idea how to find her. He was left with very few clues.

The balcony doors to his right shattered.

Ky stood, his wings spread as a figure appeared, ripping him from his thoughts.

Chapter Seven

River

She stared at the Euphrine River as they approached, in complete awe of its size. Even in the distance, she could see the way the setting sun shone off its black surface, making it appear almost as though the moon was inside rather than above it. It reminded her so much of the way the lake shone in the light.

Bass's horse began to slow as he moved toward a small outcropping of trees and dismounted. "Here should be good for the night."

"We're just sleeping here under the trees with no covering? Are you mad?" River pulled her horse alongside his but didn't move to dismount.

He ignored her and rifled through the saddle bags, pulling out the necessities. He grabbed a bedroll, unrolled it on the uneven earth, and sat down with a canteen and a purple apple tucked under his arm. "You can sleep atop your horse if you like." His head sank back, eyes closing as he took a large bite of his apple.

"There's got to be a town nearby. We could—"

"We could what? Ask for shelter and explain why the engaged Prince of Finn and the Princess of Castor are out of the kingdom alone, unchaperoned? And what is our task, River? Please fill me in."

She gritted her teeth and swung her leg over the horse, then landed loudly on the ground, her boots crunching the dirt. He didn't so much as flinch.

"It's funny to me how you throw that word in there like it's nothing. *Engaged*."

He remained silent.

River pulled back her foot, but before it collided with his side, he gripped her boot firmly in his hand.

"Oh for the saints of Heldours. River, what would you have had me do?"

She yanked her foot free. "You were supposed to do what you said you would!"

"And when my mother looked at me and told me she didn't want to rule, that she was done? That it was my turn? Was I to look at her and say, 'No, Mother. I know you're tired and old, but I'm not ready for the throne because I plan to stay by River's side until she completes the prophecy'?"

"Yes!"

Bass finally opened his eyes. In the dark, they appeared bluer and as cold as the lake in the winter. "I have a duty as well. It's not only you who's destined for something. I am the only child. That throne is mine. I have my people to think of and protect."

"Why is it one or the other?"

"Finn is the smallest of the kingdoms by more than half. Do you think I stayed home these past three moons for pleasure?" Bass stood, his face in hers. "Frick, River. I was dealing with the endless requests from the other kingdoms—they wanted my mother to give her throne to them. We can't afford to feed our people. Lilith was my only option if I wanted to feed my people and keep my throne."

The pain in his voice shook her. River hadn't known, hadn't even thought about it. She took a step back until her spine was against the horse's flank and turned her eyes away from him. "I didn't know."

"Of course not. The moment I returned and reported to the queen, she decided it was your time. My problems seemed to sink into the background because she was sending you out on an impossible journey."

River's shame evaporated as a thick bubble of anger surfaced. "Impossible because you think I can't do this? Because I'm not ready?"

He pressed his palm to the horse, pushing his face closer. "Are you looking for an apology? Because you won't get one."

River pressed her hand into his chest, forcing him backward. He didn't budge. "Of course not. Nothing is ever your fault. Not this. Not the marriage. Not that time you put a frog in my mother's chambers, or even the stupid live swollen pig at that dinner party."

The corner of his mouth lifted, and his eyes twinkled. "I don't remember you complaining when the thing squalled and nearly bit the councilman's nose. If I recall, you laughed so hard you nearly peed."

River resisted the urge to touch the scar on the inside of her arm. Her mother had made her track down the pig and kill it with only her bare hands. It hadn't died easily.

Bass lowered his mouth inches from hers. She wanted to kiss him. Needed to feel him and make the rest of the world disappear. Use him for a little while to forget all that was to come in the next few days.

"Did you bed her?"

Bass pulled back and ran his hand through his hair. "Don't be a child."

"A child! Lilith is the same age as me, Sebastian, or have you forgotten that she was born only a few moons before me?"

"Well, she certainly acts older."

His words hit like a physical blow. It was one thing for her mother to favor Lilith. For Bass to need her for his kingdom was a necessary evil, but the thought that it was more than that? It was too much.

"Well, then. That solves everything." River turned away from him as tears pricked her eyes.

He pressed his body into her back, pushing her against the horse once more. Bass's face rested in the curve of her neck. River's heart raced. She tried to calm it, tried to stay angry with him.

Bass let out a slow breath. "Kiss me."

River threw her hands up. "You are insufferable. I should have listened to Laya and stayed far away from you."

The pressure on her back abruptly retreated, and she spun to face him.

Bass's jaw clenched, working back and forth. "You don't mean that."

"Don't tell me what I mean! You slept with her. Was it before or after she presented herself as an option to save your kingdom?"

"What does that have to do with anything?"

She held her shoulders back, keeping her eyes on him. "Did you ever have any intention of wedding me?" She couldn't smother the pleading in her voice. There had been too much over the years between them for her to think otherwise, promises spoken as children.

He turned from her, walking in a few quick strides toward his pack, grabbed something, and spun back on his heels. A flash of silver flew through the air toward her. River threw her body out of the way. She heard the dagger thud in the tree behind her.

"Good," he said, coming toward her, sword in hand. The nasty-looking snake curled around the handle with eyes of ruby, a custom-made gift from her mother. The sword tip still had blood on it. River's stomach churned at the sight.

"You could have hit the horse!" she said, stomping toward the tree and pulling the elongated dagger free.

"You know my aim is better than that. You seemed like you needed this." He backed up and twirled his sword in one hand, beckoning her on with the other. "You can either keep screaming at me, or you can fight me. Which would you prefer?"

This was how things were with them. When things got complicated, they fought it out, swords in hand. He didn't speak his emotions, but she felt them every time his blade swished past her body.

She weighed the dagger in her hand. Without hesitating, she brought her arm up to block his blow. Although Bass had taught her how to wield a sword, she found the dagger lighter and easier to conceal in her daily wardrobe. River pushed his blade away, taking a step back, so she could see him better.

In the dark, with the trees lining around him, the moon shining above, his blond hair was almost gold. She focused on the fight instead of how close he had been moments ago or the smell of lemon on his breath. She moved her body under his outstretched arm, bending under the sword. They could dance like this for hours.

"You're getting slow, old man," River jested, circling. He didn't answer. "Maybe you should spend less time in bed with your lady friends and more time in the training room." The words hurt her heart even as she spoke them.

His eyes narrowed, and he lunged for her. River was caught up in her thoughts, her movements too slow as he spun and quickly switched hands with his blade, bringing it down to slam the flat side into her hip bone.

Pain shot down River's leg, and she held in the gasp. *Damn.*

"If you had been eating properly this summer, you would be even faster." His voice was dark.

River clenched her mouth shut, teeth grinding. She moved full speed ahead as she held the dagger pointed for a killing blow.

He knew her, knew her moves. He pivoted, grabbing River's left hand mid-spin and throwing her to the ground. He slammed his foot down onto her throat, knocking the wind out of her.

"Your movements are slow and predictable. Any trained fighter would've seen that showy move coming. Is that what you were doing while I was gone, practicing this?" He mimicked River, spinning around like a dancer. He made it look so girly and foolish.

She turned her face into the dirt to hide the blush. *Breathe, River.* She stood, her anger searing, and then she matched him blow for blow.

"You're moving your left arm too slowly," he chastised, swinging the sword in the same movement he had done for over an hour.

River grunted, breathing out through her nose and swinging her dagger in a circular motion around her wrist. A hard *thawp* sounded as he hit against her hip. She barely felt the pain anymore as he hit her in the same spot.

"Again," he barked, swinging his sword toward her shoulder. River was exhausted, her movements too slow, and she turned her shoulder right as his blade sliced into her arm. She swallowed the pain, pushing it deep into her stomach.

His eyes flicked away from the blood that dripped down her arm before he barked, "Again," and plunged his sword toward her.

"I am not doing this anymore!" River yelled, throwing her dagger to the left of him. "No soldier fights like that."

"And you would know that because you have been on the battlefield?"

"Let's be honest for a minute. If I come up in a fight against a Spitarian, me and a blade won't do much of anything." River turned and walked away from him.

"You might not always be fighting monsters." His words were quiet, as if she wasn't meant to hear them.

She whirled on him. "Like this man I'm supposed to kill?"

"He's a monster in his own way."

The sun pierced the horizon, sending a beam of light directly across River's face. She groaned softly, stretching out her tense body. Warm air licked at her arms.

She started before remembering where she was. She looked around the campsite and toward the dead fire where Bass was sitting, clutching his hand to his chest. He didn't seem to notice she was awake as he slowly picked at his hand, blood trickling down his arm.

She stood, approaching slowly as if he were a wild animal. "What happened?"

Bass snapped his head up, hiding his hand behind his back.

She could see a small blood puddle by his feet. "Let me see it!"

"It's fine," he said, trying to press past her.

"You're of no use to me if you have a mangled hand."

"I would never put your safety in jeopardy."

"Good, then let's see it," she demanded, reaching for his hand.

He placed it tenderly in hers. His knuckles were bloodied and swollen, maybe even broken. Wood splinters were embedded deep in his skin. She looked from his hand to the nearest trees, noticing one with a stain.

River laughed half-heartedly. "Did you punch a tree?" He didn't answer, looking away from her. "I'll need something to treat this with . . ."

She tried to remember everything her mother would have used in this situation. Her mother had been known as a natural healer in her youth. River looked around for what might be near.

"If you go find me some chancewa leaves and field moss, I can wrap your hand so it doesn't get infected by the tree's bark." It was starting to get red and puffy around the edges.

Bass nodded and did as she said without question.

The only alone time River spent with her mother was in the queen's gardens with her herbs and plants. Queen Castor felt she was the only one who could teach River properly. Her lessons were filled with survival skills—what to eat, how to heal superficial infections. She always used to tell River that one day it would come in handy. River would stand at the grinder and pretend she was a witch, mixing everything. Her mother would sternly look at her and say, "River, this is no game. You must open your mind to all the possibilities of this world." River had never truly known what she'd meant by that—it wasn't as if she'd bring about peace with healing—but she was grateful in this moment that she'd listened to what she'd been taught.

Bass returned just when she found what she was looking for: a rock shaped like a bowl. She crushed up the leaves, the liquid oozing out of the stems. The rusty goo pooled at the bottom. She broke a few pieces of the moss and added it to the liquid. It bubbled and turned inky. Crushing up the moss next, she watched as it thickened the liquid into blue tar. The smell was potent, like a skunk had sprayed.

"Bass, is there a baya leaf around here?"

Bass walked away and returned without a smile, leaves in hand.

"Sit, please."

Bass sat without saying a word, handing her his fist. She poured water over it. He winced as she cleaned out the remaining bark, picking gently at the swollen skin. With two fingers River spooned the tar onto his fist, massaging it. The swelling went down in an instant. She placed the green leaf over the paste, pressing it down on his hand, vine side up. He didn't pull away from her as their eyes met. She wasn't sure what she saw in those aqua eyes, but something was different, almost soft. River rubbed the mixture on her arm, the sword injury from practice yesterday, but he stopped her hand, dipping his fingers into the tar and rubbing her arm softly.

His hand was gentle, a light caress, as if not to give her any more pain. The swelling on her arm went down just as fast as his.

"Bass," River whispered as he removed his hand, leaving her feeling alone and not whole. He put his fingers to her lips, forgetting about the blue tar. His laugh was rich and wholehearted. She spat, rubbing at her lips, trying to remove the skunk smell that was slowly creeping up her nose.

River tried not to gag. "Oh, I am so glad you're laughing at me."

She took the small glob she still had left on her fingers and tried to wipe it across his forehead, but he was too quick. He grabbed her arm and pinned her to the ground. He lay on top of her, their faces close. River felt his breath on her face, and her heart fluttered. It was like when they'd been younger, laughing and rolling around in the grass. She could see the lines of green that streaked through his blue eyes as if they were running toward something. She could count every piece of stubble on his chin. River breathed in his scent underneath the tar, a soft hint of horse and lemon. But before she could breathe it in more, he jumped off her and stormed away.

Chapter Eight

Ky

The figure stepped farther into his room, out of the shadow and into the moonlight. The first thing Ky noticed was the mop of fire-colored hair atop her head. The second thing was her unique clothing. Her chest was covered in familiar-looking scales, black with a slight hint of orange. But he didn't have the time to ponder what that meant because this stranger had just busted through the glass balcony door with a silver glint in her hand.

"That door was thicker than I anticipated," she gasped. She doubled over, her breath coming in short gasps.

"Dragon-damned me," was all he could manage on an exhale.

Had she scaled the mountain alone? Up to his balcony? He hadn't even free-climbed that high.

"Take it easy. I'm not here to fight." Her muscled, pale arms flexed as she tossed a knife at his feet.

Ky studied her wrists—a small drop of blood beaded over a wound she must have gotten on his door. It was neither red nor blue. He cocked his head in confusion. She was most definitely larger than a human but smaller than most female Spitarians.

What is she?

Her gaze dropped down his naked body, but he didn't shield himself. It was uncommon for their people, males or females, to wear much clothing. Some dressed only in the thin layer of pict-paint.

"For someone who wears so little clothing, you seem to amass huge piles of it." She grimaced, throwing a pair of pants at him.

He caught the pants midair and slid them on but didn't move from his spot between her and the door to the rest of the castle.

The female's red hair shifted around her face as if it were alive. "I mean no disrespect showing up in your room." She bowed her head and the mess of hair flowed, obscuring her face from Ky's view.

When her head finally tilted back up, it swiveled in Ky's direction, locking on him. Her green eyes pierced right through him. "*Heiralomun* Kylane, it is imperative that we talk." The Spitarian language rolled off her tongue flawlessly, like it was her first language. "I would put my fist to my chest, but I'm assuming you would rather me not move." Her ruby lips parted, a smile spreading across her face.

He wanted to laugh at her for making humor during such a situation. *Brave female.* "And why would you put your fist to your chest? You owe no allegiance to me."

"You are right. The halfsprings owe your father nothing."

The word caught something in Ky's memory. His mother had told him stories about offspring born of a human and a Spitarian. He'd thought it nothing more than a legend—rare since the old world. But as he stared at her, he knew that was exactly what she was. Her size mixed with the fact that he could taste no magic swirling around her only proved it. He wondered what traits she carried in her blood and what color, exactly, was it that she bled?

"I would offer you a seat, but . . ." Ky gestured around. "Why don't you just tell me who you are and why you've come."

The female's head tilted slightly, her eyes narrowing. Pieces of her hair fell away, revealing a scar that fanned out to cover her whole cheek. "I'm Iris." Her voice was gentle, as if she was entirely at ease.

But the way she pronounced her name, the slight lilt, and even the elongated r's when she spoke reminded him of the accent of the Spitarian Stars. But that couldn't be—the whole kingdom was dead. He wondered if it was possible that a Spitarian Star had mated with a human to produce this halfspring.

He wanted to hear her speak more. He needed to be sure of his conclusion. "Iris, do you have a clan name I can call you by or—"

"Iris will do." She straightened her head, the red hair falling back into place over the scar. Ky couldn't help but notice how many colors were woven into it. Shades of red but also orange. Unlike anything he had seen. It reminded him of his sister's eyes, not the color, but the uniqueness of them. *How long would it take me to paint that color?*

"The Blue Illing," Iris commented as she moved to her left, toward his wall of his artwork. "You captured the dragon's likeness well. Although the coloring makes it appear far more beautiful than it truly is." A wide smile spread across her face. "This one"—she pointed to a different drawing—"is still far superior and shows the true beauty of the creature."

It was a drawing of his mother's face he had done years ago.

Ky ignored her comment as he crossed to the same dresser and wrapped a sheath around his upper thigh. He slid the unicorn horn blade into it. Its white shine caught the moonlight and cast glittering stars all over the room.

"I'm surprised you carry that thing around. It's a disgrace," she said, nearly shuddering from its presence.

"After what I did to get it, it would be a waste not to wear it." Ky pushed the images of his brother out of his mind. The black tips of his wings were reminder enough.

She made a clicking sound with her tongue. They were so close now he could break her neck in a heartbeat. Would she rise like his brethren?

She took a step backward as if sensing his thoughts and rested her hands on her hips where a belt full of weapons lay. Ky counted four silver blades, a few arrowheads, two climbing hooks, and a coiled weapon unfamiliar to him. None of which seemed to have any hint of unicorn horn, unlike his own.

"Let's not make any rash decisions before you hear me out. If you're still threatened by me after you hear what I have to say, by all means, you may try to fight me."

"I can agree to that." Ky nodded, gesturing for her to continue.

"I have some information I thought you might find valuable." She turned to Ky. "We don't have a lot of time." She let out a breath. "I need you to swear to the Fadelings, no matter what I say, it never leaves this room."

"And why should I promise you anything?"

"Because it is about your mother, and I would hate for it to fall into the wrong hands."

"My . . . my mother?" His words faltered.

She nodded.

Ky wrinkled his nose in disbelief but pounded his fist to his chest anyway.

"Rhella sent me."

Ky felt as though the magic had been sucked from him at the mention of his mother's name. "That can't be possible."

"She's alive, Kylane."

Ky shook his head. "I don't believe you." He brought his fists up to his lips, tapped gently as he thought. His heart was a wild animal within a cage, slamming back and forth, trying to get free. "We searched for her body. Everywhere. Kisling said—"

"Kisling told you exactly what your mother asked him to."

Alive. But why hadn't she come home? "And how do I know you speak the truth?"

If she were truly alive, how could she have left her offspring here to deal with the Head? How could she have left him to deal with his father alone, deal with the peace she wanted? Were they not worth it?

Ky felt like slamming his fist through the side of the castle.

Iris stood, adjusting the armor of scales she wore. "You're going to want to ask me a question only your mother would know. But I don't think even then you will believe me. You will think someone could have shared that secret."

"What do you propose then?"

Iris reached down into her armor and pulled out a small bundle wrapped in leather, then extended it to him. Ky took it, knowing exactly what it was. He had seen hundreds of these over the years. His mother's office was lined with them. She'd carried them everywhere, jotting down the bits of prophecies she sensed.

Ky opened the cover slowly, running his finger down his mother's words. A silent tear rolled down his cheek. "How did you come about this?"

"She gave it to me. Asked me to bring it here and show you a certain prophecy. The same one that has been bothering her since she left."

He still didn't believe her. Kisling would have never lied about his mother. But he played along anyway. "The one about the Castor princess?"

Iris rolled her eyes and picked at the dirt under her nails. But it wasn't the dark dirt Ky was accustomed to. It was the light sand-colored dirt that only came from one place—the Luminary Forest.

"Elora Castor has twisted your mother's words into something they were never meant to be. I folded the part you should focus on."

Ky flipped to the page she had indicated. His mother's swirled handwriting covered the journal entry. It was dated the day she'd left.

When fates collide
One red
One blue
The point they make
The war they wage
Forever it is true
She rises out of the ashes
Chosen
A flame in the mist

When death shall come
Only she will stand the fight
Only she can end it all
One war
One right
Purple shall remain
One blood in sight
Moon
Cloud
Star
Sword
Wings
Forever in flight

Rhella had marked up the pages, circling and underlining them. Small notes jotted the page.

Find Elora Castor

Ky's mind reeled. "If this is the true prophecy, why is Elora only using a few phrases?"

"Why Elora Castor does anything is a mystery to me."

Ky's hand whipped out and grabbed her wrist, examining it. "'Purple shall remain.'" He swiped a drop of her blood and smeared it onto the page, pushing it further into the light.

Iris stiffened but didn't pull away.

"This is about halfsprings? Is this why my mother has been pushing for peace with the humans? So that the combination of the bloodline remains?" Ky shook his head. "It's not possible. Spitarians can only produce with their *kupal*. You must be some sort of accident."

Iris let out a laugh that echoed around his room. "Humans are barely able to produce one child now. They're dying out. And with magic fading, the *kupal* bond will eventually fade as well. Have you noticed how few *kupals* there are? You are also a dying race." Iris shrugged.

Ky had noticed. His sister's experiments were vital. "So the prophecy isn't about peace at all?"

"It's about survival." Iris crossed her arms.

Ky shook his head. None of this was possible. Even if he didn't believe his mother was still alive, he knew that this was her handwriting, her prophecy, and most likely the reason Elora Castor had her killed—to cover the truth of the inevitable.

"Why bring this to me now?"

"I swore an oath to protect the prophecy. The most important thing right now is that Elora is ignoring the prophecy entirely and taking matters into her own hands. Her plans must be thwarted at all costs, and the girl must remain alive." Iris looked pointedly at Ky.

"So I can't kill her as my father wishes?"

"Septing Stars, no. Is that what your Head has ord—"

He whipped his head toward the stranger.

She clenched her jaw at her mistake.

"It's not possible." It confirmed what Ky had already suspected by her accent. The slang term was only used by those from the Star kingdom, but they were all dead, slaughtered by Head Axel and his sister. *Weren't they?*

Ky eyed the burn on her cheek more carefully. Could it hide who she truly was? Every member of the Star kingdom bore a star birthmark somewhere on their body.

"Who are you?"

"One day, *Heiralomun*, I hope I have the time to tell you. But for now, a warning. Be careful with the princess. She is more than she appears. Don't underestimate her."

If this woman had been able to scale this castle though his room was over the sea, then he would trust her about the princess's abilities. "Word will get to my father that she isn't dead. Her fate is already sealed."

"You can't even begin to understand how important . . ." She ran her hand over her scar. "Whatever you must do, keep her alive."

Ky held his face impassive. "You will need to help her disappear."

Iris backed up, shaking her head. "I can't."

"If my mother is alive . . ." He let out a slow breath; he wouldn't allow himself to believe it. "If my mother wants her protected, she needs to find a place for the girl. You need to."

Iris stepped over a piece of shattered glass, picking up the knife she came in with. "If I'm worrying about the princess, I can't protect your mother. She's fading, Ky. She needs me."

Fading. No, she is dead. "What the dragon-damn do you expect me to do with a human princess?"

"Just take her someplace safe. Maybe your cave. I will come for her when I can." Iris took a few more steps backward.

"It's not safe if you know about it." The thought caused something to cripple in his stomach. The only person he'd ever told about his cave was his mother. "If my mother's truly alive, then she'll need to come tell me to save the girl herself. For now, I'll head out and find the princess."

"I don't think she'll do that."

"Then the girl dies. Saving one human princess isn't worth it. I'll sacrifice her to stay on my father's good side and continue saving the hundreds—just like I've been doing for the sake of my mother's cause for years."

Iris tucked the knife back into her boot and pulled out a claw-like hook from her belt. "Hasn't it become your cause too?"

Ky's lip raised. This female was infuriating.

"Do we have an agreement, *Heiralomun*?"

"If my mother shows herself, then we do."

With a quick nod of her head, she wrapped the hook around the edge and plummeted below.

Chapter Nine

River

River's heart was in her throat as they rode. She tried not to look at Bass or notice the way the sweat made his shirt cling to the muscles on his shoulder blades or how it drew her eye down his spine. His back tightened and clenched as he bent farther over his stallion. She still couldn't seem to calm her heart rate. His face had been so close to hers, so unbelievably close, their breath mingled together. She wanted to taste his lips.

Stop.

But it was hard not to think about him or about the boy she thought was still in there somewhere, hiding.

And now, there was no telling how long this assignment would last. They were already far from home. And what would come after? He gave no indication he wasn't going to marry Lilith. River could kill Barthomule quickly, but then what? She would go home, and Bass would go to Finn to his coronation and his wedding? She pushed the thought out of her mind. River needed to focus on the here and now. She needed to focus on the murder she was about to commit.

Both Bass and River knew what her capabilities were. Despite her lack of rigorous training throughout the summer, she had still managed to lay him out a few times yesterday. She wasn't quite up to par, but she could be very quickly. River tightened her fists around the reins, the cords in her forearms pulsing. She might not always love training like a soldier, but she certainly did love the power; it made her feel as though she was worthy of her own throne. It helped that the ritual of training was the closest thing she had to ease her stomach pains and the waves of fear that overtook her.

The temperature dropped as they moved farther along the Euphrine River, and the thickness in the air seemed to lighten. River watched with interest as the water changed from clear to inky, hiding whatever creatures loomed under the surface. The rolling hills evened out into flat forests. The trees turned from green to whites and tans. There was so much of this world she had yet to see. But the terrain didn't ease her mind.

Darkness had just overtaken them when two figures around a small fire appeared in the distance. River's fingers went automatically to the dagger she had strapped to her horse.

Bass lifted his hand in greeting, but River didn't move from her blade.

The two figures stood. One was smaller than the other, but both were dressed similar to her and Bass.

"Prince Finn," the shorter one said. "Princess." They both bowed.

Bass slowed his horse and dismounted swiftly. When his hand didn't go to his blade, River removed hers and followed his actions.

"There is a fresh roast on the fire. We will let the leftenant know you're here," the shorter one said, gesturing to the fire and then hustling farther into the trees.

River arched an eyebrow. "Our contacts?"

"Yes," Bass answered.

She ignored his shortness as she pressed on. "Are we camping here for the night?"

When he nodded and sat in front of the fire, she sighed and unrolled her mat.

They sat in silence under a cluster of trees so dense that their roots intertwined. The canopy of the branches blocked most of the light from the moon above, leaving her uneasy.

River shook off the feeling, stretching out her aching body. She wasn't used to so many days in a saddle. Their surroundings gave her no hint of where they might be. She touched the bark of the tree nearest her, the dark bark hard beneath her fingertips.

"Where are we?" River tried to keep her voice even.

Bass wouldn't have taken her into the Blaque Forest. Humans didn't come back from the Blaque Forest. What little knowledge they had of it came from tales passed down for generations. It was said that there, dragons roamed free. But they would have had to cross the water to reach it.

She tried to remember the map. "Bass?"

"Outside Neven." He offered her a piece of meat, but she waved it off. "You need to eat."

He stood, alerted by the multiple sets of rustling feet, and placed his hand on his blade until three figures revealed themselves standing in the moon's glow. The two men from before, followed by a third. The two men bowed quickly and moved past them into the trees beyond. Clothes fit tight across the third's broad shoulders, though it was the holes River noticed. One was perfectly placed over his muscled stomach. River looked up quickly as the hole shifted. The man kneeled on one knee in front of her, her hand clutched tight in his.

He pressed his lips to her knuckles. "Princess, welcome."

She started at the touch. In the fire's reflection, she caught the sly grin he shot Bass before his gaze locked back on hers. She was almost lost in the thunderstorm that was his stormy gray eyes, and she swore lightning danced across them. Laya had indeed understated this man's attractiveness.

"I think that's enough," Bass barked, gripping the man's shoulder.

The leftenant hopped back to his feet, though he didn't let go of her hand as quickly.

Bass positioned himself squarely between them.

"Leon, I presume," River said, not covering the smile it brought to her lips. She couldn't quite see her quiet friend with this man, though she could definitely understand the pull toward him.

"At your service, Princess."

"I have heard many stories. I see now they all must be true."

His smile turned from a small grin to one that met his eyes. "Laya still speaks of me, then? I assumed after all these years she would've forgotten."

River laughed. She had been very wrong about Laya not understanding her feelings for Bass. She clearly had been withholding the best parts of her stories. Leon was as smitten with Laya as she was with him.

"Often and with great fondness."

"I think we should begin," Bass said, gesturing toward the ground.

Leon put out his hand and helped River to the ground. She squeezed his fingers in return before he sat down next to her. She couldn't wait to return and speak to Laya about him.

"River!" Bass snapped, and she realized she was still beaming happily at Leon. "Focus."

River schooled her features at Bass's cool glare. "Yes, right. You have information for us on Barthomule?" She did not return her gaze to Leon.

"I have been trailing the sneaky bastard." He paused. "Excuse the language, Princess."

River waved him off. "Continue."

"He sleeps in many places. One of which is here, in Neven's tavern. He has a room on the east side facing the woods. I presume it's for easy access out of the town. Though, he doesn't return on a schedule. Sometimes he is there sleeping in the morning, sometimes night, and sometimes not at all."

"Where does he go?" Bass inquired before popping a lemon grass leaf into his mouth. His jaw worked unnecessarily hard.

"That's the thing. We can't figure it out. He has been seen wandering the woods or in the other towns, though he doesn't seem to speak to many people."

"No one?" River said.

"No, Princess. Well, other than the barmaid. But I presume they are intimate. She's known for that sort of thing."

Bass cleared his throat.

"Well, then, are we sure he's the one passing the information?" River interlocked her fingers.

"I—"

"Of course he is!" Bass interrupted Leon.

River wasn't so sure. Something felt off about the whole situation. A man who was sleeping with a barmaid and who lived above a tavern was passing secret military information about a kingdom he hadn't been to in over twenty years? And he barely ever spoke to a soul?

"Surely there's no harm in making sure our information is correct. Wouldn't the Spitarians compensate him for his information?"

"They're no more than animals. They don't think as we do," Bass snapped at her. His voice was no more than a growl.

"Leon, what does he look like?" River asked.

"He's always cloaked in black with his face covered. No one has seen him up close, and I haven't been able to get a glance without blowing my cover. Though there are rumors that he has a scar, a burn. Some sort of disfigurement that he hides."

River scrunched her face. "Rumors. So there's no sure way to distinguish him?"

Leon pressed his hand to his leg. "You can recognize him from the way he drags one leg ever so slightly."

"I see." River was worried. They truly knew nothing solid about Barthomule.

"Let's get this over with," Bass said.

"Right. The faster you are back to your child bride, the better," River snapped, regretting the words as they flew out of her mouth.

Bass eyes narrowed. "This job will be easy for you. Seduce him and leave him high and dead."

"Excuse me?"

Leon cleared his throat. "I think—"

"Unless you have more information," Bass snarled, standing, "you can go back to town and watch."

Leon dipped his head in their direction, but his eyes searched River's as if requesting her permission. She returned his nod, and he silently retreated into the woods.

"You better hope Leon or the other two aren't prone to rumors because I don't think Lilith will enjoy hearing of your illicit affair with me." River remained seated, her hands clasped tightly to hide the tremor that now rattled them.

"Do you think she isn't already aware?"

River looked away. Her eyes latched onto the fire and the meat, so charred it was inedible. The smell made her want to gag. "I will not seduce him. There is a better and easier way to do this without my face being seen."

"You're a girl—use what you have. If he pays for the barmaid's services, then he would be happy for someone free. Let your hair down. You'll be fine."

River stood. "And you're going to, what, wait downstairs while I bed him and stab him in his sleep?"

"Don't be ridiculous. You won't need to sleep with him. Just get him upstairs."

River crossed her arms and squeezed her jaw shut until she knew she could form the proper response. "There's an easier way. I go in the middle of the night when he's likely asleep, along with everyone else, and I kill him. In and out quickly, and no one sees my face."

Bass stepped toward her, withdrew the dagger at her hip, and pressed it to her throat, backing her into the tree. Her nostrils flared, but she kept her face blank.

"You can't even stop me."

"I didn't try!" River wanted to slam her forehead against his. "And if you think I'm that incapable, then my plan is better anyway. I won't be fighting an awake man."

The blade in his hand fell away. "I don't think you're incapable."

"Then stop treating me as though I am."

Bass tossed the dagger, and she caught it quickly. "And what will you say if someone sees you?"

"That I need a room. I got separated from my family during a recent Spitarian attack and need a place to wait out the morning."

He nodded and lay down. "Show me how you would do it."

She let out a sigh of relief and advanced toward his unmoving body.

River's body slammed against the hard earth, her arm twisted below her. "Heldours."

Bass stood, the moonlight shining off his hair. "You're not ready."

"I'm not fighting the captain of the guard. I'm fighting an older man who's been living scarcely for years. He'll have no training." River pushed herself off the ground and stretched her back.

"What do I always say about underestimation?"

River rolled her eyes. "It'll get me killed."

"Get some sleep. We can try again in the morning."

She crossed her arms. "One more time."

Bass let out an exaggerated sigh before he lay back down on the ground.

River placed the blade to his throat for the tenth time. She closed her eyes and waited for the shift of his body. This time, as he grabbed for her wrist to flip her onto her back, she wrapped her legs around his head and flung herself to the side, her feet rolling him with her. She pressed the blade firmly until she felt it sink into skin, cradling his head in her thighs.

"I won this round," she said, feeling the slow drip of blood on her fingers. She leaned her face close to his. "Admit it."

He squeezed her backside.

River ran the flat side of the blade slowly up to the side of his face and back down until the point was on the dimple of his chin. "Say I won."

"I love you." The words came out in a quiet, exhaled breath. He raised his neck, pushing his chin further against the blade until his forehead met hers.

Small flutters of wings sprang apart in her stomach. It wasn't the first time he had said these words to her, and she hoped it wouldn't be the last.

River dropped the blade, and their lips met. Hungrily and eagerly. He rested his hands on her hips and then snaked them under her tunic across her spine. His tongue flicked against her teeth, asking for permission, and she opened her mouth, savoring the taste of lemon.

River pulled back, her hands on either side of his face. "Don't marry Lilith."

"We'll talk about this when the assignment is all done. You have too much to concentrate on now." He wrapped his arms around her until his fingers brushed her stomach. "I love how tiny you are here."

As opposed to my hips or thighs.

"Show me you love me again. Tell me it will only ever be me," he whispered against her skin.

She kissed his lips and then readjusted herself until her body lay along his, her head resting on his chest. "I do love you, Sebastian."

"Then all is right in the world again. You can kill this man, and we can go home."

Home. But he wouldn't be going home. Not with her, at least.

They were quiet for some time, and River was unsure if he had fallen asleep. "Bass?"

"Mm-hmm?" He stroked his hand down her spine all the way down to her backside and squeezed her through the tough fabric.

"I don't want to be a monster."

"Why would you be a monster?"

"If I kill him and he's innocent . . . it makes me a monster."

"He isn't innocent. He's the monster. He tells human secrets to monsters; that makes him no better than them. And if you don't do this, if you choose to go against the prophecy and not save the humans as you're meant to do, that would make you the monster."

River swallowed. "I didn't say I wasn't going to fulfill the prophecy."

"Then stop speaking foolishly. Taking this one life is easy."

"Easy?" Her stomach dropped. As if killing a man was as easy as taking a swim on a summer day.

"One quick swipe, just like we practiced. He won't feel a thing."

"And you've done this?"

"There are many Spitarian sympathizers. We've taken care of them until this point, but now it's your turn. Take care of this one, and the next, and the next, until there are no more. Until we finally learn the secret of how to defeat the Spitarians once and for all. They have a weakness. They must. Destroy them or destroy the blastful magic." He sighed. "We'll get them!"

River pulled her lip into her mouth, slowly working at the skin. "You believe that's the key to the prophecy? To win? Destroy the magic source?"

"I do, and your mother does as well. She speaks of it as if it were something that could be turned off."

"Like the stories of the old world where the Spitarians were kept in cages." Her stomach seized at the words. Humans didn't even keep their animals in cages; cows, horses, and such roamed the countryside free.

"Where monsters belong."

A root dug in her back, and she shifted, trying to get comfortable, half on the bedroll and half in the dirt. The little forest of trees blocked out most of the moon's light. It sent a nostalgic pang through her, reminding her of the fort they'd had as children.

There was another long pause before River asked, "You'll be right outside waiting for me, right?"

"When?"

"When I kill Barthomule, and then we go home?"

Bass let loose a sigh. "No, River."

"Why not? I can come to Finn with you for your coronation. I'm not needed in Castor while Mother's there."

"River."

She pulled her head away from his chest. "And I can use your castle as my home base while I search for the source of—" She slumped to the ground as Bass pulled his body out from underneath her.

"You're not listening to me."

"I don't understand."

"I'm not staying here. Tomorrow when you go into town, I'm going home to Finn for my wedding and coronation."

River shook her head. "No. Don't you see you don't have to? I've been thinking all about this. Castor is the second-largest kingdom and far wealthier than her family. So marrying me would give you everything you want."

"No, River. Not everything."

River pulled her knees into her chest. The truth began to slither down her spine, curling around her stomach. Tighter and tighter. "You want to marry her?"

"It's for the best."

"You love her?"

Bass threw his hands into the air, his untucked shirt waving across his pants. There were dirt stains on his elbows. "River."

River stood. "Do you love her?"

He readjusted his brown pants before he turned his back on her. "It's complicated."

"It's not. Not even a little."

"You just don't understand because I'm the only one you've ever been with."

She bit down on the inside of her cheek until the metallic tang of blood filled her tongue. "I understand clearly."

"She'll be a good queen for Finn. River, you have to understand."

And I wouldn't.

"You just told me you loved me. We've been intimate . . ."

He pointed his finger at her heaving chest. "I do love you. More than you know."

"Yet you're still going to marry her?"

"I don't know." He didn't need to say more. River wasn't enough for him. For him, she was nothing more than a childhood romance. Not something that could last. He needed another. *Wanted* another.

River grabbed the cloak from over her horse and rifled through the saddlebag until she found the strip of leather and tied it under her shirt.

"What are you doing?" Bass asked.

She went for the dagger, discarded on the ground near the fire.

"Get some sleep and go in the morning, please." His hand landed on the dagger at the same time as hers.

"I think you need some time to figure out what you want." River ripped the dagger from his hand and shoved it into the sheath at her waist. She threw her hood over her tousled braid and walked in the direction of the town. She would do this on her own, just as the prophecy had always said she would. Her focus needed to be off of him. She didn't need him or his half-hearted love.

River didn't need anyone.

Chapter Ten

Ky

From afar, the cave appeared to have no entrance, just an indent in the surface. But upon further inspection, one could see the half-moon crack in the surface of the rock. Ky moved toward it and pushed on the boulder slightly until it opened into a large cavern. His dragons didn't need any luxuries, so the open area was bare.

Neither one of his dragons appeared to be home. To the left was a smaller opening, an area he'd meticulously filled with dirt for them to sleep in. To the right was another outlet, though it was covered in stalagmites and stalactites and wasn't easily accessible for someone his size.

He wedged his arm in between the points and placed the bag full of *Crystolas* as far in as he could reach. Storing all the ones he'd managed to steal from the castle ensured his sister couldn't reach Belladonna.

The rising sun streamed in from a giant natural crater in the roof of the cave that made easy access for the dragons. The cave was surrounded by uninhabited mountains behind it and the sea to the north. It was very well hidden in plain sight. No one other than

Ky had discovered the entrance, and he was still quite pleased with himself.

The sunlight bounced off the most important feature of the cave—the natural *Crystolas* hot spring. It was a pool of bubbling hot water filled with *Crystolas*. The perfect place for him to recharge his magic and relax.

Ky unfolded the bedroll along the far wall under a natural indent. Hopefully, it created enough of a break from the elements for the princess to be comfortable. He set out his sheets, pillow, and blankets the best he could. He wanted to believe his mother was alive, but he also hated the idea that she would abandon her children to save some human princess. So he made an appropriate spot for the princess, but he'd learned years ago a backup plan was always a necessity.

He placed the bag of bread, clothes, and other necessities atop before he stripped off his pants and hopped into the water.

It wasn't only the warmth that invaded his body but the magical current floating in the water as the energy bounced from one *Crystolas* to the next. A rainbow of light flickered all around him every time he moved. The way the sun caught on all the *Crystolas* was one of the most beautiful things he had ever seen. Every time he got in, he regretted not doing it more. It left his head light and slightly buzzing like he was aimlessly floating in the clouds.

He closed his eyes. *Only for a few minutes, just long enough to take the edge off.* But Ky was instantly asleep, his mind filling with a black void.

The hazel-eyed girl's curly hair hung down her bare back, skimming across her spine. She smiled up at him, her eyes glistening in the moonlight. Her laughter echoed around him, and it vibrated deep in his soul. Her gown wrapped around her every curve, the sheer material shaped like feathers spread across her waist, every feather lined in gold. Hand-sewn crystals hung from a slit that ran up her leg to mid-thigh, sweeping into a train. Ky's hand moved across her hips, feeling the glitter catch across his palms. He wanted to press his lips into the curve of her neck.

It was sweet and lulling, but it didn't last long. Soon he felt it, a physical pull on his mind, dragging him down a hole.

Ky stood in Azalea's bedroom, just as it appeared in real life. Everything was perfect and untouched, blue bed made, and no clothing hung out of the drawers. He spotted his sister, her feet dangling off her oversized bed.

"It's about time you fell asleep. I've been waiting for you for almost an hour," she said, annoyed.

He looked for physical signs of exhaustion, but this was her dream, and she could manipulate it however she wanted. "Shouldn't you be bothering Wrynn? I am sure he would be happy to dreamwalk with you. I, on the other hand, just wanted a few quiet moments alone."

Dreamwalking was something only *kupals* or family members could do; it was magic that grew in the old world when family members were ripped from each other.

She waved her hand as if pushing his feelings aside. "Don't do that. Where are you?"

"Checked on the dragons quick before going out in search of the princess. Why do you need my exact plan?"

"Feisty. Who chewed your wing?" She stood from the bed, gracefully pushing down the pleats of her skirts. Even in a dream, she hid behind layers. "You took all the *Crystolas*. Father's furious."

Ky shrugged. "You seemed to have needed the break."

"He'll just have someone bring more."

"It will take at least a day. Are you going to tell me what he has you doing now?"

She looked away.

"I didn't think so. Why do you think I should feel the need to tell you anything when you don't tell me?"

She stumbled forward, catching the poster of the bed.

"Either you did that on purpose, or your magic isn't strong enough to create a solid world," Ky chastised, instantly moving toward her.

"I'm fine," she huffed, walking into the mist behind him. Slowly the room formed around her, a balcony appearing and the doors swinging open.

"That's why you won't go see Wrynn." He let his statement hang there between them. She was too weak, and her *kupal* would notice.

She bent over onto the railing, resting her head on her arms. "You don't understand. Why do you never understand?"

He moved toward her. The floor wasn't quite as solid a form as it should be; it was more of a layered mist. "Let me take over the dream. It'll take less energy."

The room began to disappear, cool mist swirling around him. He latched on, bringing the room back into focus, using his own magic to stabilize it. The balcony railing was now solid enough for them both to lean on. He turned the sky to a brilliant shade of orange like the setting sun.

"You're better at this than me, anyway. It's the painter's touch. So much detail." She sighed, sliding down the balcony. He followed her as her head flopped onto his shoulder. "Kylane..."

"Mm-hmm."

"Why won't you try and *kupal* with Belladonna? It would appease him."

Ky shook his head. "She's awful. She only thinks about herself and the kill. I can't live like that."

"Do you want to find someone?" she asked, suddenly quiet.

"Why wouldn't I?"

"I'm not sure I would've chosen to bring Wrynn into our mess if it could've been helped." She lowered her head to her knees. "Please don't ever tell him I said that. He's how I get through days like these—picturing his face. But this isn't the life I imagined when I was little." She exhaled, looking up. "Is that why you fight father's will, why you never seem to look for anyone?"

Ky shook his head, leaning farther back to look into the sky. "I have looked. I have tried, trust me. But have you ever thought that maybe my *kupal* wasn't one of us? Like maybe she's a Sky, like Mother. Maybe even a Star..." He let the words trail off. He didn't want to upset Azalea further, but he couldn't lie, either.

"Do you blame me for the Stars' destruction? Ky, you know I wouldn't have done it if I truly believed it wasn't the only—"

He placed his hand on her knee, their eyes meeting. There was so much pain in hers. Maybe even remorse. "I know." He wrapped his arm around her shoulder, pulling her closer to him. "His ways just aren't for me."

"You're like Prince Sky," she said with a small smile. "Do you remember the way Mother told his story?"

"How am I like him? I didn't cause all this—"

She patted his arm. "What do we know about him?"

"He's the reason the humans were brought to this world to begin with. They sent him back to the old world to *kupal*."

She sat up straighter. "Yes, because he had tried with every available female, and he needed an heir or his magic would die with him." She raised her eyebrows. "So maybe you need to look elsewhere."

"Go back to the old world? That didn't work out so well for him. In the end, all he did was tear the Spitarian race apart and bring humans to this world."

"Yes, but Sky isn't a whole different world."

Sky isn't a whole different world. "Are you saying fly to the Sky islands?"

His sister shrugged. "What's the harm? Of course, don't bring back a human. But there are many Spitarians other than the ones here. Plus, who wouldn't want a vacation to the Cloud Island?"

"They are heavily guarded. Is this your idea or Father's?"

The dream state became foggy. Distantly, he felt a cold nose pushing into him.

A small smile lifted Azalea's lips before she disappeared entirely.

Something moist pushed into his face, and he reached his palm up, knowing who it was by the earthy smell of the hot breath. His hand collided with a hard, smooth surface.

Ky opened his eyes to find Thumper's large juniper head pressed into him and one of his forelegs dipped into the spring. His one remaining golden eye inspected Ky's body, his nostrils flaring.

Was his sister serious? No one had spoken to the Sky brethren since the separation of their people centuries ago, though maybe it was time for a reconciliation.

"Hey, boy," Ky said, reaching up for Thumper's head.

The dragon ducked and leaned into the touch, his dark underbelly moving slowly, a noise of appreciation came from deep in his throat; a familiar rumble of pleasure.

Ky stood from the pool and instantly regretted the feeling as his brain returned to normal and his magic leveled out. He patted Thumper's impenetrable scales and shoved his legs back into his pants.

"Where's Tang?"

Thumper lifted his head to the ceiling and then back down with a grunt.

Ky pushed his hearing out and listened for the distant beat of wings. It took a moment, but eventually he heard it. "Did you two have a good breakfast?"

Thumper blew out a huff, turning his head away.

"Did Tang steal all the best parts again?"

Thumper didn't acknowledge him this time.

"I'll take that as a yes."

The sound of beating wings grew louder, and Ky looked up in time to see Tang's shadow blocking out the sun.

Tang's landing wasn't smooth. She was flying in too fast. He watched as her tiny wings folded in too slowly; her long legs weren't braced for the hard impact. She rolled awkwardly to her side, small rocks trembling in her wake. The ground erupted in a dusty puff of smoke, and the dragon let out a loud huff.

Ky had found her small, misshapen egg abandoned in a cave fifteen years ago. He had kept the egg with him in his bed until she hatched. She had been the runt of her litter, her body disproportionate. He hadn't expected her to have a long life after seeing her form, but the moment those spirited orange orbs had locked on him, he'd known he couldn't give up on her.

Tang was pure black except for a bright orange stripe that ran from the tip of her orange nose to the end of her tail. Ky bit his cheek, holding in the chuckle as she rocked her body back and forth, trying to gain enough momentum to get back to a standing position.

Ky let out a low laugh. "Did you know I was talking about you, girl? You want help?" But the low answering growl told him otherwise.

Now all he saw when he looked at his dragon was the armor Iris wore with such pride. That was a mystery for another day.

When Tang finally righted herself, Ky moved over to her and ran his hand over her belly. "Don't get too comfy. I need you to deliver a letter for me."

Tang snorted.

Ky removed paper, a twig, and ink from his pocket and quickly scrolled a letter to his human contact. They needed to meet immediately. He also requested his contact bring human coins for Ky's use.

"Can you find Blakey?" He tied a small leather sack with the note attached around his dragon's neck.

He could have sworn she rolled her orange eyes. "Please."

The dragon blinked slowly, looked over at Thumper's now-sleeping body, and took off.

Ky wrote one more note and placed it on the bedroll, hoping he and the princess would have an easier time trusting each other than he'd had training a dragon to carry letters.

Chapter Eleven

Ky

Ky's white wings dipped to the left, their black tips nearly missing the top of a tree. He had left before Tang returned, hoping his message was received. He couldn't wade in the pool forever; his responsibilities lay elsewhere.

The white caps of the Frengress Mountains sprawled across the land, morphing into the Boltos and then the Agolya Mountains. The snow decreased the farther south Ky went. He looked at the land, memorizing its beauty, the way everything had a color, no two shades quite the same. Even the snow wasn't just white; some places were bluer while others had shoots of green sprigs coming through. Ky wondered what it would have been like in his ancestors' time, when they could fly freely over the land to the sand dunes, the marsh, or even to the Sky Islands to see his mother's kin.

Peace. The word brought joy to his heart. It was all he wanted, to go back in time when the harvests were full, magic was abundant, and the Spitarians were a happy race.

He flew for nearly an hour, higher than most Spitarians flew out of caution, changing direction and speed as frequently as possible. When he knew he was finally in the clear, he made his way toward the grassy spot where the mountain finally ended. The snow draped neatly over the trees like a white blanket. He circled three times, only seeing one lone figure sprawled out on the grass.

Ky landed with a thump that shook the ground below him, inches from the sleeping man's head. The human was dressed head to toe in black; even his face was covered. He didn't stir.

"You are the laziest man I have ever met," Ky said, gently kicking at the black mass on the ground. Before his foot could even graze the man, he was on his feet, stretching.

Ky let out a soft laugh. "And the quickest. I swear your blood doesn't run red."

Blakey's crooked teeth gleamed in the sunlight below his hood. "And I would swear yours did."

Both men sat across from each other. Blakey was small, nearly child-sized compared to Ky's looming figure, and yet he'd never once shied away in fear. Ky swore even if Blakey stood in front of Head Axel himself, he wouldn't be afraid. That was one of the main reasons Ky had chosen Blakey to be his human liaison, the face of the operation. It had started small, Blakey being his first human recruit, and since then it had grown to hundreds of humans who would do anything to bring about peace between the races. No one other than Blakey knew Ky and his mother had started the crusade for peace between the races.

Blakey had been a young man reaching his prime when Ky had found him. Now at thirty-seven, Ky was still unsure how Blakey managed half of what he did. He had been living on the outskirts of the Luminary Forest, living off the land, a man outcast. Ky had only seen Blakey uncovered once, and that had been enough for Ky to know Blakey hadn't ever had it easy.

"I would ask how your family is, but I don't truly care," Blakey said, his masked face looking straight ahead.

"Then I shall not do you the courtesy of asking about yours," Ky said in a brisk tone, speaking the human's language.

"Testy today, are we?"

"The Head—"

"Ah, magic got you all backed up? Maybe you should have stopped for a release before coming here." One corner of Blakey's mouth lifted.

Ky ignored the joke. Rolling around for pleasure with a female wouldn't help his current situation. "We have some problems."

"Like you wearing your armor to a meeting with me?"

Ky crossed his arms. "More problems."

"Don't we always?"

Ky paced back and forth, his mind racing. "For starters, we intercepted two pieces of information while I was away. The first being the wedding invitation for Prince Finn, which my father has decided to use to poison everyone."

Blakey tilted his head. "Well, that is a problem."

"There's more."

Blakey let out a fake laugh. "Of course."

"The second piece of information said that Princess Castor has left the castle."

"That would explain some of the trickling of information I've been receiving about her no longer being at court. Many of the rumors stated her going north."

"North?" Ky rubbed his forehead. "My father has sent me to kill her."

Blakey leaned back on his elbows, silent.

"I'm not going to do it, of course."

"I would assume not, but why do I feel like there's more?"

Ky reached inside his pants pocket and produced the leather journal. He tossed it so it landed with a small thump against Blakey's chest.

Blakey took the book and skimmed through it slowly. "What am I looking at?"

Ky let out a sigh before filling him in on everything that had happened with Iris the night before. He hoped Blakey's eyes would give away what he felt as he spoke. But nothing changed, and with the mask on, Ky had a hard time trying to determine where this conversation was going to go as Blakey listened without interruption.

"Well?" Ky said impatiently.

Blakey scratched his temple. "I'm trying to process. And I want to make sure my translation is correct. Because if it is, everything we've ever been told about Princess Castor was that she was going to save us all. Now you're telling me you believe the prophecy speaks of a union. This is a little . . ."

"Delicate."

"I was going to say a steaming pile of unicorn shit."

Ky blew out a breath. "Well, at least it's not dragon shit."

Blakey picked up a long reed from the ground and stuck it in his mouth, rolling it slowly between his lips. "When you locate her, what are you going to say?"

"The truth?" Ky's statement came out as a question. He was second-guessing himself.

"And if she won't come with you . . . will you force her?"

Ky shook his head but then said, "I'd rather not, but a kidnapped princess is better than a dead one."

"Do you want help with the princess? I could send some of our people with you."

"No." The more people he trusted with the princess's future whereabouts, the more danger they both would be in. He trusted Blakey to keep her safe, but he still hadn't revealed where he would take the princess. The more people around when he found her, the more danger. So, no, he would do this all alone.

Blakey readjusted his hood and stood. "Well, good luck kidnapping the princess. I will do everything I can to help you from my end. Send word if you need anything in particular."

As Blakey turned to leave, Ky's voice stopped him. "I think you should spread the true prophecy."

Blakey turned around slowly. "And why would I do that?"

"If Iris's heritage is to be believed, there are already Spitarian and humans mingling. Things are already in place. Maybe with the truth out there, the inevitable will be easier when the time comes."

"And what will you tell the clan leaders at *Sensal*?"

Ky looked to the sky and swore. The *Sensal* was held every third full moon with the thirty-three clan leaders. As *Heiralomun* to the throne, it was Ky's responsibility to gather the information, grievances, and anything else the clan leaders had for their king and vice versa.

"What of them?"

"If the humans are being primed, don't you think the clan leaders should be as well?" Ky could see Blakey's yellow teeth under his hood then, an evil grin he saved for his worst enemies. Then he simply nodded and strolled toward the wood beyond, without a glance or a goodbye.

Ky raised his eyes to the distant mountains, trying to pinpoint the spot where the *Sensal* happened. He knew the clan leaders would hear about the princess's journey, knew that they would want more information, maybe even the chance to kill her during that time. Ky needed to be prepared as to how he would spin this so he seemed impartial during the meetings but would still be able to sway them with the truth of the prophecy. The ancestral hatred his people had for humans was like a disease of its own; they were killing just because of the passed-down memories.

Ky still had a hard time understanding the prophecy that had been written about the future. It was all jumbled, and the phrases and words didn't make sense. He grabbed at it where it lay in the grass and flipped through the pages slowly. Elora Castor's name was scattered throughout most of the pages, and the word "child" was circled several times.

Ky had also marked up the pages, underlining, trying to decipher the bits of texts, but only his mother would be able to understand what it meant. Pages after the prophecy, Rhella had indicated that she was going to speak to Elora Castor and her lover. Maybe his mother had given further instructions to Elora that she never wrote in her journal.

Ky sighed and stood, hoping his mother was indeed still around to provide him with direction. He pocketed the journal, then bent his knees, unfurled his enormous wings, and took flight.

Chapter Twelve

River

River stumbled over a tree branch, catching herself before she hit the ground. She let out an annoyed breath and sagged against it. She felt as though she had been walking in circles for hours. Yet the sun hadn't risen; that much she knew. She pushed on, hoping to find some glimmer of the moon ahead to help guide her path.

Just outside of Neven. The map of the countryside swirled in and out of her mind. The green-grass hill that leveled out eventually led to the Eastern Sea. Neven . . . Neven lay between the borders.

What had she been thinking? Well, she knew what she'd been thinking—she'd thought she and Bass would be walking through these woods together, at least into the town.

But instead, the princess, the only heir to the throne, the sole protector of the five Heldours kingdoms, the Peace Bringer, the Chosen One, the Savior—she couldn't even remember all of the names she'd been called over the years—was alone.

She felt like a fraud, like nothing more than a child.

What was I thinking?

The forest began to close in around her, the trees going in and out of focus as the tears came and the ball of aching expanded in her stomach.

He never meant to marry me.

That bastard.

She gasped in a breath as if the air was no longer in her lungs. The tree bark scraped along her back as she fell to her knees and closed her eyes.

River, get a hold of yourself, her mother's voice rang in her mind.

All of the information in her head rattled around while she let it all sink in deep. Then, she buried it like the remains of a decomposing animal. She imagined the soil and the grass filling in every hole and crevice until nothing remained. Until she was numb. The only thing that remained was the lump in her stomach that was growing quicker.

Her mother had always thought she was a weak shell of a human. River wouldn't sit here crying against the tree any longer. She wouldn't prove her right. She lifted her face to the sky, feeling for a breeze, searching for the way out.

A cloud shifted in the deep purple sky, and a tiny sliver of the crescent moon broke through the tree line ahead.

This is no different than the training room.

River stumbled to her feet and ran, allowing the pang of exercise and the adrenaline to hold the ball of feelings back down, tethering it like a weight in the well of her stomach. Laya might have been right about Bass, but she wasn't right about this. River could control her emotions.

She ran, jumping over roots, sticks, and leaves until she finally came to the end of the forest line.

"Oh, thank the King of Heldours," she gasped into the quiet night sky.

The small town of Neven was just ahead. A long, winding road led from the far end of the forest to the small cluster of buildings. She slowed her breathing, tucked her shirt back into her pants, and pulled the cloak closer around her face as she readied herself for her mission.

The moon was low in the sky, dipping behind a large clock tower at the end of the cobblestone street. Unlike the other one- and two-story buildings, it stood several stories high and was in pristine condition. River ran her hand along a massive hole in a brick building. The invasions had been far more brutal than she'd thought.

Although it was early evening, the town seemed relatively quiet. The unpaved streets should have been full of people. Instead, the few people around didn't even look up as she passed, their heads down, tucked into whatever clothing they wore. One woman wore nothing but faded undergarments, the fierce wind nipping at her bare legs.

The potent smell of mold and unwashed bodies did nothing to ease River's churning stomach. She continued to walk until she caught the sound of laughter. She peered through the window of the building with the least amount of damage into a room full of tables and a long bar.

The tavern?

A bell dinged loudly above her head, announcing her presence. To her relief, not many eyes looked up, and the ones that did only looked at her as if she were a fresh piece of meat they meant to devour. Hopefully, none of them recognized her for something other than a strange woman. She'd been stupid to think she could just waltz in the front door unnoticed. Several tables were scattered throughout the space, all full of men drinking and talking. Some were even sleeping. Of course, they would recognize her as a woman.

She kept one hand on her hood, contemplating her next move as the smell of unwashed bodies assaulted her nose. She tried not to show her disgust.

This is no different than our parties. I've seen drunk people before. I can do this.

"Pint," a man screamed to her left, holding his drink high. He grinned at River with a toothless mouth. His body was filthy, dirt caked on every inch of him.

River's skin crawled as she moved past him toward the one empty table in the back. At least she could see the entire room from there.

A rough hand grabbed her backside. River whirled, catching the man's hand mid-swing as he was about to do it again. His mouth dropped open. Red-hot anger flashed through her. She was a stranger and certainly not his lover. She twisted his wrist to the left, feeling the bones easily; with one more pull, she could break it without hesitation.

A woman's voice lifted over the crowd. "Now, now, Plata, play nice with the new girl." She squeezed River's arm, forcing her to let go.

River eyed them both, then noticed the tavern was now silent, all eyes on her. Slowly, she remembered her role here. She had already messed up and drawn attention to herself. River let go of the man's arm but not without a painful squeeze that would assure him and all the other eyes she was not to be messed with.

A girl no older than herself pulled her forcefully toward the bar. "Ya certainly know how to make an appearance."

"Excuse me?"

"Well, did you want the attention of every man in here? Unless ya plan on taking them all to your bed, I'd stop throwing yourself around."

Her words floored River. Was this girl implying River was asking for their attention? She shook away the words.

"Ale?" the girl asked.

River's face fell. She'd forgotten to grab some coin. How could she have forgotten people paid for things with coins? *Daft.* This was not going at all according to plan. Her stomach growled.

"And some food," the girl said and moved farther back into the tavern before River could tell her otherwise.

The girl returned, placing a bowl of clear liquid down in front of her, along with a tiny piece of stale bread and a pint full of a brown liquid River assumed was ale. She took a small sip, and the liquid burned her throat. She nearly choked, sputtering a little onto the barmaid.

The girl's pale face softened. Her skin appeared as though it had never seen the light of day, and her golden hair was swept up behind her head in an unwashed tangle.

"How could anyone drink that?" River muttered. She had never found the appeal of alcohol, though she had also never been allowed to drink it. Her mother had always told her she was afraid a drink would loosen River up too much.

"Ya'r new here." The girl's accent was thick, and River had a hard time understanding her words. How could that be? River had thoroughly studied every dialect of the five kingdoms.

She nodded, sinking her spoon in the soup, which appeared to be nothing more than broth.

"Welcome to Neven. I'm Imogen." She pointed around. "I'd introduce ya, though I'm not sure there's anyone else here worth meeting." Imogen stuck her hand out, and River grabbed it, hesitating for a second. The wealthy, especially royalty, didn't shake hands unless they were people you were intimate with or someone offering assistance.

"Ya're?"

"R—owan," River said, using her middle name

"Were you named after the princess?"

River's insides screamed "run," and she pulled her hand away quickly as if she'd been burned. The girl didn't seem to notice; she was too busy talking away to her. River only caught a few of the words as her panic and the pressure in her stomach surged then eased.

River sat for a long while sipping her soup, which had a surprisingly flavorful taste for something so thin and did wonders for her sore stomach. She looked for a man she presumed was Barthomule. Someone who never showed his face, which was only covered in black, and walked with a limp. But each of the men in here, even those who'd had a hood to begin with, had since shed it.

"Couldn't stomach it?" Imogen said, pointing to the glass.

River shook her head.

"Nor I, truthfully."

Something occurred to River. Hadn't Leon mentioned that a barmaid shared Barthomule's bed? She hadn't seen any other taverns, but Imogen might not be the only barmaid.

"Is this the only tavern in Neven?"

"Yes, ya won't find much better in these parts."

River bit the inside of her lip. "And are you the only maid here?"

"There are one or two other girls here." Imogen's eyes narrowed. "If it's a friend for the evening ya're looking for, miss, that can be arranged."

River blushed. "No, I'm supposed to be meeting a gentleman friend of my father's here. I just wanted to make sure he hadn't run off with any maids and was leaving me here waiting." River hoped her lie rolled off her tongue as smoothly as she felt it had.

"Ah, of course. What does this friend look like?"

"Truthfully, I've never met him. He was supposed to know me."

Imogen moved the rag across the bar. "Men can get distracted in these parts. This is the only tavern, but the Den is a few doors away, and some men find the draw irresistible."

River folded her arms across the bar and bent low. "The Den?"

"Where they sell Perlilium. Do they call it something elsewhere ya're from?"

The way the word rolled off the girl's tongue, it almost sounded as though she'd said Pardum, a drug the soldiers took to enhance their abilities, stay up later, gain muscles, and the like. But the girl had undoubtedly said the word with an *L*.

"Perlilium?" River questioned, her curiosity getting the better of her.

"Ya really aren't from here? Are ya some noble breed?" Imogen cocked her head as if studying River for the first time, trying to see into her.

River shouldn't have asked. Yet again, she was drawing too much attention to herself.

"I'll tell ya only because I don't want ya seeking it out on your own. It's a drug used to create a state of oblivion."

River began to stand. This wasn't why she was here.

Imogen caught her hand across the counter. "Don't go seeking out your friend this late at night. And certainly not in the Den."

"And if I do, what will I find?"

Imogen pursed her lips, her eyelids heavy. "Humans trying to forget their worries. And if your friend is one of them, he should be left at peace to do so."

"So you condone the use of drugs meant for soldiers?"

"When the crown leaves a town to fend for itself against their enemy and has boys no older than us fighting for them, it's none of anyone's business," Imogen said firmly, turning away.

River stood still for a moment. The crown had not abandoned these people. How dared this child presume to speak such things?

"Were you all not told to leave and seek shelter elsewhere? Is it not your fault for staying in a home that has been invaded over and over?"

"Ya seem to have been painted a very pretty picture of the crown as a child." Imogen *tsk*ed and placed her hand on her hip. "Yes, we were told once to walk away, abandon our homes, and leave everything. But where were the families to go? No roof over their heads, no work? Were they to raise a family on the streets and never put food in their children's bellies? Their homes still remained, their farms were still workable. What's the alternative?"

The girl spoke with a charge and authority no young woman should have.

Had her soldiers just walked away without helping? River had never thought much of it. Had they been displaced from their homes? River hadn't heard of any new developments to provide for them.

"Are all the towns that border the north like this?"

"Yes."

"And most believe as you do? That the crown cares not for them?"

Imogen shrugged. "Most."

"Is the hatred of the crown always spoken so openly?"

The girl's eyes narrowed.

"And what of the conscription age being fifteen? It is no different than the marriage age. Old enough to make an informed decision, no?" River knew she was pressing hard, but if nothing else, this trip would give her something her lessons never had. The truth. And not the truth as her mother and the other nobility saw it, but the truth from someone's mouth who didn't believe River held up the sun for them.

"Ya ask a lot of questions."

"I find myself lacking in education, it seems."

Imogen snorted and moved farther along the bar with the rag, stopping to fill another pint. When she returned, she lowered her face close to River's. "Ya're around fifteen. Do you feel ya're ready for a marriage decision? To bear his babes? To prop up a dying army? I'm not yet fifteen, and I'm not ready for any of those things. If I never see another man naked again, I'd be happy. "

River blinked, trying to keep the ever-growing shock from her face. Imogen's questions rang true. River had thought she was ready for marriage at a much younger age. Now after everything with Bass, she saw she'd been wrong. Had it only been because of the naivety of her age she'd thought those things?

"I see," was all she could manage to say.

The bell on the door rang, and River shifted to get a better look without appearing to do so. A group of middle-aged men walked in. None had a limp, and none wore covering. She let out a sigh.

"Do ya have a place to sleep tonight?"

River set her jaw. She'd been so foolish to leave without thinking this evening through better. Leon had said some nights Barthomule didn't return. If he didn't, what was she to do?

"I can't afford one. The man I was meeting was meant to pay for everything."

"We don't have any spare rooms," Imogen said, leveling her with a solid brown gaze.

River nodded, standing. "I understand. Thank you. I—"

"But I won't use my rooms 'til midday if ya want. They're yours to use."

River felt a rush of warmth. "You would show kindness to a stranger who knows so little of the world?"

Imogen grabbed the bowl of soup. "Sometimes growing up with little makes ya appreciate so much more and give even greater."

"Thank you," River said, placing her hand on top of the girl's. It felt good to touch this stranger, to be assured with the meaning of her words.

Imogen nodded. "First door on the left up the stairs." She pointed to the back corner of the tavern, where a narrow staircase led to the upper floors.

River nodded before making her way quickly past the tables and up the stairs. Leon had said the man kept his belongings here. Maybe his room would lead her to some clue. And even if it didn't, waiting for him to return was her best option.

River moved with soft feet up the stairs, then rounded the corner on the landing . . . only to come face-to-face with the gray-eyed charmer.

Chapter Thirteen

Ky

*P*lease let me find her with no trouble, Ky begged. *Fadelings, you know what I fight for. Help me.*

There were two border towns close to where Ky had met with Blakey. He would search one today and try to do the other tomorrow.

Ky dipped to the left around a knot of light trees that reminded him of the dirt under Iris's fingernails. Is that where his mother had hidden this entire time—a forest between human lands?

Centuries ago, the Luminary Forest had been full of beautiful and mysterious creatures like unicorns. That was the way of things; beautiful things killed only for the deadly to survive. If Ky wasn't fast enough, his own people would be no more than a fairy tale told to future generations. He had to find the princess and bring her to safety. If he didn't, he worried there wouldn't be a human or Spitarian left alive to tell stories of them.

Ky had never flown any farther south than the grassy plains where he'd met with Blakey. The mountain peaks slowly disappeared, turning into flatlands. Ky avoided the area in which he knew the

Spitarian hunters would be resting and veered right, heading deeper into human territory toward the rolling green hills.

The trees disappeared, and a small outcropping appeared. The sky was dark, and he kept close to the clouds, dipping in and out, hoping to avoid human attention. Even from this height, he could tell the town had seen better days. It reminded him of his castle. Most of the border towns had been reduced to rubble twenty years ago when his people had searched for his mother. They had threatened and killed any humans in their paths under the Head's orders. Neither he nor the Head had ever expected these people to be so resilient. They had remained even after the terror. To Ky's knowledge, other than being outcasts from the human lands, his father had left them in relative peace, ignoring them and choosing to kill the soldiers only . . . until recently. What had caused him to redirect his attention here?

Ky shook his head and tucked away the question for later. He didn't have time to wonder about the Head's illogical motives. Ky's wings stilled as he noticed the lack of movement in the town. It was just after dusk, the sky between a deep violet and a stormy gray. There wasn't a green-clad soldier in sight. Wouldn't the princess's soldiers be with her? Had he guessed wrong? Was she in the border town closer to the sea? He didn't expect Elora to go the extra mile to hide her daughter farther away, but now he second-guessed himself.

Dragon-damn. How to proceed?

Ky dived deep toward a small outcropping of trees. Could he quickly look? No. It would take longer, but he needed to be thorough. Ky had no way of disguising himself like his mother, who had the ability to shift her appearance.

He would walk into the town, and everyone would know exactly what he was. He only hoped that their fear of him would be all the pressure he needed to secure the information on the princess's current location.

He took several giant steps across the rubble until he reached the first semi-intact building. The streets scooped down toward a larger building with an obscure-looking circle atop it, a hollow metal sculpture of sorts. His eyebrows knit together in confusion. It was easy to see as no humans remained out. Ky knocked at the cracked wooden door. He heard a muffled voice from within, but the door remained shut, despite the small sliver of light that filtered from underneath it.

A ruckus farther down the road pulled his attention. A man stumbled out of an open door where Ky could finally hear multiple voices. The man slowly crossed the street and was swallowed by a shadow. He moved toward the noise as the door slammed shut, leaving the street quiet once more. The building was far better looking than some of the others, and this time he didn't knock. He ducked and pushed through the small doorway. A bell dinged, and all heads snapped toward him. The room fell silent except for a shattered glass and a low whimper.

The men that sat among the tables looked as disheveled as the town. One moment their hands only held glasses; the next weapons were out and ready.

Ky held up his hands. "I mean no harm. I just need some information, and then I'll be on my way."

"He speaks our language," someone whispered.

A woman in a plum dress took one step out from behind the bar. She crossed her arms. "We can't help your kind here. We paid our tax. You already took one of our girls this moon, and you won't take another."

Ky shook his head as some of the unfamiliar words washed over him. *Tax? As in, what one pays to the human crown?* "I'm not sure I understand. I'm looking for whoever's in charge."

A few throats cleared. The smell of urine was suddenly potent in the air. A young boy scurried out what Ky assumed was a back door.

"He's dead." The murmured voice was barely a whisper, but Ky's keen ears picked it up.

"I see. And who would be the leftwing?" When no one spoke, he continued. "The second-in-command? The leader?"

All eyes turned to the woman in the plum dress. She let out a sigh as her shoulders dropped. "I guess that would be me. What do ya want?"

"I'm looking for a girl. One who wouldn't be from these parts. Would have been a new arrival to the town recently—within the last moon."

"Heldours," the woman swore.

"Excuse me?"

"The tax is paid," the woman said, wringing a towel in her hands. The dress color suited her well.

"No more girls," someone whispered.

Ky eyes searched the room, looking for someone who would lock eyes with him, but not one would hold his gaze. Their heads were bowed, faces slacken. A pitiful group.

"May I sit?" He gestured toward a stool that was too small for him. The woman's eyebrows raised.

Ky took a step forward, and he felt the man closest to him flinch. Ky lowered himself to the stool. It let out a small crack that spilt through the air. He cringed, raising himself to hover over it.

"What is this tax you speak of? Is this what I must pay to get information?" He kept his eyes on the woman as she came around the bar to face him. Ky's thighs began to shake with the strain.

She pursed her lips and shook her head, her cheeks bouncing. "Don't play me for a fool. Your kind already took their one human a moon. Look elsewhere."

Ky didn't question the woman further. The rigid set of her face said she was speaking the truth. Had his people been terrorizing more humans than he thought?

"No, I—"

"I would appreciate it if you stated your business and left." She braced her hands across the bar. Her right hand slowly crept toward a hole.

Ky's eyes narrowed. "Again, I am just seeking the girl I spoke of before. She most likely was in disguise, but you would recognize her as your princess."

The woman folded her arms over her chest. "The princess hasn't left her castle in her life. Feel free to use those wings of yours and fly to her window. I hope the guards shoot you from the air. Now get."

Ky didn't know what he was supposed to say. He expected fear, but these people's reactions were hardened. Hostile. But no one had hidden from him.

He felt a pressure on his forearm as someone slid next to him. Ky followed the small, wrinkly hand up the protruding veins in its arm to an even more fragile body. The body hopped onto the stool quickly for the way it looked. He was a little shocked. Humans didn't usually live this long; this woman looked to be at least in her eighties. He waited until she was fully seated. The rags of white cloth hung off her body, and over her chest was a vest of animal fur muddied by the dirt.

"Her drink is on me." Ky laid down a handful of coins.

The plump woman looked up, her hand quickly sweeping the coins from the bartop into the hole. No wonder she was trying to protect it. Her life savings was probably under this tavern. "She can stay, but you still have to go."

The older woman's silver hair shifted from her face as she looked up at him. Her large blue eyes flickered to amber.

"Dragon—"

The old woman cleared her throat then spoke in the human tongue. "I believe you were taught better than to swear openly." The voice was merely a crackle, a whisper of what her actual voice was, but it was unmistakable.

Rhella.

Ky's heart thundered in his chest like a thousand unicorn hooves danced across it. His mother was alive. She was *alive*. Happiness spread but then died on his lips as he held in his smile.

She *had* abandoned them.

"I was also taught blood before brethren. Yet, you seem to have forgotten that."

The noise that came from Rhella's throat was like a snort as her eyes flickered back to blue. She turned to the barmaid. "I'll be back for some soup." She hopped off the stool and made her way quickly to the door.

Ky reluctantly followed her. He had so many questions. Where she had been and what was going on? Why had they never been told the truth? Why had she pretended to be dead? He was so angry, but despite his anger, the moment they passed through the tavern door and the bell stopped chiming, he bent to a knee and placed his fist to his chest.

"My Heart. *Feva da arivsam des Sparrow deseamum.*" He spoke the words each Sparrow had memorized. *We will rise again only when the Sparrow dreams.*

Small, warm hands cupped his cheeks. They weren't his mother's hands, but they would do for now. She pressed a kiss to his forehead, another over each closed eye, and then wiped the lone tear that ran down his cheek.

"My son. How you have grown. I am so proud of you. You certainly are dreaming of better." Her hands slipped to his shoulders. "Come, we should talk with fewer ears."

"Kisling lied," Ky managed as he stood and followed his mother in this strange form toward a small outcropping of trees.

She didn't speak. She only walked, as quickly as her small human body would allow. When they were within the grove of trees, Rhella turned to him. "He lied because he was my leftwing. Just as Wrynn would lie for you if you asked."

"Not to the Head, he wouldn't."

His mother let out a sigh. "Then maybe you chose the wrong leftwing. Kisling believes in my magic. More than anything."

Ky leaned back against the tree. "I don't disbelieve your prophecy. But I wouldn't lie to my Head and tell him humans murdered his wife for her gift."

"You're lying now."

He ground his teeth. She was correct. He *was* lying now and not only to his Head, but to his father and to his sister. "To protect them."

"Just as Kisling was protecting you and your sister. You each had to make your own paths." Rhella squeezed the bridge of her nose. It was a gesture he was so familiar with. The pain her premonitions brought on was unbearable. Magic always took a physical toll, but for his mother, if she didn't speak her premonitions, the pain brought her to her knees.

Rhella tugged at the small crystalline necklace at her throat, centering herself. "Did you know when Kisling and Corellie were pregnant with Emerray, I foretold that both of them would leave Kisling far before he would want? I told him to relish the moments with them while he had them."

The mention of Emerray brought a sick pang to Ky's heart. Once upon a time, Ky, Azalea, Wrynn, and Emerray had been inseparable. Ky had fond memories of growing up with her. She'd been sweet and caring and had been ripped from his life too young. When her aptitude for the sword grew, the Kulcan warriors took her for themselves. The cruel warriors were the protectors of their world and the guardians of the portal from which their ancestors had arrived. Ky refused to think about what kind of monster they had turned her into.

He shook his head but said nothing.

"I tried to tell you, but every time I would walk to tell you the truth, all I saw were the deaths of my last two offspring. When I finally decided to hold it in, you lived—"

"Is this what you call living? Az hasn't had alone time with her *kupal* in over five moons. The Head and Azalea—they are broken."

A sigh racked Rhella's body. "No, you're right. But barely living is better than dead. When I told Kisling what needed to be done, he did it without question."

"And Father? What happened when you tried to tell him?"

"Sit," she said, folding her body into the earth. Rhella pressed her fingers into the dirt and watched it slowly strain through them. "You have to understand. Things with your father were complicated. We always showed you the best. And he loves us dearly. But beneath all that, there is an evil that resides in him."

Ky remained silent. His father did love them, but he was cruel. It was evident even in the smallest things, like the way he treated his dragons. Ky had seen the cruelty, had felt it, and watched as it darkened his father's wings, reflecting the color of his soul.

"He was my *kupal*, and I did grow to love him. But it wasn't always love. I know we'd all like to think that every *kupal* is pure bliss . . ."

Ky sensed her hesitation and crossed from the tree to sit in front of his mother. He grabbed her hands. "You can tell me."

"I didn't want our offspring to fight the Head for the right to rule. I was against the whole tradition. My family did away with it. But your father wouldn't listen. He felt the strongest would survive. And that they deserved to be the Head."

"I have always hated that tradition, but I still don't understand why you couldn't tell him that you foresaw no other males were going to be born," Ky said.

"Because your sister was stronger. She has been since her powers came in. Sometimes I was afraid he would hurt her to protect your place. Or hurt you when you proved not to be enough for him."

Ky was grateful for the truth, even if it hurt.

"He never did wrong to me. Not truly. You need to know that. But he was jealous. He liked me to think the way he did." Rhella shook her head and cleared her throat. "I was in love prior to my *kupaling* bond snapping into place. We were set to be wed. But I couldn't ignore the bond. It would mean no offspring, and we were both of the original lines. We were meant to strengthen the founding families."

Ky digested the words. The *kupal* magic wasn't simple. It pulled every ounce of power from each participant; as their bodies intertwined, their magic did as well. Fighting, warring, attempting to braid themselves together permanently. They would be tied together in all ways, and it was only by this eminent combination of magic that an offspring could be born. After, they stayed intertwined for days until they regained enough strength to move. And even then, some never got up again. Eventually, the newness wore off, and the *kupal* would carry on with normal life. Until the female was indeed with an offspring, then the process of pregnancy was exhausting since the magic alone created the being. The female's body pulled power from the males as well, so much magic that if the male were in battle, he would have to remove himself. Both parties were utterly useless during the process.

"You said snapped into place? Everything I have been told from the way Azalea explains it is that it's a braid woven together of magic that tethers the two together."

Rhella nodded slowly, a small lock of silver hair falling across her cheek. "When there is love, yes. Your sister and Wrynn have been in love since they were children. What started as a love of friendship grew into the ideal *kupal* bond." She patted Ky's hand gently. He noticed then that though his mother could change her form, her veins still shone violet through her skin. "Your father's and my bond was a constant battle of wills. While they were braided together, one was always seeking dominance. And that's not how it was meant to be."

Like two fists clasped together, one constantly squeezing too hard.

"So you broke the bond." Even as he spoke the words, it hurt him to think about. What it had done to his father he had seen firsthand, but what had the consequences been for his mother?

"Yes. And what happened was so much worse than what I expected."

Ky pulled back, staring at her. He had been looking at Rhella but not truly seeing. He now studied the magic around her. His mother's magic had always been less solid than others, magic that constantly swirled around her like dancing streams of seafoam crystalline light. But now, the lines were almost frozen in the stillness. They barely moved.

Ky tilted his head, his gaze locked on his mother's now blue eyes. "You changed your eye color earlier, but it didn't stay . . . You can't change back." His own words gutted him.

She squeezed his hands gently. "Your father would tell me it served me right, that if I wanted to be near the humans so damn bad, I should stay as one. I broke the bond in this form, so must I remain in it. I can make a small change, but it doesn't last. I can feel the magic on the inside. I am fading. And in this form, I'm not sure what that means."

"You always said there were consequences for everything."

"So I did. But we don't have much time."

Ky nodded. "The princess. She must remain alive?"

"Yes, and Iris can be trusted. Though I sense that's something you struggle with, since you made me come here in person." She pointed to his heart then to his head. "Connect those before it's too late. Stop letting the past lead your future. My actions have no place in your decisions." She flicked his nose. "Iris and Princess Castor are important in the days to come. But so are you and your sister. And a few others." Her smile met her eyes, lines creasing in every direction.

"And the prophecy. Has it changed since you first wrote it?"

"Ah, what a good question. No. It's still the same, and I feel every word of it." Rhella held out her hand to her son. "Up."

Ky obliged, gently grabbing her hand and placing the other at her elbow. "Mother, I've been having these dreams . . ."

She wrinkled her nose. "Dreams? Or are they visions of your future? A hazel-eyed woman perhaps?"

Ky stepped back. "How did you know?"

The corner of her mouth lifted, but she quickly covered it with a pale, wrinkled hand.

"Am I having premonitions?"

She took a few slow steps forward, got on her tiptoes, and tried to cup his chin. Ky bent to allow her to touch his face. "They are premonitions, yes. But they aren't yours. They're mine. I've been pushing them to you while you dream. There was no way for me to speak them to you. So I allowed my premonitions to dreamwalk with you. Forgive me. It was the only way to ease my pain."

"I don't understand. So she's real?"

"Yes, son, and soon you will be united."

Ky shook his head. "No, not if she is going to die. I don't want to meet her if . . . She *is* going to die, right?"

"I've given you all you need to know. The rest is for you to figure out." Her lips were slanted down now.

Rhella's head flew back, her eyes rolling back, and her body began to tremble. She raised her hands to the bridge of her nose and let out a slow whine. Ky didn't move forward as the premonition racked her, and the magic danced around her again. And, just as quickly as it started, it faded and stilled.

"I must go."

"No, please."

"Someone is searching for you. I can't see their face, but they feel trustworthy."

Ky grabbed her wrist. She winced at the touch, and he loosened his grip. "Sorry, I forgot how frail human bodies are."

"It's okay."

"Can I tell Father and Azalea?"

She shook her head sadly. "No, not yet."

"Why?"

"I must go find Kisling. He'll be gone for a while, but when he returns to your side, you'll know it's time for us to reunite again. We'll see each other again soon."

She brought her fist to her chest, and he did the same. Then he turned away from her and closed his eyes.

He couldn't help but feel like he was losing her all over again.

Chapter Fourteen

River

River took a step back as Leon's wide gray eyes took her in. He was out of breath and his cheeks were flushed, as if he had been running a long distance, though he was on the second floor of the tavern.

"Princ—" His voice died as River put her finger to her lips.

"Leon, is everything all right?"

His shirt was unbuttoned at the collar, and his blond hair stuck out at odd angles. A small line of blush ran up his neck until it met the pink tops of his ears. "I-I just hadn't expected you to arrive so soon. Is the prince with you? I would've sworn you wouldn't come 'til early morning based on the, uh . . . tension at camp."

She felt like he was shouting rather than whispering, a loud roar in a silent hall. "Leon, where are you coming from? Where is Barthomule?"

"My—uh, what am I to call you?"

River let out an exasperated sigh. "Rowan. Now, Leon, please focus."

"Rowan . . . Ah, Rowan. Clever. My rooms. I am coming from my rooms."

River blushed. "Oh, I see."

"What? Oh, no. Not like that. I-I was chasing Barthomule. Or I thought I was. He's a tricky bast—" He slapped his hand to his face. "Oye! Sorry, my—Rowan. I'm new to all of this."

"Aren't you supposed to be a leftenant?"

"No. Well, it's complicated." Leon leaned against the wall and rubbed his face.

River studied the dark shadows under his eyes. She hadn't noticed them before, by the firelight. The man was exhausted. "Is Barthomule in his room now?"

"No, and I don't know where he is or when he'll return."

River debated what to do with Leon. "Which room is his?"

Leon pointed at a brown door with no handle a few doors down.

"You're sure?"

"Yes."

River nodded. "Go sleep, and then keep watch."

"I shouldn't." His eyes traced over the paint-peeled walls and then down the six doors that lined either side of the wall.

"It's an order, Leon. I presume you're good enough in your position to have been promoted, so with that being said, if he slipped your tail, it must mean he's on to you." She sighed. "Sadly, I don't think he'll return if he hasn't already. Which means we'll have to search him out in the morning."

"So you'll sleep as well? I don't feel right leaving you alone."

"I'll just take a look around his room, and then I have lodgings of my own. Leon, do you by chance have some spare coins? I seem to have forgotten those were needed. I'll make sure you're paid in full—with interest."

"Of course." Leon opened his cloak to reveal several knives and other various weapons hanging from his waist. He reached for his coin purse, unstrapped it, and handed it over. He seemed to really look at her then, as if seeing her for the first time. "Did you leave with any weapons when you left in anger?"

"Who said I left in anger?" She could only imagine what she looked like. Worn wool pants hung low and snug to her hips, cloak parted unevenly, and she was sure there were dirt stains in her clothes along with her hair, which she knew was falling around her face. Curly hair never stayed where it was put, especially after rolling around. She squeezed her eyes shut.

Leon shrugged and handed her a small knife and strip of leather. "For your boot."

She smiled despite herself. "Go sleep, Leon." She pointed to the door on the left. "I'm in here. First light, we move out if he's no longer here."

He nodded.

"The other soldiers who were with us in the forest. What's their watch post?"

"They watch the road out of town back into Castor."

"Both of them? Why is it that no one watches north? If Barthomule is passing messages, wouldn't it mean he's going north to do so?" She felt ridiculous even having to ask the question.

"Well, yes, but . . ."

"But what?"

"None of ours would step foot past the town's edge. Not even the queen would ask that of us."

"I see." River nodded, though she didn't see. She was here to kill someone passing information to the Spitarians, yet how had anyone ever seen them do it if they weren't watching? There were a lot of things about this assignment that didn't seem to add up. "Goodnight, Leon."

He bowed his head and turned back into his room.

A feeling in her gut told her things were different than what she was being told—about the border towns, how her people were treated, about Barthomule.

And she certainly was not about to kill an innocent man.

She moved toward the door with no handle and peered through the hole. There was no candle lit within, and the little moonlight that flooded in showed nothing under the blankets of the smooth bed.

River pushed her hand flat against the door, but it resisted slightly. She shoved her shoulder against it. Something in the room clattered to the floor, but the door creaked open enough for her to squeeze through the opening.

River moved across the room to the window and threw open the shade in order to get a full view of the space. She didn't dare light the candle on the small desk for fear it would further alert someone to an intruder. Instead, she turned to inspect the room.

It was small. A cot lay unslept in. The desk was scattered with paper and knickknacks. A chest had been pushed to block the door. *Odd.* River looked from the entrance to the window and back. She pressed her hand to the window, feeling the edges. The glass had been removed completely.

Barthomule had been using the window as a means of an entrance and exit.

Tricky bastard indeed.

Why would he need to use the window as an exit if he wasn't a spy? River felt as though her brain was getting rattled back and forth.

The papers on the desk were a correspondence of some kind. There were letters in the Heldourian addressed to a "Blakey," but they were all in code as none of the sentences made sense. She tried all of the easy codes she could remember, counting the number of letters, searching for the patterns, but whatever codes the writer had used weren't familiar to her and would take her all night to crack. She pocketed a few to decipher later, but it wasn't the Heldours letters she was worried about.

The letters that caught her attention were the letters in a language she couldn't read. Could it be the Spitarian's language? For being such feral beasts, they certainly had an elegant script with letters almost identical to her own. Some of the letters were inverted or connected to the one next to it. Some were stretched, and others were smooshed. The most interesting thing, though, was that the letter was written in swirls, not left to right. It was beautiful, almost like a picture. She picked the letter shaped like a flower and pocketed it, hoping it wouldn't be missed.

River moved her hands slowly across the wall, looking for any loose bricks or crevices to hide things in. Next, she searched the aged wooden floor, touching every crack and cranny. Finally, the furniture, though other than the glassless window and the letter with the unknown language, nothing seemed out of place.

"Oh, for the sake!" River exclaimed. She would have to climb out the forsaken window if she wanted this room to seem untouched.

River peered out the window. She was at the back of the building; below her was dirt and beyond that, trees. How had a man nearly twice her age managed to get in and out of this building? The drop wasn't high enough for death, but it most certainly was high enough to twist an ankle. Maybe that was why he always limped. Physically, she could do the drop easily, though the mere thought of the height sent a shiver up her spine.

River hated heights. When they were young, Bass had used to love to climb trees and egg River up them, taunting her until she finally gave in and proved she could climb them, which she always did with ease. It was getting down that had been the problem. Bass would simply jump, tuck, and roll. And River, well . . . wouldn't. She'd sit in the tree staring at the ground as it moved forward and backward in her vision. Finally, Bass would climb back up and hold her hand as they jumped down. As they'd gotten older, though, Bass had made it part of her training, making her climb the highest tree. He left her up there until she conquered her fear and got down on her own.

River moved back to the door, repositioned the wooden trunk, and peered quickly inside. Black clothes, slacks, shirts, cloaks, and black knit masks for the face, holes only for the eyes and mouth. *Colorful*. She repositioned the vase back in place at the edge of the trunk, from where it had fallen off when she'd pushed open the door.

A cool breeze lifted her loose hair as she braced her hands on the windowsill. She warily moved one leg over the ledge and then the next. She breathed slowly, refusing to look down. Her arms shook as she lowered her body as far as her arms could reach and dropped, remembering to bend her knees. She landed, pain jolting through her legs. She shook them out but felt nothing but the receding burn. Nothing was broken or twisted.

"Heldours!" she cursed. River would now have to reenter the tavern without being seen by the barmaid, as she was meant to be fast asleep.

She moved quickly along the back of the brick building, using it as a guide toward the front. Nothing seemed any different than before when the bell rang, announcing her presence. The eyes that had looked up before glanced down now, and she was grateful.

River searched for the barmaid, but the girl was out of sight. She sucked in her lip as she crossed between the tables toward the stairs and let out a sigh of relief when she reached them.

"Ya look like you could use this," Imogen called in her sweet voice from the side.

River started and turned to see the girl holding out a glass. A semi-clear liquid swirled inside.

"I won't ask where you were, don't worry. Though I wish you would have heeded my advice."

River blinked.

"I take it he wasn't at the Den?"

The Den. Oh, bless the saints. "No, he wasn't."

Imogen nodded and pressed the glass into her hand. "'Tis berry water. Something sweet, better than the ale if you thirst in the night. You can take it up with ya."

"Thank you, Imogen, you've been too kind." River took the glass.

Imogen stared at her expectantly, and River took a small sip of the liquid. The sweet taste clung to her tongue as it moved down her throat, overwhelming her mouth. River smiled politely and carried the glass upstairs.

She must have been more tired than she thought. She blinked her heavy eyes several times as she pushed open the door, then threw herself onto the bed fully clothed.

River stood behind a tree, its bark as black as night, looking into a clearing. It wasn't the rolling hills of her home but a small patch of grass with a little stone-and-wood cottage. Surrounded by immensely tall trees, the home appeared as though it had been built for dolls. The hunter-green door matched the shutters, which stood in contrast to the sickly forest. A small garden sat off to the side with an array of different wildflowers and vegetables. A tiny child played out front. Her hair was burnt orange, tips of fire in the sun. Her skin was milky white, layered with sprays of freckles. She spun around in her dress, a sparkling silver fabric inlaid with gold that whipped around her as she sang.

A handsome man with a distinguished olive-toned face called to the little girl. His dark clothing was discolored, with sewn patches to cover the holes. But he held his shoulders high, his wavy hair touching them. It changed as he stepped into the sun, from a deep black to almost a red sheen. His hazel eyes searched the forest before falling on the girl. He picked her up, nuzzling her in his arms, kissing her forehead.

"I have a present for you, my little Star," he cooed to her. From behind his back, he produced a set of gold and silver feathers. They overlapped each other to form a set of wings.

From River's location behind the trees, it was hard to see how they were joined together as one. She wanted to reach out and run her hands over the fluffy feathers.

"Now you can fly with me, my darling."

The little girl giggled and squealed, pulling desperately at his hands. He fastened the wings to her, somehow securing them to her back and the other pieces to each arm. He flung her up in the air, catching her on her way back down. A smile spread across her whole face.

River's chest ached, reminding her that she was intruding on a personal moment. She wanted to back away, but a twig broke beneath her feet.

The man snapped his head up, his grip tightening around the girl. Then his eyes locked with River's, taking her in. His shoulders relaxed.

"You're here." Relief was written all over his face as he loosened his grip on the girl. "One day, we'll fly together too," he promised.

"Who?" the girl questioned her father.

"Someone extraordinary," he responded, keeping his gaze on River. There was so much meaning in his eyes alone; they were hard but soft all at the same time.

"I can't see anyone, Father," the little girl said, confused.

"You'll see her one day, my little Star." He let the squirming girl go. She turned her face, and on the girl's right cheek was a tan, star-shaped mark. A birthmark, covering almost her whole cheek. She screwed up her eyes as if trying to see River, then ran back to her father, asking him to pick her up.

River's words came out before she could even think. "Why am I special?"

The man's face softened, and he took a step toward her but then stopped as if second-guessing himself. "Because you, my girl, will help change everything. Always remember who you are. You will always be a Star."

Then in an instant, he was back in the house, the little girl and her wings gone, the house in the forest getting farther as if it were running from River or as if she were being pulled away, turning back into black.

Chapter Fifteen

Ky

A sharp kick to the shin woke him.

Ky opened his eyes but then closed them again at the sight. "Well, don't you look cozy," Belladonna cooed.

He let out a heavy sigh as he eased his head back against the tree. "If I keep my eyes closed, will you go away?"

"Highly unlikely." Her voice sounded a little farther away now.

A familiar chuckle floated to him.

Ky's back stiffened against the tree he'd been dozing under. What was she even doing here, and with his leftwing, no less? He hoped he'd intercepted the letter in time. There was no way he planned on leading this hunter directly into a town full of defenseless humans.

He lifted one eyelid and peered at Belladonna. She leaned against the opposite tree, one foot propped against it. Instead of armor she wore a thin layer of coral pict-paint, which clung to every inch of her body. She had placed jewels along her arms instead of swirls of dark, patterned pict-paint. Gems twisted in her long wavy braids and matched the ones on her arms. She had even placed a jewel where her skin met her jagged yellow claws. She had two sets of human femur daggers strapped with a dragon skin to each thigh, along with two short blades.

Wrynn stood a few paces behind her. Unlike her, he wore his bone armor, every piece filled in; none of his taupe skin showed. A wry smile was plastered above his square jaw.

"Don't stand on my account," Belladonna said, but Ky had only lazily closed his eyes again. "Your sister sent us because apparently you need help and can't handle your duties."

Ky felt the disapproval like a slap. "I'm good. Go home."

"I didn't drag myself away from better things to argue with you. Stand up. Let's get this over with."

He crossed his arms over his chest and finally locked eyes with her. The pict-paint stopped at her collarbone, and her pale cheeks were flushed. The storms of coral magic ran under her almost-translucent skin, streaming out as she grew more frustrated with him.

She looked good. It was irritating that a person who looked that good could have the personality of dragon shit, though he could admit—when she wasn't scaring the pants off him—the thought had crossed his mind but only for a brief second, before she opened her mouth.

"Did I miss a celebration or something? You seem to be decked out for festivities, not hunting."

"I got called home to celebrate the festivals of the *kupaling*. My younger brother was participating." Her long, knife-like fingers curled at her sides. Spitarians took any excuse to celebrate; the festivals of the *kupaling* was just one instance. Every Spitarian who wasn't *kupaled* would gather to see whose magic theirs might intertwine with.

"You didn't participate? I would've assumed you did based on that garb. And seeing as how you nearly jumped my bones a few nights ago."

Wrynn's lips pulled in, but his eyes sparkled with unheard laughter.

Her face pinched, her voice tight as a string stretched across a bow. "That was for show. Did you not see how the hunters' eyes were on me? Everyone knows the Head wants me as the next Heart. I do my part."

Ky opened his mouth to retort but then closed it. *For show?* She had no interest in him?

"Are we going to get moving here? We're already far behind the human princess."

"You don't need to come. I can do this. How did my sister even send a message? I took her *Crystolas*."

One knife-like nail flicked the silver-blond braid over her shoulder before she pointed at Wrynn. "I believe Wrynn brought what he had from home to tide her over until he could gather more for her."

Ky shot Wrynn a glare.

His leftwing held up his hands. "In my defense, when she dreamwalked with me, she didn't mention you took them. She only said she was out and asked if I could bring more, along with Belladonna."

It pained Ky to wonder if he would have chosen his duties as a leftwing over his *kupal*'s request. "I've got this under control."

"Why are you and Az fighting? You never fight." Wrynn shifted between his feet, his dragon-scaled wings bouncing lightly behind him.

"It's nothing." Ky looked away from him.

Belladonna's eyebrow flicked up, and her face wore a wicked grin.

Wrynn crossed his arms, bulging out his muscles. "It's not nothing. What aren't you telling me? I'm your leftwing. How can I have your back, how can I lead, if I don't know what you're keeping from me?"

Ky didn't look at him. If Wrynn pushed enough, the thoughts might float right to him. Ky tried to clear his head and think of anything but the truth. Wrynn wouldn't get anything from him.

"Trust me." Wrynn's voice was soft.

Ky swallowed. Could he tell him?

Belladonna tried to cover her laugh with a cough, and Ky clamped down on the thought. "It's nothing."

Wrynn looked between the two of them. His loose blond-green hair blew across his face in the wind. "What if we both accompany you on this task? Then you don't need to be left alone with Belladonna."

She rolled her eyes but didn't interject.

"You have duties to attend. Last I checked, there was still a skirmish between a few clans to deal with."

Wrynn's green-scaled wings twitched, but he remained silent.

"And Belladonna, you're a hunter. At the border with your leader is where you belong. Not here trying to *kupal* with me," Ky said.

She bristled. "I already told you I have no intention of doing that."

"I don't think now is the time to go against Head Axel's wishes." His leftwing never pushed like this, and the pleading in his voice made Ky want to crumble and tell him everything.

"Head Axel is your blood," Wrynn continued. "You must heed that. Blood before brethren, blood before self."

Ky exhaled as he swallowed his reaction. Wrynn wouldn't choose him over his father. Their ways were too ingrained into his system. "Go do your duties, Wrynn."

"Brother, please—"

"That was an order, leftwing!" Ky snapped.

Belladonna smirked, and Ky wanted to whip it off her face as Wrynn's skin paled. But Wrynn only nodded, turned, and disappeared into the woods.

"Don't make me order you next," Ky said, though his gaze still lingered on the spot Wrynn had been.

Belladonna suddenly whipped her head to the side. Her magic moved rapidly, swirls of energy going in her ears, her eyes turning coral. Ky had never studied her before when her magic was active. Typically, he avoided looking at her altogether. But now, as she was focused elsewhere, he stared in awe.

"I agree Az uses too much. But what does this have to do with now?" Belladonna said to the air next to her.

He assumed the fadeling had been whispering about his sister's excessive use of magic, but he didn't interject. This was Belladonna's gift, not his, and he knew better than to interfere with another's magic. When the coral dancing lines moved to a normal speed and her eyes returned to their usual brown, he had the immediate urge to reach out and allow his magic to tangle with hers. Without commanding it, his magic reached a small finger toward—

Her eyes snapped to his. "Don't even think about it, *Heiralomun*. We wouldn't be a good match. And I have no desire to be your Heart."

"How—I . . . I apologize. What did they tell you?"

One brow arched in his direction as the coral slowly faded again. "They tell me all sorts of things."

"Can you tune them out?"

A knowing frown touched her lips. "No, but they try to respect my space by speaking directly to me only when they must."

"It must be annoying to have them always there. Almost as if you were living on both planes."

She shrugged and moved away from the tree. "It is, and it isn't. It's like always having my family around, always having the most interesting people, and always knowing things."

"Do you see all the fadelings from the old and the new world? I have some serious history questions if so. Like, why did only three families come over? How could they leave so many behind . . ." His thoughts trailed off, the questions bubbling to the surface. Maybe this would distract her enough so that he could get away.

"Is that a serious question? Of all the things you could ask, you want to know about the past? Not the future or the present?"

"They tell you the future?"

Belladonna smirked. "So tell me, why do you think our ancestors only brought themselves and a few others?"

Ky's mind ran through all the texts, his finger rubbing his smooth chin. "If you know the past, you can predict the future. I think the original Heads were friends. They came because they were a family."

"Right, but why not more? They could've saved at least two or three more clans." She turned away from him. Her head tilted as if someone were whispering to her, and she nodded several times before she let out a sigh and flicked her wrist as if waving them away. "Shh! I'll get there. Let me speak."

"Then why didn't they?" Ky watched her with fascination, almost forgetting for a moment that this was meant to be nothing more than distraction. He pushed himself off the ground until they were eye level with each other.

"Because, *Heiralomun,* they've learned something that you have yet to. You can't force people to think the way you do. A new world meant new order, new laws. The more families with different ideals, the more war was inevitable."

"So they brought only those they could control? That doesn't seem fair."

"If life were meant to be fair, we would be at peace, both inside and out." She pointed to her heart and closed her eyes.

Her eyes snapped open, and her head whipped to the side. "I can't tell him that," she whispered before turning back and looking at him. "I don't think I should tell you this. But they insisted. The fadelings see what you're doing. They caution you to be careful. You can't change centuries of hate and fear with one small rebellion. They don't hate the idea of you helping the humans . . . but be prepared to lose before you win."

"Excuse me?" He turned his back on her and stepped over the knotted root of a lightly colored tree.

"You aren't planning on killing the princess?"

"What?" Ky took a step forward, the words shaking him to his core. "Why would they think that?"

"So you aren't thinking about the true prophecy or even about your how your mother is alive—"

The word had barely left her mouth before both of Ky's hands and his crystalline magic lunged for her. His energy snapped against her magic the same time he curled his fingers around her throat. Her coral lines were now in his grasp, clutched in his fist, and he was snuffing them out.

"You shouldn't speak of things you don't understand. Things that could get you killed."

A smile spread over her face as she gasped, "Are you going to kill me?"

"To keep my secrets. To keep everyone safe. Yes." His answer didn't surprise him. But it did scare him a little. "Think very carefully about your—"

Pain lanced through his groin, and he withdrew his fingers for the briefest of seconds, but it was enough for Belladonna to get control of her magic again. She stepped back, and her eyes were brighter than he had ever seen. Her magic whipped in a coral hurricane around her and lifted her body slightly off the ground with its force. Energy from a hidden *Crystolas* deep in the world's core fed into the cyclone of magic that surrounded her. It grew larger as her head snapped back, the energy working through her.

"Don't think you're more powerful than me," she roared through the wind.

Ky took a hesitant step back as her hurricane of magic branched out, and several coral figures stepped out of the storm. Gradually, she dropped back to the ground as the storm seemed to evaporate, though nearly fifty shadowy coral outlines surrounded her.

"Dragon-damn me," Ky whispered as he stared into the closest fadeling's face. Each piece of them was made of fine coral cords, but the face was still as recognizable as his own.

The man who'd taught his father the meaning of cruelty, his father's father, stood before him.

"Grandspring?"

Chapter Sixteen

River

"**R**owan!"

Bang.

"Rowan!"

Bang. Bang.

"Princess Castor!"

The muffled voice cut through the fog, pulling River from her dream. The door handle jiggled back and forth.

River blinked, slowly orienting herself. Light streamed in from a small window, casting a slanted shadow on a washbasin and a wooden mirror with one jagged crack. The bed was no more than straw, and the hole-riddled blankets allowed it to poke through.

She didn't remember getting into bed. She hadn't even taken off her boots.

The banging continued. River leaned over the edge of the bed and flicked the lock. Even those slight movements sent a splitting headache through her.

"For Heldours' sake—" Leon grunted as he burst through the door. His gaze moved up and down her body quickly. "I thought you were dead! I would have to explain to your mother how I was sleeping, and you died on my watch! What do you think you're doing?"

River closed her eyes against the already risen sun. She groaned and threw her face back into the pillow.

"Are you drunk?"

Drunk? She didn't remember drinking anything last night other than the fruit water.

"Of course not," she murmured into the pillow. All she wanted to do was pull the blanket over her head and lie there the rest of the day.

"You're still dressed." He groaned with apparent exasperation.

River wanted to tell him to go away, but she couldn't seem to form the words. She squeezed her eyes closed tighter at his voice.

"What did you drink last night?"

"Are you questioning me?"

Things crashed about the room, and River squeezed the pillow around her ears, muffling his voice.

Her head thudded onto the cot as the pillow was ripped away. She finally turned to look at him.

His stormy gray eyes were large, and his face was ashen as he held up the glass to his nose. It wrinkled and then flared almost in disgust. River could have sworn last night the liquid was almost transparent, but now a pinkish slime had separated from the remaining liquid in the glass.

"Where did you get this?"

She tilted her head to the side, studying it. She didn't remember drinking so much of it. The glass was almost empty. "The barmaid.

Why? Is something wrong with it? Does it have alcohol? Is that why my head feels like this? I didn't drink that much, I swear."

Leon's long legs carried him to the window with the glass in his hand. He pushed open the window pane with one hand and dumped the contents of the glass with his other.

"Maybe it's just cheap. I'm sure there was just too much sugar in it for you," he said. "Or the fruit was bad," he added quietly to himself.

"I think I need to eat something."

Leon nodded. "We shouldn't be seen together, though. I already looked through Barthomule's door. He's not in there."

"I'll stay and eat here, then." She pulled the rough blanket over her face, trying to hide. She hated herself for the headache that led to such a lack of motivation.

"I'll check out the place down the street." Leon paused. "You sure you're going to be all right?"

"Do I look that bad?" She smoothed the hair back from her face.

Leon sucked full large lips into his mouth as if he were trying not to laugh.

"Unbelievable." River threw herself back down onto the cot.

River didn't move until Leon's heavy footsteps finally stopped echoing back up the stairs. She rolled her eyes as she pushed herself up and headed to the washbasin.

Who let that boy become a spy?

River chose a table in the back corner, though there was the same amount of people in the tavern as there had been last night, and many of them were the same customers. River rubbed her temple, trying her best to search for her target.

Target.

She repeated the word in her head over and over again as she tried to process the act of assassination. *Target* was better at the moment than to refer to him by name.

The bell above the door dinged as a large group of men entered. River leaned on her left knee, trying to appear bored as she studied each man who entered. The men gathered at the largest table, which was already crowded with other men and women. In the center of the new group, a short man clothed in head-to-toe black cotton caught her eye. He didn't remove his black hood like the rest. When he lifted his face to get the attention of the barmaid, River studied the way the black fabric clung to his face, and unlike the rest of the clothes in here, his were perfectly clean. Just like the ones from the trunk she'd searched last night.

Welcome to the party.

River eased back, away from prying eyes.

Imogen went to their table, greeting the newcomers. The man remained standing even when offered a chair. The tailored cloak he wore wasn't what she'd pictured when Leon described him. Someone had carefully crafted his outfit. Someone with money. From the fabric to the fit, it was impeccable. She wouldn't have guessed it from the trunk full of the matching outfits, but once he slipped them on, she understood the draw. If he'd chosen the look for himself, then he was dressed to make everyone fear him.

Is this the right man?

His gaze surveyed the table and then the room. River tilted her face down, allowing the loose pieces of her hair to fall, covering her face. She felt his eyes linger on her longer than on the rest of the room. She counted out five breaths before she looked up again.

An older man with dark skin and gray in his sideburns stood from his chair, scraping it backward as he gathered everyone's attention.

"Attention, sympathizers!" he shouted as he tucked his loose white shirt back into his belt, though the shirt was too short for him, and his hairy belly hung over slightly.

"Sit down, Alder!" someone yelled from behind River.

She didn't shift in her seat, wary of drawing any more attention to herself.

Alder didn't sit down. "Some of ya might've been unsure of the cause at our last meeting, but since then, I've gathered new information."

The same voice from before booed, but Alder continued all the same. "We are all aware of the Castor Princess's prophecy."

River stilled.

"But news has been sent from a trustworthy source within the castle walls that Queen Castor withheld some of the prophecy, choosing only the words that suited her at the time."

What?

"While her daughter is most certainly still the one to achieve peace, it also states that there will be both red and blue blood that will bring peace. Peace not only for the humans but for the Spitarians as well. As one."

River scooted closer. What was he saying? Of course, none of it was true. It couldn't be. Her mother wouldn't have withheld such a crucial piece of the prophecy from her. *Right?* Because this new bit changed the whole meaning of the prophecy. It didn't entail the annihilation of an entire race like Bass predicted but instead required two feuding races to cease fighting and get along.

Peace. Real peace. One the humans had never known.

River shook her head. Why would someone come up with something this crazy? To think the Spitarians—nothing more than feral animals—could keep peace.

"And Alder, how are we to have peace?" someone else yelled.

"Are we to surrender wholeheartedly? Let them devour us like they've been taking our young?" a soft feminine voice said to her left. A woman with long graying hair and a thick jawbone.

Alder whispered to the man River assumed was her target. They conversed in low, hushed tones. River wished she was close enough to hear the exchange.

"There are some Spitarians who want these senseless killings to end. They see the need for trade and cooperation as much as we do. They lack things we have in abundance."

"And we gain what?" another older man shouted.

"How about magical healing for your wife, Nesly?" He pointed to the older man. "Or crops grown rapidly to fill our starving bellies. A truce benefits us more than it could possibly do for them."

River highly doubted it.

"Can I get ya anything?" Imogen said, stepping in front of her view Alder, who continued speaking on the benefits of a truce.

"Breakfast, please. Does this happen here often?"

Imogen nodded. "Oh yes. Alder is the Sympathizer stirrer."

"Sympathizer?" The word snagged at something Bass had said; he'd killed sympathizers, he'd told her, and now it was her turn.

Imogen shook her head, putting a hand on her hip. Her sleeve moved up slightly, revealing a branded M on her forearm. "Those of us who believe in peace among all races. No fighting. Alder is good at convincing folks to see things his way. The Sympathizers' way."

River expected Imogen to have a sneer in her tone but there was none.

She couldn't believe it. Sympathizers.

"How can you possibly think peace between races is the answer?" If that was all these people wanted, why had Bass been killing them? And why would she need to?

"The same way we were raised believing a monarchy is the best way to govern people." Imogen rolled her eyes as she walked away, and River tried to conceal her disbelief. She didn't want the girl to stop giving her information, but she didn't understand. What other way was there to govern?

Alder was still speaking when River's view of the table returned. Instead of Alder standing directly in her path, the masked man now stood in front of him. The dark-set eyes under the mask were like deep holes that stared directly at her. River shifted under the weight.

Her target had seen her and taken an interest; her cover was blown.

His head tilted slightly. The mask moved with him as if it were a second skin. He pulled on Alder's sleeve, stopping the man's speech, and whispered in his ear. Leon had said Barthomule never spoke to anyone, but this looked an awful lot like speaking to those who were associated with Spitarians. It made logical sense that he was also passing notes on human movements to them. He had intimate knowledge of these towns, so maybe he was also telling them which children and families should get taken next.

Alder bent down to another man, and before River could do anything about it, the whole table was passing some secret.

Oh, for the loving saints of Heldours.

She had no idea what she was going to do now. She was utterly alone here. Leon had gone. Bass was . . . She shoved the thought of him from her head. River could try to head toward the entrance, though most of the patrons were in her way. The stairs were an option, but what would happen once she got upstairs if they pursued her?

River crossed her arms and dipped her head in acknowledgment. The last thing she needed to do was show a man fear. No. No man would ever get any sort of fear or need from her again. She had given Bass that. Desire. Fear of being alone. She wasn't afraid anymore. She could do this. She needed to do this. If everything Imogen had said yesterday was true, humans required a savior now more than ever. She could bring all of this information and lay it at her mother's feet with Barthomule's head. Then her mother would know she wasn't worthless.

She was ready.

She was ready.

Alder began speaking again. His words flowed like a song or a poem.

"*When fates collide, one red, one blue. The point they make, the war they wage, forever it is true. She rises out of the ashes chosen. A flame in the mist. When death shall come, only she will stand the fight. Only she can end it all. One war, one right, purple shall remain, one blood in sight. Moon, cloud, star, sword, wings. Forever in flight.*"

A Prophecy. The words pulled at her like she was being drawn into a trance.

The room fell silent as if they had all been caught in the same web as her. River blinked and swallowed.

"What a difference the rest of that prophecy makes," Alder said after a moment of silence.

River's skin tingled, and she tried to shake the feeling. She highly doubted the truth of the words, though if it had only been her mother and the Spitarian seer present, how could anyone else know such things? There were a few things she needed to have a conversation with her mother about when she returned. But for now, these sympathizers couldn't keep spreading these lies. It would only hurt the human race for peace and get more people killed.

In her peripheral vision, the target shifted and walked toward her. River swiveled her head toward him. She wouldn't be caught off guard. Her eyes traveled toward his leg, where a barely noticeable limp was present as he walked. Almost as if he couldn't bend it.

At least Leon had been right about that.

It had to be him.

Imogen cut across his path, bending to place a clear bowl of soup in front of her. River eyed it skeptically before standing in one fluid motion. She came face-to-face with Imogen, and over her shoulder, she could still see the man coming.

What would happen if she didn't kill him? What other problems would he cause?

"It's all we have here. Sweet for breakfast. Spicy for lunch and savory for dinner." Imogen scrunched up her nose and pointed to the bowl of soup. "Don't get your hopes up."

"Thank you. I left something in the room. I'll be back. Save this for me." River turned away without waiting for a reply. She moved quickly between the tables toward the stairs and bounded up them. A commotion started behind her, people shouting and a loud crashing, but she didn't turn to look. She threw herself into the room and slammed the door but didn't lock it. This wasn't how she'd planned to kill, but this way was better than no way.

River backed herself against the far wall next to the window. She shook out her arms and legs, trying to breathe through the sense of unease. He had seen her watching.

Footsteps thundered up the stairs before a slight shadow cast under the door.

River took a slow, steadying breath and withdrew her dagger from her waist. She balanced the blade in her throwing hand by her ear. Her fingers grazed her ear as they shook uncontrollably. She had practiced this over and over again, and yet, when it was in real life, she wasn't sure she could do it.

One dagger. One dagger right through the eye. Dead. She breathed. *He won't even see it coming.*

She dropped her shoulder and cracked her neck, trying to ease the tension that was building. The shadow shifted, and the door handle jiggled though the door remained closed.

Come on, come on.

The shadow moved away from the door, and River let out a sigh of relief just as the weight of her right hand emptied. She stiffened as it was replaced with a forceful grip on her shoulder.

The window . . .

Leon had left it open.

Chapter Seventeen

Ky

The wind shifted, blowing slightly north. Ky's hair lifted off his shoulders and then into his face. He blinked slowly at the figures. Most hung back, merely flickers of coral, while some had clear outlines of figures. But the three in front of him were almost fully formed.

"Don't act as if you don't recognize me," his grandspring scolded.

How was it even possible? He'd faded over five hundred years ago. Ky had never met him, yet the stories others told of him gave Ky enough of a sour taste.

"Bella, you have gone and scared the dragon dung out of him," his grandspring called over his shoulder.

"Serves him right," she scoffed, her eyes flashing brighter with his grandspring's every word.

"You can project them too?" Ky looked at the next face, one that had similar features to his mother's people, including the elongated earlobes with M-shaped ear points.

The male's head cocked. "I thought he'd be more attractive, the way people describe him."

Ky choked out a laugh, his hand to his mouth. "And you are?"

"*Heiralomun* Rykerson Sky, who else?" The male projection flipped his coral hair. He placed one forearm over the other and then slammed his fist to his chest, which sank through the coral mist of his body.

"Bella, you didn't say he lacked in intelligence," the feminine voice called fiercely from behind.

Ky leaned to the left to see the very familiar body of the Original Heart of the Sparrows, the one who'd saved his people from the old world. Ky got on both knees, bent his head, and placed his fist to his chest. "My Heart."

"Well, maybe not." Her voice sweetened as her magical hand brushed along his hair.

Ky lifted his head to find a female form standing over him. He gawked at how tall she was. Her long legs gave way to a body that was nearly a foot taller than him. A crown of interlaced feathers sat atop her head and her wings—oh, her wings. They were like nothing he had ever seen. Beautiful, even though they were mangled short and clipped, blunt edges of bone shards sticking straight out past her shoulders. Nothing was left of the thin wings he knew she'd been born with. He closed his eyes and pictured the blue hint of them.

Bella cleared her throat. "Ky, we aren't here to stand in your way. We're here to assist you. *I* am here to assist you."

Ky shook his head in disbelief. How was it even possible? "No one knows you can project," was all he said.

It wasn't a question. If she had shown this to anyone else, everyone would have known about it. The hunting party would have used this. But they hadn't, which meant this was her secret. She was showing him her secret because she knew his.

"I'm not sure how to believe you want to help humans. You might have left the armor at home, but I watched you pick apart the human remains barely a moon ago. You're an animal."

"Like you haven't done anything you aren't proud of to hide the truth?"

Ky studied her face. The *Crystolas* at her neck glowed, lighting up her skin, which was now utterly transparent; he could see her veins, her muscles, and in some spaces her blue bones despite the coral light of her eyes. It was incredible. Beautiful. The three recognizable faces stood between her and Ky. But many other different Spitarian forms walked around behind her. They didn't have faces, but he knew they could if she allowed them to.

Ky shook his head. "I'm sorry, Belladonna. I can't trust you. Not with this. Not with so many lives. The weight of our whole world . . ." He continued shaking his head. If he killed her, by extension he would be killing them. He didn't know much about the Frolandal clan leader, but he was certain none of their skills could even match hers. He didn't think the current clan leader had a connection with the fadelings. Generations of information would be gone if he did this. Their whole history.

He took a few steps forward, and a coral blockade of magical forms covered his path. A muscle-corded arm pressed against his chest, holding him back. It was as if the magic had become a solid form.

Heart Nomance Sparrow's voice had returned to ice. "Now I thought we agreed you were intelligent."

He hesitated before he grabbed the misty arm at his chest, which slipped through his grasp. A heavy kick from behind him brought him to his knees again.

"I think you should stay down, Grandspring."

Ky coughed out the breath that caught in his throat. "I can't." He placed one foot on the dirt and then pressed off the ground. "Please don't make me fight you all. This is between me and Belladonna."

Heiralomun Rykerson got in his face. His body was more solid than before. The tree bark of his skin overlapped his torso, legs, and arms, just like it had when he was living. The only difference was that it was shades of coral rather than the browns he'd seen on his mother's people when they'd begun to fade, their magic dying. The coral energy that composed him vibrated and wove in and out, his body shifting and reforming in front of Ky's eyes. He looked past *Heiralomun* Rykerson to where Nomance had repositioned herself next to Bella, but her body was mistier than it had been before.

The corner of Ky's mouth quirked up. Belladonna could only allow one fadeling to fully form at a time. Ky nodded slowly. He quickly ran through the ways to get to her in his mind as he watched her magic. Instead of studying her as a whole, he picked apart each energy source, watching the movement of the cords, how each flicked in a pattern as it ran from the *Crystolas* at Belladonna's throat, through her, and then into each fadeling in return. As she pushed most of the cords through Rykerson, she withheld very few for the others around her.

Ky closed his eyes. Even with them closed, he could still sense the energy around him, taste the rust of it on his tongue, through every breath of air through his nose. He pushed his power together, weaving it in his mind into his magical crystalline hand. With his eyes closed, the magic was nothing more than that. No faces. No feelings. Just power.

His crystalline hand snapped behind him and grabbed onto the weaker cords that made up his grandspring. He grasped on, snuffing them out.

His grandspring chuckled from behind him as the cords reappeared. "Did you think it would be that easy?"

Ky's face fell as he opened his eyes. He'd hoped it might work, but he'd guessed wrong. He had to touch Belladonna to make them disappear.

He let out a sigh, hating himself as he swung his leg parallel to his grandspring's body, lifting his leg and kicking him square in the jaw.

Belladonna gasped at the same time his grandspring grunted.

Interesting. The hits would wound them both.

Ky righted himself and charged straight for Rykerson's gut, dipping his shoulder down and then upward with the impact, hoping to hit below the bark rather than against it with his bare skin. His skin shredded on contact. He felt it like tiny knives peeling back his flesh. One glance at his shoulder proved that though it had hurt like a damned dragon claw, not one drop of blood had been shed. That was good; humans didn't need to find his blood in these woods.

"My mother said you could be trusted, Belladonna." He grunted as she pushed back the *Heiralomun* another inch. "This tells me otherwise."

"Stop fighting and talk, then!" Belladonna's voice rang out.

Ky didn't look up as he slid his blade from the sheath at his thigh. The metal end of the blade was cool to his touch and felt heavy in his hands, and he took two quick jabs to Rykerson's unprotected side between two overlapping bark pieces.

Breath whooshed from the *Heiralomun* as he turned to mist and disappeared.

"Please tell me I can't kill him?" Ky said, out of breath as he stood, now nearly a few stick lengths from Belladonna.

"You didn't care about that two seconds ago." Her voice was harsh and breathless. One of her hands clutched at her side, though Ky saw no blood.

Good.

The features on the Heart became more apparent as she stepped in his path next. A staff formed in her hand. "I am looking forward to seeing how our species has weakened over the years."

Ky sheathed his blade. "Please don't make me do this. I respect you too much. It would be like killing my childhood fantasy."

"Then you should have listened to reason." Her long fingers spread as coral electricity ran between them and over her staff, charging the air around her. She slammed it to the ground, and Ky dove out of the way to avoid the lighting-like current.

"Come on. You can do better than that."

She twirled the staff between expert hands, faster and faster until it was like a weaver's wheel. She pushed the current forward directly to his chest.

The shocks racked his body as the electricity crossed through him, causing spasms until his body locked in pain. He nearly lost control of his bowels. Ky gasped for breath, trying to move through the bone exhaustion her power had just caused.

"You've got to be kidding," he stammered. How was it possible for a fadeling to have control of their own magic on this plane? The Heart certainly had her powers no matter her form.

Ky was barely able to drag himself to a tree, using it to prop his body up before Nomance was on him. She gripped both of his shoulders, and another round of electrical currents ran through him. The spasms started all over again.

"We don't have to do this. We can still just talk," Belladonna called to him, though her voice sounded farther away. He blinked back the darkness that tried to overtake him. "I only want what is best for our people."

"I don't think you do," Ky gasped as the spasms eased. "I think you are clouded by hate and past prejudices."

The lighting currents started again, and Ky relaxed his body against it, not fighting it this time.

"Enough," Belladonna said.

Ky opened his eyes, and Belladonna's coral eyes hovered above his head. He didn't hesitate; he leaped for her throat. Nomance was quicker, and she slammed her hand down on his chest, the electrical current causing his hand to stop just shy of her throat.

His breath stopped, the world turning black as his heart stilled. The magic running through him was the only thing sustaining him from fading. He felt . . . nothing at all.

"Did you kill him?" Belladonna asked urgently.

"Don't be dense. You know I can't kill him like this." Nomance's voice was angry and disapproving.

A finger pressed to his chest as another jolt restarted his heart.

He gasped for air, his limbs still immobile. Slowly, the pins and needles feeling told him his mobility was returning. He flexed several times, waiting for his body to respond to the movements.

Nomance clicked her tongue. "You are so blinded by your lack of trust you can't see what's in front of you. She's a friend, not a foe! Do you think I would risk all that I helped build for anything less? Don't become your father by thinking you are always right."

Ky grimaced as her words hit their mark. He still needed the upper hand, so he kicked her legs out from under her. The Heart tumbled backward. Ky caught her hand, pulling them both to their feet at the same time. He looked straight into Nomance's eyes. The coral of them made him feel as though he was looking at Belladonna rather than her.

He tried to focus. "Then explain it to me."

One eyebrow formed and then raised. "We shall, gladly."

Ky whipped his left hand out and clapped it on Bella's wrist. He didn't take power. Instead, he just held on. "You have very little time to explain why I should trust her," he said to the Heart.

The magic shifted in the air around him. Shining coral cords drifted lazily back toward Belladonna as all fadelings but one returned to her. Shivers ran up his arm as they passed through him and into her. Belladonna's shoulders relaxed, and a small sigh left her parted mouth. The *Crystolas* at her throat looked a little duller.

Ky's eyes narrowed. "You okay?"

Her head bobbed slowly up and down, and she blinked lazily.

"Are you going to pull back the Heart as well? You might feel better."

The Nomance huffed to his right. "The Heart has things to say."

"Carry on then." Ky gestured for Nomance to continue, and he loosened the grip on Belladonna's wrist. "Shall we sit?"

"I'll make this quick. *Heiralomun* Rykerson Sky brought humans to this world to satisfy the human he fell in love with. He thought he could hide them and shield them from the other Spitarians who still hated those who had enslaved them. It didn't work. The humans hated us, and we hated them. It was a silent war of sorts. For some years, we completely ignored the existence of the humans. Other years, we slaughtered whole villages. We are a moody sort."

"Mm-hmm," Belladonna agreed, her body slowly relaxing.

"When the Skys and the Stars agreed to have peace, the Sparrows didn't, so we split. The Stars wanted to separate but keep peace with the humans. The Skys wanted to live among one another, and the Sparrows wanted them gone."

"I know all this," Ky said, already losing his patience.

"But we always agreed to stay to ourselves. Your father saw to it to destroy a whole section of our race because the Stars decided they no longer wanted to live separate from the humans. One of the *Heiralomuns* of the Stars began speaking about taking a human for a wife. Your father lost it. We fadelings have tasked Belladonna to help right that wrong."

Ky looked from Belladonna to the Heart. "And why is it that she would listen to that? Better yet, even if she listens, it doesn't mean she believes it's right."

"Walker Lukon of the Stars was my *kupal*," Belladonna whispered.

The pain in her voice made Ky release her wrist and step back to search her face. "You were *kupaled*? I didn't know."

"Ten days." A small smile lifted her lips. "It wasn't even long enough for us to tell our families yet. He left me in the cave so he could bring it to his Head's attention first. That was the same day your family decided the Stars were a problem." She swiped at the tears that fell down her cheek. "Do you have any idea what it felt like to sever a newly braided bond?"

Ky shook his head, watching her pale throat bob.

"I felt it as he died. We were still so connected; I felt every shuddering breath he took as the unicorn dust circled his bloodstream and finally settled in his heart. I didn't move for days. My brother found me two moons later, frozen solid in a few feet of snow. It took the healers another five moons before I would move again."

"But you were already in the hunting party."

"I was, and because of that, I remain with them just as I was before. They believe a human party wounded me. The fadelings didn't give me this task because they had no other choice. They gave it to me because it was the only thing that finally got me back on my feet."

Ky turned to Heart Sparrow to confirm, but she was already gone. Belladonna's eyes had returned to their usual brown.

"Let me help you save the princess from your father and herself."

Ky cocked his head. "Herself?"

Belladonna chuckled. "That stupid Queen Castor has sent her only daughter to thwart all that you have worked for."

"What do you mean?"

"The fadelings say she sent River to kill Blakey."

Ky's wings sprawled to their full length. "Why the dragon would she do that? Where is the princess? Why didn't you lead with that?"

Belladonna crossed her arms. "Am I coming with you?"

"Fine!" Ky shouted, his nostrils flaring.

She pointed southeast toward Neven.

"Keep up, and at any point, if I think you are lying, I will kill you to protect them."

"You could try."

Chapter Eighteen

River

The pressure increased on River's shoulder. She lurched forward as the figure behind her propelled over her.

"Hel—" River tried to swear as her face hit the floor.

"Does Elora allow you to speak like that, Princess?" The figure in black spun her dagger gingerly between his fingers before he tossed it to his left hand.

Heldours. Not only had he spotted her, but he recognized her.

He balanced the blade on two fingers. "Decent weight. Have you ever actually used it, though?"

River righted herself and took one small step back to brace herself into position, one foot planted behind the other, accidentally knocking it into the mattress. The room wasn't big enough for the kind of fight that was coming. She raised a fist in front of her but kept her arms loose.

"Don't worry. I won't use it." The blade landed with a thud in the wash bucket to his left. "Not really my style."

"What exactly is your style, Barthomule?"

A visible shudder ran through him. "Call me Blakey."

"Are you not the former prince of Morsaw?"

A dark laugh came from behind the mask. He opened his mouth, and yellow teeth shone. "I have as much claim to the throne as any of the bastards who came after me."

"You murdered your mother and tried to kill your father. Now you run around sharing information with Spitarians and spreading lies to my people. I would say you abdicated your throne a few times over."

He took a step closer, rubbing his covered chin, and she realized he wasn't much larger than her. They were almost eye-to-eye, although he was slightly broader.

"You seem to think you have it all figured out. Though the notes you stole from my room tell me otherwise." He crossed his arms, muscles bulging through the fitted black cloak.

"Do you deny what you're being accused of, then?"

"I don't deny anything. You and the rest of the crown scum can think what you want of me. I couldn't care less, though we had high hopes for you, River. We thought since the prophecy spoke of you, maybe you would be more open-minded than the rest of the fools. I'm disappointed."

Her spine stiffened. It irritated her how deep and rough his voice was, like gravel scraping against the ground. She feared she would dream of it long after he was dead, haunting her every waking moment. She didn't have time for this.

River planted her foot on the edge of the bed. "This blasted boot." She fiddled with the strap and looked up at him. "Since you seem to know who I am, you wouldn't happen to want to surrender and head back to face your punishment, would you?" She silently pleaded with him to say yes.

"Had I done something wrong, I would gladly. Though, Princess, I would consider the reasons you're here." He cocked his head .

He said "princess" like it was an insult.

"Do you think you're on some mission for the greater good? Or is it merely to silence the truth?"

River's nostrils flared. Did this man think he was spreading the truth? "A princess isn't sent to silence a thug. I'm here on royal business."

"Then you wouldn't mind sharing it with a fellow royal."

This had gone too far. The man was talking in circles, and she couldn't get a read on him or, furthermore, this situation. She slipped her fingers lower into her boot until they grazed the cool metal. "Your mother was known for being regal and poised, with deep blue eyes that almost appeared black. Did you stare into them as you shoved the knife into her belly over and over again?"

Blakey stiffened.

"Were her eyes still open when you set the place ablaze with your father still sleeping?"

He lunged for her and wrapped his hand around her throat. He was quicker than she expected, and as he squeezed tighter, she didn't fight him.

"Do you want to know the part of the story they don't tell?" Blakey pushed his face eye-level to hers, and she could see his eyes weren't black but a deep saturated blue, just like his mother's.

River grabbed the knife. *One strike to the kidney. That's all it would take.*

"My mother was pregnant." His hand loosened around her throat.

Pregnant? She'd never heard that.

"It wasn't my father's primary intention to kill her. It was just a bonus, he said. Because the babe wasn't his, and they both knew it. By the time I heard her screams, the blade had already found its mark. I begged him to call help to save her. But he refused. I even threatened to never take the throne." He scoffed, but River saw the tear slide from his eyes beneath the mask.

He cleared his throat. "Before I could call for help, he sliced his knife across my throat. His aim was off." Blakey stepped back, releasing her throat, and instead reached for the top of his hood and pulled off his mask. "You see, I wore a necklace of fire stones, which protected me."

His hair was thin and gray, and his face was still handsome, despite the sickly pale of his skin and eyebrows that never seemed to see the light. A significant slash zagged around his neck. "He thought we were dead and set fire to cover his tracks." Blackened skin like burnt meat dipped beneath the collar of his tunic.

River gripped the knife so hard she felt the side as it bit into her flesh. She couldn't believe it was true, but she knew he wasn't lying. His wounds weren't self-inflicted. King Morsaw had no wounds from that night. She had met him on several occasions, and he was the sort to boast about his injuries and his accomplishments, not remain silent. She looked away from Blakey.

"Do you want to know who saved me? Healed me and brought me back? Cleaned my wounds every few hours? Held me when my body throbbed from fever or when the tears wouldn't stop?" He replaced the hood. "The father of my unborn sibling. A man with wings the color of the night sky, feathers for eyebrows, and webs between his toes. You would call him a monster. A demon. But I called him Papa."

River had no words.

"Now you can take that knife in your boot and try to finish what some other royal started, or you can listen and open your eyes to the world that's screaming for peace and begging for assistance."

River withdrew the knife from her boot but didn't aim it. Even though he had somehow known her intention, his words struck her core. "How do I know you speak the truth?"

"What you've been led to believe about the Spitarians isn't the full truth. They operate out of fear just as much as we do. The ancient history of the past world no longer has to affect the future. They still see us as their slave drivers, but they needn't, just as we needn't see them as monsters with magic."

Ancient history or not, they were still the bad guys here. River swung, aiming for his side.

Blakey jumped out of the way and backed toward the window.

"Do you not see how devastated this town is? If the Spitarians hadn't terrorized these people and other towns like it, our farmers wouldn't be eating soup three times a day." River huffed.

Blakey let out a low chuckle. It was a fake, disgusted sort of laugh. "And if the humans hadn't pulled back and only guarded the rich, they wouldn't have been such easy pickings."

She heard her mother's voice in her head reminding her of her duty. He was a liar, and he was going to get people killed with what he was doing—if he hadn't already.

River didn't hesitate as she ran for him, her arm flying, seeking any flesh she could find.

A wave of something powerful almost knocked her off her feet. Fear licked up her sides, ran through her mind. She tried to shake it off, but it was uncontrollable. It stilled her every movement, flushing all sensible thoughts from her head, and filled her with the panic of choosing wrong.

Confused, River stumbled and clutched the wall. She'd been so sure of her actions moments ago. But now, she only felt fear.

"Whoa, are you okay?"

She gasped and pushed it away. She wasn't afraid of making the right choice. She knew what it was. She stalled and pushed whatever it had been deep down and threw her body forward.

Each step brought him closer to the window until he sat on it entirely. He ducked his head out the window and reached above his head.

River's knife vibrated in her hand as it found a home. She pulled back, ready to strike again. But he was gone.

River stuck her head out the window to see him being hauled up by a rope. One hand on the rope, the other at his bleeding side.

She threw one leg out the window, pushed her body up until she was crouching, and jumped.

Don't look down.

Reaching one hand out, she grasped onto the fabric of his pants. Blakey kicked wildly—he was no longer being pulled up. A small red droplet landed on her face.

"Let go!" he wailed, his breath ragged.

Blakey kicked furiously at her hands, then her head. Pain lanced through her skull as one blow landed directly on the side of her face, but she didn't let go. She blinked away tears that stung her eyes. He knew who she was. Regardless of anything else, he couldn't leave here.

"Swing!" Blakey shouted upward.

He threw his body to the wall. River slammed against it, hearing something crack as her arm shook. She grunted in pain. Something was certainly not right with her shoulder. Pain crawled up her hand, and she could no longer feel her fingers. She watched in horror as Blacky bent his knees and pushed off twice as hard. He intended to knock her off the wall again. She couldn't take another collision.

She would fall.

Just as she was about to hit the brick wall again, she flung herself toward the windowsill. Hands outstretched, one gripped the ledge, but she heard the *pop* as her shoulder gave way, and her body slipped to the earth.

She was in the forest again in front of the cottage with the green shutters. It was almost so perfect it appeared fake.

"River," said a pale woman with fiery red hair, a speckle of freckles across her nose. She cupped River's cheeks with warm hands, and her piercing green eyes locked her in place. "River, listen. You're in danger. You need to figure . . ."

Her mouth continued to move, but River could no longer hear her words; her familiar face was blurred. The words were all twisted in rhymes, and she couldn't understand them. The language turned into vines that wrapped around her ankles and legs, tangling with her body. River was unable to move, unable to breathe. The house started to burn, crumpling to ash and smoke, and it suffocated her, covering every surface. She screamed soundlessly.

The redhead shook her. Pushing away the smoke, the words turned into a language she could no longer understand. An older woman appeared, one hand on the girl's shoulder. Long silver hair billowed out around her. She seemed unaware of River below despite the redhead pointing in her direction. They spoke back and forth, and the words were a musical, yet guttural noise.

As the smoke and the vines continued to spin around River, closing her in, every word began another vine, another piece of ash being shoved down her throat. River was going to die. Right here in this forest, where a peaceful child had once played with her father.

"I can't breathe," she screamed over and over, but only her ears could hear.

Her focus moved in and out as the older woman's eyes finally landed on her. Her long crooked finger pressed into River's heart. She pulled her finger away slowly as a line of black mist followed behind, pouring out. But she shook her head, saying something to the redhead.

Stop! *River wanted to scream.* I don't know what you mean. *Her anger flared, and the vines shot off. They hung limply on the ground at first, torn between them. But her anger was potent. The vines crept toward the redheaded woman, slowly at first but then gained speed. They encompassed her body, and River laughed as they started to strangle the redhead. Her face turned blue, gaze pinned on River.*

Somewhere in the distance, a husky voice of pure velvet spoke. The older woman's face twisted in confusion.

The old woman walked forward, put one hand on River, and shoved.

Before the darkness overtook her again, a flash of white wings wrapped around her, the husky voice lulling her to ease.

Chapter Nineteen

River

River woke gasping, her fingers digging into the hard earth below her. She blinked rapidly at the lowering sun and took in a few short successions of breath.

"Oh, thank the king," a male voice said. A face appeared in her blurred vision. "I would've been hung for treason if I let you die." Leon's voice cracked in a panic. His calloused hand touched her forehead. "And if I wasn't, Laya would've done it for sure. Where does it hurt?" He prodded at her legs first, then her arms. "They don't feel broken. Your shoulder looks out of place, though. Can you move your body?"

She had no idea what he was prattling on about or why her back felt so stiff.

"What if you can't walk? Heldours. I'm in so much trouble." He touched her neck gingerly. "Can you feel that?"

"For pity's sake, Leon, back up," she groaned.

He did as he was told, taking a giant step away from her.

River blinked several more times. "Why do I feel like . . ."

Like she'd fallen. Everything came flooding back.

"Oh, ow," she said, trying to lift her head.

Leon moved toward her and extended a hand. She looked between his dirt-caked hand and hers, then winced.

"I think you're right about my shoulder."

Leon's long fingers dropped to his side before he kneeled next to her and pushed her into a sitting position. "This is going to hurt."

River grunted.

"Try not to kill me for this." He wrapped his hand around her wrist and, with one quick pull forward, her shoulder slid and popped. Pain raced through her in a whoosh as he pushed her wrist to her chest. "Hold it here for a minute."

He ripped a piece off the bottom of his shirt, revealing a stomach laced with muscles. River averted her eyes. No wonder Laya was so smitten. River found herself partial to the man.

Leon delicately wrapped his shirt around her, securing the wrist to her collarbone. "Leave this on."

River snorted. "I'll be useless like this."

Leon rolled his eyes. "If Prince Finn didn't teach you to fight one-handed, then he didn't do his job." He grasped her good elbow and pulled her to her feet. "You want to tell me what happened?"

"The tricky bastard."

"Ah. I see you met Blakey."

River's eyes widened. "Blakey? You seemed to have left a few things out of your report, Leon."

"I mean, Barthomule. I just recently learned of his nickname."

River eyed him skeptically.

"You have blood on your hands. Are you hurt?"

River held up her hands, noticing the dried smears of red. "It isn't mine."

He nodded. "Why don't you get inside and clean up."

"How did you find me?"

"I was delivering something to your room and noticed you were missing. Came looking and, well, I put a few things together. I'm going to search the forest to see if he left town. Do you want to recheck his rooms?"

River swatted at her filthy cloak and nodded, then touched her throbbing head.

Leon hesitated, searching her face. "Do you want me to walk you back?"

"That wouldn't make either one of us very good at our jobs."

He shrugged. His smile was large. "That would be the first time a woman said I wasn't very good at something."

River rolled her eyes. "You are quite the charmer. No wonder Bass hates you."

A rumble of a laugh rolled from his chest as he walked backward a few steps. "I think that might have more to do with you than anything else." He turned on his heel and strode into the forest.

River entered the quiet tavern. Most of the tables were empty, and a new barmaid had begun serving, this one far older, her creased face set in a harsh line. River hurried past her and upstairs. She paused outside Imogen's door. The girl had said River could have it until the afternoon, and she was most likely sleeping now.

She knocked lightly before she removed Leon's shirt from around her. Her arm throbbed at her side, but she couldn't appear weak.

"Come in," the soft voice called.

River opened the door quietly, hoping to not disturb her. "I'm so sorry. My friend left something for me here. I just came to retrieve it, and I'll leave."

Imogen sat on the floor in front of the mirror, brushing her freshly washed hair. "Quite handsome, that friend." She motioned with the brush toward the bed.

"He seems to think so." River leaned down, her mouth hanging open slightly at the pile on the bed. The leather one-piece was smooth to the touch, yet stiff, almost like armor. On top lay two elongated daggers with amethyst jewels in the hilts. She wrinkled her nose. Only a Finn could get their hands on these royal stones.

"There's more under the leather." Imogen didn't raise her head as she worked her wet hair into two braids.

River pushed aside the leather to reveal a bronze box tied with a navy ribbon. She pulled off the lid. On a silver chain hung a large amethyst about half the size of her balled fist. A cluster of tiny cloudy crystals dangled on either side of it. She had never seen them before, and they were surprisingly ugly. Maybe they were expensive, because whoever had designed this piece had surely not done it for its looks. Her fingers warmed as she touched the cloudy crystals, trying to place them.

But why would he give her such an expensive gift while she was here?

"The note's sweet too," Imogen said.

River looked over her shoulder, scowling. "What note?" She pushed aside the clothes until she found the unfolded note. That nosy child had read her letter.

She resisted pulling it to her nose. It would smell like lemon, and she didn't want to miss him.

The note was written in his small, elegant hand, though smaller letters were scrawled hastily in the corner.

There's so much you don't know, and so much I wish to tell you. Maybe one day I'll be able to. I ordered this for your birthday and figured there was no better time than now.

Below, in a more elegant hand:

Every girl deserves jewels in her favorite color. You always said yours was the purple the sky turned right before it was too dark to see. These stones reminded me most of you. – Bass

River's heart ached in a way she didn't think a seventeen-year-old's should. She loved him, even though she knew she shouldn't, even though he was no longer hers. She loved him and hated him all at the same time. Hated that he didn't think she was worthy of his love or capable of genuinely doing things herself. Hated the way he treated her like she was disposable one moment and the only thing on his mind the next. He was a complete mind snake, sinking his fangs in her just to watch her squirm and then sucking the venom back out to do it all over again. Tears pricked her eyes, but she wasn't crying for him. It was for the little girl and little boy with big dreams that would never come true.

"I'll leave you to change. It seems the outfit couldn't have come at a better time." Imogen pointed at the tears in her slacks River hadn't noticed before. A large one at her thigh revealed her tan skin. "And ya should try to do something with that hair while you're at it." Imogen's face crinkled. "You have leaves in it."

River grabbed at her head as heat flicked to her cheeks. "May I use your brush?"

Imogen shook her head, coming toward her. "Ya shouldn't use a brush. Ruins the curls." She rummaged through her drawers until she produced a comb and a small bottle of clear liquid. "Sit. Let me."

"You don't have to."

"And let you go out there with a rat's nest atop your head? With those jewels and that leather? You'll look like an easy mark."

Why had he gotten her jewels? It wasn't like she wore them often, and they would do her no good here.

"I can take care of myself." River crossed her arms over her chest and winced.

Imogen pushed at River's spine, and she allowed herself to be moved in front of the mirror. Did anyone believe she could do anything herself? Bass had sent her new weapons. This girl she barely knew was doing her hair. She had still yet to kill Barthomule—Blakey. How was she going to kill the man now that she had heard his story? It had felt too real in the moment. Could someone fake that much pain?

"Used to comb my sisters' hair every day before . . ." Imogens picked up the clear liquid.

River raised an eyebrow, but before she could question further, Imogen lifted a finger, silencing her. She poured a little liquid into her hand. The smell of lavender and something else tickled River's nose as Imogen rubbed it into the ends of her hair. She ran the comb through it, slowly and gently.

River closed her eyes, her body relaxing. "Before what?"

Imogen cleared her throat. "Before the fire that killed my whole family."

River's stomach seized, and her hand tightened around her leg. A wave of fear racked her. Flames rose up in the mirror as if they were everywhere in the room. She had never experienced anything like this, where she knew what she saw wasn't truly happening, yet the flames seemed so real. As real as the fear that now seized her. Her nails drew blood from her thigh.

River tried to breathe, but it felt as though a boot was pressed against her chest. The edges of her vision blurred as her breathing became short rasps. She pulled her knees to her chest, cradling them. She couldn't do this. Couldn't handle this fire. Be here. Or leave here and do what she needed to do. Maybe she should just lie here and let the flames take her.

A hand touched her shoulder lightly.

"Breathe. Focus on the pressure of my hand." Imogen's voice was soft as she bent down beside her.

River felt the weight of the hand.

"Only on my hand."

Her actual hand, not the imaginary foot on River's chest. Only the visible hand on her shoulder. She pushed all her thoughts toward that hand.

"Slow your breathing."

And River did, focusing on Imogen's hand and the gentle breaths next to her ear. Eventually, the weight lifted from her chest, and she could breathe again.

"Thank you," River said, looking up at Imogen. The flames were now gone, and relief washed over her. "I will celebrate your family.

Imogen nodded. "Next time, ignore the negative and replace it with the positives. That's what my gram told me." She smiled.

"Easier said than done."

"Emotions are tricky bastards."

River nodded, thinking this girl and Laya would get along well.

"The man who brought the gift. Is he the friend of your father's?"

River tried to keep her face impassive as she blanked. She had forgotten all about the lie she had told. "Mm-hmm."

"Well, with a face like that and gifts like those, I can see why your father would want you to be together. Though I'm not sure I would trust someone who dresses like a poor man and gives gifts like a prince."

River's eyes found Imogen's in the mirror. The girl's brown eyes sparkled. She suspected something.

"Thank you," River said curtly, taking the comb from her hands. "I've got it from here."

Imogen nodded, a smirk still playing on her lips. "I'll leave you to change, then. I have some errands in town." She grabbed the black cloak off the back of her door and was gone.

River combed through the rest of her hair quickly, doing her best to braid it the way Laya had taught her, though each new strand caused her further difficulty as small curls kept popping out.

How in Heldours was she going to kill a man if she couldn't even braid her own hair?

The leather fit her like a second skin, sliding over her legs and clinging to her lower half. It showed off every curve and every inch of the figure her mother had wanted her to hide. River pushed back the fear she felt all around her, stuffing it deep down. The fear of wielding a weapon against someone, killing someone whose story about a controlling father had struck a chord with her. But was it truly possible a human woman could fall in love with the magical race? She shook her head.

She let out a sigh as she cradled the warm necklace in her hands. What was she supposed to do with this thing? She certainly couldn't leave it here. She clipped it around her neck, feeling a warm buzz run through her.

She pushed her shoulders back, staring at herself in the mirror. A flicker of movement outside caught her attention as three figures emerged beyond her window at the edge of the woods. The three huddled together, one with a familiar-looking gait. She grabbed her weapons, slipping them through the holsters in the uniform, and without thinking or festering on her fear, she flung one leg over the window and dropped.

The moment she hit the ground, she regretted the decision. Her head throbbed. The fall earlier had certainly affected her worse than she'd suspected.

The three figures moved farther ahead and into the trees. Her feet didn't hesitate as she followed after them.

Chapter Twenty

River

River's boots crunched against the ground beneath her as she ran. She didn't have time to second guess chasing after three criminals. This was her chance to kill him and get it over with. She needed to go home. Clear her head. But really, she wanted to know what was truly going on in her kingdom; it had become apparent things weren't as they seemed. Maybe then the council would finally realize she was ready to handle this and understand everything that was going on with her kingdom, ready to rule—and maybe even better than her mother.

The black-cloaked figures stopped, and she slowed, pressing her back against a tree to stay hidden. She might be able to take one on, but she wasn't dumb enough to take three of them, let alone take an innocent life.

Innocent. The word brought her up short. He couldn't still be innocent. The story was true. The heat at her chest thrummed.

No. She would do this.

River peeked around the tree in time to see the group split, each running farther into the woods but in different directions.

"For the love of . . ." Her eyes darted back and forth between the path, trying to focus on the legs and detect a limp. They all ran perfectly.

She moved forward through the trees, following the slowest one. If they were trying to throw her off their tracks with the legs, it would still be the slowest one. She had injured him earlier. The blood on her hands was enough to prove it.

She pushed herself as hard as she could, just like in the training room. The way Bass made her when they raced the horses. It wasn't long before she was closing the distance between herself and the man. Her arm throbbed, limp at her side, but fortunately it wasn't her dominant one.

She threw Leon's knife, and it sailed past the cloaked head and thudded into a tree behind him, right where she'd intended.

The figure stopped, spinning toward her.

He let out a low whistle, which echoed from somewhere behind her. A sliver glint flashed, and the figure ran toward her. She blocked the knife with her amethyst dagger.

River grabbed his wrist, but he twisted and pulled, broke free, and backed up a few steps.

"I don't want to hurt you, Blakey. I was assigned to kill you, but if you just turn yourself in, all will be righted," River said, studying the mask, hoping for any flicker of emotion, but she could barely make out anything but the light of his eyes.

The figure only grunted before he moved toward her.

River blew out a breath. "I don't know why you want to make this hard for me."

She twirled her amethyst dagger around its hilt before she threw it at his knife. At the last minute, he moved his hand, and her blade sank into his shoulder. Bass would have made her throw again and again until she hit the proper target. He would have said she'd judged the man's movements wrong, but Bass wasn't here, and she could do this without him.

A fierce pang throbbed through her bad shoulder. She wasn't sure how much longer she had it in her to keep fighting.

The man pulled her blade from his shoulder and ran for her. River spun out of his grasp at the last minute, away from the blade. She pulled the second amethyst dagger from her waist. He lunged again. The strikes were uncoordinated and untrained. She would've figured a prince had better training than this. She blocked every one, though the speed of the blows was uncanny.

He was undoubtedly mad that she'd gotten him with a blade twice now.

There was a whoosh of breath hot on River's face as he landed a punch to her gut. She stumbled back but not before she punched him square in the nose.

The man lifted his hand to his face and wiped at the wet spot on the mask. His hand came away bloody. He pointed the blade at her.

"You don't have to do this," she said. She didn't want to kill him. "Please don't make me do this."

The man whistled again, and another higher-pitched whistle echoed his.

"If you're waiting for your buddies from earlier to ambush me, I'd suggest you not. Be realistic. I have men stationed in these woods," she lied. No one even knew where she was.

Sharp pain sliced her cheek. Liquid slowly dripped down her face. She blinked. Blakey no longer had a blade in his hand. She'd been so worried about killing him, she'd forgotten he still had a weapon. Forgotten that he'd tried to strangle her earlier.

She pressed her hand to her face, and blood oozed from it.

He charged and threw her against the ground. The weight of it sent her dagger flying. He pummeled her left and right, in the face, in her sides. She bucked her hips and swung her arm, flinging him off her right to her dagger.

A quick flash of silver pressed against her throat.

She had been willing to give him mercy. Be fair and just. The serpent of anger and confusion in the pit of her stomach struck. The rage filled her up inside, churning, a warm buzz spreading from her chest down to her arms.

"Do it," River said. "You'll just prove to everyone exactly who you are. Pathetic. You should've let the fire consume you."

It was almost instantaneous. The moment the words left her mouth, she felt a wave of fear, of burning alive, wash over her. River's chest burned and sizzled as if the fire already surrounded her. And she latched onto the fear, gripping it tight and riding it instead of pushing it down. This was just like before. It would disappear. It wasn't real.

"Stop," the man growled as his dagger dug deeper into her neck, drawing blood.

White flecks floated down around them, catching on the man's clothes. Her skin heated as if she were on fire from the inside, flaking away to ash all around them as the air became unbearably thick.

River gritted her teeth and arched her neck to push it harder against the blade. She blinked; a fire burned behind her eyelids. The ash floating in the air begged her to ignite. She wanted it to engulf them both, burn them to ash. She had failed. She would lose, and with it, the prophecy would fail.

She would burn everything.

River barely heard the whistle above her, and she wasn't sure if someone answered this time, but she didn't care. She relaxed her mind, allowing the burn that started in her chest to spread to her limbs as a dark mist clouded her vision. She imagined flames roaring to life from the little drifting ember that landed on the man's shoulder. The fire erupted to life behind him, and her insides hummed.

Her throat burned as the blade heated, turning orange around its edges.

The man wrenched his hand away, dropping the dagger. His weight lifted off her chest as he backed a few paces from her.

She stared in disbelief, and a small cackle released from her mouth. She slid her eyes to the right, watching the flames follow her command as they silently crept along the ground as though alive. The flames licked at the leaves and the branches. Like a child, they crawled, then stood.

The man shook his head, whistling in earnest as his head swiveled all around him, but the fire spread quickly, consuming the forest floor. The red-and-orange blaze was alive all around them. They were River's, burning inside of her, her fear come to life. Her mind went numb as her limbs burned not from the heat but from the unusual strength that seemed to well up inside of her.

The figure stumbled away from River. His eyes alight with the fear that was no longer in her heart. She drew a large circle in the air, and the fire encircled him, getting closer and closer as her circles became smaller. Her good arm reached instinctively out to the side as if grasping for something. Power coursed through her. The flames were an extension of her finger, her body, and it was all-consuming.

Fire nipped at his toes, moving farther up his legs.

"Princess River, please stop!" a girl shouted, raising her hand and removing the mask.

Distantly, River recognized the girl's voice, her face. It wasn't Blakey.

She knew she should stop, but something more powerful in her didn't care. It was like expelling the storm she had been drowning in her whole life, finally calming it, taming it. Turning the storm into a raging fire.

The girl tried to back away, but there was nowhere to go. River turned away from her face, only watching the flames dance. She couldn't feel the heat from the flames or hear the screams, but she knew the girl was screaming.

It was all a dream. If she closed her eyes, it would all go away.

"Please," the girl begged. She clutched her chest, and before River knew it, she was completely engulfed.

River couldn't stop, the woman's face not registering until it was too late, and she couldn't pull it back.

"Imogen . . ." River whispered before she collapsed onto the ground as the fire continued to rage around her.

Chapter Twenty-One

Ky

"Stop moving so much!" Ky growled as Belladonna wiggled against him. He tightened his grip around her waist. They had been flying a while, high above, and had yet to find anything. Ky was about to drop her off and make her walk back home. His arms were tired from carrying her.

"It's not my fault I don't have wings," she snapped.

It was a great mystery to all why females were no longer born with wings. Ky supposed it was because in the old world, the females' wings were clipped by the humans to keep them weak. Most females were more dangerous than males. Belladonna scared him already, and with wings, she would be a beautiful monster.

"There," Belladonna shouted and pointed toward yet another cluster of trees.

"This is like, the twentieth time you've said 'there.'"

She pinched his arm. "Before I said, 'that looks like something.' Now I'm telling you they're there!"

As much as the fadelings' general information had been helpful, it hadn't been quick. What Ky hadn't realized hours ago was that the fadelings had to walk to find the information just like they did, as

Belladonna had explained it to him. Their plane was just like Ky's. If he had to walk or fly to find things, so had they. It was like having many eyes in many places, but the information was slow, and the princess's whereabouts had changed recently, messing everyone up.

"I don't see anything!" Ky retorted into her ear. Her arm wrapped around his as she wiggled. He half wanted to strap her to him.

"They said look for the magic."

"The fadelings are losing their minds. Why would we look for the magic when I'm searching for the princess?" he yelled.

But just as he finished, he saw a flicker of movement. Ky sent out his own magic, searching the forest floor. A vital untamed energy source was directly below him. It skittered and thrashed against his. Whatever it was, it wasn't supposed to be here this close to the humans. Had an offspring wandered too far from home and into the humans' forest?

"There's something there. Let's check it out."

"Land there. Let's go on foot." She pointed farther away from the source, but it was a brilliant tactical move. If it was an offspring wandering too far from home, they would see a hunter and their *Heiralomun* and run, afraid of getting in trouble.

Ky did as she said, pulling back his wings and touching down in a precise spot between the trees.

"What do you feel?" Belladonna asked, her hands on the axes in her weapons belt.

Ky pushed his senses a little farther. "Something untamed. What are we walking into here?"

Shrieks of terror or pain rattled his ears.

Belladonna pulled out the ax from her belt and ran. Ky chased after her, but her long legs moved her faster.

He stared down the scene ahead where two figures were, one crouched over the other's still body. The sheer power drew his attention toward her. The magic wrapped darkly around her, but loosely enough he thought he could blow it away, like a dark cloud. Everything in Ky froze as his eyes traced up and down the female.

Her deep brown hair was matted to her skull, leaves and twigs collected in the thick mane. He had memorized every curve of her body, though she appeared far smaller in person. He could almost feel his hand glide down the dress she'd worn in his dreams, his calluses catching on the sequins. He could still taste her sweet mouth.

He swallowed.

She was unmistakable. His dream girl—real, still alive.

Close enough to him that he was starting to have trouble breathing.

She was screaming as her magic exploded all around her. Black puffs of it choking his senses.

"Kylane, wake up!"

"What?" He whipped his head toward Belladonna, who stood eerily still, not stepping closer.

"You dragon-damned idiot, touch her!" Her eyes glowed coral.

Ky took a few quick steps toward the girl, dropping to his knees, and wrapped his arms around her at the same time his crystalline fingers snatched the magic from the air.

The hazel eyes he never thought he'd see in real life looked up at him as a slight gasp left her lips. She relaxed in his arms as her head lolled to the side.

"That bloody screaming was . . ." Belladonna shook her head, looking over his shoulder. "The fadelings are telling me this is the princess, but please don't tell me she's a halfy!"

A halfspring?

"I don't understand," Ky said, looking from her to the body on the ground. "Check for a pulse."

Belladonna ignored him. "What the dragon is a halfy doing parading as a human?"

"Bella, check the other one!"

She pointed her ax at him. "You just called me Bella."

"I am going to hit you if you don't check her."

She grinned at him. "I'd like to see you try."

"Belladonna!" Ky growled.

"She's dead."

"You can't know that."

She replaced her ax into her belt. "I've killed enough to know. She's dead."

"Don't make me command you! Just touch her neck. Look for injuries."

"Like you could." But Belladonna bent and did as she was told. "No pulse. Dead, as I said." She gently flipped the human girl over. "But there isn't anything. No stab wounds—nothing. What can that little thing do?" Her eyes were now on the girl in his arms.

"I—" Ky fumbled for his words.

"The necklace," Belladonna said the same time Ky noticed the *Crystolas* necklace wrapped around her neck. It had to be amplifying her powers. "Whoever gave her this wanted to see what she could do." She pointed to the metal spots of the necklace that were now empty.

He traced his fingers carefully around her neck until he reached the clasp. Brushing the mess of curls aside, he yanked her free of the chain and threw it as far from them as he could.

"Well, this changes things," said a familiar yet out-of-breath voice behind them.

Blakey appeared from behind the tree. He halted in front of the dead girl and bent, touched her face softly, and swore. "She's one of ours."

"I'm sorry," Ky said, shaking his head. "I don't . . ."

"Put the princess down," shouted an unfamiliar voice from behind Blakey. "I need to take her home."

A blond human stepped between the trees, his slate-gray eyes pinned to them. Ky took in his pressed-back shoulders; he was skinny in a muscled way. Definitely a soldier.

"She's not going home, especially now that we know she isn't human," Ky said dryly.

"For King's sake, yes, she is!" the gray-eyed man argued.

Ky cocked his head. "Who are you?"

"Leon. I'm a Castor personal guard—"

Blakey placed a hand on Leon's shoulder. "He's also one of us. But who is she?" He pointed to Belladonna, whose coral eyes were focused on the distance. Her head whipped quickly from one side to the next.

"Ignore her."

"I can still hear you, Kylane," she growled.

"I don't understand. How did this happen?" Ky pointed at the girl with one hand but kept the princess's magic locked with the other. How was the princess the same one from his dreams? The one from the premonitions his mother had been sending him for months. He couldn't wrap his head around it. Each time he grasped for connection, it slipped through his fingers like smoke.

Blakey cradled the dead girl in his arms as he stood. "Leon came to warn me that they had sent the princess to kill me. She was more physically capable than I anticipated, and she wouldn't hear me out. I wanted to come tell you. So we split up, hoping to confuse her. It worked." He looked down. "A little too well."

Ky's brain moved quickly. Keeping her alive was the most important thing. Not just for the prophecy but his own sanity. "We need to follow through with the plan. It's even more important now. You have to go back and say she's dead."

Even as he said the word, it haunted him. Dead. It made him want to hide her in his cave and never let her return to the world that would kill her.

"We can't do that. Castor would go into chaos," Leon interjected.

"I'll take care of Imogen's body and spread the rumor." Blakey's hands tightened around the dead human. "I didn't mean for her to die like this."

"We know," Leon said, patting Blakey's shoulder. The two were clearly close.

Belladonna stepped forward, her brown eyes back to normal. "The body needs to come with me."

"What?" Ky and Blakey echoed in unison.

Belladonna placed her hand on her hip. "You think Head Axel is going to believe the human princess is dead without proof? I'm sorry, but that body is going to buy us time."

"She doesn't look like our princess," Leon said.

"It doesn't matter. He won't know the difference," Ky added, nodding at Belladonna. It was a brilliant plan.

"Ky, you can't be serious." Blakey's voice rose in a way he hadn't heard before. "This child has people who love her. Ones that will miss her. She was one of our own. We owe that to them."

Ky wanted to pace, but the unconscious princess was still in his lap. "I am sorry. We'll have to help the family in another way. Give them coin—"

"A child's life is priceless!"

Ky felt Blakey's words more profoundly than he cared to admit. None of this was supposed to have happened. Something deep within him was struggling against his own. Was it the girl's magic? Or the fact that this poor human child was dead?

And why hadn't his mother told him? The girl in his arms wasn't only the princess who was supposed to help integrate the two races, but she was also the girl he was supposed to love. The girl he was supposed to watch die.

Ky shook his head, trying to clear it. "I'll do what I can to bring the human's body back to you." He lifted the cloak away from the sleeping princess. A leather one-piece clung to her skin almost like pict-paint, and he cocked his eyebrow. "Where are her human clothes? Her dresses?"

"This can't be happening." Leon stepped forward.

"Leon," Blakey warned, but his eyes were on Ky, who had tightened his hold on the girl. "Their leader wants her dead. We can't have that."

"I'm trusting you here, Blakey. I've never questioned you before, and I'm not going to start now. But I don't like this. I'd like it heard that I disagree with whatever plan you all have here!" Leon took another step toward Ky and kneeled at the princess's side. "Her dresses are all back at the castle. Wherever you take her, you'll keep her safe, right? She had some misinformation about Blakey that was fed to her by her mother, but she's a genuine person, and one day she'll make a great queen."

"I will do everything in my power. But for now, I need to pull off her death in order to keep her safe." Ky sent his magic to prod at her gently, then put his finger to her neck. Both beat slowly. "I need wealthy royal clothes."

"There's an abandoned manor not too far from here that should have something passable. But I also want to say I'm against using Imogen as a replacement. Wholeheartedly," Blakey said.

"I don't have any other options. I'm sorry." Ky looked at Belladonna. "Treat her with care. If we can return her, we need to."

Belladonna nodded and stepped forward, gently taking the girl into her arms. She looked ridiculous, almost like it was a baby in her arms rather than a teenage girl. Is that how he looked with the princess in his arms?

"Blakey, can you get the clothes?"

"I'll do it. It is on my way back," Leon said, stepping forward.

Ky nodded. "Bella, listen to Leon, work together. Don't get caught." He turned to look daggers at Leon. "I'm trusting you. If you get Belladonna caught, you'll be damning your princess to death. Do you understand that?"

"She is chosen," Leon said.

"What?"

"The prophecy. It's what we call the princess." Leon rolled his eyes. "I've got this."

Ky cocked his head toward the south. Neither Belladonna nor Leon looked back as they headed toward the manor on foot, disappearing farther into the forest.

"I'm not sure I can forgive you for this," Blakey said. "But I hope it all works out for you. I truly do." He turned his back on Ky.

"Where are you going?"

"To do what I must. For the family. For the now dead princess. And for the prophecy."

And with that, Ky was left alone with the unconscious princess.

"Am I supposed to just kidnap you?" he said to her still body. "This would've been much easier if you were awake to understand your own death."

He wished he had a yoligs leaves candy shard, something to help him bring back this girl as he'd done for his sister so many times.

"Okay, Princess, please don't freak out." He stood, cradling her carefully to his chest, making sure the sharp edges of his armor didn't cut into her. "Let's do this."

He spread his wings wide and began to push off the ground. He felt a small shift in his arms and plastered on a smile so as to not freak her out.

But it wasn't needed.

Hazel eyes stared into his as the tip of his unicorn blade pressed into his neck between his armor.

"Drop me, demon, or I will slit your throat."

Chapter Twenty-Two

River

River woke up in a tight embrace. She let out a small breath.
Bass.

She hadn't thought she would be happy to see him. Maybe he'd changed his mind. Her eyelids were heavy, so she kept them closed for a minute to take in his scent. Her nostrils flared in anticipation of the familiar smell of horses and lemon but instead, what went up her nose was something she couldn't quite place. Almost salty and rusty like metal left in the rain.

She stiffened as she pried her eyes open. Her stomach sank.

Oh, saints of Heldours.

She blinked slowly, trying to stay still. She was in a man's arms. *No*, not a man. She was pressed against bones. Cold bones.

This was no man. It was a monster. A demon.

A Spitarian.

She fought every instinct to scream and swallowed it. All he had to do was squeeze, and he could pop her like a fruit. Something white glinted in her peripheral as she shifted to a new position.

She relaxed her body, allowing her arm to flop over his as he continued to reposition her. She let her other arm slide down farther between their bodies. This monster was cold like death. She flexed her fingers. She couldn't believe she was considering it. *But he has to have a male organ, right? Grab and twist.* That was her plan. Her fingers scratched farther, and she felt him crouch. She touched something cooler than him. Hard, like a . . .

Weapon.

In a quick movement, as he stood, she pulled it free and swung it to where she hoped his neck was.

"Drop me, demon, or I will slit your throat."

Her body shifted, and with a thud, she was on the ground, staring up at his entire body. Her stomach dropped, and she froze, breathing slowly. It was made entirely out of bone.

The pictures in her schoolbooks hadn't done these creatures justice. There was nothing human to this thing. Every inch was bone, but the bones didn't seem to connect or form together in any logical way. It was as if someone had taken them from multiple different creatures of all sizes when they'd created this . . . thing. Its body stood large and hulking, twice the size of a normal man in height and broadness. Its face was pure white bone with black irises and massive ivory spiraled horns protruded out of its head. Large feathered wings sprawled behind its shoulders, white as snow until the color met the tips and darkened.

River's knees shook as fear ran up her spine.

She stared at the creature. It didn't move as tendrils of steam rose from its mouth. Its giant wings shifted around it, the leaves and twigs moving around the ground.

It lifted its hand, raising it toward its head, and River scooted back, its weapon still in her hand. In one quick movement, bones began to fall to the ground. She realized with a start it was shedding his armor—a skull helmet, a bone chest piece, and the rest of the bones that covered his body.

A large man stood before her, bare-chested, his brown skin beautiful and sun-kissed, a few shades darker than hers after a long summer's day. The muscles of his chest and abdomen were well defined. Black pants were tailored to fit his lower half just right, slung low on his hips. He was still tall, but with the armor gone, he seemed less beast-like, especially without the height of the added horns, though he still was much larger than her. Fine midnight hair fell askew around his shoulders, some pieces held back behind his head, and his prominent jawline was clean shaven.

He was beautiful, from his head down to his bare toes. He couldn't be real. He looked too polished.

He stood, unmoving, staring without blinking. His eyes looked less black without the shadows of the helmet. Instead, they were a deep brown.

Something about him seemed so familiar.

His deep, soothing voice startled her. "I'm sorry to have frightened you. I mean you no harm." The use of her human tongue was flawless. "Do you mind putting that down? I don't want you to hurt either of us." His eyes were pinned to the weapon in her hand.

"I am capable of wielding a weapon."

The corner of his lip rose in a half smile. "I bet you are."

River wouldn't let her curiosity overshadow her common sense. Even if all the stories about their race weren't true, she didn't doubt the ones about strength. Her eyes traced over his smooth chest. Without the bone armor, he didn't look evil. He looked like a fairy-tale prince from a book.

"As I said, I won't hurt you." He took a step forward, hands splayed in front of him as though she were a creature about to flee. She wouldn't give him the satisfaction of a chase.

The breath left her lungs slowly as her eyes moved back up toward his face. His brow arched as if waiting for a response.

"I'm not scared. The armor startled me, but I've come across your kind before," she lied. *How did I get here?* She racked her head, trying to come up with her last memory. She gulped away the sour taste as flashes came back to her in waves. "Where is the girl? Imogen?" River stood, taking the weapon with her.

Ky didn't back up a step, but his eyes kept flicking back and forth between it and her face. "She's dead."

"I don't . . . I don't understand." In one blink, the images came back, one by one. The girl's face in terror, her screams, the fire . . . But it couldn't have been real. She looked down at her unscathed skin. No, none of it had been real. River shook her head.

He took one step forward, and she took one step back, her spine brushing against the trunk of a tree.

"You're lying. I didn't kill her. It was a dream."

He cocked his head, studying her, and then his lips turned down. "I'm sorry. It was no dream. The girl is dead."

River pointed to the forest floor. "If it were a real fire, everything would still be burning. It was a dream . . ."

The pitying look on his face confused her. "Is that what you were seeing? Fire?"

No. River couldn't have killed her. The girl was younger than her. Had been kind. Offered a room, food, brushed her hair. What had she been doing running around in black, dressed like the enemy?

River squeezed her eyes shut, her breathing quickening. She pushed it aside. She couldn't do this now. A much greater threat was in front of her. She would deal with those feelings later. She focused on her breathing, trying to will herself to slow and hide the clawing sensation away behind something else within herself. Just for now.

She swallowed, trying to keep her eyes focused on the enemy, but the power that had coursed through her earlier . . . had it been real? If it had been, she had killed with it. Then maybe she could use it again to get her away from this monster.

River clenched her fists together, willing the feeling from earlier to return. She pumped them several times. How had she done it before? How had the fire come?

"I will not harm you. And whatever you're trying to do with your fists, you should know that your power will be of no use on me." He backed up a step as if trying to prove his point.

"Power?" *No, not power . . . magic.* This was wrong. He knew. Everything in her was screaming. Adrenaline started to course through her. *Run.*

He laughed. "It's swirling all around you. But I can tell you don't have control of it yet. It's like steam after a hot bath, easily wiped away."

Sweat ran down her spine.

"I can help you control it."

Control it? She didn't even know what it was. How was it possible she had power? What did that even mean? She was human.

Right?

Her stomach rolled as if she had just swallowed a large amount of acid.

She needed to get out of here. Someone would come for her. They still needed her to fulfill the prophecy. She would do her duty: kill Barthomule, save them, not die, and hopefully get her throne. She just needed to keep him distracted long enough. But she was still so confused. The ball of dread climbing back up inside her like a living being.

"How did she die?"

He studied her. "I don't know. There were no visible wounds upon her. But when we arrived, your magic was surging out of control." He pointed to his throat. "You had a necklace on. The stones were making it worse."

River shuddered. "The clear ones."

He nodded.

Bass. But why?

"You said 'we'?" She looked from him then to the armor. "No, no, her body needs to go back to her loved ones. I need to explain. I didn't mean to kill her. They must know that." Her breathing picked up again. The sinking feeling in her gut like a dark pit inside herself eating her whole.

He put his hand out as if to comfort her then put it back down to his sides. "That was your first time, then?"

River's eyebrows knitted together. "I don't make it a habit of killing people."

Ky held up his hands. "Dragons, no. I meant your magic."

She sucked in her lip, biting hard. This couldn't be happening. She had killed that girl. Yes, she had been fighting back, defending herself, but still. Imogen was no more than a child. She had helped River . . .

I killed her.

She gripped the weapon in her hand tighter.

"I am terribly sorry for what you endured. No one should have to learn of their magic that way, let alone have it come in like that. If I'd been aware of your abilities, I would've found a way to remove you and teach you. I failed you." His voice trembled. "It must have felt like this deep dark hole, as if something were always eating you alive."

The pain that laced his words wasn't for show. "Like I was drowning," she whispered.

He nodded before raking his hands through his long black hair.

He had apologized to her. No one else had ever done so. But here, with this stranger, a man who was supposed to be her enemy, she felt . . . seen.

"Taking a life isn't something that's easy to live with. It changes you." He lifted his fist to his heart. "It affects this."

It was true. Her chest hurt like an animal had sat on it while her stomach tried to climb out of it. She felt terrible—worse. She'd killed someone, someone's daughter, someone's sister. Someone's friend. It left its own kind of weight behind.

River imaged the whole forest burning down around them, willing it to consume her too. She deserved it. She could take out two monsters with one mighty firestorm.

Because that was what she was.

A monster.

"It takes us years of training to master our magic. Don't force it. It'll come when you're ready."

She didn't want to learn to control it. She wanted nothing to do with it. All it had done for her was kill someone. She'd spent years learning how to fight as a human, and now she would need years of training to learn to control . . . this. She didn't want it.

He took another step forward.

River pressed her back into the tree. "Stop doing that. If you're not here to harm me, then stay put."

As he got closer, though, his features became less dreamlike. His face was flawed, dark circles under his eyes, and a scar ran from the left of his neck down to the top of his right pectoral. He was still handsome, but as she got closer, it was a darker kind of beauty. River felt smaller with his body towering over her.

He let out a laugh that echoed around the forest. "Fair enough. I'll stay put if you won't run. I'd hate to have to chase you, and I'm exhausted from looking for you. You didn't make it easy."

River inhaled. *Looking for me?* Not important now. "So Imogen's body?"

He gestured to the ground. "Do you mind if I sit?"

River shook her head but remained standing.

He folded himself cross-legged onto the forest floor. "This is a long and complicated story. So I'll try to make it as easy on you as possible, River."

"I'm sorry—you have me at a disadvantage. You clearly know my name, but I don't know yours."

He laughed. "My friends call me Ky."

"Friends?"

His eyes searched her face as if he could read her every thought and feeling.

"Continue."

"As I'm sure you're aware, there's a prophecy that states you'll end this war."

"So I've been told." She didn't move. It would take him longer to stand, and she could use that to her advantage if running became her only option.

"But that isn't fully true. My mother was the one who spoke the prophecy over your mother. The prophecy doesn't state you'll end the war. It states that you'll help bring the races together." He recited the prophecy by memory.

River shook her head slowly. "There was a man in the bar who said the same thing."

"Yes. I spread the true prophecy to some humans I trust. One of those humans is Blakey. You know him as Barthomule Morsaw."

"Heldours." She squeezed the weapon in her hand tighter.

Ky nodded. "And I think the King of Morsaw wanted him dead because he was working with me and about a hundred or so other humans who believe in peace, maybe even integration. That piece is new." He shrugged. "My mother asked me to help the humans—and you. I don't want to disappoint her."

River nodded slowly, understanding the need to impress a mother. "And you're saying my mother only told me one piece of the prophecy." She didn't want to believe her mother was capable of lying. But after everything she'd seen and heard from Imogen the past few days . . . And Bass had lied to her as well. It was possible that this monster—or man, Spitarian, or whatever he was—was telling the truth. Even so, he was still dangerous, and she needed to stay far away from him.

He grabbed two sticks from the ground and began twining them together. "Imogen was one of these humans who believed in peace. She was helping Blakey avoid you and get to me. But there's a little more to the story."

"Of course."

"My father, Head Sparrow, wants you dead. He wants all humans dead. I was ordered here to kill you. But I can't because you're important to the peace. So I had Imogen's body taken to him in your place. He won't know the difference. And I had Blakey spread a rumor that you're dead."

"I'm dead?"

Ky nodded slowly.

"I can't remain dead. I must rule my kingdom when my mother dies and do whatever it is I am supposed to do that leads to that prophecy." River threw up her hands.

His thick shoulders shrugged. "I hadn't really thought that far into the future."

River wanted to laugh, but instead, she pulled at the skin on her lips with her teeth, peeling away the dry, cracked layers. If they thought she was dead, no one was coming for her. She had meant to keep him distracted, but the more they talked, the more River felt at ease, almost as if somewhere deep down she trusted him. Maybe it was because, for once, someone was telling her the whole truth. Plus, there was something about him, the cadence of his voice, that felt so familiar to her. But she couldn't place his face. A face that was filled with a sense of deep sadness, permanent creases that showed he frowned more than he smiled, like the weight of the world lay on his shoulders as well. A familiar spirit.

"Clearly. Well, you did think about where I can stay for the meantime, no? Or am I to wander the woods until I'm discovered?"

"I have a cave . . ."

River pressed her lips into a thin line. *A cave? For a princess?* What did he take her for, an animal? A monster? A Spitarian? Is that how they lived, in caves? And what did that make her? She had magic, but she looked just like her human mother. *Mother is human, right?* Her head spun.

"Fine, then. Let's get this over with." She began walking in a direction she hoped was north.

He chuckled behind her. "We're going to need to fly."

"I don't fly."

He held out his hand, and she hesitated. "If you'd like to keep that weapon you can . . . as long as you promise to never stab me in the back with it."

She wouldn't make that promise but nodded. "If I don't come with you and run, what will you do?"

Ky let out a sigh, his hand still hovering between them. "I would have to give chase."

"So I don't have a choice. You're taking me against my will." She pointed the weapon directly at him.

His eyes remained locked on hers. "I'm saving you."

She scrunched her face. "Whatever you have to tell yourself to sleep at night."

Somehow, she knew if she took his hand there would be no going back.

Chapter Twenty-Three

River

River stared at his outstretched hand and swallowed, trying to clear the dryness in her mouth. Ky's large wings beat slowly behind him. His feet hovered off the ground.

She couldn't outrun him, and she wouldn't win in a fight. His father had sent him to kill her, and she doubted he would send anything less than his best after her. What choice did she have but to go with Ky? If it turned out he was untrustworthy she could run off while he slept. He couldn't watch her at all times.

"If I go with you, I want a say in what happens next. A say about every decision before it is made."

He cocked his head, his gaze sliding over her slowly. She was suddenly very aware of the leather she wore and how it fit her body.

"You're coming with me either way, yet you make demands?" He grinned slyly. "I see the tiny human likes to joke."

"I just figured a cooperative captive was better than one who stabbed you in your sleep."

A low chuckle rumbled to the ground. "I was already warned not to underestimate you. I should have thought of your size as an asset rather than a disadvantage. Forgive me."

She placed her hands on her hips. "So are we in agreement? I have a say?"

"Okay," Ky said, a small smile lifting the corners of his mouth. "Anything else?"

"I want my voice to matter."

Ky chuckled.

"Don't laugh!"

He nodded, pinching his lips together.

"I want to know what's really going on in my kingdom and the other human kingdoms. I want the knowledge your spies know."

"They're not spies. But fine."

River stepped tentatively toward him. "And I want you to teach me how to use my . . . my stuff and what it all means."

"Your *stuff*?" His brows rose. "If you mean your womanly wiles, I can't help you there."

"Don't be crass. Plus I'm more than capable of that myself." She gestured between them.

"I can see that. I guess if you mean your magic, then, yes, I or someone I trust will teach you. I'm not an expert, but we'll figure it out."

River sighed. "And when I say it's time to go home? It's time to go home."

"Yes, Princess."

"Don't call me that!" she snapped as she stalked toward him, trying not to trip over any exposed roots.

"What am I to call you?"

"My name." She stopped in front of him, looking at his outstretched hands.

"Is everything all right? They're no dirtier than you are."

River looked up at him and blushed. "No, it's not that. It's just that . . . We humans don't touch strangers often, and you are . . ." She gestured to his chest. "Naked."

"Just be glad I'm wearing pants."

She blanched, pulling back.

"May I please touch you, tiny fierce human?"

She rolled her eyes. "Since you said 'please.'" River ripped a piece of her outfit and twisted it around the blade before shoving it into her boot. She placed her hand in Ky's. His wrapped entirely around hers, covering it. The sensation of his cold skin against her warm palm sent a shiver down her spine.

"I am going to pull you against my chest. Is that okay?"

She nodded, still staring at his hand.

He gently pulled her to him, her face pressed right below his pectorals, her breasts pushed up against his abs. He snaked his arm around her upper back and tightened his grip. She was thankful her leather protected her from most of the coolness of his skin.

"You ready?" His voice had turned deep and throaty, and it made a rush of fear go through her.

"Don't drop me," she whispered.

"Wouldn't dream of it." With three powerful beats of his wings, they lifted from the ground and into the air.

From the gap under his wings, she could see how the plants and leaves shuddered, and they soared higher and higher. River took in a sharp breath as they moved quicker above the trees. She could see the whole forest.

If this weren't so scary, it would be beautiful.

She shook. What if she fell?

"You're going to want to wrap your legs around me," he said into her ear.

This time River didn't hesitate and wrapped her legs around his, clinging to him.

His chest rumbled. "I'm going to scoot you up a little."

Her body heated as she realized how she was positioned on him. "Okay."

The arm that wasn't wrapped around her back moved underneath her and scooted her farther up him until her thighs were notched just above his hip bones.

He grunted.

"Am I heavy?"

"No."

River stared up into the blue sky, soaking up the sun. They rose higher and higher above the clouds. She clung to Ky, her arms wrapped tightly around his upper back, and his arms encircled her waist. She was glad to be facing this direction, watching his wings move rather than watching the ground sprawl beneath her.

"You're missing all the best parts. Would you like me to turn you around? I can hold you facing forward. It's how I fly with my sister."

"No, heights haven't always been my friend." River paused. "Wait, your sister doesn't have wings?"

"No females do."

"Why? That seems a little unfair."

"They did once, beautiful ones from what I've read. Not feathers but ones made of a material comparable to silk, smooth and thin . . ." His voice trailed off.

"What happened to them?"

"Our history is . . . I'm not sure how much humans know. Before this world, we inhabited another, and it was an awful place. Females' wings were cut in order to control them. Some males as well. After a few generations, females were born with none. Maybe they were no longer necessary for survival, or their bodies didn't have enough magic to produce them. It's hard to say."

River felt the heavy breath in his chest more than she heard it. "I'm sorry. That's terrible." She swallowed. "How do they get around now? You carry them?"

"Or they use creatures." His grip around her waist tightened.

Did I say something wrong?

"Don't panic and do exactly as I say."

"What?"

He readjusted his hold on her. "Slowly move your arms around my neck."

She stiffened but did as he said.

"Don't look down. I need to put you on my back. Something's approaching."

"Something?"

"Go," Ky said, wrapping his finger around her ankle and giving her a push. Her legs swung free. She gripped his neck tighter as he flung her around to his back. The world spun.

"Wrap your legs." He reached for her feet and pulled them above his hip bones. Her face lay flat against his back in between his beating wings. The muscles on his back rippled with each beat. The air shifted around them.

Don't look down. Don't look down.

Ky's arms tightened. "I am going to have to fly really high and really fast. Close your eyes."

River did as she was told. Her fingernails dug into her arm. She felt the wings under her shift fast, and the wind bite at her face as they flew faster. The air chilled, and the breath from her lungs became shallower.

After several minutes, he squeezed her arm. "We're in the clear."

She let out a breath, opening her eyes. "What was it?"

"A dragon. A small one looking for food. He didn't even bother to look up."

River loosened her grip but only a little. "That's comforting."

"See there?" He pointed toward a long mountain range. "Those are the Boltos Mountains, and farther out is the Frengress Mountain range."

She lifted her head slightly off his shoulders. "Much more extensive than our hills." Her gaze followed the white-capped mountains. All different sizes and colors; some pure white, others browner. Some with trees, some without. Nothing like the sprawling green hills that were just that—green.

"Is that mountain red?"

"I'd say burnt orange. But it's not the mountain. We have crops growing on that one. They're brashen bushes, so it appears like it."

"Brashen bushes?"

"How do you describe them? It is a . . . What's your word? Vegetables. They grow on a large bush almost the size of a tree. They taste like your carrots but look like . . . What's the fruit you have, the one that comes on trees? The red or orange ones."

"An orange," she said, smiling.

"Yes. Mm-hmm. Right, well, they look like that, but they have a nice spicy tang."

River tried to imagine the taste. "I'll take your word for it." She shivered.

Ky sighed. "You're going to need a coat. I should've thought of that. After I drop you off, I'll try to bring something."

Drop her off? Wasn't he staying in his own cave? Maybe it was better this way. If it turned out she couldn't trust him, she could always leave.

"So you don't wear much clothing under your armor. Oh, your armor—we left it behind."

"It's okay. I'll go back and get it. It would've been an uncomfortable ride for you."

"So dragons really do roam these parts?"

"And many other creatures. It's best if you stay in the cave, okay?"

She pressed her face to his back, seeking warmth but finding none. "Where will you be?"

"I need to go make sure that Belladonna made out with Imogen's body, and my father is pacified."

River wasn't sure why, but the thought of another woman as large as this man scared her to death. She shuddered.

"We're here." He pointed to a black mountain, and in the distance, it appeared to be one large one. But as they got closer, it was a bunch of smaller mountains all clustered around one.

"Is that water?" she asked, looking past the mountains. She sniffed the air. The salty smell she caught on him early was the briny scent of the water.

"Yes, the Norta Sea."

"I didn't know there was a sea in the north. Is it cold?"

"Yes. Deadly cold." Ky circled the cluster of mountains, and each had a large heaping of snow on top. "It's getting close to the time of the harvest, so the sea will change color as we go into what you call winter."

"Change?" River wondered if it was like how the Euphrine River got blacker as one went farther north.

"If you're still here by then, it is certainly a sight. It's sea dragon mating season. They all surface to mate."

He said "mate" so casually. It made her stomach squirm. River tried to see his face because it sounded like he was smiling. "And how does that change the, uh . . . color?"

"The magic the mating puts off. It lights up the sea." He pointed. "We're here." He flew them closer to the mountain and circled to a platform that jutted out of its side. "I should warn you. I do have two dragons in here, but once you get to know each other, you should get along."

"Get along? Are you insane?" River huffed. "They aren't pets."

"They are to me." And now she knew he was smiling. "Brace. I'm landing."

She gripped her hands tighter around his neck as she felt the world straighten and rumble under her body as he landed.

He tapped on her arm. "Release my neck before you kill me," he rasped.

She let go quickly, dropping the last few feet to the ground and landing on her backside. She looked up at his face, feeling the blood drain. "I am so sorry."

He chuckled. "Don't worry, I was just kidding. We can't die that way."

"You can't?"

"You have a lot to learn. We're very hard to kill. Only one thing truly does it." He pointed to her booted foot where his blade was stuck.

The mouth of the cave seemed shallow. She followed him and ran her hand over the rough rock where an apparent crack led to an opening. The entrance was almost too small for him as he pushed through. She easily moved in after him. It was clever. Someone passing by wouldn't notice it because it would appear from a distance like it was closed off.

After a short, narrow hallway, the cave opened up into a large cavern.

"Welcome."

Right away, she noticed the smell and the warmth. It was oddly stuffy and smelled of ash, sea, and rust.

A loud growl thundered through the cavern, bouncing off the walls as it echoed around them, and she grabbed onto Ky's arm.

"Easy, Tang!" he shouted to his left as a giant black beast pounded toward them. Its scales along its side were each larger than River's head, overlapping into hard armor.

The dragon dipped through another opening to her left. It skidded to a stop and plowed its head into Ky's stomach. Its orange eyes looked like tangerines. They were larger than her fist and focused solely on her.

"Tang, this is River. She's going to be staying here for a little. Play nice." He cleared his throat as he rubbed its snout lovingly. "And be gentle girl." He flicked the dragon's nose, who snorted and shook its head.

River let go of Ky's arm but didn't back up as she held her breath. He was leaving her with two dragons. Was he insane?

"I think we need a different location."

"They can understand everything you say. Don't insult them. Be nice to them, and they'll treat you nice."

A growl came from the depths where Tang had just been—a deeper rumble that shook the caves—and River did back up this time. A dragon twice the size of Tang came barreling out, elongated teeth flashing.

Ky stepped in front of River and bent down slightly, arms out. "She's mine," he growled.

His?

The dragon came up short, closed its mouth, and River could have sworn it nodded. It bent its knees until its head touched the ground.

"That's Thumper," he said and pointed to the long forest-green tail that jumped loudly back and forth.

"Is it going to eat me?"

Ky let out a laugh that echoed around them. "You're too scrawny. Not enough meat. More likely, he would just bite off your head and leave you to rot."

"Comforting."

Ky held out his hand again, and she took it, feeling like a child. "I made you a little bed, and there's some food." He rubbed the back of his neck, dropping her hand. "It was the best I could do on short notice. If you're still cold, the dragons are a great source of warmth." He let out a breath. "Oh, and stay out of the hot spring. I'm not sure what effect it will have on you."

"The what?"

He pointed farther into the cave where steam rose. Colors glinted and bounced off the surface onto the wall like a rainbow.

"Okay." She looked around, wrapping her arms around herself. "How about a fire?"

He shook his head, pointing at the ceiling. "I don't think it's a good idea."

She nodded, understanding. The smoke would go right out the hole, alerting them of their presence.

"You should try and sleep for a little."

She looked toward the bed and then back to him. "I think I'm okay." But even as she said it, her bones ached from exhaustion.

"If you insist. But magic is very draining. When I came into my magic, I slept for days after I used it the first time. And mine certainly didn't come in anywhere close to as powerful as yours."

She had so many questions, but she held them all back. "If I sleep, what will you do?"

"You'll need to eat when you wake. I thought maybe I could find some meat."

She eyed the dragons behind him. "They'll go with you?"

He chewed the side of his cheek. "No, they'll stay here and have you for lunch."

Chapter Twenty-Four

Ky

She rolled her eyes again—those damned enchanting hazel eyes—and Ky couldn't help it as his mouth turned into a lopsided grin.

"Go." He pointed to the bedding. "Sleep. I'll be back soon."

River's gaze darted to the dragons, then to him as she backed up a few steps and ducked into the alcove.

"Behave," he growled at his dragons before he made his way back through the cave.

The cold harvest air whipped in his face, and he breathed it in, trying to calm himself. He still couldn't wrap his mind around it. She was the same girl. The princess. His dream. He tried to keep his mind from running away from him. He couldn't separate his feeling for the girl in the cave from the one in his dreams. The one who looked at him alone as if there was no one else, like he'd turned the sea pink, versus the girl in there who, half the time, looked like she'd like to stab him in his sleep.

She probably could too. He saw the look in her eyes—the same look he saw in Belladonna's, in Azalea's, and, a few times, in his mother's. Within, she held a monster at bay that could destroy the world if she wanted it to. Her magic, the well inside her, was only a glimpse of what she was capable of. Even without it, she could do damage. He was afraid it meant someone had destroyed her, which tore him to shreds.

He didn't even know this girl.

He looked back toward the cave entrance and wondered when she would leave. He knew she would; it was only a matter of time. She'd leave this cave and then him.

As everyone had.

Everyone chose. And so far, they had chosen anything and everything but him.

Ky removed his trousers, enjoying the breeze. He raised his hands above his head, bent his knees, and dove. The wind rushed by him, his hair flapping in every direction until his body plunged into the sea. He had told River it was deadly cold, and even against his extra thick skin, he felt it like tiny little knives piercing him. It was precisely what he needed to get out of his head.

Ky opened his eyes, and the salt of the sea burned until they adjusted. The water was dark and cloudy. It was the most challenging time of year to fish with no new life yet. He pushed deeper into the water keeping his wings tucked tight behind him so they didn't slow him down. He kept going even as the air ran out of his lungs, his head becoming light. He kicked on.

Finally, he reached the warm spot, his body easing into the new temperature. He stopped and spread his wings to stabilize himself. Ky remained perfectly still as the sea resumed life around him. A few small pink fish were the first to investigate. They swam between his toes, tickling his skin. Next, a larger skeleton fish with no meat on its bones swam over his feathers. The light touch sent shivers down his spine. He waited, blinking slowly; his lungs burned. He wouldn't be able to hold out much longer.

The pressure around him shifted. The smaller fished scurried past him. Ky kicked his legs out in an arc just in time to miss the shark's teeth. He had underestimated its size; the thing was half his length. The beast darted forward, turning back on him to attack, teeth flashing, and stopped. It blinked, recognizing another predator when it saw one, and charged. Ky tucked his wings, sinking out of the shark's way. He flipped himself over, wrapping his legs around the upper half of the shark, and squeezed until he felt the flesh give way.

Ky could no longer hold the breath in his lungs. He released the shark's headless body until it floated in front of him and guided it with his head back toward the surface.

The moment they breached the air, he gasped, gulping down air. He blinked out the salt of his eyes and allowed his soaked wings to carry him back to the ledge with the shark's body in his arms.

Ky hoped she liked shark. He hadn't bothered to ask before he left, and as he moved back through the cave, he felt a little crazy.

His gaze landed right on her. A blanket was wrapped around her shoulders, and her knees were pulled to her chest in one of the coldest spots. River's eyes were bloodshot as they found his, and it pained him to see her that way. Was it him? Had he been wrong to bring her here? Ky had insisted she come, insisted she pretend to be dead for her own safety, but she had people who loved her. Missed her. Maybe even a beloved. She was around the age of marriage.

"What is that?" she asked, her voice raspier than it had been earlier. Ky must have looked confused because she continued. "In your arms. Is that your idea of meat?"

"Do you not like shark?"

Her face scrunched up, and she covered up her nose. "It's bleeding all over you, and you're wet."

"I'll dry. It is kind of you to be concerned."

She pulled the blanket around herself tighter.

Tang's head popped out of the sleeping cavern, and the dragon's eyes pierced the shark. At least someone appreciated him.

Ky jammed his hand into the squishy meat, grabbing ahold of the vertebra, and yanked, pulling it free. He extended the body to her.

"You can't be serious. I can't eat that."

Now Ky was the confused one. "Why not?"

"It's raw."

He could have sworn the girl's face turned a shade of green. *Raw. Right.* "The princess only eats cooked meat, Tang. What do we have to say to that?"

River stood, glaring at him, the blanket falling away from one bare shoulder. Ky couldn't pull his eyes from her tan skin. "I told you not to call me—"

Before she could finish her statement, Ky threw the fish above his head, and Tang took his cue, shooting out a huff of heat from her mouth and a tiny bit of fire.

The shark fell to the ground with a splat.

Ky looked back toward River, hoping for approval. Instead, he found the girl flat on her back, bare legs sprawled and her face ashen.

Dragon-damn. He had scared her. She would undoubtedly leave now. And why was she naked? Ky's gaze found the leather balled up near the farthest wall.

"Are you trying to kill me?" she snapped.

"No more than you are me."

She pulled the blanket around herself again. "What?"

"Nothing. The meat is cooked now."

She scoffed. "Clearly."

He clenched his jaw and rubbed his forehead, trying to keep his eyes off her. He had never felt so awkward about nakedness before. But she had been so concerned and even offended by his touch. He didn't want her to hate him or mistrust his intentions. He turned his back to her, searching the through his bag of supplies for a small knife, and cut it the shark meat into cubes. He offered one to Tang, who swallowed it in one bite, and threw another one toward where he could hear Thumper breathing.

"Do you want some or not?"

"Not," was her muttered reply.

"Fine. But it would keep you warm and help replenish you after you used so much energy."

"I said I'm fine."

Ky cracked his knuckles. This human was certainly infuriating.

He grabbed a chunk for himself and sat next to Tang, who peered over his shoulder eagerly. He ripped a small piece away and tossed it to the dragon before risking a glance at River.

Her chin was tucked between her knees, the blanket wrapped like a cloak around her. Her hair, which had long since fallen out of the braid, fell in kinked waves around her, leaves sticking out in places. Her hazel eyes were fixed on the spring, though he could tell she wasn't looking at anything in particular as silent tears fell down her cheeks.

"Her death weighs on you."

River jerked as if his voice had startled her. Her gaze fell on him, and she swiped at her cheeks quickly. "I killed her."

"Yes."

She blinked, startled by his words.

"And you will always hold that with you. The kills don't get easier. If they did, then you would be a monster. Like my father."

"I don't think that's how it works."

"I can still picture the face of every Spitarian, human, and creature. Even that shark. When I close my eyes, I see him. I see the unicorn from which I took that horn." He pointed at the ground where it lay.

"It's not the same." Her voice was a whisper, and her eyes were no longer on him.

"I see my brother's face when we were boys, and I see it again as I drove that horn through his heart. It was a sneer. He thought he was better than me. Better than Azalea. I saw the flicker in his eyes when he realized he wasn't, and the joy as he welcomed the blade." Ky's voice trailed off, and he looked up into the night sky. A few stars shone through the clouds above the hole in the cave.

"You killed your own brother?"

He could almost picture the disgust on her face, and he couldn't bring himself to look at her. Ky swallowed. Why had he shared that with her? He had never spoken with anyone about it. Not Wrynn, and certainly not Az.

"We all have things that weigh on us heavily. All we can do is carry them. Don't bury the emotions, but don't ride away on them, either." Ky stood and finally looked directly into her eyes. "I don't see a monster when I look at you."

Her mouth opened as if to speak, but then she closed it.

"I packed clothes in one of the bags. You should wear them, or you'll get cold."

Ky unfurled his wings and leaped for the hole in the ceiling, leaving the gaping girl behind.

Chapter Twenty-Five

River

River stared at him, slacked-jawed. The muscles rippled on his back as the wings extended and lifted him from the ground. His black-tipped white feathers caught the gleam of the moon as he disappeared through the hole and into the sky.

She hadn't known what to say to him. He'd killed his brother. He was a monster. Was she safe here? Was she . . .

She laughed at herself. *Safe?*

She was as safe here as she was anywhere else. Deep down, everyone was a monster, including her. Hadn't she proved that?

Imogen was dead. And River had killed her.

She pushed it down, balling it up with the rest of the stuff she couldn't deal with.

A cold gust of wind blew in, and River looked up to see the sky. A shadow was perched on the ledge, but in the next blink, it was gone. She was exhausted. She pulled the blanket tighter around herself and willed the tears to end.

The green dragon's tail had stopped thumping the moment Ky had left. He returned to where it had come from, farther down a passage of the cave. Tang, however, had decided to lie between her and the entrance. Its—no, her; Ky had called it a girl—orange eyes followed River's every movement and sniffed at every gust of wind.

Is the beast sniffing my blood because it's hungry?

The walls of the cave were lighter in some areas and darker and rockier in others. The place where the bedroll was tucked was a light section. It was like a little sleeping cove with rock on all three sides. She lay down and ran her hand over the stone. Small flecks of something scattered down on her face, and she coughed. She licked her lips, tasting salt. Were these salt rocks? She licked her finger and scratched at the surface and returned it to her mouth. It was definitely salt. She had never heard of such a thing. Logically it made sense. At one time, the sea must have carved this cave and left a piece of itself behind.

She closed her eyes and winced. The ball in her stomach was leaking, seeping memories through her. Every time she closed her eyes, she saw Imogen's face.

River scrambled out of the blankets and retched. Bile spewed onto the rocks. She tried to stop, but it just kept coming, burning her throat as it exited her trembling body.

She wiped her mouth with the back of her hand as she eyed the mess.

"Don't look at me!" she snapped at Tang.

The dragon obediently averted her eyes.

River deserved this. She had killed an innocent girl. It might have been an accident, but she'd been about to kill a man because her mother had told her to, which was just as wrong. All to get her throne . . . a throne she no longer felt worthy of. What had she been thinking?

River hugged her body tighter, but she just couldn't get warm. She sat up, bringing the blanket with her as she walked past Tang, whose orange eyes popped open.

"If you are going to kill me, just get it over with." She squared her shoulders. The dragon didn't move. "That's what I thought."

Tang sniffed the air and turned her nose from River.

"Are you telling me I smell?"

The dragon let out a short huff. She could swear the thing was speaking to her in her own strange way.

"Fine." River looked between the dragon and the glittering pool, the silver moon lighting it from below. Steam rose from the bubbling surface. Ky had told her not to, but what the Heldours? Nothing more could truly go wrong.

She walked toward the edge of the pool and looked in. The large crater in the rock was filled with gems that all glowed a different color. They changed with every ripple of the bubbles that poured up from the deep. She could feel the heat as the steam rose to touch her face.

The bubbles slowed for a minute, long enough for River to see herself reflected. She was a mess, her eyes dark-rimmed and her hair . . .

Are those leaves?

She pulled them free. The reflection rippled, and River watched as a small black vine shot out of her hand and moved up her arm, around and around. It tightened around her skin, pinching as it went. She tried to clench her fist, and thorns cut into her skin. Black blood dripped as if the poison leached from inside of her. She swore, holding in a scream, her body unable to move. She ground her jaw as every muscle tensed and stared at herself as her eyes flickered to an opaque white, all color vanishing. Her flesh peeled away as glistening teal scales grew in its place. She breathed slowly, trying to calm her nerves, forcing all of her willpower into closing her eyes against the pain of seeing herself turn into a monster.

A low growl startled her.

She opened her eyes, but there was nothing there, nothing but the bubbles formed into a shape of a star, reminding her of the birthmark on her neck.

She looked over her shoulder. Tang was on her feet now, eyes pinned on River. Another growl, this one louder, but it wasn't enough to stop her as she jumped in.

The water swallowed her. Warm tingles of heat ran up and down her arms like a current. River touched the bottom of the pool, hard gems cutting into her toes. She pushed herself back toward the surface. Her head broke the surface as water dripped down her hair.

Pins and needles spread through her arms. Her skin was aglow, a golden light shining through her as if she were being lit from within.

"Wow," she whispered.

"Get out of the pool." Ky's voice was a low growl as it echoed around the cavern.

River whipped her head behind her, and she covered herself, making sure her breasts were below the surface. "What are you doing? Get out of here!"

He let out a long breath. "I don't care for one second that you're naked, Princess. Get out of that pool now."

She pushed herself to the far wall. "I will do no such thing. You won't let me build a fire, and it was—"

Her stomach seized as the pit in her stomach exploded from within her. She threw her head back and screamed, light flashing from every surface. Her eyes became blurry as the world around her shifted.

Two Kys stood before her. One as he was now, shirtless, and another in full armor. The full-armor Ky was screaming, bent over a woman. No, not any woman. It was River. She was practically naked in a layer of . . . mud? She couldn't be sure. But she was older. There were silver streaks in her hair, and her chest was covered in blood. It pooled from a hole in her chest.

"What the Heldours?" she said to the real Ky, whose eyes were also trained on the vision next to him. He was saying something, but over the bubbles of the pool, but she couldn't hear what.

River's breath hitched as the warm tingles of the water turned to pain, like little teeth chewing at her. Her body began to thrash, and she started to sink.

"Dragon-damn!" he growled as she fully submerged.

She couldn't catch her breath; the water filled her nose, her mouth. Her chest tightened.

Good. This was what she deserved. She relaxed into pain and gave in to the pull of the dark.

Strong hands gripped under her arms and pulled her up.

No. No.

"Let . . . me . . . die," she croaked as water leaked from her mouth.

"Not today."

One forceful blow to her back expelled the rest of the water from her lungs.

River sputtered and coughed. She tried to clear her eyes. His hand clamped down on her neck.

"Oh!" River tried to wriggle free, but his grip tightened around her wet skin. She swung her arms wildly as a roar of frustration escaped her chest.

"Stay still, you feisty human."

Her arm collided with his face, and she threw herself from him.

Her body was on fire, burning from the inside. She clawed at her skin. Something was slithering beneath it. She felt like little worms were just beneath her skin. She scratched harder.

"Get them out!" she cried, tears streaming down her face.

Ky's deep brown eyes pinned her in place as giant arms wrapped around her body. She stumbled at first as her wet flesh slid against his bare chest.

The feeling of worms vanished. Nothing was in her skin.

"Look at me, River. Look at me." Ky's hand forced her chin toward him. "It's the magic. You can't control it yet. That pool. I told you not to go in it. It amplifies you. Refreshes you. But you're part human. It's too much magic for you."

She breathed slowly. "Let me go. I'm fine now." She tried to pull herself from his grip.

"My magic is holding yours at bay. If I release you before it has time to settle, it'll start up again." He sat, pulling her with him.

Her mind was at war, and she squeezed her eyes shut. She was being held by a Spitarian. Her magic was out of control. She had nearly just drowned, and she was okay with it.

Oh, Heldours.

"And you have to hold me like this to do that?" She regretted the words the moment they left her mouth. It felt so nice to be held.

"Would you like me just to touch your finger instead?"

She shook her head, afraid of saying the truth out loud. She didn't want him to let go. She pulled her knees to her chest.

"Okay." One hand released her, but the other tightened as he wrapped the blanket around her and turned her body so the blanket was between her bare back and his chest. She pulled it around her chest, covering herself. Her heart hammered in her chest.

"May I?" Ky said, his hand hovering over her hers.

River nodded.

He gently picked up her hand and placed it on her heart. She felt the elevated rhythm beneath her palm. "Do you feel this? This right here? This is real. You are real. Whatever whispers your mind is saying, whatever distortions it's trying to make you believe, it lies. Your heart is the only real thing; feel the beat of it. Don't ever let anyone make you think you aren't real or worthy. Or that you have done something so bad that you don't deserve to live."

His eyes met hers and held it as she let out a long breath and nodded again.

Her wet hair dripped down her back as he pushed it aside. Ky traced two fingers down the extensive scars on her back. She shivered under the light touch. His breath came in shorter bursts, and she could have sworn she felt his heart beat twice as fast. His fingers dropped away as he pulled the blanket tighter around her shoulders.

There was a long stretch of silence before his chest rumbled behind her. "When you were in the pool, you saw yourself dying on the ground with my arms around you."

River remained silent.

"When you were in the woods with the girl. What did you see then?"

"Fire," River breathed.

"Fire," Ky repeated quietly, his lips above her ear. She felt his every breath.

He shifted slightly but kept his arms wrapped around her body, clasped around her curled knees.

"Your magic is curious. I can't get a read on what it is. I can tell it's magic of the mind. Those were my images you were projecting. But the fire . . . I suppose it was the girl's. I just don't know. Maybe memories."

"But that hasn't happened. My hair was gray, and I was dying," River pointed out.

"Right."

River shifted at the heat of Ky's breath on her ear. She felt almost as if she was betraying Bass. It was uncomfortable but only for the briefest of moments. This was a necessary means to an end.

"—sense. Still, she would know best. Tracking her down to train you is the wisest choice, I think."

River realized she had missed half of what Ky had said to her. "What?"

"She's not easy to contact. She's in hiding from her *kupal*. Or maybe from her choices. I just think . . . no. She'll be able to teach you about this better than I. I think it's best if you and I part ways."

Part ways? River was so confused. "Who would be able to train me best?"

"Rhella."

River turned her head to see him, though his eyes were focused on the distance and not on her. Was her human body so unappealing to him? "And you trust her, this Rhella?"

"Yes. She helped me when my magic came in. It'll take me some time to contact her. I'm sure she'll agree." His chest heaved.

"What's your magic?"

Ky chuckled. "I guess I should've explained that earlier. I'm not sure what the word is in your language. I doubt there is one. But my magic is . . . like I can see a candle, a living flame within every Spitarian. I can sense how the light of the flame moves, telling me what type of magic the flame is. Also, how the smoke moves and rises tells me what they're doing with it."

"Others can't?"

"No."

River sucked her lip into her mouth, thinking about it. "But that's not all?"

"No. I can, with physical touch of the person, snuff out that flame as long as my flesh touches theirs."

River pulled the blanket around herself tighter, though she made sure not to shift the arm that touched her skin. "Everyone's magic is different?"

"No two Spitarians have the exact same magic," Ky said. "Why?"

"I guess I was trying to figure out why I have magic. Where it might have come from."

Ky cleared his throat. "Rhella would be the person to ask about that as well. I think your magic is okay now. I am going to release my hold on your powers."

Ky shifted behind her, and her flame reignited inside her. A tingle started near her heart and ran down her limbs. The pit in her stomach was no longer a giant ball but the size of a seed. A kernel of a flame.

"You okay?" Ky's voice was gruff as he released her, backing away.

River nodded slowly.

"I think you should put your clothes back on and get some sleep." She heard him rustling around behind her before he reappeared in front of her, holding a bundle of clothes. "I . . . you should wrap your hair."

She grasped at the ends of her hair, keeping a hold of the other side of the blanket. Her hair was a solid clump of frozen braid. What had she been thinking?

"I need to get going. Will you not go in again?"

"I won't," she promised, though the weight of everything still hung on her like a blanket. River had been born for so much more than this. She had no intention of dying like that. Or on the ground, for that matter, bleeding from her chest. She was going to die saving her people. That was how she was going to go. She owed it to herself. But she especially owed it to Imogen. She repeated the words over and over again until maybe she would start to believe them.

"I'm okay. Are you sure about them?" She pointed toward the dragons.

River heard a loud, almost indignant, snort.

"They might just ignore you now that I laid down the law. Get some sleep. I'll try to be back as soon as I can."

And with that, she watched muscles ripple on his back as he walked to pick up his blade and sheath it, then shoved his hands deep into his pockets. His white feathers caught the gleam of the moon, and then he was gone.

There was a huff of heat behind her, and she stood quickly, realizing Ky must have been leaning against Tang because the dragon was almost directly behind her.

"I'm just walking to warm my blood. I'm cold." She stood, walking away from the water's edge and toward the pile of discarded clothing. She had been foolish to take her clothes off, though she hated the sight of the leathers as they reminded her of Imogen. She quickly put the black leather back on, knowing it would keep her body heat in. She hated the feeling of them almost as much as the stiff formal dresses her mother forced her to wear. Neither of them felt like her. She just wished she knew what would feel like her. She took the longer dress Ky had given her and wrapped her hair in it as he suggested. How had he known? He most certainly had a woman in his life if he knew about hair.

River let out a sigh. "Is it always so cold in here?"

The dragon let out a snort as she shifted, her black scales catching in the moonlight that now hung somewhere over her. Her front leg was now open, her head tilted almost as if in invitation.

"You can't be serious."

The dragon's mouth opened, her tongue coming out, but her teeth remained hidden.

"I'm going to be that stupid girl they tell stories about because I trusted a dragon, aren't I?"

Tang rolled her orange eyes toward the ceiling.

"Did you just roll your eyes at me?"

River shut her eyes and debated. Well, she was dead anyway. What harm could it do?

She walked slowly toward the dragon, her hands on the blanket, her arms spread wide. "Don't eat me." She tried to imitate the way Ky had shouted at the other one.

The dragon didn't move as River slipped between her front legs and her neck. Heat radiated through her. Tang was warm like a log fire. River guessed it made sense since the dragon was filled with fire, but she no longer needed the blanket. The soft rumble of the dragon's breath was soothing. Tang inched her head closer until it nudged River's arm. She didn't hesitate this time as she placed one hand on Tang's head and ran it down the bridge of her nose, making sure not to run her hand the other way and catch the sharp edge of the scales.

A low rumble started around her, and Tang let out a soft puff of hot air.

"I see you like that. Now don't eat me once I fall asleep," River said softly, patting the dragon's smooth nose. It was black but had tiny specks of orange on closer inspection. "You are a pretty little thing. I'm not sure I've ever seen a color orange like that. So bright."

Thoughts of Imogen weren't the only things that plagued her mind. It was also thoughts about how it was possible for her to have magic. She had killed a girl with magic. A human had magic. Something deep down told her if she had magic, she couldn't be human. Then what was she?

River closed her eyes.

The ground shifted behind her, and River woke with a start. Her eyes opened as she hit the hard earth.

Tang was growling, and then something else was growling.

Something hard wrapped around her stomach—Tang's black tail. River couldn't move, and she could barely breathe. But Tang wasn't facing her; she was facing the entrance of the cave.

River couldn't see past Tang, but she noticed a green-scaled body she assumed was Thumper standing to the right. His spikes pointed and his leathery wings flared.

"Easy there," an unfamiliar voice called.

River elbowed Tang in the tail just enough for her to wiggle out of its grip. She dropped into a crouch to peer between the dragon's legs.

A tall, muscular silhouette stood at the entrance of the cave.

Chapter Twenty-Six

Ky

Ky had watched and waited above the cave until River had finally gone to lie next to Tang. He was in awe of her, of everything she could do. Everything she was. He was even a little jealous of his dragon at the moment. He wanted her to be at peace in his arms as she was against his dragon. The few minutes his arms had been wrapped around her hadn't been enough. The smell of roasted sugar assaulted his every sense and made him want to kiss the soft dip of skin where her shoulder met her neck.

He had to get away. She wasn't his, though he knew her smell would haunt his dreams. Maybe if he never went near her again, she wouldn't die. Maybe if he could stay away and keep his distance, he would save her.

He hesitated before taking off this time. He couldn't risk being far away if she decided to be reckless again.

He hadn't known her magic would explode the way it had, but he also should have guessed. Curiosity was going to kill him. He wanted to go back to his books because he couldn't remember everything he had learned about halfsprings. He wanted to be able to give her all the answers she would seek that would allow her to learn how to use her magic without exploding and harming herself or someone else. He could already see the toll the girl's death had taken on her. Her lips seemed turned down preeminently.

And why had he opened his mouth about Fiskane? Even after he'd told her, River hadn't asked about it, nor had she seemed scared of him. He was scared of himself, yet after a brief slack-jawed moment, she'd seemed to accept it. Accept him. Even his own family wouldn't do that if they knew the truth, that Ky had trusted his brother. Even though he shouldn't have, and he had paid the ultimate price. They both had.

Ky flew straight for Head Axel's balcony after circling the cave several times to make sure he wasn't followed.

No candles lit the side of the castle, though he could still see the vines that grew along the edges of the door. He landed with a soft thud, but the scene through the glass brought him up short. Belladonna was on the ground, kneeling next to Imogen's lifeless body. Her coral pict-paint had been peeled from most of her skin, leaving behind a bloody mess of welts. Axel's dark hair hung loose around his bare shoulders as his foot pressed down into her neck. His sister sat cross-legged in a *Crystolas* circle. Wrynn looked exhausted. His long blond-green hair lay loose, the soft waves touching his bone armor, and his face was the color of snow.

Ky ripped the vines off the door and flung it open. "What the dragon-damn is going on in here?"

All heads turned to him—even Bella's tilted up toward him. A large bruise covered the side of her cheek. Ky clamped his teeth together.

Axel's stunned mouth turned into a smile. "Kylane, my son!" He stepped away from Belladonna, who didn't rise, though her body twitched every once in a while. Axel placed his hands on his son's shoulders. "Where have you been? You look exhausted."

"I'm fine. I can't say the same for my comrade. What is going on?" Ky reached out his power, searching for Bella's, but her magical energy was missing. He met his father's eyes. "Return her magic. You're hurting her."

"We became concerned when you didn't immediately return with her," Azalea said, rising to her feet. Her large brown and gold dress swirled about her.

Ky pushed past his father and went to Bella's side, wiping the blood from her lip. "I had something to take care of first, but I thought you would want the princess, so I sent Bella ahead. I worked with her just like you asked. And this is how you treat her?" Ky lifted her to her feet, though she was a dead weight on his side. Her face was paler than usual, and her brows knitted tightly.

"I can't hear them," she gasped. "I can't feel him."

Ky's heart broke for her. It must feel like she was losing her *kupal* all over again. "I am not going to ask again. Or I will fly her far enough away from your hold."

Head Axel flicked his hand in annoyance, and Ky saw the energy as it rippled in the air. Her coral rope untangled with the Head's, and it flowed back into her body. Her body thrummed, and she let out a soft gasp of almost pleasure.

"Something's not right with her," Wrynn said, pointing to the other body on the floor. "It isn't the princess."

"You can read dead girls? Since when?" Ky asked.

Wrynn crossed his lanky but muscular arms. "No, but look at her nails, her hair, even her skin. That's no human royal."

Bella's eyes didn't slide to Ky's but the grip she had on his hand tightened.

"Go," he breathed into her ear. "Take the human."

"She isn't going anywhere!" Axel shouted, going toward her. "We need Bella."

Ky stepped in front of her. "This doesn't concern her." And then he turned to Wrynn. "You read her without her permission?" Ky shook his head in disappointment.

"You can't be serious," Wrynn said. "We had no idea if you were alive."

Bella shifted from behind him and grabbed the human, but she stumbled a little. Ky grabbed one of *Crystolas* off the floor and placed it onto the dead body hoping it would give Bella enough energy to get them both to safety. "Go."

"Kylane!" Azalea said indignantly.

"I trust her."

Axel's eyes narrowed at the door. Ky didn't turn, but he felt the coral magic behind him as it disappeared farther into the castle. "You didn't *kupal* with her, yet you're protecting her? What happened out there? Where is the princess? And don't try to convince me that child was her."

Ky narrowed his eyes at his leftwing. His own man, his best mate, had foiled his plans. Maybe if he'd trusted Wrynn with the truth from the very beginning, then none of this would be happening. It was his own fault. Now he had jeopardized everything. The princess was in danger.

"Kylane, where is Princess Castor?" The Head's voice came out slow and collected. "Don't make me force it out of you, son."

Ky shook his head. "I have recently come to know some things, and the princess has nothing to do with this. She is insignificant. Innocent. She doesn't need to pay her mother's crimes."

Head Axel stepped toward his son, his hands balled at his sides. "I always knew you were sympathetic to the humans, but I passed it off as you being your mother's son. I allowed it. But this? You disobeyed an order. Not only that, but you are allowing your mother's killers to get away with this and not holding them accountable. You are putting humans above your own blood." Head Axel shook his head as he beckoned Wrynn forward. "You will tell me what I want to know, son. This is for the best. Trust me."

"Wrynn, don't," Ky said, looking at his comrade. "Please."

"Just tell him what we need to know," Wrynn pleaded, his round face looked concerned, pale lips slanting down.

Ky remained silent.

"Then you leave me no choice," Head Axel said. "Read him, Wrynn."

Wrynn stepped forward, but he hesitated, keeping his emerald magic at bay. "I am his leftwing. If I do this, he will never trust me again."

Ky stilled, his eyes shooting between his leftwing and his father.

"Did—"

Azalea stood, interrupting Head Axel's words, and strode to her *kupal*. "This isn't a choice, Wrynn. You will do this."

Wrynn stiffened under her touch. "Az, please. Don't make me."

Her soft pink lips pinched together, and she squeezed his forearm.

Wrynn's eyes locked on Ky's, and he saw the moment the walls closed behind his eyes as he accepted the inevitable.

Ky threw his fist, knocking it into Wrynn's face. His friend fell back, but Ky threw his hand out, clamping his hand over his leg. Ky ripped the magic from him and pulled the green energy into him.

The air swirled with black mist. It formed a hand and yanked the green streams from him, as well as his own crystalline ones. Ky's eyes widened as it left him just as quick. He felt it as the magic was sucked from him, leaving him empty. He fell to his knees, gasping for breath, his chest exploding without his magic.

Axel bent down, his face level with Ky's. "This is for your own good. You will learn the humans aren't worth your pity."

He wanted to reach out and use his magic on his father, give him a taste of his torture, but he was powerless. Ky's magic was similar but different from the Head's. Ky could remove someone's power by touch. The Head needed only to be in their presence.

"How does it feel to be human, Kylane? Do you like it? Does it give you a thrill? I don't see the lure . . ." Axel trailed off, his eyes focused elsewhere. Ky knew he was thinking about Rhella. She'd thought being human was a fun game. "Wrynn, read him."

Ky searched Wrynn's face, but he had gone blank. Only a small trickle of blue blood leaked down his nose. Head Axel placed a hand on either side of his son's shoulders, holding him down. Wrynn's magic worked without touch, but for deeper digging into someone's brain, skin-to-skin contact strengthened it.

"I'm sorry," Wrynn said as his cold fingertips pressed to Ky's forehead.

"No, you're not," Ky growled as he felt Wrynn's magical fingers seep into his brain. It felt as though one of his index fingers was running along the inside of his skull. He shuddered as Wrynn reached his memories. Green fingers weeded through them as Ky watched images flash in his mind. He was seeing precisely what Wrynn was seeing. He tried his best not to think, not to conjure his most secret memories.

Wrynn's magical finger slowed on a harrowing memory of the day Emerray left their lives. Ky wished he could close his eyes and not see the look of pain in hers.

But Ky was powerless, and Wrynn continued on. His mother leaving was next. Ky struggled under his father's grasp. It was of no use. Ky saw his mother again in the bar as he had seen her only two moons ago.

Ky stared directly into Wrynn's diamond-shaped pupils. "Did you find what you're looking for?" he growled.

Wrynn blinked, and his green fingers began to shuffle again.

Until the hazel-eyed princess swam in Ky's mind.

Ky tried to think of anything else; he pulled up images of Tang and Thumper. Wrynn's fingers ripped away the images, searing Ky's mind. Ky's heart ached as every dream he had ever had of River flickered across his vision.

Ky ran his hand over her hair, and he attempted to smooth out the pieces that stuck straight up. She turned to face him, her smile wide and her eyes bright from the newly risen sun. She pressed toward him, held at bay by her swelling stomach. She rolled her eyes. Ky bent down, placing a kiss on either side of her belly. His hazel-eyed love patted his head gently.

"Do you have to go?" she whispered in his ear as he straightened, her voice as sweet as a kiss.

"I won't be long." He cupped her delicate cheek in his hand.

She crumpled at his touch, her body falling with a heavy thud onto the ground. Bright light flashed all around him as he moved with her. Blood seeped from her chest out an open wound. Ky's large hands instinctively pulled out the sword, a serpent curling around the handle before he covered the hole.

Then her face in real life, when he had first seen her, dark brown waves matted with leaves, the power pouring from her. The way the leather clung to her breasts. Her fresh mouth. The feel of her skin as he ran his fingers down the scars of her back. And Ky's last image of her, the lavender dress around her hair as she leaned against Tang. Her face had been so peaceful in sleep.

Ky wanted to curl in on himself.

She was going to die.

He had failed her.

Chapter Twenty-Seven

River

River stared at the figure as it shifted and stepped farther into the cave. The moon's glow revealed a tall, muscular woman. The orange stripe in her scaled armor brought out the orange in her red hair. The scales stopped halfway down her pale, milky arms. Even there, she was somewhat red, as if sunburn was a permanent thing for her. A weapons belt slung low on her hips held an assortment of shining weapons. The orange and black scales fanned out in a long skirt, revealing muscled calves. Bright green eyes flicked up to River—in question or recognition, River couldn't tell.

Her eyes were captivating.

Despite her size, pale skin, and angular cheeks, River didn't feel afraid because the woman looked . . .

The woman's eyes narrowed.

Those eyes.

She looked exactly like a younger version of River's mother. The only difference was the fiery flame of curls that billowed in the wind. She had only ever seen that color once. It reminded her of the girl from her dreams. The little girl with the wings and the father with dark red-brown hair.

River swallowed and pushed her shoulders back. "If you're here to kill me, I think you'd better turn around. Unless you want to be a dragon's dinner." River moved under Tang's front left leg, resting her hand on it casually. She traced the outline of the scales, counting them and trying to calm herself.

"I'm not here to hurt you, River."

River scoffed, pointing at the woman's waist. Strapped to the leather strip around her waist were hooks, a whip, and a few thin blades. "Could have fooled me."

Her eyes followed River's down to the belt she wore. She slowly unhooked them and tossed them at River's feet with a loud clank. "Now do you feel better?"

"Who are you?" River placed one foot on the weapons belt.

"Iris. I'm the daughter of the late Star *Heiralomun*. The heir to the Star throne."

River's face scrunched up in confusion, and she shrugged. "Well, I'm not sure what that means or has to do with me."

"The Stars are a Spitarian family that ruled alongside the Sparrows. They were killed because they began to sympathize with the humans, forming intimate relations with them."

Iris moved the hair from over her cheek, revealing a large, blackened mark that took up the whole left side of her face. "I used to have the mark on my cheek in the shape of—"

"A star."

Iris's lips lifted into a crooked smile. "Yes."

River remained silent. The woman was beautiful, and her black-and-orange armor, muscular physique, and the weapons under her feet indicated she was a warrior.

"It's a mark all those who belong to the Star family have. The clans who chose to live under their rule also carry it but in a different form. Ours is a natural birthmark. Theirs is a magical one. A birthmark we are all born with somewhere on our body. A symbol and a way to unify us."

"What does any of that have to do with me?"

Iris pressed her lips together. "My mother was human, but my father was a Star prince."

River stared at her. She was smaller than Ky but still bigger than River. But those green eyes. Those cheekbones. It wasn't possible.

"Have you ever wondered what happened to your father?" Iris said. "Or where that mark on the back of your neck came from?"

River touched the star on the back of her neck. She shouldn't have. But she couldn't help it.

"My mother is Elora Castor," Iris said slowly. "I am her firstborn."

River stepped back. "I don't think—"

"The man in the dream I pushed to you. It was a memory mixed with a little dream. I wanted you to know him. Your father, Rowan."

"Rowan," River repeated the name and tears pricked her eyes. "My middle name is Rowan."

Iris stepped forward, but both dragons let out a growl. She held up her hands. "I won't hurt my sister," she reassured them but didn't move closer. "He wanted you to have a piece of him even though he would never see you grown."

River shook her head. "Why would he leave me?"

"Oh, River." Iris's green eyes were cloudy with tears, but none fell. "He didn't have a choice. Elora made a lot of mistakes. She convinced him it might be the only way for both of his children to survive. For her to marry King Castor and convince him you were his. Have an heir."

River's mind spun. The magic. Her "father's" distance as a child. Why he always looked at her sideways.

Because she wasn't his. Because she was half-human.

"Where is he? My father? Our father."

"He's dead. There was a brutal massacre—all our people, almost. Our father was away visiting Elora while it happened. He lived for years in hiding, pretending to be dead. But Head Axel found out about his hiding location and had him killed."

"So he never knew me." River stepped closer to Iris, but Tang shifted, so her leg blocked the path. "This is all too much."

"I understand. I do. It was a lot for me when I learned about it as well. And I wish I had time to let you digest it, but you're in danger."

"Ky said I was safe here."

"Not anymore. I'm sorry—we have to go."

River took a few steps back, and Iris advanced. Thumper stomped his juniper-green foreleg, and the cave rumbled around them. The dirt and rocks scattered.

"Don't hurt her," River said, "but don't let her come closer."

Thumper's beady eye looked from her then to the girl and dipped his head. Had the dragon obeyed her? Was it because Ky had claimed her? She pushed the question aside for another time.

She turned her back on Iris and moved toward the glitzing light of the pool in the back of the cave. The moon reflected off the stones, sending multiple-colored beams all around it.

"I wouldn't get any closer to that if I were you," Iris said.

River ignored her. The power had overtaken her last time. But maybe if she only touched the water rather than her submerge whole body, she could control it better. Control it enough to get this girl claiming to be her sister far enough away from the cave for her to escape and find Ky. He was who she really needed.

"River, don't!" Iris shouted as River bent and stuck her finger in the bubbling water.

Heat spread up her finger through the rest of her body; the now-familiar tingling feeling accompanied it. A sensation of fear washed over her quickly, like a fresh sea wave smacking her square in the face and taking her under. But this time, she broke free enough to taste the fear. It tasted like losing control.

But it wasn't her fear. This fear belonged to her sister. Iris.

Ky had been wrong. These weren't memories; they were fears. Other people's fears. All her life, River had felt like she was fragile, like she couldn't handle the emotions. But this wave of fear didn't belong to her, and for the first time, she could truly tell the difference between other people's fears and her own. Almost like for the first time, she could keep her head above the water rather than letting it pull her under. It was an enormous relief.

"You're afraid of losing control," River said, one finger in the water and her head cocked to see Iris.

Iris's green eyes brightened with a twinkle before they darkened again. "You have power?"

"Don't you?"

"No. I mean, other than my size, and the extra strength, speed, hearing, and things like that. I have no other power. None that I can control or manipulate. I wasn't expecting that."

"So I don't have the size, the speed. I'm a normal human in that way, but I have power." River tried to process. Something inside her told her it was true. It all made sense, the heavy burden she'd carried. The magic. How she'd always felt different. How her mother treated her. The scars on her body. The way she had always been bent and shaped to appear human, to act human. Every time the wood cracked across her knuckles for allowing emotions to control her. River wanted to laugh aloud. She didn't want to believe it, but she did.

"Put us together, and we would be a full-blooded Spitarian." A short laugh escaped River's mouth. Iris smiled. "I feel it stronger here than ever before. I can sense the power differently."

"There are *Crystolas* in that water and being closer to them is probably increasing your abilities. It's what fuels magic."

"So you really are my sister?" River stood. The moment her finger left the water, she could still feel the fear coming off her sister, but it was all muddled with her emotions again.

"I am."

River walked toward her. This time, the dragons didn't get in her way. Ky was right; they understood every word. She stepped up to her sister and looked up into her green eyes. Her mother's eyes. River touched her sister's cheek, and Iris flinched before she leaned into the touch.

"We have to go."

"Can we wait 'til Ky returns? I owe him a thank you."

Iris shook her head. "But I promise we will find him and thank him another time. Right now, we must go. Trust me."

"Where are we going?"

"Away from here." Iris smiled. "I think it's about time we both had an honest conversation with our mother. Do you think these dragons will let us ride them?"

"Ride them? Are you insane?"

Two low rumbles gave River the answer she was hoping for. Iris was undoubtedly insane; even the dragons thought so.

Iris shrugged. "Only a little. But I climbed here, and it was a lot of work. I don't think you could handle it."

"Who says?" River placed her hands in the crock of her hips.

Iris held up her hands. "It wasn't meant to be an insult. Gather the blankets and food while I coax these beasts into flying."

River ignored her, gathering the bags. She didn't want Ky to worry about her. She wasn't quite sure why, but she felt a connection to him. What she had seen in the pool wasn't memories; it was his fear, and for the smallest of moments, she thought his fear was losing her. She shook that line of thinking away. They barely knew each other, and she certainly had no intention of becoming more familiar with the Spitarian than she had already become. She blushed. She at least owed him thanks.

"Maybe we can leave him a note."

"Why do you care so much? I mean, you've known him for like—hey, ouch!"

River looked over her shoulder to see Iris had pulled her hand away from Thumper's mouth. "I don't care. I just think he should know what's going on."

"Mm-hmm," Iris said, moving toward Tang instead, whose black body circled around her, dodging her outstretched hands playfully. "Okay, you little rascal. You have to let us ride you."

"Have you ever even ridden a dragon before?"

"No," Iris grunted. She ran full force at Tang, then turned at the last second and headed for Thumper. It happened so quickly River barely followed her movements as she flung her hand out for one of Thumper's side spikes and hurled herself over his side. The dragon roared and threw himself from side to side. "But it can't be too hard."

River crossed her arms. "You're fast."

"Not as fast as a full-blood, but I can hold my own." Iris held on through every buck as the dark green body arched under her.

"Are we just going to steal his dragons and fly them into the human territory? Doesn't sound like a well-thought-out plan. They'll shoot at us."

Iris shrugged. "They know their way home, I assume."

"And you think my soldiers—"

Iris arched one red bushy brow.

"Our soldiers, sorry. I just . . . I think I need to hear it from her first. The truth."

"I take no offense to that. She has a lot of explaining to do. Like why she stopped visiting."

"Visiting?" River stepped forward and placed her hand out to Tang, who ducked it as she came close.

"She came about once a moon until I was twelve. Shortly after that, she stopped."

River closed her eyes, trying to remember the times her mother had been out of the castle, but it was foggy. "Twelve . . . that would have made me—"

"Close to eight," Iris said as the green dragon sank to the ground in defeat. "Hand me that stuff."

River passed up the bags full of food. She had left one behind just in case. "My—King Castor died my seventh year of birth."

Iris nodded. "So she was a full-time queen. A little hard to play house in the woods with her secret family once all the responsibility was hers."

"The cottage with the little green door? And the black trees?" Even as River said it, she knew Iris would confirm it.

"And the garden. It's the memory I sent you."

"Sent me?" River was confused. She'd thought Iris didn't have magic but now didn't feel like the time to ask. "That was a private moment with your father. The wings he gifted to you. You didn't need to share it with me."

A small, sad smile shifted on Iris's face. "He was your father too, and you deserve to know how good he was. He would've wanted to give you the world."

River's throat swelled as her heart pounded in her chest. "So you didn't know about me?"

"Not until he was dying. He told me. And Rhella, Ky's mother, filled in the gaps—"

"Rhella?"

Iris gave her a somewhat puzzled look. "Yes."

The woman Ky wanted her to train with was his mother. Why hadn't he just said that?

"She took me in when I was fifteen. Left her family behind and took care of me." Iris shifted and loosened something around her, a thin belt and a leather strap with a knife. "Use the step to secure the blankets around yourself. This is going to be a cold ride. You think you can get on that thing?"

Mothers leaving children behind didn't seem natural to River. She had always thought she and Bass would have children in the future. They had spoken about it often. But she wouldn't wish an absent mother on anyone. She knew how that felt. She wanted nothing more than to comfort her mother about everything including how her people were fairing on the border. Make her mother do something about it.

"I think I'll manage better than you, sister," River said, turning to Tang. "May I ride you? And then you can tell Ky you got me safely home?"

The large orange eyes came close until the dragon's nose pressed into her chin. Her front legs shifted and bent.

"Then let's fly." River extended her hand toward the dragon. Her mother had a lot of explaining to do. "To Elora Castor."

Chapter Twenty-Eight

Ky

Ky's body screamed.

His heart raced as everything came crumbling down around him. He did the only thing he thought he could do with Wrynn's fingers in his mind.

He pushed every thought toward Azalea, pulling at his own memories of his sister. The ones of her killing the Star people. All those times she had passed out from exhaustion. He flooded his mind with the life they'd been living, of the secrets she'd hid from her *kupal*, the ones that made her look every bit the monster their father was. About how her power and using it for the Head was killing her slowly.

She would never forgive him. But he didn't care; she would be alive. They all would. Even if it hurt Wrynn, he didn't care. He pushed it at him. Wrynn needed to understand why Ky had done it all these years. Maybe he would even help.

I was only trying to protect her, Ky whispered into his mind, hoping Wrynn could sense it. His sister wasn't blame-free in all of this, and if she continued down the path she was on, he was afraid she would never come back from it.

Wrynn's fingers withdrew from inside his head. His round face puckered with anger. He looked over his shoulder at his *kupal*. She cocked her head as he stared at her.

Azalea brought her hand up to her lips as her skin paled. "Wrynn, I can explain."

Axel stepped forward. "Whatever secrets Ky has shared, I'm sure you're aware we do what is necessary to protect this kingdom. And you would be wise to keep those secrets to yourself. We wouldn't want your father to find himself with one less son."

"Father." Azalea's gasp was merely a whisper.

Wrynn turned back to Ky, his face turning to stone. "Of course. I have seen all I need to."

Head Axel stepped away from his son, and Ky felt his magic slowly trickle back in. Head Axel patted his son's back gently, but Ky shook his hand off.

Axel ignored the insult. "And where is she?"

"In a cave by the sea. It shouldn't be too hard to locate." Wrynn stepped back, placing his hand on Azalea's shoulder. He shook his blond-green head slowly at Ky.

"Good, go get her," Head Axel growled.

"I'll do it." Ky stepped forward. "It'll be shorter. I know where it is."

"No," Wrynn interjected. "I think it would be better if you stay here and tell your family about your mother."

Ky's lips curled, his nostrils flaring.

"Rhella is alive," Wrynn added, his back to Ky as he walked toward the balcony doors. His emerald wings spread wide.

The door flung open, and Wrynn was gone.

"What did he just say?" Azalea said, staring after her *kupal*. Her eyes slowly turned to her twin. "No, you wouldn't keep that from me. From Father."

Ky swallowed. He had no idea how to play this.

"Tell me this isn't true!" Azalea demanded. As she stepped forward, the long dress she wore swayed.

Ky slid his eyes to his father, who had sunk back against the sleek black desktop, his eyes on the palms of his hands.

"Kylane!" His sister's brown and gold dress swished at her hips, fanning out as if expanding with her anger.

Ky worked his jaw back and forth. "She's alive. I saw her while looking for the princess. She told me the true prophecy about the princess, not the one Queen Elora portrayed."

"No." Head Axel's voice was low, but it broke over the simple word. "No."

"She asked me not to tell you. She had visions that if we knew, it would be the death of us."

"No," Axel said a third time, his eyes still on his fist, which he opened and closed several times.

Azalea sank to the ground back in her circle and closed her eyes. Ky felt the magic shift around the room. Crystalline cords bounced from one *Crystolas* to the next and then into his sister.

"What are you doing?" Ky said. "Az, whatever you're thinking, let's talk about it." Ky's heart pounded in his chest. He wanted to scold himself for it, but part of him was afraid of his own sister.

"I am going to find my mother," she snapped.

"She doesn't want to be found," Ky spoke softly.

Head Axel stepped between Ky and his sister. "She is my *kupal*. I would know if she was alive. I don't feel her. Someone tricked you."

Ky should have thought of that. Of course. He could have spun it into a lie. But it was too late to go back now. Azalea would locate her if she was using her magic. "She faked her death to protect us. Had Kisling lie for her."

"You saw her?" Axel asked.

Ky nodded slowly. "She's in her human form. I'm not sure you'll find her, Az."

"Why?" was all Axel said.

"The bond snapping messed with her magic." Ky sank down next to his sister, disrupting the circle. "Az, this is what she wanted. She's trying to protect us. Aren't you both sick of fighting with the humans? Of living in fear based on an ancient battle that wasn't even ours? They didn't kill her. They've never killed one of our kind in this world. But we've killed hundreds, maybe even thousands over the years. The prophecy is meant for all of us to live together in peace, coexist, maybe even procreate. We don't have to live in fear if we live together."

Azalea gripped his chin hard, her cobalt eyes pinning him in place. "You're talking crazy."

"I'm not—"

Head Axel stepped forward, kneeling in front of his son. "I understand your mother has filled your head with all these lies. But we will never be safe to live and coexist. One human will turn against us, learn our secrets, and know how to kill us. We will be finished. I'm doing this to protect us."

Ky shook his head. "Don't go after her. You would be killing us all. She said if we knew, we would die."

Head Axel ignored him, stepping back. "Find your mother."

"Az, please. Listen to reason. Do you really want to do what you did to the Stars to all the humans? Don't you feel bad? It was wrong. This is all wrong. You can't win. Kill entire races or groups of people because we're different from them? We should embrace those differences, benefit from them."

"They have nothing we can benefit from." Her eyes cooled to a deeper blue.

Ky stumbled back at her words. He'd thought she could be reasoned with. "We're dying off. Our magic is dying off. We could procreate with them. Save our race."

"That's not even possible," Az snapped without looking at him. Her power began to spin again, flicking right through him.

"It is. I've done the research. It happened in the old times. And it's happened here. I met a halfspring—"

"They're abominations!" Head Axel said. "Kylane, stop speaking of such things."

"They are *good*," Ky finished, backing toward the open doorway. If his family wasn't going to listen, he would have to stop Wrynn from bringing River here before it was too late. "I'm doing what I think is right."

Pain lanced his left shoulder, and he flinched, his eyes flicking between the blood leaking from a fresh wound on his shoulder, the edges of the cut turning bleached white, and the unicorn blade stuck into the wall behind him. Ky's arm was on fire.

"I don't want to hurt you, Kylane. Please, listen." His father's face was pale, his hands out to his sides, pleading. "I'm only doing what's best."

Ky took a step back, covering the wound with his hand as blood pooled and slipped down his arm. He felt the poison of the unicorn blade eating away at his flesh. He was careful not to let his finger touch where it had also touched.

"You should be fine if you just sit here and let it heal. I can even help it along." Azalea's voice was soft as she held up a *Crystolas*. Her eyes were round moons.

"You tried to kill me," Ky sputtered at his father.

"No, Kylane, I would never. I was only trying to prove a point. Please sit down and let your sister look at it."

Ky scoffed. "Like you didn't kill my brothers before me."

"That was different." The Head's hands flexed at his sides. "You know it has always been tradition to allow the strongest to live. How else would we know who was right to rule?"

"Right, because that makes sense. And what point were you trying to make by hurting me?"

"That we aren't invincible, son. Suppose a human got ahold of these? We would go extinct." Axel stepped toward his son again, but Ky took a step back.

"You ordered all the horns to be stripped from the poor creatures and brought here. I don't think there are any unicorns left. What's the harm if you have them all right here in this office?" Ky showed him his bloody arm, and Axel flinched. "We're going extinct anyway. Our magic source is fading. You both can feel it. In a few hundred years' time, we won't be able to produce any more offspring the way we're going. Where does that leave us then?"

His father would have to kill him to stop him from going after River. He turned his back on Axel and took a few steps before his arm felt as though it was going to explode. His father's cords wrapped around his crystalline flame inside and snuffed it out.

Ky fell to his knees as the poison spread down his arm fast. Without his magical healing ability holding it at bay, the poison rocked through the rest of the body as his skin leached of color.

"Az, knock him out and heal that wound before it kills him."

"No!" Ky's whisper was a gasp as the world turned black.

Chapter Twenty-Nine

River

A smile lit River's face as she pulled herself up and onto the dragon's back. She bent toward Tang.

"Thank you. I didn't think I could jump as high as her." River hoped her words were whispered.

Iris chuckled. Her hearing was undoubtedly superhuman.

Tang let out a low growl, and then Thumper followed.

"Oh stop!" River said, patting gently. "This ride won't be that bad."

"Septing stars!" Iris swore. "We are too late. Get her out of here."

River looked from the cave of the entrance, where the dragons certainly couldn't exit, and then toward the mouth at the top of the cavern. A shadowy figure covered the hole, wings spread wide.

"Run," Iris breathed.

River slid off Tang's back, and the dragons repositioned themselves between her and the cave's entrance. River could run, but there was nowhere for her to go. The entrance to the cave was a drop-off to the sea, and Ky had warned her it was deadly. She was stuck.

"No." Even if she wasn't stuck, this woman was her sister. She wouldn't leave her. Not because she knew her or loved her, but because Iris knew parts of her story River didn't. Maybe one day they could be sisters; it was a hopeful prospect that made River want to smile. But for now, this woman was all she had left of the missing piece of herself.

Neither dragons' teeth were bared, but they were still growling. The moon glinted off emerald scales. This Spitarian had wings that looked like Thumper's stomach and almost the same color too. It certainly wasn't Ky.

Tang's tail whipped out and pushed River toward the small alcove covered in long, rock-like spikes from the ceiling and the ground like a row of teeth. This cave had jaws. River pressed against Tang's tail, but the dragon didn't budge. Instead, she blocked River in, pressing her back farther until she had to squeeze into the small space between them.

Tang's growl deepened. River suspected the warrior was getting closer.

"Tang, Thumper. Don't be like this. You know me. I'm just here for the girl. Ky asked me to retrieve her."

Ky.

For some reason, she had a hard time believing Ky would send anyone but himself to retrieve her. From her spot, River saw her sister slip off Thumper's back. One second her red hair was in the air; the next, she was gone.

"I know you," the male said.

"Oh yeah?" Iris replied. "So then I think you'll understand why the human will stay with me."

River bent, trying to get a better viewpoint. She certainly wasn't going to hide while her sister was out there fighting her battles alone. If the dragon-man wanted her, he would have to fight her as well.

River ran her hand down Tang's stiff tail. The way the dragons were growling gave River a strange feeling that regardless of whether or not they'd been friends before, they wouldn't let her go without a battle.

River bent her legs, about to dart out between the small crack, but something brushed the back of her calf. She spun and bent her finger, grazing a bag stuck between the formations a little farther back. She squeezed her arm through the opening, her face squished against the formations. She licked her lip. These were more salt formations. She grasped the bag and pulled it toward her. A cloudy gem the size of her fist tumbled out, and she grabbed it. Heat tingled quickly up her arm, straight to the center of her chest.

Had Ky stashed this whole bag of Crystolas here?

The tingling increased the longer she held it, throbbing near her heart until her whole body no longer shivered with the cold but vibrated like it was coming to life with a fierce heat. She closed her eyes, enjoying the sensation. It was similar to the feeling of the hot spring but less intense.

Fear surged all around her. Fear that didn't mingle with her own. Each tasted different. Iris's fear tasted of bitterness, of losing. So different from the man's burnt cloves. Then there was her own.

But it was in the back of her throat. It was almost inconsequential compared to theirs.

Tang's tail whipped fiercely back and forth, but she stepped over it.

The dragon's orange eyes pinned her in place, but River stood beside her sister and squared her shoulders.

"I don't think you thought coming here through. You're scared of betraying those you love. But I think you know that by coming here, you already have. And that scares you more."

The male's eyes went from the glowing stone in her hand to her face. His clean-shaven jaw dropped, and he mumbled, "Dragon-damn."

"The only dragon around here about to be damned is you, dragon boy."

Iris snorted beside her.

One tame blond eyebrow went up. "I can see why he's so anxious to keep you hidden. And you," he said, looking Iris over top to bottom. "You're the one who knows where Rhella is. I'm sure the Head would love to get his hands on you."

Iris smirked as she pulled a thin, silver blade no wider than a stick from her belt.

"And what do you expect to do with that thing? Pick my teeth?"

She flicked her wrist, and the front part elongated into a shiny metal ax. "It parts skin from bones easier." She shrugged. "The only way I like a male is thin sliced." Iris twirled her wrist, and the ax spun over it and into her other hand.

"I would say fight until neck break, then? But I have a feeling neither of you would wake up," the male said wryly.

Iris charged, ducking low and swiping his feet. The winged man lunged, going for her throat.

"Wrynn, I think Rhella would be quite disappointed in how you turned out," Iris growled, his hand on her throat.

His nostrils flared. "You have no right to speak of her."

River took a few quick steps forward. She switched the glowing stone to her nondominant hand before slamming her fist into the base of his spine, making Wrynn curve inward.

Iris reached for her belt and whipped out a long rope. Its silvery length unraveled at her hip toward the floor. She flicked it at his feet. Gold barbs shot out of the smooth surface, tearing at his bare feet. He stumbled backward, the barbs releasing but pulling his flesh with them.

"You play dirty," he said, "using weapons. You aren't a Spitarian." Wrynn balanced on the balls of his bare feet, avoiding the fresh blood that poured from them.

"I am a halfspring, after all. My moves reflect my upbringing." Iris flicked the whip at his bare feet, catching the skin on top and yanking it free. Droplets of blood flicked off the whip. She cracked it off the ground next. The noise sounded like thunder echoing throughout the space.

He backed right into Thumper. River hadn't seen the dragon move, but there he was, snapping over Wrynn's shoulder.

"You don't know me." He didn't balk at the dragon, almost like he knew it would never hurt him. He didn't fear it, but River knew precisely what he did fear.

"You are Azalea's *kupal*—" Iris began.

"Is that the pretty woman with crazy blue eyes?" River asked her sister.

Wrynn cocked his head and stared at her. "You want to go swirling around in my head? How about I swim in yours?"

River felt fingers move across her face. She swatted them away, but nothing was near her. Her skull throbbed as the invisible fingers slid inside her mind. Imogen flashed before her eyes. Her mother. Bass. Then back to Imogen and her death. The fire that had consumed her. The fire that was fear come to life.

"Imogen, huh? You like killing humans? Maybe you halfys are more like us than I thought."

River took a step back. The fear she could taste now was her own. The smell of burning flesh clung to her nostrils, invading every sense. She heard Imogen begging for help. Pleading for River to stop. River's fear consumed her, a fear of what she was becoming or what she already was . . .

She squeezed her eyes shut as the feeling overpowered her.

Behind her closed eyes, she saw herself the way she had in the hot spring, as the monster she was. Horns and scales. Magic and death. Pain and suffering. Grief and more death. Blood. Blood covered her body, her hands. She bit the inside of her lip. Her fears had already come true. All of them. She wasn't worthy of the crown. She wasn't worthy of Bass. She wasn't worthy of anyone. Anything.

Someone shouted her name.

River pried her eyes open and tried to steady her breathing. But her chest rose and fell quickly, her pulse racing.

"River, listen to me!" Iris grabbed her face roughly. "Whatever happened with that girl Imogen. I'm sure you didn't mean to kill her."

"It was an accident. I didn't know it was her." Though she would have been just as guilty if she had killed who she'd intended. River's gaze flicked between the two, but she felt the fingers slide away.

"You have something dark in there," Wrynn said. "I don't want anything to do with it. Head Axel should dispose of you when he's done before that contaminated magic spoils us all."

"Shut up! Don't let him into your head." Iris pressed her fingers harder into River's skin. "Don't let him near us," she shouted over her shoulder to the dragons.

River stared into her lush green eyes, and it was like the rolling green hills of her home. There was something comforting about it.

"Listen to me. Your magic works differently than theirs. It's not predictable because you've never used it. Because you've stamped it down your whole life. It's a part of you. It's the scary, dark part of you. But still *you*. If you don't learn to understand and accept that part of yourself, you'll never be in control. Trust me." Iris growled—a fierce, deep noise that erupted from her stomach. If River wasn't so deep in her own monster, she would have been afraid of Iris. "I won't lose you too!"

"Is that why you fear control?" River gasped, trying to reel herself back in. When she closed her eyes, all she could see was Imogen's crying face.

"She can't control that!" Wrynn yelled, trying and failing to edge around the dragons toward the sisters. "I've seen a magical possession before. My brother had it. She won't last."

Iris's bright green eyes stayed locked on her sister's in the cocoon the dragons had created between their bodies. "Don't listen to him. Focus on me. On my words."

River shivered as the magic coursed through her body.

"Would Ky have brought you here if he thought you couldn't figure it out? He brought you here, not to Head Axel," Iris breathed. "You want to know why I fear losing control? It's because when I do, when I can't control myself, I lose things. People. Like our father. I won't lose you. I'm here now. Focus on me."

River tried to focus on the emotion in Iris's voice, but she couldn't get past the wall of fear holding her down. It was as if the ball of emotions she'd stuffed down was floating in front of her face, suffocating her. It was so heavy. She wanted to feel the warmth her sister's words should bring, but nothing could move past the emotions clawing inside her already.

"Everything feels wrong."

"Let go of the *Crystolas*, River."

She looked down. She had almost forgotten she was holding it, though the thing still glowed. The rock was certainly dimmer than before. River breathed and focused on the fear inside her, placing each back where it belonged. Her sister's fear, her own fear of becoming a monster like the childhood stories. And Wrynn's fear of betrayal.

She placed the tip of her tongue on it until the words flowed from her mouth. "It's you and me, my *kupal*. Until the end. No matter what, beloved are those with bonds like golden rainbows and Sparrows who have dreams." The voice wasn't her own. It was honeyed and melodic as it left River's mouth.

Wrynn froze, and Iris leaped at the opportunity. She ran full speed at him as he whipped around and looked above, searching for the voice. Azalea, his *kupal*'s voice. The crazy blue-eyed girl River had seen in his fears.

Iris lashed out with the ax, cutting at his stomach. He grasped at the wound. River could have sworn she saw a blue bone where his rib cage should be as deep blue blood spilled over. Were Spitarian insides like hers?

River squeezed her hand, the gem giving way. It turned to dust in her palm, scattering as her breath whooshed from her.

"Get on the dragon," Iris roared, throwing herself onto Thumper's back.

River ignored her, springing back toward the cave's jaw and pushing through the salt formations. She grabbed the bag full of *Crystolas* and hurtled toward Tang's kneeling body.

She didn't even need to utter a command. The dragon took off, nearly flipping River off before she wrapped herself around the dragon's neck.

River watched from above as they flew away. Wrynn stumbled to his feet, but she could have sworn he smiled at her, his white teeth flashing in the moonlight as a small trickle of blood leaked down the side of his mouth.

Chapter Thirty

Ky

Ky woke to loud voices. The pain in his arm had dulled, but it was still there. He had healed fully, his skin back to a normal color but his chest felt empty, his magic missing. His arms were stiff at his sides. Something burned against his back, eating away at his flesh.

He cracked his eyes open. The floor was beneath him, but his back leaned against one of the legs of his father's unicorn desk.

Of course.

He was tied in place. Not by ordinary rope or any that could be seen by the naked eye, but by a thin crystalline cord that had a slight blue tint. His sister's magic was roped around him, keeping him in place.

He let out a huff as he stared at the people in front of him, the ones he'd once called his family. Now he wasn't so sure. Blood was supposed to surpass all else. He had walked away from that a long time ago. At least, he thought he had. But here, in this moment, as he stared at his father, who screamed at Azalea and Wrynn, a hand squeezing on each of their arms, he knew the truth. Blood could never overpower what he knew deep in his bones was right. His magic and his blood sang for it. Blood wasn't stronger than this. Had it ever been?

Wrynn shook his head. He held his stomach where dried blood crusted over a thick slice that ran from his ribs to his hips.

Interesting. Someone had tried to filet Wrynn . . . but Ky hadn't left River with a weapon. *Tang?*

"Father, please stop. I don't have enough magic to heal this after taking care of Ky," Az said. Pain laced her voice. She touched her stomach as if she too were in pain. "I'm sorry."

Wrynn kissed her cheek. "I am already healing."

"I don't understand," the Head growled.

"Father, please, this isn't his fault." Her hands fisted in the gold flowers of her dress. Dark circles shadowed her eyes; she was exhausted.

Wrynn, Ky growled inside his mind. *Where is she?*

Wrynn whipped his head in Ky's direction as he answered the question aloud. "A redheaded thing—the one from your memories—saved her, and they flew off on your dragons."

"And you didn't go after them?" the Head demanded.

"Why not?" Ky asked, though he was so glad the male hadn't.

Wrynn turned away from Ky to face Head Axel. "Princess Castor has powers. She's not human."

Ky stiffened. He'd wondered if Wrynn had believed the memory. He hadn't said anything before, but Ky knew Wrynn must have seen it for himself this time.

"She was out of control," Wrynn added.

The hot spring. The *Crystolas*. Ky had worried, knowing if she was close enough to the bag he had stashed, it might become a problem.

"It's not possible." Head Axel paced, his gaze flicking between the two males.

Ky scoffed. "She's a halfspring. I told you it was possible years ago after I read the records."

"Who's her father?" Head Axel finally turned to look at his son. "Who's the mother?"

"Elora Castor is her mother, no doubt about it," Wrynn said, scratching his hairless chin. "She looked like her. Human. And I read her mind."

Ky stiffened at the thought of Wrynn's fingers on River, inside her. He seethed. His leftwing had utterly betrayed him. There was no coming back from this. It was Ky's fault. Maybe if he had trusted Wrynn, this wouldn't have happened.

"And the father?" Axel directed the question again at Ky.

Ky felt the bands tightening around him. He focused on his sister. Her face was blank, impassive, but fire raged in her eyes. He noted the rigid set of her jaw, the fists pumping at her sides.

"Can you stop?" he said.

Her eyes widened, but the hold on him released slightly. "I should pop you."

"I would still be here, and you would only have a mess on your hands."

"I know," Az said, looking away from Ky.

"Are you two finished? The father?" Head Axel bent down to his son's eye level. His deep brown eyes were clear, and his nostrils flared slightly as if searching for the lie himself.

Ky's head spun. "I was going to look into it. But you scared her off before I could do any further investigating. Maybe you should have listened to me."

Axel stood. "I want her dead."

"No!" Ky shouted.

"What?" Wrynn's face paled.

"You both heard me. She shouldn't exist." Head Axel placed his hands on the desk above Ky. Ky wished he had enough strength to kick his legs out from under him.

"What if she belongs to one of our own?" Wrynn's voice was quiet but firm as he threaded his fingers through Az's. "That could cause civil war. Worse if she belongs to the Skys, and they find out we killed her. That war would divide our people. I doubt we'd win in the end."

"He's right." Azalea brought their joined hands to her heart. "We can't fight the Skys. We would be far outnumbered."

"You took on the Stars, daughter. You can do this too."

Azalea stiffened, her eyes flicking to her *kupal,* who flinched at the words. "At least let us figure out who she belongs to first, and then we can deal with her."

"Fine." Head Axel said, throwing his hands up. "If that's what you wish, daughter."

"Wrynn and I will go at once then." Azalea looked at Ky, then back to Wrynn.

"No. If your brother wants the child to live so badly, he and Wrynn will go while we go after your mother."

"Will you be okay?" Azalea said, her hand cupping Wrynn's cheeks.

"Yes. Mere flesh wound. It'll heal." Wrynn kissed her gently on the lips. "Good luck finding your mother. We can discuss the rest at another time." His smile was tentative.

Azalea turned her cobalt eyes to Ky and bore into him, cold as ice. "If you allow anything to happen to him, Kylane, I will make you suffer."

Ky felt the threat run up his spine. His sister had never spoken to him that way. Had never looked at him as though he meant nothing to her.

"I understand," he said to her retreating form.

"Where's your armor?" Wrynn asked.

"In some woods near the Castor border."

"We can get it on the way," Wrynn said as he grabbed his bone armor from the corner. He slid it over his taupe-colored skin, clearly ignoring the pain in his stomach as he put it on piece by piece. "Those dragons of yours better behave."

"Someone going to untie me?" Ky asked, ignoring Wrynn. He hoped his dragons didn't, and that Iris and River were hidden safely.

Head Axel walked to his son, Ky's unicorn blade in his hand. "I am going to trust that you do good by your family. By your blood." The magical cord that held Ky's magic released it, and it rushed back into him. Ky's chest heaved with a deep breath. "Can I trust that?"

"Yes," Ky said, keeping his gaze level with his father's. He extended his hand for his blade.

His father placed the blade in Ky's hand, then pressed his fist to Ky's chest. "Good. We will bring your mother home."

Ky strapped the blade back onto his thigh. "Let's go," he growled at Wrynn over his shoulder.

He'd do what was right for his family even if they didn't believe that. He just hoped that one day they'd all understand and maybe forgive him.

But if not, he would live with that weight like he lived with the weight of what he'd done to his brother.

Chapter Thirty-One

River

"Let's land here!" Iris shouted over the wind.

River's hands still shook, as they had through the whole ride. She tried to pull herself back into control. Not by shoving everything down, but by truly feeling it, letting herself ride through the emotions. Sensing the waves of fear from her sister every time she turned to look at her. It hadn't become easier to tell the difference between the emotions, but now she at least knew the overwhelming ones that seemed to come out of nowhere weren't always hers.

She might be a monster, but she wasn't going to be an out-of-control monster. She'd learn to control this, to channel it and deal with it like she'd always done with everything else in her life.

They landed on the edge of the lake within the castle gates.

A mass of emerald uniforms ran toward them, spears and swords drawn and pointed in their direction.

River let out a deep breath as she took in the faces that approached them with wariness.

"Let me do the talking," she said as she untied the blanket from around her shoulders and adjusted the small weapon at her thigh she'd taken from Iris. The ground barely shook beneath her as she dismounted the dragon.

"Yes, Princess, whatever you say." Iris's sarcastic tone was evident by the massive grin she spread across her face and the bow she gave upon her dismount.

River shot her a glare over her shoulder. "You're a princess too. I wouldn't be so quick to run that mouth, sister."

Iris smirked.

The first face she saw was gray-eyed, and his grin spread from ear to ear with a thunderous laugh.

"You're supposed to be dead. But the princess lives!" Leon shouted the last part to the rest of the men. A round of cheers went up all around. Leon's nose had recently been broken; it sat crooked on his face, and fresh bruises lined his cheeks. Somehow, she knew it was her fault. He was supposed to be guarding her, and she had turned up dead.

"Fly high above in case we need you," River whispered to Tang before patting her side. "Thumper, find Ky."

The dragons didn't wait as the humans got closer. Their giant wings spread, and they were in the air.

"Let them be. They saved me," River commanded the men as they got closer, directing arrows toward the sky. Two giant blotches blocked out the sun for only a few moments before they were gone.

"And her?" a soldier said, his gray hair slick against his skull.

"She has business in the castle. You'll escort us both." The men hesitated, but River glared at them the best she could, trying to make her face as impassive as her mother's. "Was my command not clear?"

"You heard the princess. Let's get to it," Leon shouted to the men. "It's good to see you alive," he whispered.

"Mm-hmm," River said, trying to keep in step with her sister's long legs.

"We can't let her in here." The gray-haired guard ran ahead of them, blocking their way around the lake.

"I think you'd better move before I decide you're no longer fit for duty." River brushed past him and moved around the lake closer to the castle. The sun glistened off it, though it wasn't nearly as pretty now that she'd seen the sea.

River eyed the stone buildings. One large structure anchored the center, and three newer gray stone wings bordered the original building. Small buildings scattered the rest of the lawn, but nothing was near the lake. Large balconies lined every window off the front, giving off the feeling of iron cages. Everything that wasn't stone or iron was glass.

"It's bigger than I imagined. She always told stories about the castle. She complained about it being too confined," Iris murmured under her breath.

It had always been a cage, and each step River took toward it made her stomach sink more. She shot Iris a sideways glance, but no one said anything else as they made their way across the grass and onto the stone pathway that led to the stone castle.

"Riv!" a familiar voice shouted.

River turned in time to see Laya barreling toward her, her arms as wide as her grin.

"Oh, Riv!" Laya's voice cracked. Tears streamed down her face and she pulled River into a hug.

"Laya." River pulled back and wiped her tears. "I'm okay, I promise. We'll catch up soon, but where is my mother?"

"The sunroom with Bass." Laya nodded toward the closest balcony.

Two new guards stood at the front door, both clad in ruby red. River frowned in confusion. She stood for a minute, looking up at the large marble doors. She waved her hand and then arched an eyebrow at the soldier before he finally opened the doors for them. They entered the main door, crossing the checkered tile floor, and headed up the first set of stairs to the left. It was only five small stairs up to the sunroom, but with each step, she closed off the emotions that bubbled within her.

"Keep them all down here," she whispered to Leon. He nodded but shot wary glances toward Laya, who leveled him with a fierce gaze.

River didn't wait for the guard to announce her before she flung open the large oak doors.

The room had the second-biggest windows in the whole castle. They ran from the ceiling to the floor and looked out over the front gate, though if one pressed their face to the glass or stepped out the balcony door to the left, one could see the lake to the right. The room was furnished in plush red velvet. Black chaise lounges scattered the room, and tasseled pillows lined the floor. It was her mother's favorite room. She'd had it designed so she could sit in the sun without the harsh rays ruining her delicate skin.

"This is certainly a welcome sight." River's voice was level, almost bored, as she took in Bass's tired face, Lilith in her thin silk gown, and the queen outfitted in the greenest velvet dress River had ever seen. It looked like the one she'd worn to King Castor's funeral.

A long table was laid out in front of them with teacups and breads of all sorts. In the center, a fountain of chocolate spilled down onto more delicate pastries.

River's mouth watered. She hadn't had sweets in some time. *Quite the tea party for just the three of them.* She wanted to reach out and run her finger through the fountain but knew the moment the sweets touched her tongue her mind would hate her, and her stomach would revolt.

The queen's pale face seemed to blanch of any remaining color. Her jaw dropped, and she blinked several times at River and then at the woman that stood behind her.

"I—" she breathed. "Iris?"

"Hello, Mother," was all her sister said as she positioned herself next to River.

That was all River needed. Seeing them in a room together—the way her mother's eyes gleamed with moisture. Even at the king's funeral, her mother hadn't shed a tear.

Iris *was* her sister. River no longer had any doubt.

"Don't worry, Mother. I'm alive as well. Not that you ever bothered to check," River said, feigning nonchalance.

"You shouldn't be here, Iris. It's too dangerous for you," the queen said. She didn't look in River's direction. Her gaze was locked on Iris.

Bass stepped forward, hands extended toward River until they were face-to-face. He ran a thumb down her cheek, then eyed the leathers with approval and desire. "I didn't believe it. Your mother said you were dead, but I never saw your body. I knew it was a lie."

River pulled back from his touch, a sadness overshadowing any previous feelings completely. "Let's talk after this."

Bass's face pinched, but he nodded, searching her eyes for something.

"This monster doesn't belong here. Get her out," Lilith shouted as her thin gown swayed with every step back she took.

"Dearest cousin. I would have expected a warmer welcome from my own blood." Iris moved over to the seat closest to Lilith. "May I sit? I think I will sit. How about you, sister?"

Lilith shook her head, staring between Iris and the queen. Her eyes grew wider by the minute.

River stepped forward and placed her hands on the red velvet chaise lounge Iris had chosen. She gripped tightly, afraid she was going to fall over or fling it. She wasn't sure which.

"Mother, I think there are some things we need to talk about," she said. "Maybe send my human cousin elsewhere."

"I'm not going anywhere," Lilith said, though her back was now closer to the wall and the door that led into a different sitting room.

River cocked her head, studying Bass, who had moved to stand between River and Lilith. He didn't wear his customary uniform; instead, he wore a jacket of purple and red with black fitted slacks. His half-lidded blue-green eyes were bloodshot as he looked at her.

They narrowed slightly as if he were trying to figure her out. Was he scared she would attack the queen in the sunroom?

"Royal matters don't include you, Lilith," River said.

"I'm the heir to the Castor throne. Everything includes me." Lilith's sneer was visible over Bass's shoulder.

River stiffened. The words cut her in half like being stabbed in the back.

"What?" Iris and River said at the same time.

"Why is she claiming to be the heir?" River directed her question right at her mother.

The queen's delicate throat bobbed, but she recovered quickly, leaning back in the lounge she sat in. She stretched out her legs, the slit of her dress opening to reveal her pale, unwrinkled skin.

"You were dead. I had to do something. I couldn't not have an heir. This strengthens everything. We have the two kingdoms married." The queen waved her delicate hand before her eyes flicked once again to Iris.

Iris was still seated, though River took note of her finger, which was slowly stroking the still-bloody ax on her hip.

River looked around the room and then laughed. A cold, hard, fake laugh. One that built up from deep inside her and bubbled over. "Sebastian. How funny! Wasn't that the argument we were going to make to my mother about our engagement? Oh, how the tables have turned."

"River, I—"

"Don't. I really, truly don't care right now." River felt a brief wave of fear. It was of loss, and she didn't know whether it had been from her or someone else.

"I think it's time you restore the rightful heir to the throne." River said, pointing toward her sister.

"I thought you were dead. I thought you died in the fire with R—owan." A small noise caught in the queen's throat as her body shook with silent sobs.

River had never seen her mother cry before. And, she noted, she was crying over Iris, again. Not over River coming back from the dead. But Iris, the true heir of Queen Elora.

Iris didn't flinch. Her face was impassive as she watched her mother cry. "I don't want the throne. I don't want anything to do with Elora. The crown is River's, as it always has been."

"Iris." The queen shook her head. "You don't mean that. I am sorry. Please."

"You didn't do what was right back then, so you'll do what is right now." Iris stood then. Her body towered over the queen's.

Bass stepped in her path, his calves brushing against the low chaise lounge. He fit here and River felt as much an outsider as she always had. This had always been more his home than it had been her own.

Iris smirked. Her eyes twinkled, and River could have sworn she was enjoying herself too much.

The queen grabbed Bass's hand and squeezed, pulling him over just enough for her to keep an eye on her daughter. "Even if I wanted to, I won't put a bastard on the throne." The queen cleared her throat. "Lilith is a full-blooded human. This is the best thing for the humans."

Iris's lips pinched together as she nodded, her nostrils flaring. "If that is how you want to play it, Elora. Then—"

"Wait... What? No one outside knows the truth but us. No one even suspects. If Iris doesn't want the throne, I certainly do." River was shocked at her own words. She had thought she was unworthy. But the people needed someone who could look outside her perfect little bubble, and that certainly wasn't Lilith. River would do her best to make sure it was her, even if she had to surrender more of herself—because that was what a good queen did. "And I have a plan that will save the humans."

"You have found a way to kill the Spitarians?" Bass asked, his gaze softening on River.

Iris leveled River with a glare and shook her head slightly.

River opened and then closed her mouth. Iris shot a glare at her mother, green eyes locked on her like they were horns about to attack.

The queen tilted her head. She'd had a Spitarian lover. There was no way she didn't know more about them than she was letting on.

"I have always known—" the queen started, taking a small sip of her tea.

"I was talking about the prophecy," River said, cutting her off. For some reason, Bass knowing how to kill Ky didn't feel right. Did she honestly even know? She thought about the weapon she'd held when she'd first met Ky. There had been genuine fear in his eyes when she held it in her hand. But she had no idea what they even meant.

"What about it?" Elora questioned, straightening in the chair.

"I have heard the whole thing, Mother. When were you going to tell me that the prophecy was about bringing the races together for peace and not about the annihilation of one race or the other?"

"Probably the same time she was going to tell you that she was shoving you into a role that was never meant for you," Iris said bitterly.

"What're you talking about?" River said, her face scrunched in confusion.

"Iris . . ." her mother said in her oh-so-familiar warning tone.

The corner of Iris's perfectly shaped mouth lifted. "Oh, did you think I wouldn't tell her? Did you think I'd run from my destiny? I have more honor than that, Mother."

"Iris, I was only doing it to protect you."

"Can someone fill me in here?" River asked, stepping around the chaise toward her sister.

"The prophecy was never about you. It has always been about me. You're only a part of it, just like Ky is. But the chosen one to rise from the ashes is me. You've been carrying a burden you were never meant to carry," Iris said, cool and calm. "It was always mine."

River shook her head, trying to clear it. But then the pieces became clear: twenty-one years ago the prophecy had been spoken. *Twenty-one years.* "You're twenty-one."

Iris nodded.

River whipped her head to her mother. "You were pregnant when the prophecy was spoken over you. The daughter the prophecy spoke of wasn't about me . . . all this time . . ."

The queen sank back into her seat, her shoulder slouching. River hoped it would swallow her whole. "Iris, I was only trying to save you. Protect you."

"So instead, you forced my father to have another child. Just to saddle her with something she couldn't possibly carry." Iris pointed to River, the sunlight from the glass catching off her armor. "Look at her. Look in her eyes. Don't you see what you've done to her? Forcing her to hide the other parts of herself so much that she's drowning inside?"

River couldn't breathe. Her sister's words. They'd been her whole life. She had thought she wanted more answers from her mother, but she wanted nothing more from her. She didn't need any further excuses.

River eyed the woman who'd made her childhood a nightmare, who'd forced her into a box. She didn't deserve River's love and devotion.

She didn't deserve to wear the crown.

Crash.

Glass shattered all around them, scattering down in tiny pieces of crystal. Lilith let out a high-pitched scream.

"Get down!" Bass shouted, covering the queen's body with his.

River and Iris ran to the balcony, ignoring his warning. Bass shot a hand out to try to pull River toward him, but she sidestepped his reach.

On the ground below, a broad man with dark hair and feathers as white as snow and another blond male with green scales threw punches at each other left and right. Dirt flew up all around them as they tackled each other to the ground. Rocks sprayed in every direction.

A thorn of fear and anger pierced River's side. She squeezed her eyes shut, trying to decide to whom it belonged.

Chapter Thirty-Two

Ky

Ky's feet slammed into the ground just outside the castle, startling the two guards in front of the iron gates.

Thumper had found them midway to the south, pointing them in the right direction. Ky guessed it didn't matter now that his father knew River was alive. Why shouldn't she alert her kingdom to the same thing? He was sure many had been upset by her death, and he hoped this would give them comfort.

"And why couldn't we have just landed inside the gates?" Wrynn deadpanned.

Ky shot him a glare. Thus far, he'd refused to answer any of Wrynn's questions. His leftwing had even gone as far as to provoke him into a physical battle in the skies. Ky had dodged every move, ignoring him completely.

"I think you should point that spear elsewhere before it ends up in your eye, human." Wrynn batted away the spear of the emerald-clad guard with one light swipe.

"We are guests of the princess," Ky said to the other guard, whose face had begun to drip with perspiration. "We respect the customs."

"Of our enemy?" Wrynn asked, confused.

Ky finally spun and faced his friend. He couldn't control the growl in his throat as he answered, "They aren't our enemies. They're my father's enemies. Though I suppose since you chose him, they *are* yours. Feel free to remain out here."

"Can we stop this now?" Wrynn said under his breath. "This is getting ridiculous. What's between us can be resolved later. Alone."

Ky whipped back around just as the human guard advanced toward them, spear raised.

"Please." Wrynn pointed toward the guard, who was shaking. "They'll want to kill us if we aren't together on this."

"We aren't together. You chose Head Axel," Ky snapped before eyeing the guard again. "If you would please inform the princess we're here. She's expecting us."

"I'm your wing," Wrynn whispered from behind him, pain lacing his voice.

"Not anymore. I'll choose another."

A bell tolled in the distance.

Wrynn kicked at the gravel below his feet. "I think that was an alarm bell. Do you have another brilliant plan? Or were you going to leave me out of this one too?"

His stomach sank. Wrynn was right; this was Ky's fault. If he had trusted Wrynn from the beginning, maybe this wouldn't have happened.

"Fly," Ky commanded as he saw the mass of emerald-clad bodies running down the sloping hill toward the iron gate. Both males unfurled their wings, lifting themselves into the air.

"Arrows!" Wrynn yelled, pushing his body in front of Ky's. He spun in a quick circle in the air, deflecting the arrows with his dragon's wings.

Ky tried not to be impressed by the male. They had practiced that move for years and had never been able to use it in battle. It had been perfectly executed, almost beautiful.

In the back of Ky's mind, he felt the awareness of another's magic as they soared over the gates farther toward the stone castle. His gaze flicked toward one of the many balconies.

"There," Ky yelled over the roar of the wind and the shouting humans below. He stretched his hand toward the balcony. He could feel River's magic pulsing in.

Wrynn reached out, grabbed his foot, and slammed them down into the earth, dirt and rocks skidding all around him.

Ky twisted, trying to wiggle his way free. "What the drago—"

Wrynn's face was above his, his dragon's wings covering their bodies. "Bolt arrows from the towers," he said with a wince as they pinged off his wings.

"How many?"

Wrynn let out a sigh, his face inches from Ky's. "We'll be like this for a bit. Why don't you tell me what's really on your mind, brother?"

"You told him. Everything. Even after I showed you all my memories. After all he has done. Don't you understand what he's been doing? Making *her* do?" Ky squeezed his fists together, resisting his innate urge not to throttle his former friend.

Wrynn's knee pinned him down by the wings. The feeling of his feathers being held back sent them twitching. "I can't control what your sister does any more than you can. They had a right to know about your mother. Az has the right to make her own decisions, as she's been doing for years. He's not brainwashing her. She's making her own informed decision; you just don't like it that you disagree with them."

Ky glared into the male's eyes. He'd thought this was his best mate. His brother. He shook his head. "Don't you see? This is the way it has to be. We must make peace."

Wrynn shrugged. "I didn't tell him everything. I didn't tell him where to find your mother, though I know where she is because you suspect. And I didn't tell him about the redhead. Though I should have since she is something special."

"I thought I could trust you."

"You want to talk about trust?" Wrynn laughed and stood, helping Ky to his feet, his wings moving fast around them. Ky heard the arrow notch and shifted Wrynn an inch to the right as the arrow flew by them both. It was like the humans thought they didn't realize they were there. "You could have trusted me from the beginning about what your mother asked of you. About all she told you about the humans."

Ky shook his head at the truth behind his words, but he didn't say anything as Wrynn shoved Ky aside just as an arrow shot for him.

"Do you mind?" Wrynn growled over his shoulder at another emerald-clad human about to nock another arrow. "I'm trying to have an important conversation here." He turned back to Ky. "You could have trusted me when Iris came to you about the prophecy. But you chose not to. This is all on you."

"I couldn't."

"Why?"

They both sidestepped another few arrows. The voices around them began to pick up, shouting for their death.

"At first, it was just mere curiosity as a kid, learning the human language, gorging myself on their stories. I even followed my mother when she left. As far as Kisling let me, at least."

"Humans are interesting, and I thought you loved the research of it." Wrynn grasped an arrow out of the air. "This is getting tedious."

"I did. I do. But I trusted her. I trusted my mother when she said she'd always come back. When she said this mattered. She lied. She knew she wouldn't come back." Ky shook his head as the sound of ten arrows notched and flew toward them.

Both males leaped and jumped at the same time, their wings lifting them in the air to avoid the arrows.

"You could've told me. All of it."

"I trusted you not to read my mind. Look where that got me," Ky yelled over the wind.

"Some things are for your benefit. You can't hold it all on your shoulders, Kylane. It's not how the world works. I wouldn't have, if Azalea hadn't asked . . . hadn't demanded."

Smash.

Glass shattered down from above. A high-pitch scream ripped through the air. Both males' heads swung up.

River!

"Are you trying to kill your own princess and queen?" Ky growled at the soldier whose arrow had broken the window just as a figure appeared on the balcony above.

Wrynn dove for Ky, taking him to the ground again. "You need to trust me here and now."

"How can I?" Ky squirmed to try and search for River, but Wrynn held his neck.

"Because I believe you, and I believe the prophecy."

Ky blinked. Had he just heard him right? He swallowed. "Why?"

Wrynn growled as Ky bucked under him. "I have seen things in other minds you wouldn't believe, and soon I'll tell you about it. But I know our magic is dying, and so we will die off. If this is the way to save us, save Azalea, I am with you."

"Even if it is against the Head? And your *kupal*?"

"She'll come around." Wrynn hopped off Ky's back a moment before he was about to be bucked.

"If you play me, I will take your wings."

Wrynn nodded. "To the Sparrows who dream."

"And the Sparrows who fly," Ky said, finishing the old phrase used by those who had escaped the old world and forged a way to the new one.

Ky looked up, and his gaze locked onto the hazel eyes he thought he'd only see in dreams. A small smile lifted the corner of River's mouth.

Chapter Thirty-Three

River

He'd come for her. Ky had found her. She wasn't sure whether to be terrified by the prospect or elated.

A smile lifted the corner of her mouth for the briefest of moments before a hand wrapped around her wrist, pulling her away from the balcony and the shards of glass that were scattered about her feet. Fear slammed against her back like it was warring with her. River shook off the feeling as best she could and pulled her arm from the grasp.

"Inside now before anyone sees her here with us," Lilith hissed, her hands fisted in her skirts.

Iris shot a glare in her cousin's direction before she strode past River and Bass toward the balcony herself. "Well, if it isn't Kylane and Wrynn. Come on, let's see what they want." She placed one hand on the balcony and pushed herself over, landing like a cat on the balls of her feet two stories below.

River leaned over as Iris beamed up at her. *Show off.*

"Hurry up. They certainly aren't here to see me." Iris waved her forward.

She looked over the edge then back to her sister before shaking her head and taking the cobbled stairs of the balcony that led to the sprawling grass.

"There were steps, you know," River muttered.

Emerald-clad figures swarmed her the moment her feet left the last step. She wasn't sure for a moment if they were there to help her or stop her.

"Stay back, Princess. We just got you back. Let's keep you out of danger," one soldier said, his mustache pointed in several directions.

Another soldier with brass on his shoulders turned to the group. "Nock. Fire!"

The order sent a curse of annoyance through her. A feeling that was undoubtedly her own.

A large shadow suddenly blocked the sun, turning the grass into night. A roar ripped through the sky only moments before Tang's sleek body landed outside the ring of soldiers, blocking River's path.

The cluster of soldiers stepped back, pushing her spine to the wall. She stiffened.

"Cease your fire!" River shouted over the throng of frantic soldiers. "That's an order, and unless you want to be burned alive by a dragon, stand aside."

The dragon dipped her head in acknowledgment, the orange strip that stretched from her nose seeming to ripple with every movement. Her armor-like wings fanned out in front of Ky, blocking River's view and most of the archers' as well.

Iris's fiery head was there one moment and then gone the next as she stepped under the dragon's protection.

Good.

One loose arrow flew, lodging itself into Tang's right wing. The dragon barely flinched, but her eyes swung in the direction from which the arrow had come.

Tang's belly must be brimming with fire because River's certainly was. She shoved at the soldier closest to her. She heard cries of protest but started swinging her fist.

"Princess," a green-clad soldier with one stripe warned.

"What are you—" A gruff voice was cut off as her fist connected with his jaw.

She heard Tang's warning growl and swung around in time to miss the butt of a sword at the back of her head.

"You lay one finger on me, even if it is to protect me, and I will take your hand." River shoved her foot behind a soldier's knee, ripping the dagger from their belt.

She pointed it in the soldiers' direction, a mix of emotions on their faces. "I think I'll greet our guests myself. Thank you."

Orange eyes were level with hers. For the briefest moment, she thought she was a goner, but then Tang nudged River's forehead with her nose.

"I think I like having you as a friend," River said. She nodded toward the arrow. "Want me to get that for you?"

The dragon dipped her body toward her. River pushed herself onto her tiptoes and yanked the arrow free. Milky blood oozed from the wound.

The dragon righted herself, the wound sealing over slowly. River patted Tang's side as she worked her way around the dragon moving with her.

A blade rested in Iris's relaxed hand.

"If you had chosen not to wear your armor, you both would be less frightening," River said, taking careful note of the fact that neither male had bothered to raise a blade, though she saw blood leaking from both of them.

Wrynn turned toward her and shrugged. River noticed an arrow lodged in his shoulder. "I didn't think it was right to raise a weapon when we came seeking peace."

River raised a brow. He certainly hadn't wanted peace when he'd sought her out earlier. What could have changed?

Tang growled again.

"Ceasefire, or you'll have to shoot me," River said, stepping in front of Ky and her sister, though both towered over her.

"What are you doing here?" River asked over her shoulder.

"I promised to train you on how to use your power."

"You promised someone would train me. And him?" River pointed to Wrynn, who had begun to argue with a guard closest to him. "He tried to capture me."

"She likes you." Ky nodded toward the dragon.

River ignored him. "Why are you here? Did your father send you?"

"He did, yes. But I had to make sure you were okay for myself. I hope, in time, we might be able to convince him that there's a world that both our people can reside in."

"I'm not sure it's possible. Look how my people . . ." She shook her head. "These soldiers reacted to your presence. I think my place is here until I can teach them otherwise."

"It seems to me the throne is no longer yours." Ky's gaze shot up to the balcony where her mother stood with Bass on one side and Lilith on the other, a tiara upon Lilith's head that hadn't been there before. Silver and gold spun together with the Castor emeralds and the Devlyns' rubies hanging off swoops and swirls.

My tiara.

"Because you told them I was dead," River snapped.

Ky's brown brows knitted together. "To protect you."

"You tried."

Ky nodded. "I did. And now I'm saying don't hide anymore. Let them see who you are. Lead your people the right way with your whole self."

"I can be whole here."

"Can you?" Ky pointed toward the swords and the notched arrows. The humans' faces were etched in anger, fear. Disgust.

River knew the truth.

"My sister's out looking for my mother now," Ky said. "She can train you like she trained Iris. She can tell you of the true prophecy. Come with us. Learn about yourself. And if you want to come back here, you can."

"And what of your father?" River said.

"We'll convince him. Convince my sister. Once my mother's with him, he'll change. She'll help. I know it."

"River."

Bass was suddenly by her side. She hadn't even noticed him leave the balcony. He snaked his arm around her waist and pulled her against him.

She shoved against Bass, her body stumbling back and into the saddlebags on Tang's side. Heat rushed up her body, a warm tingling up her limbs that danced near her heart.

Fear swirled all around her. Bass's fear for her.

No . . . of me.

She squeezed her eyes shut. She saw his fear as if it were a memory in her mind. She saw herself. What he feared she was. Eyes that glowed red and black, mist pouring from her mouth. She had bones instead of flesh, and red blood dripped from them.

"We can fix you. We can fix this," Bass said. His lip curled at the sight of her.

"River. You okay?" Ky said. Gently, he reached for her shoulder, his face openly concerned. His fear tasted of flowers. He wasn't afraid of her. Ky's fear was for her. It was gentle and coaxing.

He stretched out his hand, and she allowed his fingers to close around her, pulling her to her feet. The heat and tingling disappeared. She smiled up at Ky and wondered if he knew how good it felt to have the magic lifted, as he'd just done, for even the mere moments of their touching.

"River, it's okay. Step away from him. Come back inside. Come home." Bass stepped forward, his hand outstretched, his snake sword in his other hand.

"You will never love me, all of me, for who I truly am. Not even as the friends we once were." River's voice almost broke as she spoke the truth.

"You are the Princess of Castor. Nothing else matters. We can still fix this." Bass's voice was cold. A warning.

River shook her head. "There's more to me than that. I don't want to hide those parts of me anymore."

"Those aren't who you are," he snapped with a growl.

"I have a sister. And stories of a family I've never met. You want me to push that all aside to be some talking puppet? To destroy goodness, to never learn my magic?"

"Magic is a poison. It will consume you."

"Damn," Wrynn whispered.

Iris chuckled.

A sad smile lifted River's lips. "It's been consuming me for years. Eating away parts of me because I was trying to hide, to be who everyone else wanted me to be." River pointed to herself. "It's hurting me, trying to be something that I'm not."

"No, no, we can still fix this. Fix you. Lilith will give your throne back." Bass looked over his shoulder, and Lilith shook her head in disagreement. His eyes snapped back to River's. "She will. I will convince her."

River looked to Ky, whose lips were turned down as he stared at Bass. To Iris, who was now yelling up the balcony obscene phrases at Elora that River had never heard before and didn't think were in the human tongue.

Iris, who wasn't bad. Who had been honest from the beginning. And Ky, who also had been forthcoming from the start. A supposed bad guy who wasn't bad at all. A male who was afraid for her, not of her. And her mother, whose fear was of losing Iris again but nothing for the daughter she'd raised the past seventeen years.

The weight of it all seemed crushing. She wanted to bury her face under the dragon's wing and sleep until all the feelings disappeared. But she couldn't. She had to make a choice. One she knew would change the course of her life.

Chapter Thirty-Four

Ky

Ky heard the panting breaths of the human and the accelerating beat of his heart as if it were about to run away from him. River called him Bass, but Ky could think of a few other choice names to call him. His hands felt empty without the unicorn knife. Ky wanted to impale it right through the blond-haired, blue-eyed demon who kept reaching for her.

Dragon-damn.

It took everything in him not to sweep River up into his arms and fly her away from here, but this wasn't his fight. Her choices had been taken away her whole life, and he wouldn't do that to her again.

So Ky planted his feet and waited as the blond man shoved off the soldiers who tried to pull him back. River's shoulders relaxed, all tension going out of them. Her fighting stance loosened as she crossed her arms like a defiant child.

"Get away from her," the man roared, reaching for his sword.

Ky felt the urge to roll his eyes. *Humans.*

The gleaming steel whipped free, and Ky saw the pommel, the ruby snake eyes stared at him.

"River, come to me," the man spat.

Ky could barely hear the words she spoke in return as a loud roaring filled his ears.

It was him. This man. The flashes from his dreams flooded back, overwhelming his senses. He couldn't see around him. Rust filled his mouth as his magic roared. All Ky could see was River's blood on his hands and the coldness in this man's blue eyes.

This blue-eyed human was going to kill her.

It didn't matter that she was a chosen princess or that Ky didn't love her yet. But the dreams, his premonitions—he knew he would. He saw the swell of her belly between their interlocked fingers. Something inside Ky broke, a piece of his heart he'd no longer believed he had. Ky wanted to fall to his knees, ask the fadelings for wisdom, beg them to save her life, even if it meant forfeiting himself.

But instead, he remained standing. And tried to focus on the words coming out of Bass's mouth as he yelled hateful and hurtful things at River.

She didn't deserve this, and he didn't deserve her. Ky could tell there was something off about him as she pulled away from him and stumbled into Tang's side.

River's magic exploded around her. The dark swirls around her seemed to move away from him and farther into her depths. It was like even her magic knew something was wrong with Bass as he tried to convince her that she needed to stay and reclaim the throne.

Elora's pleading voice pulled Ky's attention from River for a moment, into another conversation.

"You had no right to make this her life," Iris yelled, her red hair moving as if of its own accord.

"Better her than you." Elora's face was bone-white, her emerald eyes locked on the redhead.

"How could you do that to her? Father would hate you for this, if he knew what you've truly done to his youngest daughter."

"Father?" Ky muttered to himself.

His mind reeled. If River and Iris were sisters with the same father . . .

A Star! One daughter raised by the mother, the other raised by the father. It made sense. The more human-looking one passed off as the human heir. But then the prophecy . . . Iris looked to be in her twenties. Was *she* the one meant to rise from the ashes?

He felt like he'd been sucker-punched. Rhella had said River was important, but she hadn't specified she was *the one*. That was why she was doomed to die—because it was Iris who would rise. Not River. The smiling face from his dreams and the blood-soaked chest. Red blood. In the vision, her blood was always red.

Ky's body stiffened, his heart constricting.

"You don't understand," Elora begged, reaching toward the balcony for her daughter's hands.

Iris moved farther from her, stepping closer to Bass's back. "Don't. The prophecy was never about her."

Ky let out a breath as Iris confirmed that she was the chosen one. His mother must have told her that she was the one who would bring their people together.

River had held the world on her shoulders without reason.

"We need to go. Take the girl, and let's go." Wrynn shoved his shoulder and pointed to the humans who were becoming increasingly agitated.

"We can't. She has to choose us."

Wrynn reached up to his shoulder and pulled an arrow free. "And why would she do that?"

"Because before now, she's never been given a choice. She needs to choose."

"Choose to go to her death?" Wrynn said with disbelief.

"Choose to believe in herself and her sister, my mother, and us. We can all make a difference. Prophecy or no prophecy. That's what I want. How about you?" Ky growled out the words. He hoped there was still something he could do to avoid the death he knew would break him in the end.

Wrynn threw the arrow to the ground at his feet and shoved his finger through the hole in his shoulder. "I want my *kupal* to come back from the brink of destruction. I want her to stop worrying about magic disappearing. I want to breathe for once without thinking someone I love is going to die. Or that I'm betraying them."

"So?"

"Peace sounds pretty good. It sounds like it might give me all the things I want." He pointed at River, who stood still, her body covered in a dark mist.

Ky crossed his arms. "Then she must choose. We have to give her that."

The soldiers began to close in.

"Kill them. Kill them all! Did you see that one with her hand on the queen!" a blonde wearing a tiara on the balcony screamed, her dress almost as pink as her face.

The soldiers drew their bows again. Silver glinted all around them.

"Oh hell." Wrynn pushed Ky out of the way as he took a dagger to the arm.

Ky growled, ripping the blade from Wrynn's arm.

"I'm done waiting," Wrynn spat as blue blood gushed down his arm. The circle of humans began to get smaller around them.

The blonde's voice was a shrill anthem of *kill them all* from her perch above them.

"Iris!" Ky yelled.

The soldiers had swords pointed at her throat. Her gaze locked on her mother, a wicked grin spreading over her face.

Elora was crying, her face tear streaked. "No. No," she breathed, but the word was barely a whisper compared to the pink fury of the girl beside her.

Ky's hand shot toward the ground. He grabbed the dagger he had pulled from Wrynn's arm. In a few swift steps, before any human could track his movements, he slammed the butt of the dagger into the soldier's nose, pulling Iris back with him. He tried his best not to draw unneeded blood and backed away farther. Iris didn't fight as they returned, as one, to River's side.

"What's wrong with her?" Iris asked, wide-eyed.

River, whose hands were on her head, unleashed a blood-curdling scream. It ripped from inside her like it was tearing her apart.

Maybe it is shredding her apart?

Ky clasped her hand in a moment of desperation, stilling the storm and his own beating heart. Her warmth spread through his fingers as they slid into place.

Chapter Thirty-Five

River

His fingers tugged gently and pulled River from the depths of the emotions and decisions she had been swirling in. Drowning. Wasn't that how Iris had put it?

The corner of Ky's mouth quirked as she squeezed his fingers gently. Something fluttered deep within her belly as a grin spread across her lips. His deep brown eyes were warm and welcoming.

"Were you just going to let them kill us both? Some queen you are!" Iris shouted close to her, her words a froth of hate and anger.

Elora lay crumpled and crying on the balcony floor, guards blocking her as Lilith stood tall, barking orders.

River could just make out Wrynn; he clutched a bloody shoulder with a weapon in his hand, keeping emerald-clad soldiers away from Tang's backside.

Ky tried with one hand to keep the soldiers away from Iris and herself. River released his fingers with one last squeeze.

A soldier grabbed at Iris's ankle and yanked her, though her sister's eyes were still locked on their mother.

"Let her go!" River screamed. "Don't touch my sister."

Iris waved her off as she met River's eyes. "I'm okay."

"Mother!" River pleaded. "This isn't how it's supposed to go. This isn't what you want, I can tell."

Iris scoffed, stepping alongside her sister. "Come with me. Meet Rhella. Learn about your family."

"No!" Bass shouted. "If you go with them, you're no better than the monsters."

"I'm not the monster here. Not the one you fear. There are good parts and bad parts of me, and I'll never let myself deny any part of me ever again."

Bass took a step away from her. His sword raised, for the first time, in her direction. He pointed it directly at her chest. "You are nothing without this throne. Without me."

It was as if, in that single moment, he had cut away all of her good memories with him, leaving behind what she would have been without him.

River clutched her chest as a nasty, cruel laugh erupted from her. "I see how you see me now. My people will love me for me. Or they aren't my people."

A large hand extended to her.

River's gaze shot, one last time, toward the mother who had burdened her with so much more than lies, who had taken her family from her and made her feel as though she wasn't enough. "Mother. You'll revert the birth order back to Iris when I'm gone."

"I don't want this throne," Iris said.

"I couldn't explain Iris's parentage. And everyone has seen you with them." Her voice was weak, her eyes finally meeting River's.

"So you won't do what I ask?" River said, allowing the hate to seep into her features.

Elora shook her head. "Not if you go with them. I can't explain any of this."

"Then I'll return and take my throne back." River placed her hand in Ky's. "With or without your help. Iris?"

River looked at her sister, who elbowed the closest soldier in the mouth and pushed away the blade. With her right hand in Ky's, River extended her left toward her sister. Iris's hand was warm as Ky yanked them both closer to Tang's side.

River clung to him as he wrapped his arm around her waist, and his large wings began to beat.

River let go of her sister's hand, and she propelled herself onto Tang's back.

"You'll regret this! I'll kill you all!" Bass swore from the ground.

It was a promise she thought would strike her heart. But as she looked into Ky's gentle face, his eyes locked only on hers as they rose higher and higher, she didn't seem to care that the first man she'd ever loved was now set on her demise.

Let him try.

Chapter Thirty-Six

Ky

River.

His heart hammered harder in his chest as he studied her face. How was it possible he didn't know her, and yet he felt like she had always been a part of his life? It was the premonitions his mother had been sending him. All the nights he'd dreamed of her, and in them they were . . . in love? Was that even possible? He'd need to be careful with her. It wouldn't be fair to her for him to cast all of these feelings onto her.

He still couldn't believe she had chosen to come with them. He shook his head. He wouldn't let any harm come to her. Not from him, and certainly not from Bass with his snake-handled blade. Maybe her decision to come with them had negated that premonition, but he knew deep down that the last words he'd heard as they'd flown away weren't likely.

Bass had said he would kill them all.

Ky would lay down his own life before he watched Bass stick a sword through River's heart. Physically or metaphorically.

River's hazel eyes locked onto his. In the light, her eyes were different than what he had initially managed to see. He wanted her to sit in the sun for hours just for him to get the color right. A line of green circled the iris, almost a yellowish gold fading to brown. She opened her mouth then closed it. He wanted to wrap both hands around her face and get lost in her eyes . . . or maybe her lips.

I am in so much trouble.

He finally broke eye contact and doubled his speed flying, beating his wings faster.

"Can you flip me? I want to see."

He did as she requested, spinning her body so her back was to his chest. His hand wrapped around her middle. She flung her arms out to the side as if they were her own wings, and she laughed. He wished he could see her smile.

"I could get used to this flying thing." She sounded as if the world had been lifted off her shoulders. And in a way, he knew it had.

"You'd look good with some glitter wings," Iris called over her shoulder.

The sisters exchanged knowing smiles before Iris lifted her arms on Tang's back. These two were undoubtedly going to be an interesting pair. Add his mother into the mix, and he didn't think even Belladonna would cross them. The image made him smile. He thought Belladonna would fit right in. He just wished he had as much confidence about his sister.

"I hate to do this, but I think we should land soon. Come up with a plan." Wrynn spun in the air then pointed down into a clearing. Ky was happy to see a small smile play on his lips as he looked between the sisters. "Regroup now that there are no longer arrows or screaming people."

"Agreed," Ky said, though River's shoulders slumped a little, her arms going back down to her sides. It twisted his heart. "Do you trust me?"

"No." The word came quick, but there was laughter in her voice.

"Well, that's disappointing. You should hold on tight anyway and keep your eyes open."

She stiffened, but as Ky wrapped his hands around her waist, she gripped them tighter. When he knew she was positioned securely, he tucked his wings and dove.

The wind ripped through them both and she screamed, but the screams turned into laughter the moment they were close enough to the trees for her to reach out and touch. He flung his wings out as they glided slowly down.

She was still laughing as they touched the ground. Her legs gave out, and he went for her, but she slapped him away as she rolled in the dirt laughing. It changed her whole face. He wanted to make it happen again and again.

Through gasps, she said, "I am scared of heights, you know." She flung her body onto the dirt, closed her eyes, and smiled.

"I think I'll take you flying more often if this is you scared."

Beautiful. She was breathtaking. He knew it wasn't just the dreams now, though those didn't hurt. When he'd first seen her, it had been the dreams that pulled him in. The dreams and the magic. Now? Now it was like seeing her for the first time with his own eyes. His real eyes. Without the weight that had been set on her shoulders for years. She was free. It did wonders for her face. The mouth set in a terminal frown now tilted up as she lay in the sun.

But he couldn't keep her. He knew it. He would lock up what he felt because she didn't need any more burdens in her life, and that was all he would be to her. He would protect her, and that meant keeping her far from the dragon-damned mess that was his father. He would send her with his mother, where she would be safe.

"Well, that looked like fun!" Iris called down to her sister as the dragon landed much slower, carefully controlling her landing so as to not roll Iris off her back. He was impressed by Tang's care. "Maybe Wrynn will take me next time."

Wrynn rolled his eyes. "Not likely."

River finally rolled, patting Tang's foot. "I think Tang could show us how to deep-dive and roll."

Wrynn and Ky exchanged worried glances. It was unlikely.

Tang nudged River's hand with her nose as Iris dismounted gracefully. Like a Heart. That was what she was. Iris outranked him. The two of them were the last of their people. Convincing his father to work with them was going to be complicated, almost as hard as ending his war on the humans.

He let out a sigh, enjoying watching these simple moments. River had bonded with Tang, and it was nice to see her like this. River enjoying his dragons as he did sent a thrill through him. His ancestors had said dragons could sense the nature of one's true self better than any other creature. He hoped that was accurate.

"This place has seen better days," Wrynn commented.

There wasn't grass, just dirt and rocks. Ky looked around the surrounding area. It was as if the roots from the trees around them had choked all the life from the earth, not allowing anything to grow.

Tang shook out her back and then curled up, closing her eyes the moment her head hit the ground.

"I think we broke your dragon," Iris mused.

"She'll recover." Ky smiled, stepping over to pat her head. "You good?" he asked River, who had slowly gotten to her feet.

River finally spun on her heel. Her smile vanished as she looked at Wrynn in disgust. "I think you should have killed him, Iris."

Wrynn crossed his arms. Though the armor shifted slightly, it was an awkward stance that pushed his chest plate out too far. He didn't meet her eyes. Instead, he looked to Ky as if expecting him to vouch for him.

Iris broke the silence between their stares. "Wrynn, can you be trusted now?"

He finally turned to meet her eyes. "I was never *not* trustworthy."

"Could have fooled me," River bit out, pushing the curls that had broken free from her braid out of her eyes. "Do you trust him?"

River directed the question at Ky, but for once in his life, when he looked at Wrynn, he wasn't one hundred percent sure. In the past, he would have instantly said yes. That was why he had chosen him as his leftwing, to fly along him in battle and defend his flank. But here, in this moment, he wasn't sure he did trust Wrynn. Not with River. He swallowed this reaction. Wrynn had said he was in, so Ky would have to give him the benefit of the doubt.

"I believe Wrynn will look out for our people's best interests. I also think he will look out for me and my sister. Even if we disagree about what that looks like all the time."

Wrynn nodded and placed his fist to his chest.

"That's reassuring," Iris said sarcastically.

River pulled her lip between her teeth absentmindedly, and Ky watched with fascination as the tender skin was sucked and bit and turned a deep red. He gulped. This woman was killing him, and she had no idea.

"I guess it'll have to do for now." River nodded toward Wrynn. "But if we ever feel like your beliefs aren't aligned with ours, I will have no choice but to deal with you myself."

"Why dirty your hands, sister? I would be happy to dispatch him for you." Iris's smile was large as she ran her finger down her blade slowly.

Wrynn rolled his eyes. "Doesn't she kind of remind you of Belladonna?"

Ky laughed. "I was thinking these two would get along well with her. It's that crazy bloodthirsty look in her eyes. I'd be careful if I were you, brother."

Wrynn scowled.

"So what now?" River slid down again, leaning against the sleeping dragon.

"River and I will meet with Rhella," Iris said.

"And if the Head has found her? I'm not sure either of you are safe." Wrynn moved to study the ground. He ran his fingers over the dirt and smelled it. "At least not until we know his intentions."

"So what do you expect? For us to just go into hiding?" Iris crossed her arms.

River watched the exchange, but she sank further into the dragon's side, her eyelids heavy. Ky wondered when the last time was that she'd had any proper sleep or a hearty meal.

"I think it's best for you both to go back to the cave. At least until I can find the Head and my sister. Get a reading on where they are at."

River nodded slowly.

"Eat well, rest, and then head out to find my mother once I know my father hasn't."

"Why are you so sure he hasn't?" Wrynn asked. "Your sister's pretty resourceful."

"Rhella's been avoiding him and everyone else who could recognize her for more than twenty years. I think avoiding those two would be easy." Iris pulled a blade and began working it along a rock.

"You don't know my *kupal*," Wrynn said, resigned. "Plus, would it be so bad for the Heart to be returned to her throne? She could help us get Head Axel on our side."

"Are we so sure that's a good thing?" Iris muttered.

Small thoughts flitting around in Ky's head, but mostly he was thinking about how he wanted to curl up with the now sleeping River, tucked under Tang's wing.

"Look at your sister, Iris. We can at least let her get a good night's rest. She doesn't have our stamina. She's running on fumes," Ky finally said.

A sad smile fell on Iris's face as she looked at her little sister. "I guess I forgot."

"We all did. She hasn't had a full night's sleep in days. Let's regroup at the cave in a few days."

Iris nodded. "Is it safe to stay here?"

"An hour letting those two rest up is in everyone's best interest." Ky pulled in his wings before he walked over and leaned against Tang's hind legs, making sure not to disturb River with even so much as a slight touch.

"Well, I guess I could try to dreamwalk," Iris said, leaning down along Tang's other side so they flanked her sister. "Who's taking the first watch?"

"First watch?" Wrynn said. "I thought you were raised by our kind."

Iris muttered something under her breath but stopped.

Wrynn, Ky, and Iris heard it at the same time. The beat of distant wings.

Ky rubbed River's arm gently. She jerked awake.

"Dragon—" Ky's swear caught in his throat as a giant black dragon appeared in the distance—just as his magic was ripped from him. He let out a gasp and crumpled.

Half aware, he felt River's hand squeeze his bicep.

"What's going on?" River yelled, pain lacing her voice.

Ky didn't take his eyes off the male descending from the sky next to the giant black beast whose scales rippled in the sunlight. The black beltron was his father's pride and joy. And the enormous membranous wings that flew next to them were his father's.

Wrynn was on his knees, choking on his own breath.

Ky tried to reach out with his magic, but it was a hollow hole inside of himself.

Iris stepped in front of her sister, who had gotten to her feet. Tang's short black legs rumbled the ground as she stood ready to flee or fight.

"Kylane," Head Axel bellowed from the sky.

"Iris," Ky croaked. "Take Tang and get her out." The words were barely a whisper from his lips.

"No," River said, shaking free of her sister's tight grasp. "What's going on? Ky, get up!"

Ky hated the worry he heard in her voice.

"Head Axel can yank power," Iris said. "We aren't safe here. You aren't safe here."

River backed up a few steps closer to Tang's side, and Ky let out a slow breath.

Good. Go.

"Kylane, why stop here? You could've brought them all the way home."

"Father, is this necessary?" Azalea said as she kneeled in front of her *kupal*, who still gasped for breath. Ky hadn't even seen her dismount. "Father, let him go. You're hurting him."

Ky's head was yanked up. His gaze met his father's dark glazed eyes.

"I didn't find your mother. And that is a problem, my son. For both of us."

Chapter Thirty-Seven

River

River wanted to scream.

"No matter how much magic your sister used"—Axel's fingers were threaded through Ky's hair, pulling his head back—"we couldn't sense her. So I came looking for you to give me more answers. If she is alive, why can't your sister sense her?"

It took everything in her not to react. She didn't understand how he could steal Wrynn's and Ky's powers with less than a snap of his fingers. His power was, as Iris had explained, his own but more potent as both writhed under the weight of it.

"I told you. She doesn't want to be found," Ky croaked.

"Oh, I will find her." The voice was a deadly promise. "We'll discuss this without your company. So which one is the Castor Princess, son?" Axel asked, his charcoal eyes on his son.

"Head Axel," Ky gasped.

The look in Ky's eyes as his father yanked back his son's head made River clench her jaw to hold in her scream. The pit in her stomach grew.

"One is large, but the other has power . . ." Axel gaze moved between River and Iris.

"Neither of us," Iris said, crossing her arms.

"Neither . . . well, you aren't human." Axel dropped Ky's hair and patted his cheek. "You brought me two halfys instead of one?"

"*Halfspring*, I believe, is the word you're looking for. Because I am not half of anything," Iris corrected, inching closer to River's side.

River stretched her fingers out, grazing her sister's weapon belt as Iris stood eerily still.

"I'm guessing it's the brunette. She would be the only one who could pass as human all these years. But you aren't, are you?" Axel flicked his wrist in an odd hand motion; his fingers grasped at the air as if he were feeling something. He pulled slowly, and River felt something within her chest tug toward him.

She let out a hiss.

"There's definitely magic in you. Who's your father?"

River remained silent, but her eyes flicked to Wrynn. She wasn't sure why, but she thought he was the weakest link.

Axel's eyes followed hers. "Wrynn, is there something you need to tell your Head?"

Wrynn gasped, and as he picked his head up from the earth and stared at Axel, his trembling fingers dug into the rocks as if that could hold him in place. The woman River assumed was Azalea kneeled next to Wrynn and pulled his head in her lap. He relaxed at her touch as her blackish-blue hair fanned out around them. Every piece of him seemed more at ease, though his face contorted.

"Father, return Wrynn's magic now. I'm sure he will answer you." Dark circles ran under Azalea's eyes, and her nose was crooked.

Axel flicked his fingers. Wrynn's eyes widened as he took a giant breath. As if breathing was the only thing holding him in this world.

"I don't know," he lied on an exhale. His gaze locked on the Head's, but he remained in his *kupal*'s lap.

Axel's glare remained on Wrynn. He didn't believe Wrynn. His eyes traced down Iris's cheek, and his hand which was rested on her neck, began to squeeze.

"Elora is our mother." River wouldn't protect her mother any longer, just like her mother had never protected her.

Iris's eyes flashed as Axel chuckled darkly. His face pinched, as if considering Wrynn's betrayal.

River's finger slid to her sister's waist and she palmed one of the weapons, a small dagger that fanned into an ax. She quickly slipped it up her sleeve.

Axel spun back to Iris. "Interesting. But your father . . . Read her, Wrynn. The redhead."

"No." River stepped in front of her sister. Her palms twitched to use the dagger, but it wasn't the right moment.

"Oh, interesting. Do you know who you are, child?"

Iris flung her arm over her sister's shoulder, pulling her back from the Head's stare. "We are your daughters. Or Wrynn's, or Kisling's, or . . . oh, Hunter Victumis's." She shrugged, though her arm remained over River protectively. "What does it matter to you whose daughter we are? We're the solution to all of your problems."

"She's right, Father," Ky began, though his words tumbled out slowly as he tried to get to his feet. "We're losing our magic. Az knows it. You can feel it. We won't be able to reproduce soon. But they can. With whomever they want. No magical bond needed."

River wondered what that meant. *No magical bond?*

"Are you suggesting we sully our blood with red?" Axel said to his son. "Your grandspring would be appalled at that. Halfsprings should be thrown to the depths of the sea where they belong."

"What happens if Ky doesn't find a *kupal* before you die?" Wrynn asked.

"Wrynn!" Azalea said. River didn't know her, but by the look on her face, she was shocked, as if Wrynn had said the most absurd thing. "You can't be serious. You agree with this?"

Wrynn gripped Azalea's face, pulling it to his. He began to whisper, but River was unable to make out what he was saying.

Axel scoffed, and Iris stiffened beside her. Her gaze moved to Ky, whose face was white as a sheet.

Ky's mouth hung open. "No!"

"Is it true? A child?" Axel said, his eyes on River.

"No, Father," Ky said as if trying to regain some footing with his father, whose eyes seemed to have turned into an inferno.

"Well, that can't happen." Axel stepped closer, and Iris shifted her body to cover her sister's. "What can your magic do, little girl?"

River felt it return to her like a weight thrown back on her as he asked the question. Her body shuddered, and her face pinched at the feeling.

"Do you want to find out?" Axel asked.

"No," Ky and Iris said in unison.

Axel whipped his head to Iris, then back to River. His hand jumped out too quickly for River to stop. The grip on her chin was like a death grip holding her in place. She wanted to slam the knife through his eyes. But it still wasn't the right time.

"Where is it?"

"What?" River asked.

"The mark. Your sister was smart enough to burn hers. But where is yours?" Axel lifted her shirt, inspecting her belly. He spun River, and her hand flew to her neck automatically.

Stupid.

Axel caught her arm midair, pulling it to the side until her shoulder popped, the same shoulder as before. It sent a storm of pain through her body, and she yelled.

Axel hissed as his other thumb pressed into her neck. "Az, do you see this? You missed two Stars. We'll have to kill these two as well."

River tried to force the pain away and focus on the fear around her. But it all swirled together. She hadn't known the particulars about who had killed her family, but the fact that Ky's sister was in on it . . .

Had Ky ever killed a Star?

"Now that I know where you two came from, I no longer have to worry about it being any of my men. I wonder, do you die the same as us? Or like humans?" Axel dropped River. She hit the ground with a thump, landing on her arm. She could no longer feel it. He stepped back, staring at her body in a way that made her squirm.

River screamed in frustration, pushing her power, trying anything to grasp onto a fear that would get them out of this.

His cackle was an animal-like howl. "Little girl, you aren't even stronger than a new offspring."

Something rippled inside of her near her heart. She felt it like her own arm was being yanked away, but instead of pain, it was a relief. As if a wet blanket had been removed from her head. She felt light as air. She sucked in a breath. It was how she had felt after Ky had touched her. Like nothing was in her anymore. While she still felt her emotions—and they were as heavy as ever—the tingling feeling she'd always thought were part of them was now absent.

"That is what it feels like to be human, child. I'll allow you to die feeling the pain of emptiness," Axel said.

River scooted back using one arm until she touched Tang's front leg. The dragon gave a deep rumble in response.

River clutched her arm and stood, bracing her back against the dragon to hold her up. She drifted into the feeling of weightlessness. She didn't even care that her arm had lost feeling; besides, the contact pain was nothing like the pain of emotion. He had shut it all off. This wasn't what it felt like to be human; this was what it felt like to not feel other's fears. Simply her own, and it was glorious. She began to laugh.

"River!" Ky called desperately.

Iris pressed into her side. River didn't fight her as the strange laughter rang through her. This guy had messed up. He had given River exactly what she needed.

"Oh, a tough one, are we?" A smile spread over Axel's lips. "Then I'll make you watch as I kill your sister."

He stepped forward and grasped Iris's throat. She kicked out at his kneecaps but not before he threw her to the side, faster than River could blink. Iris's body landed on the ground a few feet away with a sickening thud.

"I doubt she'll get up after that."

Rage filled River as she stared at her sister's unmoving body. It was an all-consuming emotion with the lack of fear that filled her up inside and rolled through her like a thunderstorm. She kept her face neutral as she blinked, ever so slowly, cocking her head. The sky opened up and rain began to pour down. The earth cracked and then lit up as the lightning flashed overhead, brightening her skin.

Head Axel arched an eyebrow. Behind him, Wrynn moved slowly on quiet feet to check on Iris. When his eyes met River's, she couldn't tell whether he was telling her Iris was gone or still living. Axel couldn't take Iris from her. She had just gotten a family.

"River." A hand grabbed her ankle. "Don't do this, Father. We're following the plan. The prophecy, Mother's, your wife's—*Rhella's* plan. She has a plan for both of these girls."

"They aren't girls. They're half of that. Nothing. And as for your mother, she is gone. If she wanted to help, she would be here." Axel stepped closer to River, completely ignoring everyone else. His fist cracked into her jaw.

River's eyes went in and out of focus. Her jaw ached, but she laughed again, spitting blood onto the ground. Her sister's crumpled body appeared to double in front of her.

"Az!" Ky's voice was strained. He stumbled to his feet. "Don't you understand? Mother did this for us. So we could survive. So all this could happen—and you won't even stand up to him long enough to see what's right? Please."

Azalea slowly shook her head, a strange, pained look on her face.

Ky flung himself at his father, knocking him sideways.

They tumbled in the dirt, splashing into the mud. Axel landed on top of Ky, both hands around his son's neck.

"Stop fighting and submit!" Head Axel bared his teeth. "This is all for your own good. She isn't good enough for you. No pathetic human or halfy will ever be good enough. They are the muck beneath our feet. Not meant to live in our world. Not meant to breathe. Let them suffer as those before us suffered."

"Father. You're wrong—"

Ky didn't finish before Axel took the unicorn blade from Ky's side and pressed it just below his throat.

"Father!" Azalea screamed, running for her brother, Wrynn right on her heels. "What are you doing? He is your *Heiralomun*. Your last son!"

"No son of mine would choose this halfy, a mere piece of a Spitarian, over his own blood."

River shook her head. "Clearly, you have things a little twisted. You'd get along well with my mother," she said with a laugh.

He pressed the blade harder against his son's throat until blood spotted under the edge. "I would stop laughing if I were you, girl."

But River kept laughing. She couldn't control it now. Her whole life, she had been made to feel like less than nothing. Like she could only ever amount to the one thing they needed her for. And now no one needed her. But for the first time, she wanted to truly live. So she kept laughing.

Axel hopped off his son and strolled a few feet toward her, stopping to kick Iris in the face. A blow that snapped her neck back.

"I'll be glad when you end. And the rest of the humans with you. Your mother killed my *kupal* without a second glance back. I'll make sure I leave both of your corpses on her gates." He gripped her throat and squeezed.

The feeling of metal was cool against her palm. She had no idea how to kill a Spitarian. But it would have to do.

"Maybe your daughter should stop healing my sister then," River bluffed.

Axel whipped around at River's words, and she grabbed the knife from her dead arm sleeve and transferred it into her working fist. When his head swung back, River didn't hesitate.

She slammed the skinny blade right into his eye, piercing it as though it were a fruit on a tree. The sound was similar. Her hand vibrated from whatever bone she hit.

His head flung back, and his body hit the ground, mud splattering up all around him.

Chapter Thirty-Eight

Ky

Ky's eyes widened as his father splashed in the mud next to him. The lightning flashed once more in the sky to reveal the glint of silver. He opened and closed his mouth at the metal plunged through the Head's eye, then looked at the shaking girl whose hand was still raised.

"River, what have you done?" He scrambled to his feet. Axel was going to kill her slowly for this. His sister's surprised gasp, followed by Wrynn's choke, sent Ky on a tilt. He had his magic back, but it wouldn't last long. "Get on Tang and go now."

"I won't leave Iris," River rasped.

Ky heard the squelch first. The sucking sound of a blade being pulled from the depths. He didn't even have time to get to his feet before he felt a piercing blade enter his throat. The heat seared through him as the unicorn blade pinned him to the ground. His chest ripped apart once more, his magic leaving him.

Ky gasped. He couldn't breathe. The dagger was implanted right into his trachea, cutting off his air and his voice. Without his magic, he wouldn't heal, and eventually, though it might take hours, he would die.

He blinked slowly and craned his head. She was going to die right along with him. If he was going to die, he wanted to look into those hazel eyes one last time. Wanted to blink and remember her hand over the swell in her belly. They would never make it that far.

Head Axel was on her again, this time without relenting. River's hands beat at him, scratching and pulling at Axel, kicking for air. Those beautiful hazel eyes bulged slightly as she struggled for breath.

Ky felt as though his life and everything in him were being shattered.

He pulled himself slowly onto his forearms, allowing the dagger to pull through him where it remained anchored in the ground, ripping from his throat. Pain exploded through him, but he barely noticed it. He dragged one forearm over the next, pulling himself across the mud as quietly as he could. Until he reached his father's ankles and bit down into the flesh, pulling the tendon with him. Warm blood splattered across his face.

His father screamed in frustration and then crumpled before him, dragging River with him. Axel released her long enough to throw himself onto his son's body, his knees pressed firmly into his chest.

Ky's vision darkened around him. He had lost too much blood, and the unicorn blade had certainly poisoned his bloodstream by now.

"Do you know what happens to your body if I take your head here and now, son? Without your magic, you won't come back." Axel gasped as he held Iris's bloody thin silver dagger in his hand. It was still coated in his dark blood. "Don't make me do this. Don't choose her."

The blade pressed into the gaping hole in his neck. Ky's gaze didn't remain on the Head; it wandered, seeming to always seek River. Was she still breathing?

Please.

Head Axel let out an anguished scream. "Why would you make me do this?" A small tear landed on Ky's face. "I thought I taught you better."

"Father! Release him now!" Azalea's voice was pure panic.

Ky tried to look for his sister, but he couldn't see past his father's shoulder. He could only feel the weight of him stiffen above him.

"Az," Wrynn whined. "Put it down."

"Step away from Ky, or I will do it," Az said.

Head Axel's weight left Ky's chest. "Azalea, put down the blade."

Ky blinked slowly, his head lolling toward his sister.

Azalea stood frozen as the rain pelted down all around her. Her too-thick dress was soaked, and it clung to her as if weighing her down. A flash of light and the clap of thunder illuminated what Ky feared: his unicorn dagger was pressed into her chest by her own hand. How had she gotten Ky's dagger without notice?

"Father, listen to me. We've spent barely a day looking for Mother. And if what Wrynn says is true, we owe it to Ky to allow the girl to live. This isn't our way. At least, it shouldn't be. If this is what Mother was fighting for, we owe it to both of them to at least hear them out."

"*No!*" Head Axel bellowed, taking a step toward her.

Azalea stepped back. "I will pierce this knife through my heart. Release Ky's magic."

Axel's meaty fists clenched at his sides, but they shook fiercely. "Why? Why would you do such a thing?"

"For all your talk of blood over everything else, you are so quick to throw him away just because his ideas are different than yours." Azalea stepped back again, pressing it closer until the tip pierced the first layer of her flesh. "Don't come any closer."

"You can't be serious."

"He is my brother and your son." Her nostrils flared. Wet chunks of hair stuck to her face. "I don't think you want to tempt me in this."

"But he is wrong."

"Az," Ky croaked. He didn't want her doing this, not for him.

"Wrong as he may be, I still want him around. Plus, if you kill him, you will have no *Heiralomun*. Our people will have a civil war. We'll fall into chaos just like we did when the families split all those years ago."

"I—" Axel began but with one look from her, he stopped.

Azalea took a step toward him. Her bare feet slapped mud up her dress, and she snarled. "Is it blood over everything?"

"It is."

"Then release his magic." Her hand was steady.

Ky didn't think she would do it, though. At least he hoped she wouldn't, and even more that their father wouldn't call her bluff. She was just like their mother, holding him by the strings. What a pair of twins they were.

Axel's hand twitched, and Ky felt the power rush back through him. He stood slowly, his legs nearly giving out beneath him. He could already feel the skin knit together, slightly pulling.

"Thank you, Father. I promise the world will be better," Ky said quietly.

"Just because I released you doesn't mean I agree with all this." His gaze locked on Azalea, who hadn't dropped the blade. "I released him. Now hand over that blade."

She didn't move. "What of the girls?"

"They die."

"Please!" Ky screamed.

"Father," Azalea said, almost bored. She began to turn the dagger slowly at her heart. "Let them go. We can still continue with the plan for the wedding if you want. But let them go. Clearly, they mean something to Ky. And maybe they mean something to Mother."

"No. They die." Axel turned back to Ky and began walking toward the girls.

"Axel, that is quite enough."

Ky and Axel stared toward where the voice was coming from. Out of the storm, dry as day, thick black hair flying all around her as if she were the storm herself. His mother, in her Spitarian form, stood just beyond Azalea's right shoulder. Her head cocked as if studying them all.

"*Momaza*," Az choked, using her pet name for their mother.

"Axel, you have driven your own daughter to place a blade to her chest to get what she wants?" She clicked her tongue. "And your son has blood on his neck that came from you."

Ky blinked rapidly. The voice was hers. But she had said she couldn't change because she'd broken the bond . . .

"My Heart, my beloved, is it really you?" Head Axel's voice shook, and he took a tentative step forward.

"Who else would it be?" his mother snapped and crossed her arms.

Ky couldn't see his father's face, but the pitch in his voice told him all he needed to know.

Ky looked behind him. Iris was still crumpled in the mud, unconscious, but River had a glowing *Crystolas* behind her back. Her white teeth clenched, glowing through the storm. She was projecting his mother. But what exactly was she? The fire for the girl . . . the images from him . . . and now his mother?

"What do you have to say for yourself? I trusted you with my children, and look what you've done." His mother's voice was calm but cool. Angry. "Were the other deaths not enough?"

Axel fell to his knees. "My Heart, please forgive me."

Fear.

River projected fear.

Ky didn't wait to see if he was right. He lunged forward and grasped his father's shoulders. He tugged at the cord of his father's powers, ripping them from him.

Axel sucked in a breath as the air left him.

"Azalea, your brother is right. This was my will. Listen to him," Rhella said, turning to her daughter. "And you too, Axel."

"Wrynn!" Ky yelled. "Dagger."

Wrynn leaped for his *kupal,* yanked the blade from Azalea, and threw it over Axel's head into Ky's outstretched hand.

The blade landed just as his mother disappeared.

Ky grasped the blade in his shaking hand. The Head yelled and struggled underneath him. Ky didn't hesitate. He sliced the blade down either side of one of his father's wings. He sliced through the bone at the base of his back. Ky's hand shook as he moved to the second one. The sound and smell nearly made him stop. But he kept slicing over the screaming. The skin on Axel's back where the poisoned blade sliced turned his dark skin a sickly pale.

"Ky!" Azalea yelled, but the words were lost in the storm and in his father's sobs.

Ky wasn't sure if his father cried for his *kupal*, his wings, or his magic.

He looped one arm around his father, flipped him onto his back, and sat on his chest. He placed the blade to his father's heart next. "Father. I don't want to do this. You are still a loved ruler, and I have no *Heiralomun*. Civil war will break loose."

The Head's lips circled, and his teeth lashed out for his son. Ky held him still, his powers also in his grasp.

Ky turned to his sister. "Azalea, I don't want to kill him. I don't want civil war. But I will if you don't help."

Azalea stepped closer to Ky, a hand on her elbow as Wrynn whispered in her ear in earnest. Ky didn't bother to listen. Wrynn had told her earlier that River was to carry Ky's baby from premonitions from their mother. That was what had set Axel off.

"Az, please," Ky begged again. He moved the blade to his father's heart.

"River, throw me one of those *Crystolas*," Azalea finally demanded, devoid of any emotion.

River hesitated, but Ky nodded his reassurance, and the *Crystolas* soared over his head.

Az cleared her throat and then sighed. "I can bind his powers in this *Crystolas* for now." She looked at her father. "I will only do this until we can all come to an agreement without hurting one another." She looked at Ky. "Do you agree?"

"I agree," Ky said, though he would break that promise if it came down to life or death, and Azalea must have realized that as well because her nostrils flared once more but she didn't argue.

Azalea closed her eyes, and she reached for Ky's hand. Ky felt his father's powers being tugged from him as if a long string pulled from inside himself, untangling from his father's. It flowed smoothly into the *Crystolas* in her other hand. Ky only panicked for a second that she would take his as well, but when her hand dropped, she tucked the gem under her arm.

"Now what?" Wrynn asked. "We can't let the Head bleed out here."

Ky's eyes fell to his father's blue blood still pooling under him from his back. "Az, can you use a *Crystolas* to stop the blood for now?"

"Yes. River, another, please."

River walked across the distance slowly. One of her arms hung limply at her side; the other cradled the bag to her chest. "You can have this. If you help my sister first."

Az's face blanched. Her nostrils flared.

"Az," Ky warned.

"Fine," Azalea said, throwing her hands up and stomping in the mud toward Iris.

The rain slowed. The smell of rust permeated the air as his sister bent toward Iris.

"You two take him to a healer. I'll get the girls. Can I trust you to do that?" Ky said to his leftwing. He still hadn't gotten off his father, who hadn't stopped struggling. An angry slew of curses left Axel's mouth every so often.

"What did I miss?" Iris's voice croaked.

River's body shook as she threw her arms around Iris.

Az moved to Ky's side. "I'm going to knock him out first."

They all looked to the Head, whose eyes slowly closed.

Chapter Thirty-Nine

River

River pulled her knees up to her chest and wrapped the blanket around her shoulders, bracing against the wind. The edge of the cave provided little comfort from the chilling breeze that whipped up from the water. The sea rolled and churned below, banging up against the rocks like an angry song.

"How long have you been out here?" Ky called as he landed with a crunch next to her. "You're going to freeze."

"It's peaceful. How was getting Axel settled in the castle?"

Ky shrugged. Today he had at least bothered to put on both a thin pair of pants and a thin white cotton shirt. The material was almost see-through, and it was rolled up to his elbows hastily. She knew it was for her benefit. His hair was pulled back into a knot at the nape of his neck. "The healer gave him something to settle him, so Az didn't have to use so much power. She'll have to slip it into everything he eats and drinks."

"And how long is this supposed to go on? You can't keep him like that forever. It's inhumane."

Ky sat down next to her, and his body blocked the wind slightly. "We aren't human."

River laughed. "Right. Well . . ."

"I don't know. I'm hoping we can get through to him."

"You cut off his wings, stole his power, and are drugging him to make him more cooperative. You think he'll be willing to listen to you after all that?" She had her doubts about this whole plan. Truthfully, she knew none of them would kill him, and it would be up to her and Iris to do what must be done.

"No." Ky shook his head and picked up a rock tossing it across the water. "I'm hoping your sister has luck finding my mother and convincing her to come home."

River nodded slowly. She sucked her lip into her mouth and chewed on the skin.

"And you? What's your plan? I mean, after my mother teaches you to control your power."

River had tried several times to pull her power to show Ky what she had done in the few days since they'd returned to the cave, but every time, it resulted in her curled in a ball and him pulling the power from her to give her relief. She couldn't replicate what she'd done to Axel or even Wrynn no matter how she tried.

River released her lip along with a sigh. "I go home. Show my mom and my people that I can do this."

"My human contact, Blakey, can help you with that. The rebellion they've created—I think you should take it over."

She drew her eyebrows together in surprise. They had spoken in great detail about the people who sought truth and peace between the races. She was rather impressed by the whole thing. She tried to hide the guilt she felt for nearly killing the man and ending an innocent life.

"Why?"

"Because I'll have so much on my plate with my father. I'll need to rule in his stead, in secret. I won't have time to run around chasing humans to keep them safe. That's your job now. I've never trusted anyone to do it the way I trust you."

"So we no longer matter to you?" River asked, arching her brow.

He slowly moved his head toward her, and a small smile spread across his face. "I didn't say that. But I think you'll be better at it than me. I'll help where I can. I'll send word of danger if I hear of it."

"So like partners?" River's hair blew fiercely around her face. It felt so good to have it free of its restraints.

"Partners. Yes, I like that. Partners for peace."

River trembled, and Ky wrapped his arm around her, pulling the blanket tighter.

"You work on your people, and I'll work on . . ." Her words trailed off. *Mine?* But the humans weren't hers. She wasn't a human. She wasn't a Spitarian. Where exactly did she fit in?

"River?" Ky's face pulled with concern, but she didn't want his pity. "All of us are your people. It's okay not to fit exactly where everyone wants you to. You don't have to be anyone. When you stop trying to shove who you are down and stop hiding, you'll shine brighter than the rest."

River nodded slowly, trying to absorb it all. Even with all the unknown and all the challenges that lay ahead, she felt hopeful for the first time in her life. She didn't feel like she was heading down a path to prove something. She felt strong, like she was finally filling the role she was meant to. Not her sister's role of savior and chosen one, but her own role, for her own goals— help all races, become the woman she always knew she could be.

She had an ally in an *Heiralomun*. One she hadn't seen coming when she'd set out a few weeks ago. Blakey, who she'd been sent to kill, could be her biggest supporter for her throne and to help her people finally stop a fight they should have never been in.

And to top it all off, she had a sister. Blood who was willing to die for her. To teach her. And hopefully, love her. She had a family history to learn about.

"I do think all I have seen will help my people. I think I can rule. And if, after I learn to control my magic, I don't feel like I'm the best for my people, I'll make sure they have someone who is."

Ky smiled at her, catching a few strands of stray hair that clung to her lips, and pushed them aside. "I have complete faith in you."

River hoped he was right. "It's years . . . decades . . . centuries of biases to overcome."

"And we have all the reasons to squash that."

"*We,* huh?" River grabbed a stone and chucked it. "You have purple blood, and I don't know about it?"

Ky laughed and shrugged. "Something like that."

"I don't get you. But I think I'm very excited for the opportunity to learn what makes you this way."

Ky grabbed her hand and placed it to his chest. "It would be a great honor to call you a friend, River Rowan Castor, the brightest of the lost Stars."

Heat flushed River's cheeks, and she suddenly felt timid. She didn't pull her arm from his grasp. They had a lot of work ahead of them, and the they would do it together. Tooth and nail, they would do it.

Wing and Sword.

Cloud, Star, and Sky.

Epilogue

You will be pleased to learn I have found the last Star. Not only that, but something else as well.

Send someone to get me out of this ridiculous prison my offspring think can hold me, and I will share the information with you then.

Keep an eye on the Devlyn problem. You made the mess. I won't be helping you clean this one up again.

Don't make me regret this arrangement.

And do not go looking for the Star. I have a feeling with all the commotion you're stirring up she will be headed straight for you.

- Axel

JR Szpila

Want to know what happens next? Will Ky and River stay just friends?
Get the next book here –

http://www.jrszpila.com/thesparrowswhodream

Love this book? Want an exclusive illustrated edition?

http://www.jrszpila.com/thesparrowswhodream

Acknowledgments

Oh man! After eight years of writing this book, I can't believe I am finally writing this. I will do my best to remember everyone, but if I forget you, please forgive me; eight years is a long time.

First, I need to thank Jesus because nothing would have happened without utter grace and the words that flowed every time I begged him to help me. All of my creativity came from Him. He was the reason these words helped to heal me.

Thank you again to my mother. Denise, I don't have enough space to list all you have done for me and this book. Nothing, and I mean nothing, would have happened without you. I love you more than the moon and the stars, mom. Thank you for being a super mom and my hero.

Joshua, thank you for loving me and giving me all the time and space I needed to get this book and all future books out of my head. Thank you for supporting my dreams and our family.

My kiddos, I know it is hard to understand when you are a little, but I hope one day, when you read this, you will learn how much I love you. I hope you see that all dreams, no matter if someone tells you they are unreachable, aren't. You can do anything you set your mind to. You are warriors. Thank you for the time and grace.

To the rest of my friends and family, thank you for the congrats, the love, the encouragement, and for watching my little monsters.

Serene, my writing bestie, thank you for always encouraging me, reading all my work, and making it better. I would not be the writer I am without you. I am forever grateful for your witty remarks and your friendship.

Sophia man! You made my book bleed, tore out its guts, and then helped me sew it back together in the right order. You are beyond talented. Thank you for always being honest with me.

My forever favorite group 14, (Tina, Sammie, Sophia, Marena, Clare), each and everyone of you is so crazy talented, and it is an honor to share stories and our worlds.

The super cool writing group, to current members and past members, you have been with me since the beginning of my journey, and you all have made me a better writer.

To all my early readers over the years who read the first drafts. Thank you! From the bottom of my heart, thank you! You all helped shape this story. I am sorry that I can't name you all after eight years. Please know how each of you impacted this story.

About the Author

JR Szpila is a mermaid in disguise and walks on two legs only because it's more socially acceptable. She is a lover of photography, chocolate milk, pasta, and Jesus. JR graduated from UAlbany with a bachelor's degree in psychology and is currently pursuing a master's in clinical mental health counseling. She writes and reads in every spare moment she has, including the dinner table, the beach, and even at sporting events. She lives in Saratoga, NY with her husband, two boys, and two cats, Luke and Leia.

Want exclusive and free content?
Sign up here

http://www.jrszpila.com/newsletter

www.ingramcontent.com/pod-product-compliance
Lightning Source LLC
LaVergne TN
LVHW091700070526
838199LV00050B/2217